DEADLY GIFT

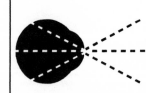 This Large Print Book carries the
Seal of Approval of N.A.V.H.

DEADLY GIFT

HEATHER GRAHAM

THORNDIKE PRESS

A part of Gale, Cengage Learning

GALE
CENGAGE Learning™

Detroit • New York • San Francisco • New Haven, Conn • Waterville, Maine • London

Copyright © 2008 by Heather Graham Pozzessere.
The Flynn Brothers Trilogy #3.
Thorndike Press, a part of Gale, Cengage Learning.

Thorndike Press® Large Print Basic.
The text of this Large Print edition is unabridged.
Other aspects of the book may vary from the original edition.
Set in 16 pt. Plantin.
Printed on permanent paper.

LIBRARY OF CONGRESS CATALOGING-IN-PUBLICATION DATA

Graham, Heather.
    Deadly gift / by Heather Graham.
      p. cm.
    ISBN-13: 978-1-4104-0890-7 (hardcover : alk. paper)
    ISBN-10: 1-4104-0890-6 (hardcover : alk. paper)
    1. Private investigators—Fiction. 2. Serial murders—Fiction.
3. Haunted houses—Fiction. 4. New Orleans (La.)—Fiction.
5. Large type books. I. Title.
      PS3557.R198D4358 2008
      813'.54—dc22
2008042628

Published in 2008 by arrangement with Harlequin Books S.A.

Printed in the United States of America
1 2 3 4 5 6 7 12 11 10 09 08

In memory of my mom,
and the Irish contingent —
those who believed in leprechauns
and banshees and that all things
could be possible.

ACKNOWLEDGMENTS

And for some folks who are amazing all year:
Dave Simms, F. Paul Wilson,
Harley Jane Kozak, Alex Sokoloff,
Jason, Shayne, Derek,
Chynna and Bryee Pozzessere,
Connie, Scott, Al, Josh, Stacey and
Kaylyn Perry, Helen and James Rosburg
and Ali DeGray, Brian and Kristi Ahlers,
Lance Taubold, Rich Devin, Kenny Jones,
Debbie Richardson, Mary Stella and
Beth Ciotta, Mr. Mark Johnston,
Bob and Sandra Levinson.
The inimitable Kathryn Falk,
Lady Barrow and
Jo Carol Jones and Carol Stacy,
Cindy Walker,
Pat Walker and Patty Harrison,
Kelli Salkin and
CJ Hollenbach and Kevin and Nate Beard.
Kevin, you are my true hero!

7

PROLOGUE

Narragansett Bay, Rhode Island

The sea was a beautiful thing, and being on the water was absolute heaven.

Eddie Ray felt the air on his cheeks and knew that they would be turning red soon with windburn. It was a winter's day, but off the coast of Newport, Rhode Island, the seas were deceptively serene. He loved the sea in winter, with its changeable moods. He wasn't a fool. He didn't intentionally run out into dangerous storms, but he'd brought more than one boat through a heaving nor'easter, and he loved the churning waves, the wind, and even the cold that came with the driving rain and stole into a man's bones.

But today was sweet! Crisp, cool air, the temperature hovering near forty degrees. A soft breeze, just enough to fill his sails and power the *Sea Maiden,* who rode the water as if she floated on air. She was his favorite of all their boats. He even had her name tattooed on his arm.

He hadn't needed to take the *Sea Maiden,* of course. She was a sixty-footer, and none of those nouveau riche boys who earned their money in the city and came to Rhode Island to flaunt it would have taken her out for one passenger.

One strange passenger.

Eddie sat at the helm and glanced around. He had taken the man on at twelve o'clock sharp, just as the guy had asked, and they were going to be back at the marina by two-thirty, because his partner Sean and his wife would be heading out at four to Ireland, and Eddie intended to be there for the send-off. It was a big deal; Sean hadn't been back to the country in which he'd been born for years.

And not since his honeymoon to the Caribbean had he been on a trip with Amanda.

The new wife. The "trophy" wife, as Kat, Sean's daughter, called her. Well, if a man was going to marry a woman less than half his age, he had to expect some backlash. Then again, Sean O'Riley had always re-minded Eddie of an old-fashioned kind of pirate. Not a real pirate. The kind in the movies. Captain Blood. Heroic, bold and determined. Sean would manage to keep peace in his own house by facing it the same way he faced the wind: legs firmly spread on the deck for balance, hands on his hips.

Kat was off chasing her music career most of the time these days. She was good, and they were all as proud as they could be. But Sean wasn't good at living on his own. He needed someone else around the place, preferably a woman to take care of all the details he had no interest in handling himself. Kat's mother had died long ago, and now that Kat wasn't around, Sean needed company. Company other than his old maiden aunt, as sweet a woman as Bridey might be. Company other than Clara and Tom, who looked after the big old house. Marni, who was married to Cal, their newest and youngest partner, was always willing to play hostess when Sean needed to entertain for business, but Sean had needed more than that, ergo Amanda.

Whatever made Sean happy was, in Eddie's mind, good. And if Amanda made Sean happy, then Eddie was happy — though, God knew, he couldn't figure out *why* she was enough for Sean. He'd finally decided she must be a dynamo in bed, because she didn't have the brains of a clam, and she barely pretended to be nice to Kat, who was the light of Sean's life. But Sean was his best friend, as well as his partner. They'd traveled life's seas together, the rough and the calm, the good and bad, the happy and the tragic. So if Sean was enjoying this particular voyage, then Eddie was glad for him.

This Christmas, though, Eddie had already arranged to give Sean the one thing he'd been hunting for as long as he could remember.

They had read all the books, reliving history from before the Revolution, looking for clues, all the while building up their charter business together, and on top of that, Sean had fought to keep up the big old house his grandfather had built.

Eddie smiled suddenly. Yes, they were friends.

And he was pleased, pleased as all get-out, to think that he'd gotten the best Christmas gift in the world for Sean.

But for the moment . . .

He was happy to bask in that knowledge and wait for the holiday, only a few weeks away now.

For now, he was glad he'd accepted this charter, even if his passenger was more than a bit strange, all muffled up in a huge sweater, and wearing a trench coat that looked like it was at least one size too big. John Alden, he'd said his name was, without so much as a smile. It was certainly a damned good name for a New Englander, and Eddie wondered if the guy was descended from his Pilgrim namesake. You certainly wouldn't think so from his appearance. Short, with a funny mustache, oversized heavy-framed glasses and a husky way of talking, he reminded Eddie of a terrier. The kind of feisty little dog that wouldn't accept the limits of its own size and would challenge a mastiff. But the terrier's money was as good as anyone's, and Alden had wanted a two-hour cruise around the little islands out past the sound and into the bay. No problem.

Eddie knew those islands like the back of his hand.

Knew the secrets of those islands.

He wondered if this strange little man knew anything of the history. If he was familiar with any of the old Rhode Island tales of daring revolutionaries.

He certainly didn't seem to know much about sailboats. You chartered a boat like the *Sea Maiden* because she was a beauty, because she was sleek, because you could unfurl her sails on a day like today, with this gorgeous breeze, and fly.

And what the hell had this guy wanted?

For Eddie to drop the sails and run the motor.

Oh, well. It took all kinds to make the world.

Eddie glanced at his watch. He'd been cruising slowly around the islands for a while now, and it was time to get back. He meant to see Sean off and enjoy the party. Kat was already home, in preparation for Christmas. It was sweet to imagine her pleasure when she saw the gift he had for Sean come Christmas. Kat would play the piano and sing the traditional Christmas songs, along with some she'd written herself. They would all join in, him with his worse-for-wear baritone and Sean with his tenor. And Bridey, despite her age, with her clear soprano. They would make hot Irish coffee, slathered with whipped cream, and Sean and Amanda-the-trophy-wife would regale them all with tales of their trip to Ireland.

But first he had to get back for the big send-off party.

Where had his passenger gotten to? Eddie figured he would just start back, since the guy must have gone forward for the view and the helm was aft. The guy wasn't in the cabin, that much he knew, because he'd

14

locked the forward hatch. He might have taken the *Sea Maiden* out by himself, but he wasn't a fool. No stranger was getting into the cabin by himself. There were too many official papers and personal belongings in there, since the *Sea Maiden* was the favored vessel for most of them.

"I'm heading back now!" Eddie called, hoping John could hear him. "Like I told you, I have someplace to be tonight!" He needed to get back, take a shower. This was going to be a proper bon voyage party, and he planned to show that uppity trophy-blonde that he cleaned up well.

"Hey! Did you hear me?"

Nothing.

He squinted. The blue was already leaving the sky. Night came early to New England in winter. Like a massive bird's wing, it swooped in, a single shadow falling silently across the sky.

He started to rise, then sank back in his seat, a perplexed frown knitting his brow.

"What the hell?" he muttered.

At first he was confused.

Hell, yes, the guy was strange, but . . .

"What . . . ?" Once again, he began to stand.

Eddie wasn't a small guy. He wasn't muscle-bound, but he'd worked the sea all his life, and he was no weakling. He even carried a small gun.

Which was in the cabin.

And nothing — nothing — had prepared him for this.

He felt the air move as the man did, but he didn't have even a split second to brace himself against the on-slaught. He had barely begun to rise before he was falling.

The icy chill of the water numbed the searing pain. He was falling, falling into the darkness of the ocean, but something was billowing up in front of him, like a shadow, only . . .

It was red.

It was his own blood, he realized with a strange sense of calm, and it was pouring from his chest, spewing out like a geyser.

He was numb, frozen; only his mind was capable of functioning at all, and then only to realize sadly that he was dying.

What a fool he'd been. He should have seen.

But he hadn't, and now it was too late.

Yes, he was dying. He couldn't feel his hands or feet. His lungs were burning, and his blood was still spreading through the water, clouding his vision. He thought his lungs had probably been punctured, not that he'd ever known much about anatomy.

16

He knew enough to know that he was dying, though.

Being on the water was absolute heaven. Wasn't that what he'd been thinking earlier? How about being *in* the water, and praying that it would indeed be heaven when the dark and the numbness and the red pool of blood were no longer a part of him?

I had so much more to do, to see, to live, he thought. Too late.

What a fool he'd been.

Blackness began descending, tamping out the streaks of light that flashed through his head. The darkness was oddly gentle. The last of the light began to fade, so quickly. Seconds passing, milliseconds . . .

A lifetime. His lifetime.

Death was a certainty. He was a strong man; he thought he had been a kind man.

But he was afraid.

A strange sound roared through his ears, one that was oddly out of place in this watery realm. It was like the whip of the wind, and horses racing across wind and waves, horses as black as night, yet somehow silhouetted against an even greater darkness. There was something terrifying about it, and yet also beautiful . . . calming.

And then, through the darkness, a hand reached out. . . .

1

Dublin, Ireland

"Clear!"

"What's happening? Oh, my God, my husband! Let me get to my husband!"

Caer Cavannaugh was aware of the woman screaming beyond the emergency room curtains, just as she was aware of the triage nurse speaking to the woman in a calming way, trying to keep her from interfering with the doctors who were working desperately over the man.

He had come in with strange symptoms that had apparently appeared within twelve hours of his arrival in Dublin. According to his chart, he was in his seventies, was usually in good health, and he and his wife had checked into their hotel, shortly after which he'd become desperately ill. First he'd complained of terrible pain in his stomach, then of a weakness so overwhelming that it was close to paralysis sweeping over his limbs. And then he'd started having problems with his heart.

By the time he'd reached the emergency room, he'd collapsed. The doctors, not finding a pulse, had started treatment instantly.

"Charge!"

The man on the bed bucked, his back arching, and then a reassuringly regular beeping began. His heartbeat was back. Orders were shouted; Caer obeyed them. She'd been summoned to the emergency room just minutes before the man had arrived. In her work for the Agency, she never knew quite where she would be when, or what she would be expected to do, but she'd been well trained to deal with whatever she faced in any new situation.

This, however, was unusual, even for her.

The pulse on the screen jumped erratically for a few seconds, then steadied. The man blinked and looked at her, then smiled weakly. "Angel," he said, and then his eyes closed again and he slept, attached to an IV, a heart monitor and a blood pressure gauge.

The team in the room congratulated one another. A moment later, Caer heard the man's wife, sobbing and still upset, as a doctor explained to her what had just happened, even though they still didn't know the cause of the problem. He told the wife that she needed to calm down and give them some answers. Caer, waiting as orderlies were summoned to take the patient up to intensive care, watched and listened, putting together the details.

The patient was Sean O'Riley; his wife was Amanda, and she was substantially younger than he was.

She was going on and on about their wonderful day and how happy Sean had been. He'd been born here in Dublin, but been living in the States forever. He was always strong and healthy; since he was a charter captain, he had to keep himself fit. When asked what he had eaten, she said they'd had breakfast on the plane, lunch at the hotel, and dinner at a place on Temple Bar. They'd eaten the same thing, and she felt perfectly fine, but it was soon after dinner that he'd taken ill.

"I have to see my husband!" she insisted then.

Soon, she was promised.

Caer studied the woman through the opening in the curtain. She was petite, with a nice figure and disproportionately large breasts. Caer couldn't help but wonder if they were real. Blond hair, pretty hazel eyes, but a slightly sharp look to her. Gold digger? And if so, was she somehow responsible for her husband's condition? But could anyone, even the best actress, fake such a look of tragic hysteria?

The doctor suggested sedation. Amanda nodded, and a nurse gave her a shot.

A police officer arrived. *Interesting,* Caer thought.

"Cavannaugh."

Caer started and swung around to face the male charge nurse who'd called her name.

"You're on. He's assigned to ICU for the next few hours, and you're with him."

"Right. Thanks," she murmured.

He looked at her curiously, as if he wasn't sure he recognized her.

No surprise. It was a big hospital. Anyone could wind up working with anyone else on any given day.

He smiled, as if deciding he'd seen her before after all.

"I'm on it," Caer said, greeting the two orderlies who showed up to move her patient, checking lines and his oxygen intake as they made their way down the hall from emergency to the elevators to intensive care.

He was to be kept alive. There seemed to be no reason for his life to be in danger, but it was, and he needed care and protection.

■ ■ ■ ■

Zach Flynn was sleeping deeply when his cell phone rang. What might have proven to be a tragedy, the case of a missing boy, had been neatly and happily solved in a matter of days. Sam, the ten-year-old, had been angry. His mother had remarried and had a baby, and the baby had been getting all the attention. He hadn't been kidnapped, despite the open window and the mess in the room. He'd staged the event and gone to hide out in his father's old hunting lodge. When Zach had found him — tracking him down through his emails to an Internet buddy in China — he'd been ready to go home. No heat, running out of food — it hadn't been half the fun he had expected. All had worked out well. Sam's mother and stepfather had been so relieved that they'd welcomed him back with tears and enough love to make him believe he was as cherished as the new baby.

And so, with the "real" business — the private investigations firm he ran with his brothers Aidan and Jeremy — in good standing, Zach had planned on spending a chunk of December on his side business, checking out some of the musicians hitting the Boston clubs. Years ago, he'd begun investing in music studios, producing promising acts on his own label and watching with pleasure when they were picked by the major players. It had made a nice break from his job with the Metro police in Miami, and it was still a good way to wind down from his day job.

He was exceptionally good with computers, and had become their three-man firm's tech guy for his ability to hack into all kinds of systems. His street instincts were good, too, though, and he found his life fulfilling, even if not every case ended as well as Sam's had.

Then again, some of their cases would have made a statue smile, like the time Mrs. Mayfield, of the Mayfield Oil Group, had hired them on for a fantastic sum to find Missy.

Missy was a cat.

Easily done. Missy was found with six little puffs of fur, and the Flynn brothers were all offered kittens.

Music was his love, though. Music was something that pulsed in his blood and echoed in his mind, not to mention the way it eased and cleansed his soul. It was something beautiful when he saw so much that was ugly.

So he'd claimed December for himself — a chance to get back into that other world where no one went missing and no one died.

Last night, after arriving in Boston, he'd started relaxing with a vengeance. Not that he got drunk, because he didn't drink to excess, having learned long ago that the temporary high wasn't worth the loss of control. But he'd run into a bunch of old friends at a pub on State Street and downed a few Boston lagers. Still, he was instantly aware at the sound of his ringer, and he answered the phone automatically. "Flynn."

"Zach, oh, Zach, thank God you're there. Eddie has disappeared, and now Dad is in the hospital over in Ireland. I was going to fly over there, only Bridey said I shouldn't, but Dad —"

"Kat?" he asked, cutting across her uncontrolled flow of words.

"Yes, it's Kat. Oh, Zach, it's awful, you have to help. We don't know what's going on, and my father is all alone over there with *her.* You have to go over and see what's happening, Zach. I need your help, and so does Dad."

"Okay, slow down and start at the beginning. What's wrong with your dad?" Zach asked, coming thoroughly, instantly awake. Sean O'Riley had been one of his father's best friends. Even after his dad had passed away, though Sean had been in Rhode Island and the Flynns had been in Florida, Sean had been there, like an uncle, ready to offer a hand to Zach and his brothers. Then Zach had gotten involved with Kat. Not romantically, but she had the voice of a lark, so he'd given her some help professionally, put a band together for her, and now she was starting to soar. She was like a long-distance little sister, most of the time.

"She did something to him." Kat went on frantically. "She's a monster with a bad dye job and veneers over her fangs." She paused for breath and managed to calm down a bit. "Bridey said you should go over there right away and see what's going on. She's afraid for me to go. You know how she is, worrying that something will happen to me. Probably afraid I'll wind up in jail for killing Amanda. Zach, please. You have to go and bring Dad home safely."

"Whoa, wait a minute. There are excellent hospitals in Ireland, and I'm sure —"

"He needs to be *here.* So we can all be with him. Please. I'll hire you. Zach, I'm scared. Eddie is missing, and I'm afraid he's dead, and now someone's after Dad, I'm sure of it. It's got to be *her.* You know I've never trusted her, and now I think she's really done something." She had worked herself into a frenzy again and practically sobbed out the last words.

"Kat, if Sean is in trouble, I don't need to be *hired.* I would do anything for him. But you've got to calm down. And Bridey is right, you can't start wildly accusing Amanda."

"But I'm right!"

"Then you need proof."

"My father won't believe me."

Zach understood Kat's feelings about her stepmother. Amanda wasn't much older than Kat herself was. But he hadn't seen anything himself to suggest that Amanda meant to do away with Sean. Sure, she enjoyed the fact that he was well off and probably wouldn't have given him a second look otherwise, but that was a far cry from murder.

Frankly, he just didn't think the woman had the brains to be capable of planning a murder.

By the time Kat finished talking, he knew she was right about one thing. She should *not* go to Ireland — she might well wind up in jail — and he should. Actually, he thought, he should be heading straight to Rhode Island, where Eddie Ray and his boat had gone missing. But Sean was alive in a hospital in Dublin, and he needed to come home. Kat was too emotionally involved, too convinced that her stepmother was evil, to see to that. Sean, for whatever reason, loved his new wife. He also loved his daughter. And a blowup between the two women could be dangerous to his health.

Zach picked up his watch from the bedside table. He could be in Dublin by morning. How soon he could head back, though, would depend on how well — or poorly — Sean was doing.

"What about your father? Is he well enough to travel?"

"Yes, with a nurse or something. I didn't understand it all, just that, yes, he could come home. Please, Sean, bring him home. And when he's safe — or at least at home, where I can keep an eye on that woman — you can find Eddie. I've talked to Dad, and he thinks he just ate something bad, but he's worried sick about Eddie. Just book a flight to Dublin, then call me back and I'll handle the rest of the details. You're free right now, right?"

There was a movement on the other side of the bed, and he winced. It wasn't as if he didn't know the woman's name. He did. But there was nothing between them other than the fact that she liked a dimly lit bar and some good music after a long day at corporate headquarters, and so did he, so he'd ended up here at her apartment. Truthfully, he was beginning to think he was meant to wander aimlessly and restlessly through life — focusing on work, but never finding what it was that he really wanted to come home to.

He wished right now that he had woken up alone.

"Yeah, I can leave today, and I will. I'll get a flight," he said to Kat, going over what she had told him and wondering if something dangerous really was going on, or if he was letting Kat's suspicions get to him.

He reminded himself of just how much hostility she bore Amanda, even though, for her father's sake, she kept it hidden most of the time.

It was perfectly possible that Sean had simply fallen ill or, as he'd said himself, gotten a nasty case of food poisoning. As for Eddie, well, that *was* worrying, but maybe he was just playing a prank.

No. Eddie would never play that kind of a practical joke. Something else had to be happening, and once he got back, he would have to find out what.

He started to tell Kat a quick goodbye, but she stopped him.

"Wait, Zach."

"What?"

"Please, I know I must sound crazy, but . . . God, I feel it. Like a chill in my bones. It's like . . . like something evil is out there. An evil shadow. I'm worried sick about Eddie, and . . . I can't let anything happen to my dad. I can't."

"Kat, I'll get to him as quickly as possible and I'll get him home."

"Something really bad *is* happening, Zach. I don't understand it, but I'm really afraid. And I'm not a coward, you know that."

"I know that, Kat. Just stay calm. I'll get Sean home."

"And you'll stay with us until you get this figured out?"

"I'll stay until it's all figured out," he promised, then said goodbye at last and hung up.

He slipped from the bed, showered, then dressed in the bathroom. When he went back into the room, his bed partner was still stretched out on the mattress, a lithe and well-manicured thirty-something blonde.

"Call me when you're back in my neck of the woods," she said huskily.

He ought to tell her he would. That would be the polite thing to do.

But he didn't want to lie, so he didn't say

anything.

"You're not going to call, are you?"

"No," he said softly.

For a moment she stared back at him with tawny brown eyes that registered what was at least an honesty between them. Then she smiled, something dry in her gaze. "Nice night, thanks. Have a good life."

"You too," he told her. It was the truth. It *had* been a nice night, and he wished her well, but their lives weren't meant to intertwine.

He dialed the airport as he left, and headed back to his hotel to pack up as quickly as he could.

The air was soft and sweet, redolent of flowers, the sky blue, the hills emerald beneath the sun. She could feel the damp blades of grass beneath her bare feet, and she reveled in the sheer joy of being alive and feeling the silken breeze lift her hair until the sun kissed the back of her neck just so.

She could feel the beat of her own heart, and she ran in her dream as she had once run in life. She laughed out loud at the promise she felt all around and in her love for the land itself. She had come from the city, just as she had when she was a young child, free and strong, believing that happiness lay ahead. She knew that when she crested the next hill, she would see the cottage with its neatly thatched roof where it waited in the valley. A fire would be burning in the hearth, and at night, the men would drink their ale, play their tunes, sing of the maids they had loved and lost, and speak of times gone by. The old cottage would be filled with those she had loved and everything she herself had lost.

She realized that she was quickening her pace, and it troubled her at first. But then she decided to simply exult in the strength that filled her limbs. It was wonderful to run so, with her senses so alive and in tune with nature itself, the grass beneath her feet, the air, the sun, and even the distant sounds of music, like a siren's song, beckoning her onward.

Then she looked back — and she knew. Knew why she was running faster. *Had* to run faster.

There was darkness behind her. The darkness of night, of billowing clouds, of shadows against the sun.

The sweet music that had called to her gave way to a roll of thunder, and she knew that she had to run, for like the sweep of a tidal wave, the darkness was coming. In that thunder she began to hear the drumming of horses' hooves, and when next she dared to look, something was breaking through the clouds, rushing ahead of them.

A coach. Dark, massive and beautiful, yet terrifying, and drawn by huge, elegantly plumed black horses.

And she knew — somehow she knew — it was coming for her.

She turned away and began to run harder. She was young, she told herself, beautiful, and the world was hers.

She saw someone there . . . ahead of her. She knew him, she was sure of it, but she couldn't place him. There was a sad smile on his face, as if to welcome her. Something told her that he shouldn't have been there. She knew him. A friend, not a lover. And yet a friend who did not belong here, not in this Ireland she had known and loved as a child. He waved, and she couldn't tell whether he was welcoming her or warning her away.

It didn't matter. She had to escape the darkness, and the only way to run was forward.

And the thunder of those hooves! She didn't know, either, whether that great coach was meant to save her from the darkness or if it was part of it.

And so she ran, picking up speed, her

heart racing, her calf muscles burning along with her lungs. She prayed, as she raced to stay ahead of the darkness, that the coach was coming to save her. To hurry her onward toward the emerald-green beauty of the day, and the warmth and the love of the cottage and the one who waited for her there. He was speaking now, and though she couldn't hear the words, somehow she knew they were a warning.

"Eddie?" she cried out, recognizing him as she drew closer.

"It's all right, Bridey. I'm fine now. Fine where I am. But you have to watch out for the shadows and for the wind that howls."

"Eddie, for the love of God . . . what happened?"

"Would that I knew. I saw the shadow."

And then he was slipping away from her, fading. Shadows were falling around him, but she needed to reach him.

And so she continued to run. . . .

Eager and, despite her fear, so alive, so desperately alive.

She could feel the dew beneath her feet. Feel the strength that powered her young muscles. Heart, lungs, mind: all were keen, and simply being alive was so sweet. . . .

Bridey O'Riley woke with a start.

34

Barely had she blinked before she felt the arthritis crippling her hands, bowing her back, even as she lay in her bed.

Ah, dreams.

In dreams, a woman could be young again. Beautiful. Back in the Ireland of her youth, away from the strife of the city, just a lass playing in the hills and dreaming of love.

She smiled as the light of day crept in through her windows. There would be no racing down the hills and across the velvet green dales of Ireland today. Her home there was as much a part of the distant past as her youth. If she were to rise and glance into a mirror, no brilliant eyes, radiant smile or porcelain skin would meet her stare. She would see an old woman, wrinkled and weathered, one who had lived, survived tragedy, known ecstasy, and knew now that death could not be far away. She could look out a window and see rocks, gray in the thin light of winter, jagged and wild and, perhaps, even exciting. This was America, the shore of Rhode Island, the place she now called home.

And a fine home it was. Sean William O'Riley had done himself and his family proud. The sea was his heritage, sweeping through his veins, and he had come to this place, this granite shore, and made himself a fine living chartering beautiful ships with high masts and billowing sails. They lived in a stately mansion and wanted for nothing, and the respect he had shown her, caring for an old relation all these years, was proof that he was a good and loving man.

He was a good businessman, too, working with that new young fellow, Cal, and with Eddie Ray. . . .

Her smile faded as she remembered seeing Eddie in her dream.

Eddie Ray was missing.

One of the best captains on the Eastern Seaboard, he had taken out his favorite vessel, the *Sea Maiden,* and he hadn't been heard from since. He had disappeared.

But he had been in her dream, standing in front of the cottage and warning her, though there was no reason for him to be there, when he had always lived here, in the States.

Even as that thought came to her, the door to her room was flung open and Kat stood there for a moment, posed in the doorway, like a regal figurehead standing strong against the rise and fall of the sea. Katherine Mary O'Riley, her great-niece. She was Sean's daughter, and as young and beautiful as Bridey had once been herself.

"Oh, Aunt Bridey!" Kat cried, clearly upset.

"What is it, child?" Bridey asked, sitting up against her pillows.

Kat flew across the room and threw herself down next to Bridey on the bed.

"They found the Sea Maiden floating out by one of the islands."

A tremor shook Bridey's heart. Hadn't she just seen Eddie, captain of the Sea Maiden, in a glen in Ireland, where he shouldn't have been?

And hadn't he just been warning her about the shadows?

"And Eddie?" Bridey asked softly, dread knowledge filling her mind.

Kat looked down at Bridey with troubled blue eyes.

"Not a sign of him," she whispered, close to tears, and then she sat up straighter.

"It's her," she said grimly, staring at Bridey through narrowed eyes. "That bitch. I don't know how, but somehow Amanda did something to him."

"Ah, now, lass. Your own dear mother would'na' mind that your father found happiness with another."

"Oh, Bridey," Kat protested. "That's a crock! Amanda is barely five years older than I am, thirty-one. She married my father for his money — you know she did. And now Dad is in a hospital in Dublin and the boat has been found, with no sign of Eddie, and I know — I just *know* — she did it. . . ."

"Now, lass, how can that be? Your da is in Ireland, and Eddie went missing here right before the party, and you know Amanda was with your da that day," Bridey said softly.

"I don't care. She did it — somehow. She poisoned my dad," Kat insisted. "She's evil. Pure evil."

"Now, Kat."

Bridey tried hard not to betray any emotion in her face, but her mind was racing. Why on earth had Sean taken it upon himself to marry that young blonde . . . what was the word they used over here? Bimbo. That was it and it described Amanda O'Riley all too well.

She couldn't say such things to Kat, though, or she would only make things worse. She smoothed her great-niece's hair. "Don't you worry, now. Didn't you tell me you were going to ask Zach Flynn to see that Sean comes home safe and well?"

Kat nodded. "I called him this morning, and he'll be on his way today." Then she offered Bridey a smile. "And *you* were the one who said I should ask Zach."

"And you did right to listen to me," Bridey told her. "He'll get your da home, that he will." She was grateful that Kat had practiced enough control to send Zach for Sean. Amanda was Sean's wife. If he was incapacitated, she called the shots, and having Kat there spewing accusations wouldn't help anything. Not only that, if there was something to be discovered, if there *was* a threat, Zach was trained to handle such a situation.

"I should be with my father," Kat said softly.

"But you're with me," Bridey said, and smiled. "And blessed I am, child. Zach will bring Sean home, and he'll get to the bottom of whatever is going on here, I promise you."

But Bridey knew. He would not find Eddie. At least, not alive.

She had seen the dark coach, and the plumed black horses.

Eddie was dead.

And the coach of Death was still thundering down on them.

2

"You should see it at Christmas," Sean O'Riley said, and his eyes were bright, despite his weakened state as he lay in his hospital bed. "We're on the coast, so there's no guarantee of snow, but it's crisp and cool, always, and the breeze comes just right, and it's just beautiful."

Caer smiled, impressed by the old man's vigor. Being assigned to him had been a pleasure. He still sported a cap of thick silver-white hair, and he was watching her with eyes as bright a blue as the sky over Tara itself. If Sean O'Riley said that the weather at Christmas was crisp and cool, it probably meant people froze their buns off. She liked him, liked hearing the story of his life. He had been born here in Dublin, in the very hospital where he now lay, but home to him now was across the Atlantic Ocean. A city called Newport, in Rhode Island, known for fierce weather, including

40

crippling nor'easters. He hadn't even been back in Ireland a day before he'd been rushed to the hospital, but already, a bit of a brogue was returning to his speech, even after the years he'd been gone.

"I'm sure Newport is lovely," she told him.

He nodded, satisfied by her agreement, then winced slightly, adjusting himself on the bed.

He had a strong constitution and had gone quickly from ICU to a regular room. Dr. Morton, the internal-medicine specialist, suspected some kind of food poisoning, but Sean had eaten the same meals at the same places as his wife, and an inspection at the restaurant where they'd dined had turned up no bacterial contaminants. Amanda remained fine. In fact, she was at the hotel spa right now, having declared that she needed a massage to ease the tension that had filled her because of Sean's illness.

Sean was seventy-six.

Amanda was thirty-one.

That made her stomach forty-five years younger than Sean's, so perhaps that had helped her. Then again, the doctors weren't sure what had brought Sean to the hospital. They had checked his heart — which was healthy — and performed scans, and they had no real answers. They were pleased with his progress, but he was weak as a kitten right now. The kind of pain he'd endured had put tremendous pressure on his heart, and that had nearly taken his life. But as to what had caused that pain, they still had no good answer.

"It's been good to come back to Ireland," he said quietly, then smiled in realization of how strange that must sound. "Despite . . . this." He gestured to include his hospital room and all the monitors still hooked up to him. "We saw a terrific production of Brendan Behan's 'The Hostage' at the Abbey Theatre. A matinee, luckily."

"You haven't been back since you moved to the U.S.? Fifty years ago?" Caer asked.

He shook his head, and he looked at her, but it was as if he were looking back in time. "Caer," he said, pronouncing her name correctly, "kyre." "It's so easy to get caught up in life, so you plan to do things, but . . . well, at least I made it back at last. But," he said, and wagged a finger at her, "you've never been to the United States, have you, young lady?"

"No," she admitted, smiling. "No, I haven't. I tend to be busy right here."

"Nurses are always in demand," he said.

She felt a bit guilty as she replied, "Yes, nurses are always in demand."

"Used to be, we had tons of Irish nurses and Irish priests in the U.S., but they say that the economy here has gotten so good that they don't need to come over to find work anymore."

"I never thought about it. I've always had plenty of work here," she said.

"Well, someday you must come to the States. And not just New York or California, either. Take Rhode Island, you take Rhode Island, now. We have a wealth of beauty and culture and history. I went over because my grandfather died and my father wanted to stay here. I understood how he felt — even shared his feelings, to be honest — but my grandfather had built a magnificent house and begun a business that someone needed to take over and make it into a solid, profitable enterprise. So I did. And when I saw where the house sat, atop a cliff, high above the water, with the wind whipping up sweet and wild, well, I knew it was the home I wanted. Here . . . the world is progressing, and it's right for Dublin, but in Newport I found the past, somehow. When I'm not on the water, I'm following the trail of one Revolutionary fellow or another. Ever hear of Nigel Bridgewater?"

"Who?" Caer said.

Sean laughed. "No, of course not. You'd

have learned Irish history in school. Besides, Nigel died too quickly to have made it into most of the history books. He was a great patriot, though, sailing out in secret one night with a delivery for the Continental army. He was young, just twenty-six, and they said he could navigate the sometimes-treacherous seas of New England like a fish. But he was caught, and executed by the British. Anyway, for years, Eddie — he's been my partner practically since the beginning — and I have tried to follow his trail. Apparently he knew the British were hot on his heels, and he managed to hide not just some of his treasure — funds collected for the struggling patriots — but also dispatches, letters that named names and would have led many of his fellow patriots to the gallows for spying. Maybe it sounds silly, I've always loved tracking a good historical mystery."

He looked up at her, and she stared into his eyes and assessed what she saw: a man who had spent a lifetime working hard, a man with zest and energy, an all-around good guy.

His gaze turned inward then, and he said, clearly upset, "I've got to get out of here — got to get home. Right away."

Caer looked at him curiously and asked

gently, "I know I don't understand your business, but why do you feel you have to get home so quickly? You do understand that you'll be taking a chance, right? The doctors still haven't figured out what made you so sick."

"Why do I have to get back?" he asked, as if the answer should have been obvious. "Eddie is missing."

"Your partner," she said.

"One of my partners," he said gruffly. "There's Cal, too, but he's young and hasn't been with us that long. But Eddie . . . Eddie joined me right after I moved to the States and helped me modernize the business. We added year-round dinner cruises, and he worked like a son of a gun right beside me to handle all the business we added. He lived in the little house out back — well, little by Newport standards — and we worked like dogs, maintaining the boats, captaining them, doing the paperwork at night." He grinned wryly and went on.

"Eddie . . . he lived my dreams with me. A lot of people thought I was crazy — still do, but I'm rich now, so I get to be eccentric — but I study the past, and Eddie and I . . . we've followed Bridgewater's trail. He was heading south with dispatches for the Continental Congress and a hold full of

45

English coins, and he managed to hide both before the British caught up to him. He was hanged without ever giving up the secret of where he had stashed everything. There's bravery for you. You see, I don't think he was just holding out on the money. Like I said, I think the papers he was carrying would have condemned some of his fellow patriots, so he died in silence. I mean, that was honor. Real honor. I've always dreamed of discovering just where he hid that cache, and maybe even writing a book about it." He laughed suddenly. "Listen to me. I'm just a rambling old man, taking advantage of a beautiful young woman who has no choice but to sit and listen to me."

"No, this is fascinating," she assured him.

"But you have other patients," he reminded her.

"The floor is well staffed. I'm all right, really. Trust me, if someone wants me, they'll find me."

His story *was* fascinating. She liked him, and she enjoyed sitting with him. She wasn't quite sure why he had wanted to acquire a wife like Amanda, but then again, who was she to judge?

"I'm worried about Eddie," he said, and there was a deep sadness in his eyes. Then he saw her watching and tried to make himself look strong again, but he couldn't hide his troubled thoughts. ". . . I have a bad feeling something's happened to him, and I owe it to him to find out the truth," he said firmly. "They've found the boat — and no sign of Eddie, I have to get back. I should have known something was wrong when everyone was there to see us off — except Eddie. He never missed a party, and he'd promised he would be there. . . . Something must have happened. Maybe he's in hiding."

"In hiding? Why?"

Sean waved a hand weakly. "Who knows? I just know I have to get home, though I'll bet I won't find a nurse like you back there."

Silently, she agreed. No, he would never find another *nurse* quite like her. Deciding she needed to change the subject — now — she said, "Tell me about your family."

"Family. It's really all that matters in the end," he said softly.

She felt a tug of emotion at her heart. She felt a strange ache to belong to someone's family and be spoken of with such love. She'd never really known a family.

"They were what called me back," he said.

"Pardon?"

He glanced up at her sheepishly. "It was strange, when they brought me here — to

47

the hospital, I mean. I suppose I was dreaming, but I felt like I was a boy in the hills again. I'd forgotten how right they are when they call this the Emerald Isle. The wind was blowing, setting up a real howl. And I was running back to the cottage where I grew up, like I was a kid going home. I heard someone — I think it was my mother — singing an old Irish song, crooning in the old Gaelic. The sun seemed to be setting. There were bursts of light, and shadows falling, but I didn't feel scared of them, even though I knew I should. It was beautiful, and I felt like I could run forever . . . but then I heard my daughter's voice, and suddenly I was aware that I was in the hospital, and that I had to fight, had to live. I had to live because I had to go home. To my daughter."

"Ah," Caer said.

"Caer?"

She started, looking up.

Michael was standing in the doorway, summoning her. He was in a white lab coat with the name "Dr. Michael Haven" embroidered on the pocket.

"Excuse me," she said to Sean.

"Oh, Lord, forgive me. I *have* taken up too much of your time," Sean told her.

"No, no, it's all right," she said as she rose,

then smiled and squeezed his hand. "I'll be back."

"And glad of it I'll be, lass," he told her.

Her smile deepened; he was sinking back into a few Irish cadences in his speech.

"I'll just talk to the family a bit," he told her, and nodded toward the picture at his bedside.

She had to laugh, though looking at the happy grouping made her feel . . . as if she were definitely missing out. In the photo, Sean had his arm around a beautiful young woman in her early twenties, who looked up at him with all a daughter's adoration of her father. Then came a woman — his wife, but not the girl's mother. Sean had told her that his first wife had passed away. His new wife was only a few years older than his daughter. On the other side of Sean were three tall — and, she had to admit, handsome — men, all clearly related to one another. Brothers, Sean had said. An old woman sat in a chair in front of the rest. Bridey, Sean's aunt, who lived with him.

Bridey had the same bright blue eyes as Sean and his daughter. Her expression held a mixture of wisdom, kindness and compassion. Caer knew she would love Bridey, were she ever to meet the woman.

But it was the brother standing closest to

Sean who never failed to attract her attention.

She figured that he had to be about six-two, and his hair was a light auburn. His eyes were direct and seemed to look right out at Caer. Every time she found herself staring at the picture, she was startled to feel a little tug at her heartstrings; she was sure she'd never seen such eyes before. They weren't blue, weren't green. They were the true aqua of the Caribbean, startling against his tanned features, arresting, piercing, and even, despite being only a photograph, assessing.

She had thought at first that he was Sean's son-in-law, but he'd told her no, the Flynn boys were like the sons he'd never had.

"He's on his way here," Sean told her now.

"Pardon?" Caer drew her eyes away from the picture, embarrassed that she'd been caught staring.

"Zach Flynn," Sean said. "Kat convinced him I need an escort home." He sighed dispiritedly. "We look like a nice family in that shot, huh? Not quite so, I'm afraid. You marry a younger woman, and everyone thinks she's a gold digger. Who would have thought I'd spend my golden years trying to be a peacekeeper?"

"Well, I'm sure things will work out for

the best," she said. Which was a crock, she knew, but most of what people said in the hospital was a crock. It went with the territory.

"Caer?"

She heard her name again. Michael. She should have followed him by now, she realized.

"Excuse me," she said again to Sean, and left.

Michael was heading down the hall, and she quickly followed him.

He stepped into an office, waiting for her to join him. As soon as she did, he closed the door. She felt him at her back — not a comfortable feeling.

He walked around and stood behind the desk. "What are you doing?" he asked her.

"What do you mean, what am I doing?" she demanded, determined not to let him put her on the defensive.

"Just what I said — what are you doing?"

"Talking to Sean O'Riley," she said.

"You're supposed to be observing, trying to find out what's going on."

"Well, if I'm trying to find out what's going on, talking to him seems like a good strategy to me," she said flatly.

He shook his head and began pacing, running his fingers through his hair, glancing at her with irritation.

"You're getting too emotionally involved."

"I am not!" she protested.

"Excuse me. I am the one in charge here," he told her.

She fell silent.

"All right. You'll have to go to America with him," Michael said. "You can be his private nurse."

"What?" she gasped, stunned. She worked here. In Dublin. She always had.

"I . . . don't want to go to America. There's plenty of work for me here, and I don't have a passport. I don't even have any nursing credentials."

Michael waved a hand dismissively. "I'll take care of everything you need." He reached into a nearby bookcase, grabbed a huge volume and tossed it to her.

"What's that?"

"A nursing manual. Start studying."

"But —"

"Start studying. You're going to America. Remember, there are rules in the Agency, and *I'm* in charge."

She knew there was resentment in her eyes.

"What's your problem with America?" he asked her, aggravated.

What *was* her problem?

She inhaled. She didn't know. Maybe it was . . .

The man.

The man with the sea-colored eyes. *He* would be going to America with them.

Something about his stare unnerved her, even in a photograph. She couldn't imagine facing it in real life.

He would find her out.

She told herself not to be ridiculous.

Besides, hadn't Sean just said that he was coming *here?*

So she was going to have to face those eyes no matter what.

Michael must have thought her silence meant she was still objecting to his order. "Caer, you *are* going," he said with patience — and authority.

She forced a smile. "Can't wait," she told him.

"Caer," Michael said softly, "something's wrong. Someone is after his life. This is serious."

"I know," she replied, her voice equally quiet.

Resigned. No, not resigned. She just didn't have a choice. Michael really did call the shots.

"Hey, it's the Christmas season, and the

Americans go all out to celebrate," he told her.

Michael would know. He had been just about everywhere.

"Yeah, great. Ho, ho, ho," she said.

"Go on, I have arrangements to make," he told her.

"Sure. I have some affairs left to handle here, as well," she told him tightly, as she walked to the door.

"Routine," he said.

"Routine does not negate the importance of any assignment," she said, and glanced at her watch. She had a matter to handle now that she considered just as important as any other.

Even Sean, no matter how much she liked the man.

"Caer," Michael said, as she turned to leave.

She paused at the door, her back to him. "Yes, sir?"

"Don't forget the nursing book. There's an envelope there, as well."

"Oh?"

"You'll want to go shopping for your trip, after all," he said.

"You can just bet I'll shop."

He appeared amused rather than threatened by her words. "Do your worst. Or your best," he told her. "This could be a great vacation for you, if you just look at it that way. Oh, and Merry Christmas," he said pleasantly.

She went back for the book and her travel allowance. With one last evil glare at him, she left the office, closing the door behind her.

America.

In the end, it didn't matter. Sean O'Riley was in danger, and she had to find out why, and from whom. And she had to stop whoever it was from causing him any further harm.

As she moved away from the door, she realized that the soft music playing in the hallway was a Christmas melody.

It was almost Christmas, and she was being forced to leave.

To go far across the Atlantic.

To find a would-be killer.

And the man with the extraordinary eyes would be there — just as he would soon be here. And she was afraid, she realized.

Afraid of being found out.

No, she told herself. It would never happen. Michael would never *let* it happen.

She took a deep breath. She was going to be a nurse in Rhode Island, and that was that.

It would be fun, she told herself. This was the holiday season, and she was going to spend it in America.

Oh, yeah. Ho, ho, ho. Merry Christmas.

She glanced at her watch again and knew that she had to hurry or she would be late for her other assignment.

And there really was no such thing as being late.

It simply wasn't accepted.

Not for this assignment.

3

Zach stared thoughtfully out the window as he felt the plane's landing gear slip into place. Dublin. He hadn't been here in a long time, but it was a city he loved, where the old mingled with the new, and history, some of it painful and all of it a lesson in the ways of man, seemed to be waiting around every corner. But there was one thing he especially adored about this capital city of the Irish Republic. The music. He'd encountered some of the most melodic voices he had ever heard in the Dublin pubs. There was real heart in Irish music, heart and passion. What could be wrong with coming to a city where he was guaranteed a good pint and fine music?

Nothing.

Still, it wasn't the music that had brought him here, it was his friendship with Kat, and his fear that maybe she wasn't over-reacting because she hated her stepmother, that someone really *was* after Sean.

Right now, as much as he loved Dublin, he was chafing to get Sean O'Riley safely home, then find out what the hell had happened to Eddie. He'd been just about to board the plane when Kat called him — hysterical — to tell him that the boat had been found, but Eddie had not been aboard, and there had been no obvious signs of what had happened to him.

Zach had also talked to Sean, who was convinced that it was just exhaustion from the flight, combined with something he'd eaten, but nothing the least bit threatening, that had caused his illness. He knew his daughter distrusted his wife, but Sean himself was quite certain he was in no danger from Amanda.

He *was* worried about Eddie, and that only made Zach worry more.

He, too, was far more worried about Eddie than he was about the possibility of Amanda trying to kill Sean. The way he saw things, the woman didn't have the intelligence or the nerve to be a cunning killer.

"Ah, there's my Dublin," said the elegant older woman at his side, interrupting his thoughts.

"It's certainly a beautiful city," Zach said,

turning to her with a smile. She'd spoken only four words, but there was a lilt to them, a melody in every word that made the Irish accent different from all others.

She smiled back, and he saw the plethora of wrinkles — many of them clearly laugh lines — in her face and wondered just how old she was.

It was as if she read his mind. "I'm ninety-two. Old enough. And weary. But glad to be home." She pointed out the window. "Many a protest was held there, and blood flowed in the streets, but that was a long time ago. We're finding peace now. Even in the north, we're finding peace." She flashed him a knowing smile. "Can't be havin' tourism without peace, and can't be makin' good money without tourism."

"It's the way of the world," he assured her.

"American-Irish?" she asked him, indicating his auburn hair.

He laughed. "We're all a bit Irish in America, I think — at least on St. Patrick's Day. My name is Flynn, but my father's family goes way back in the States. My mom was Irish, though." He frowned suddenly, looking past her. It had seemed as if a shadow had walked by, down the aisle of the plane. It must have been a trick of the light, he thought, as the plane canted, turning for its final approach to the runway.

"So are you coming home, then?" she asked.

He shook his head, but something about her expression touched him. "I'm only here to travel home with a friend who got sick right after he arrived." And whose daughter thinks her stepmother is trying to kill him.

"I see. Bringing him home for Christmas," she said softly.

"Well, bringing him home, yes. And it is nearly Christmas," Zach agreed.

She offered him a hand. "I'm Maeve."

"Nice to meet you, Maeve. I'm Zach."

"Well, I'm comin' home for Christmas," she said. "The old music, the old ways." She smiled at him. "Home is a fine place to be."

"Isn't home where the heart is?" he asked her with a smile.

She laughed quietly. "Aye, and my heart and home are both here, and that's a fact, lad. Those I love are here, and Dublin . . . it's what made me, and my lads and lasses are here, and their lads and lasses, and their little ones, so . . ."

He nodded his understanding.

"And where is home for you?" she asked him.

He hesitated, surprising himself. Home.

Where *was* his home now? Interesting question.

"My folks passed away a long time ago," he told her.

"Ah," she said softly, understandingly.

"I have two brothers, and they both have great wives. We grew up in Florida, and now one lives in New Orleans, and one is in Salem, Massachusetts. I still spend a lot of time in Miami."

"And you miss your brothers," she said sagely, nodding.

He laughed. "No, I see them all the time. We work together."

"A family business," she said with delight, then frowned, confused. "But however do you manage that, all livin' in different places and the like?"

"Computers. And . . . we were all in law enforcement, then left what we were doing to form an investigative agency, so we're traveling all the time anyway," he explained.

"Delving into the unknown," she said.

"The unknown is usually known — by someone," Zach said. "We find the things that someone else missed or overlooked." He was startled when she reached for his hand and studied his fingers.

"A musician, too," she told him.

He laughed, surprised. "Maeve, you ever

61

need a job, you call me. You're good."

"The singing detective?" she suggested.

"Nothing like that. I play guitar. I suppose I can carry a tune. But I run a small record label and a few studios. That's where my talents lie."

The flight attendant came on the P.A. to welcome them to Ireland. There was a jolt just as they landed, and Maeve, who still had his hand, grasped it tightly as her cheeks turned ashen.

"It was just a gust of wind as we came in," he assured her.

She flashed him a smile. "Just felt a shade o' darkness there, that's all, lad. A shadow on the heart."

He squeezed her hand in return. "It was just the wind," he repeated.

A shadow on the heart? he thought. Well, she *was* ninety-two, he reminded himself.

Odd turn of phrase, though, considering that he'd thought he'd seen a real shadow in the aisle.

Their flight had been an overnighter, and when he looked out the window again, the sun was coming up high.

A few seconds later, the sound of a hundred seatbelts unbuckling was like a strange, offbeat chorus. He stood and helped Maeve get her small bag from the compartment above her seat, then bade her goodbye and good luck, and went for his own suitcase. He strode off the plane, thinking he would head straight to the hospital and check in on Sean before doing anything else.

It had been several years since he'd been in Dublin, but the airport hadn't changed. He headed for customs, and watched as Maeve made her way toward the line for nationals. He blinked, thinking that he saw a shadow hovering near her. A shadow? In the brightly lit airport?

Jet lag. Had to be jet lag.

He turned away, then turned back.

Odd, out of the corner of his eye, he'd thought that he'd seen something else. An impression. A woman's face. Beautiful, with pitch-black hair and cobalt eyes, and features like Helen of Troy, pure perfection.

There were women all over the airport, he told himself dryly. A dark-haired woman rushing by Maeve, a young blonde excusing herself as she, too, moved quickly, and a fortyish matron who paused to speak. Zach couldn't hear her from where he stood, but from the looks of things, he was pretty sure the woman had asked Maeve if she needed any help. He would have helped her himself, but he was a tourist and had to go through a different line.

Maeve accepted a hand from the woman, and Zach smiled. Every once in a while you saw something that restored your faith in humanity. His smile faded. He hadn't seen it all that often lately, though maybe that was due to the work he'd chosen.

He'd worked forensics in Miami, and what he'd seen there hadn't been good. But he'd put in his time, and he'd been damn good at his job. But when he'd heard his brothers' proposal to open an agency, he'd been ready. He'd told Aidan he was ready to throw in with them the same day a crackhead had decided that microwaving his infant son would make him quit crying.

But there were decent people in the world, too, and he had to remember that. Like the woman who had helped Maeve. Like Sean O'Riley, who had been there after his parents had died, when Aidan was struggling to keep himself, Jeremy and Zach together as a family.

The woman was still there helping Maeve when he made his way to baggage claim. She was the one who cried out when Maeve suddenly fell.

There were no velvet ropes, gates or nationalities separating them then. Zach raced to Maeve's side. She gripped his arm when he bent to help her, and he knelt by her side, his training kicking in as he loosened her collar, testing her pulse.

She smiled up at him. "I'm almost home," she said. "And it's all right. I can hear the music, and the banshee's whispered in my ear. It's time. The luck o'the Irish be with you, my fine, kind lad." She reached up and trailed a finger over his face, then shuddered, and her eyes closed.

"Maeve?" He gently leaned his ear against her chest. She wasn't breathing, and the quick pressure of his fingers against her throat told him that she had no pulse. He told the woman who had helped Maeve to call emergency services, then started counting, pinching Maeve's nose shut and breathing into her mouth. He kept at it, but well before the emergency crew came to take over, he knew she was gone.

He stood there, watching the men work, watching as the sweet woman was declared dead at the scene. She'd wanted to come home, he told himself, and she had.

He had a sense of someone watching him, which was a little ridiculous. Half the people in the airport had been staring at him. But he turned and thought that he saw someone slipping around the corner.

Of course, he thought irritably. Lots of people were slipping around the corner.

They were leaving the airport.

He spoke with the authorities about Maeve, and they thanked him for all that he had done, though he hadn't really done anything, he thought in disgust. Maeve was dead.

He told himself that it had been her time. She had lived a long and good life.

Still, he couldn't just shake off her death. He collected his luggage and headed around the corner himself, in hopes that the car he had reserved was waiting.

As he exited the building, he saw the sign in Gaelic and English.

Eire. Cead mile failte. Ireland. A hundred-thousand welcomes.

Outside, he breathed a sigh of relief when he found his car. It was parked right next to a sign that advertised a pub whose slogan was *Paddy's! May the luck o' the Irish be with you.*

He greeted the driver and slid into the back of the sedan, thinking that he didn't believe in luck, Irish or otherwise.

He *did* believe in the good and evil that resided in men's hearts, and he was anxious to reach Sean, anxious to get him home, anxious to find Eddie. That was what he needed to concentrate on right now.

He checked his phone for messages. There

was a text from Aidan, who had contacted an old associate in Dublin, who was keeping an eye on things at the hospital. The man's name was Will Travis, and he was posing as an orderly to see that nothing else happened to Sean while he was there. Zach clicked his phone shut. He enjoyed working with his brothers. Their past careers made for good contacts in their present one. Aidan, as a former FBI agent, had some particularly useful ones.

He tried to keep his mind on the current problem, but as they drove to the hospital, he found that he was mourning Maeve, a woman he had barely known, and who had, in her own words, gone home.

"Hey there, you're not looking so bad!"

Caer had been sitting at Sean's side, listening to his tales of Rhode Island, when she heard the voice. Deep, resonant, pleasant. A rich tenor. No real accent, other than American.

At first he didn't even seem to notice her. He just strode into the room and over to Sean's side, which gave her a chance to examine him.

Tall, lean, clearly well-muscled but not bulked-up. She knew him immediately, of course, from the photograph and the color of his hair. Like his voice, something about that deep, rich color was compelling in itself.

"Zach, you've made it, lad. You didn't need to come, you know. That girl of mine, such a worrier. Bothering you to come over here when I'm right as rain," Sean announced. But his pleasure at Zachary's arrival was evident in the broad smile and the fact that his eyes had brightened like diamonds.

"Not a problem, Sean. Hey, who's going to complain about a trip back to Dublin? It was just a good excuse for me to come over for a few days," Zach said easily in reply to Sean. He, too, was smiling, and it was obvious that his words were genuine. Caring for an old friend was clearly not a bother for him but a pleasure.

Finally his eyes lit on Caer.

He started, as if he recognized her, as if he'd seen her before. Maybe not. Perhaps he was just startled by anyone else being there at all. Or because she was there, not Sean's supposedly loving wife. Or maybe, there was just something about her that looked familiar to him.

She recognized his eyes, though. They were the same true aquamarine she had seen in the picture, but even more powerful in person, as hypnotic as the sea, as deeply changeable. She felt as if he had the ability to look right through her.

She stared back, forcing herself to remain serene, expressionless, and prayed that her own eyes were every bit as enigmatic as his. Still, it felt as if time had stopped for a moment, for just a heartbeat. *Should* she know him? He'd been in Dublin before. Maybe it was one of those things where she had passed him once in the street and somehow the image had remained in her mind.

"Hello," he said.

Maybe she'd imagined the whole time-had-skipped-a-heartbeat thing. He sounded friendly but nothing more, certainly not as if he thought he should know her.

She rose from the bedside chair, extending a hand. "Hello. Welcome to Ireland. I'm Caer Cavannaugh. How do you do?"

"Zachary Flynn. And fine, thank you."

Naturally he had a great, firm handshake, she thought as she returned it.

"Caer's the world's loveliest and most patient nurse," Sean explained.

"Thank you," she murmured, her attention all for Zach Flynn, who was definitely studying her now. She felt as if she were blushing. Good God, how ridiculous. She didn't blush.

"Mr. O'Riley's too kind," she said smoothly. "Well, I'll let you two get on with it. A pleasure to meet you, Mr. Flynn."

"Zach," he said.

"Zach," she repeated.

"Caer is accompanying us home," Sean told Zach. He sounded gleeful. Like a little kid who had just acquired a toy that would make all the other kids jealous.

"Yes, Kat mentioned something about you traveling with a nurse," Zach said, still looking at Caer. "Have you been to the States before?" he asked her.

"Never. It will be quite a journey for me," she told him pleasantly.

"Quite an opportunity," he said.

Still that smooth tone to his voice. Lulling. But was there also a note of suspicion in it?

"Indeed," she agreed. "Well, if you'll excuse me . . . ?"

She left the room, but as she slipped out, she heard Sean say, "This is foolish. You having to come all the way here, just for me."

She paused in the hallway, just out of sight, to listen.

"Kat is worried about you."

"She should have come herself."

Caer sensed Zach's hesitation. At last he

said, "She didn't feel it would be in anyone's best interest if she came."

"Oh, that child! I love her, but she's absolutely convinced that Amanda married me for my money and is just waiting for me to die."

Zach didn't bother to deny it.

"She's overprotective," Sean said.

"She loves you," Zach told him.

Caer could see Sean, in her mind's eye, waving a hand impatiently in the air. "She should have a little faith in me. I'm not a doddering old fool. I'm not desperate for love and affection — or sex." He paused, then went on. "The thing is, you're here — where you shouldn't be — to protect me, when I'm not the one in trouble. Eddie is. You should be in Newport, trying to figure out what the hell happened to him."

Caer continued to hover just outside the doorway, listening.

"Sean, the sooner we can get back, the better chance we'll have of discovering what happened," Zach said.

Caer heard just a hint of impatience in the man's tone, telling her that he felt he should already be on the trail of the man who had disappeared.

"Eddie's *got* to be all right," Sean said.

There was silence. She knew that Zach

71

didn't think Eddie was all right, and he wasn't going to lie to Sean and say that he did.

Sean spoke again. "Who the hell would want to kill an old geezer like Eddie? He's never hurt anyone. People love him. Maybe he was swept overboard and picked up by someone else. Maybe he lost his memory."

"Amnesia?" Zach offered.

"Yeah, amnesia. It's possible."

"Sean, I've checked all the area hospitals. No one has admitted anyone who fits Eddie's description."

"And you've checked the morgues, too, right?" Sean asked hesitantly.

"Yes."

"And no Eddie, right?" Sean asked.

"No," Zach agreed.

"Maybe someone kidnapped him," Sean suggested.

"Yeah, sure. Maybe," Zach said. He sounded unconvinced. "So where's Amanda?"

"At the hotel. She was feeling all wrung out from the stress of worrying about me, taking care of me . . . you know. Anyway, I told her to take some time today. Get herself a massage. She'll be around later tonight. She's anxious to see you."

"I'm sure," Zach said, not sounding sure

72

at all. "What about the doctor? I have to talk to him. Kat will have my head if I don't come back with a full list of all your medications, what you can do, what you can't do."

Caer heard footsteps in the hall, probably Sean's doctor on the way. She slipped around the corner and headed for Michael's office.

"Help. Is anyone out there?" came a weak cry from one of the rooms.

Caer paused, turned and headed in. A frail old woman was lying in one of the beds. She looked as if she had lived several lifetimes, all of them tough.

"Hi, what do you need?" Caer asked gently.

"Just the telly thing, there, dear. I hate to ring the bell and be botherin' a nurse for such nonsense, but I can't get the thing. It fell."

Caer smiled and stooped down for the remote. "It should be on a string, attached to the bed," Caer said. "I'll see that someone comes in and fixes that for you."

"Ah, bless ya, lass," the woman said. Caer looked at her. She was old and worn, but her eyes were bright. Her hand, as it fell on Caer's, was all bones and age spots, but it felt surprisingly strong. Her eyes narrowed as she looked at Caer, and something seemed to disturb her, but she offered a tremulous smile. "Gentle and kind, you are."

Caer squeezed the woman's hand and backed away quickly, glancing at the woman's chart and her name. "Mrs. McGillicutty, when you need something and you can't get it yourself, you ring that bell, do you hear me?"

"I don't like to be a nuisance," Mrs. McGillicutty said.

"You're not a nuisance, so get that thought right out of your head," Caer said firmly. "And I'll send someone in here right away to fix that remote."

As she started out of the room, another woman came in, moving quickly. She was perhaps forty or so, and pretty, except for her look of fatigue and stress. She smiled at Caer hesitantly. "Is everything all right? Mum is . . . ?" Her smile was beginning to fade.

"Fine, fine. She just needs a bit of very simple technology — a cord for her remote," Caer assured her, and the other woman let out a sigh and went to the bedside, kissing the old woman's cheek as she took her hand.

"Mary, me love. So good to see ya."

Mrs. McGillicutty took her daughter's hand, and her eyes were bright.

Caer was surprised to feel a sting of tears come to her own eyes. She was startled by her own show of emotion and swiped impatiently at her cheeks. But it was beautiful, the loving bond between mother and daughter.

"That pretty nurse is just going to be seeing to it that I can reach my telly-thing here," Mrs. McGillicutty said happily, then turned to Caer.

"Mary took over my husband's pub when he passed away," she said proudly. "You'll have to stop in — it's just down the street. It's called Irish Eyes."

"Mum," Mary said, "I'm sure she has better things to do."

"I'd love to stop by," Caer said. "I'll come tonight." She smiled warmly.

Mary flushed slightly. " 'Tis just a working man's place," Mary said.

"And a working woman's, as well," Mrs. McGillicutty chastised.

"I just meant that . . . well, it's a pub. Family style. Nothing fancy," Mary explained.

"Nothing fancy needed. I'd love to stop by."

Caer had the feeling that it would be old-style and charming, not like all those soulless new bars taking over the city.

And, she thought, irritably, if she was

heading to America, Michael could stuff himself if he didn't think she deserved a night out before she left. She had that envelope full of money to spend, straight out of petty cash, and she didn't see any reason not to spend some of it at Mary's pub.

She hadn't checked the amount, of course, but she doubted that it was too "petty." She would spend the afternoon of the day shopping and doing a bit of research on another O'Riley, and then she would stop by the pub.

"I'll see you later," Caer said with a smile.

"Lovely," Mary told her.

Caer left the room at last, seeing to it that a nurse's aide went to take care of Mrs. McGillicutty's remote control, then quickly changing out of her uniform. On her way out, she stopped by Sean O'Riley's door. He was still in conversation with Zachary Flynn, but their voices were too low for her to hear.

Caer left the hospital and wandered the streets, shopping for what she thought she might need in America, though quite frankly, she had no idea what would be stylish for a Rhode Island winter. She did the best she could, though she was handicapped by the fact that she seldom dressed in normal street clothing.

With her purchases made, she went on to the hotel where Sean and his wife were staying. Amanda wasn't in her room; at least, she didn't answer when Caer called her on the house phone. Deciding that the other woman must still be in the spa, Caer decided it was time to find out what the ritzy establishment had to offer.

It was all on Michael's euro, after all, she thought with a satisfied smile.

She checked her purchases with the bell desk and headed for the spa. Apparently, everyone felt the need for something exotic, since Mandarin specialties were prominently advertised. She managed a quick look at the register and discovered that Amanda O'Riley was in the orange-herbal baths. Happily, she was able to arrange for a walk-in treatment for herself.

She was escorted to a room where sitar music played softly, and she was offered slippers, a bathrobe and herbal tea. She asked if they had Irish breakfast tea, instead, which the consultant prepared for her, but only after looking at her strangely. Apparently few people turned down the herbal variety. Then she was served strawberries, which were delicious — she could barely remember tasting anything so sweet — and then she was whisked off to the bath, where she shed her robe and slipped into a giant tub filled with hot water, herbs and orange peels. Now she was listening to harp music, and luckily, she was in the tub right next to Sean's wife.

The blonde was lying back in the water, her hair wrapped in a towel to keep it dry, just as Caer's had been. A pillow rested beneath her head, but she had removed the cucumbers she had been given to set on her eyelids and was chatting to the woman on her other side.

The water was soothing, and a series of small jets kept it in constant motion. That, combined with the orange peels and whatever concoction of herbs floated in the water, intended to soften the skin, was extremely pleasant. She allowed her cucumbers to remain on her eyelids and listened in, though she hardly imagined that — if Amanda had indeed caused Sean's illness in some way — she was going to blurt out a confession to a stranger.

"Eddie is such a nice guy. It's too bad he's the one who's missing, not Marni, Cal's wife. Talk about a piece of work. She has a husband of her own, but she's always looking to sweet-talk *mine*. Not that I blame her, really. You'd have to know Sean to understand just how fabulous he is, even though he's so much older than I am. He's got the constitution of an ox. He's never ill — well, usually. Honestly, I don't understand what could have happened." The woman sounded genuinely puzzled, Caer thought. "All this has really upset me. I needed today. Absolutely *needed* a break from the depressing atmosphere of . . . that crummy hospital."

Caer almost sat up in indignation. The hospital was understaffed, admittedly. But it was a good hospital, and the employees worked very hard. It was more than a job to the people she had come across there — it was a caring way of life. . . .

And depressing? Crummy?

Christmas was still weeks away, but in their free time, the staff had put up trees on every floor and in every ward. They had festooned the walls with decorations, and done everything they could to brighten the patients' rooms for the holidays, so those stuck in bed to while away their hours of pain and sickness would have something cheery to look at.

Well, she hadn't cared much for Amanda when she had met her, and nothing she was hearing now was doing anything to change her opinion. She certainly didn't seem like the kind of woman a man like Sean would choose to marry.

"You know," Amanda said to the woman on her far side, "he may be older, but all those years of experience certainly pay off in bed." She giggled. "I mean, he's *hot.* Maybe that's what I should do," she said, considering. "Something risqué, like making it with him in his hospital bed."

Far more than Caer wanted to know.

But the woman on the other side of Amanda was apparently perfectly happy to discuss other people's sex lives.

"If the man is ill and, well, *older,* that might not be all that good for him," she said.

"Really?" Amanda said thoughtfully. "It could be just what he needs."

Amanda's cosmetician came by then with a massive towel to help her out of the water, informing her that it was time for her sea-salt scrub.

Caer sank deeper into the water, grateful now that the woman hadn't noticed her, since she was going to be traveling with them, and Amanda might not be best pleased if Sean's nurse knew all about her love life.

Caer opted against the sea-salt scrub herself, and quickly dressed and headed downstairs, where she pulled out her cell phone and dialed Michael. When he answered, her heart sank. It sounded as if he were at the races. "You're not at the hospital, are you?" she asked.

"No, but I made sure someone's there," he told her.

"Sean needs to be watched carefully tonight."

"He's your assignment," Michael told her.

"Yes, but if I'm leaving tomorrow, I have things to do," she informed him.

"What's the problem?" he asked.

"I think that his wife might actually try to kill him tonight."

"How? A knife? A gun? More poison?" Michael asked sharply.

"No. With . . . kindness, you might say."

"What?"

She groaned inwardly. "Michael, she was talking about shagging him in the hospital. If that causes any kind of a strain on his heart, it could be dangerous for him."

"Mmm, but what a way to go, huh?" he said lightly.

"Michael!"

"Sorry, sorry, just thinking it might be just the thing for a lot of poor blokes out there."

"Are you taking this seriously at all?" she demanded. "Because if you're not —"

"If I weren't, you wouldn't be going to America," he told her. "But don't worry,

81

get your shopping done — and whatever else it is you intend for the night."

"I intend to learn how to blend in like a normal person," she informed him. "God knows, working for you, I seldom get that pleasure."

"Go on then, blend. I have someone at the hospital, and I'll see that Sean's not left alone with his devoted spouse. But once you leave the country, he'll be your responsibility. What will you do then?" he queried. "Sleep on a cot in the marital bedroom?"

"You really should think about stand-up comedy," she said irritably. "I just think that he needs to be a bit stronger before he . . . you know."

"Jealous?"

"Of what?" she demanded.

She heard the laughter deep in his throat. "A good shag?"

"I'm hanging up now, Michael," she told him, but he stopped her before she could make good on her threat.

"Caer."

"Yes?"

"After you left, they finished their arrangements. You will be leaving tomorrow. Zach Flynn met with the doctor, and O'Riley's records have already been transmitted to the States. Mr. Flynn seemed to have no problem with a nurse attending Mr. O'Riley — in fact, he seemed to think it was a wise decision. He even appeared amused when he discovered it was you. He teased Mr. O'Riley that his wife might not be pleased. So there you go. She definitely won't be happy at all about that cot in her bedroom."

She took a deep breath, ready to tell him what to do with himself, but he went on too quickly for any interruption.

"You leave the hospital in a limo with the O'Rileys and Mr. Flynn at 8:00 a.m. sharp for an eleven-forty-five to New York City, where you'll transfer to a flight into Providence."

"No problem."

"Don't be late."

"I'm never late, Michael. Being on time is a requirement of the job, after all."

"Yes, so I need to get on this right away. Flynn has left the hospital. In fact, he should be arriving at the hotel any minute."

As Michael spoke, Caer saw the American walking into the lobby.

"Right. He's here."

They said goodbye quickly, and she hung up, wondering if she should try to hide behind one of the pillars and avoid him. But she was too late. He had seen her. He'd walked in with his head slightly lowered, as

83

if he were in deep thought, and when his eyes fell on her, they seemed to fill with a touch of annoyance as well as curiosity.

"Hello, Miss Cavannaugh," he said.

"Hello," she said, inexplicably at a loss for conversation.

"I understand that you're flying with us tomorrow."

"Yes."

"So what brings you to the hotel?"

"The spa," she said quickly.

"Oh?"

She blushed. Dammit, she didn't blush, and now he'd made her do so twice in one day. It was the way he was looking at her, as if she were a typical woman, as if creature comforts and looking pretty were all that mattered to her.

"I've never flown before," she said. Stupid admission! But he seemed so suspicious of her from the get-go, as if she couldn't possibly be what she claimed to be, so she felt the need to convince him. "To be honest," she added ruefully, "I've never been outside the British Isles. I'm a bit nervous about the plane ride, and I thought I'd try something to . . . not be nervous."

"Ah."

"Well, I'll let you get to your room," she told him.

"I'm not in a terrible hurry," he said.

Great, she thought. So they were just supposed to stand there, staring at one another?

He smiled slowly, as if aware of her discomfort and trying to put her at ease. "Are you set for the trip?" he asked her. He was staring at the shopping bags she had retrieved from behind the bell desk.

"As set as I can be," she replied.

He studied her again. "Are you free for a bit?"

"Free? In what way?" she asked cautiously.

"I was thinking of checking on Amanda, then getting a bite to eat. I was hoping you would join me."

"Oh, well, perhaps Amanda's hungry, too," she suggested.

"I'm assuming that Amanda will want to see Sean sometime today."

An unbidden image of Amanda's plans for the evening popped into Caer's mind. But Michael would see to it that Sean was kept safe from his wife's "ministrations," she thought.

She blinked to dispel the unwelcome image and was staring at the face of the man before her. A striking face. Strong features that helped to define the sea-colored eyes and auburn hair. His was a face that offered a grave maturity along with youth. She didn't think he could be much more than thirty, and yet something in his eyes made it appear that he had acquired the knowledge of a lifetime.

He was a private investigator. He'd been in law enforcement, forensics, before that. No doubt he'd seen far more than he had ever wanted to of the dark side of human nature.

But surely not even he could know about Michael and the Agency.

"You *were* going to eat this evening, right? Dinner?" he said.

"I was going to a pub," she said. "To see friends," she added quickly. Saying goodbye to friends would be the natural thing to do before taking a long journey.

"If you know a good one and can bear the company . . . ?" he asked.

"Of course," she said stiffly, wondering how she was going to handle the question of friends if he actually insisted on accompanying her. In fact, she thought, this was where he should have politely let her off the hook, seeing as she hadn't replied with anything that resembled enthusiasm. But he didn't.

"Sean's welfare is of the utmost concern to both of us," he said.

"Then maybe one of us should stay at the

hospital," she suggested.

He smiled. "Not necessary."

"Oh?"

"One of the orderlies is actually an associate," he told her.

"An associate of what?" she asked, frowning.

"The family business," he said lightly, and shrugged. "You'll be getting all the family dirt soon enough, might as well start off knowing the full story. As you may have realized, Amanda and Kat don't get along. Kat believes Amanda caused her father's illness."

"And what do *you* believe?" she asked him.

He shrugged. "You've met Amanda, right. Flighty? Yes? Clever enough to pull off the perfect crime? Not unless she's an exceptional actress. But right now, I'm not sure it matters so much what I believe. It's better to keep all bases covered and just see what, if anything, happens." He had been speaking relatively lightly, but he sobered as he added, "One of Sean's partners has gone missing, so all precautions should be taken."

"I see," she said.

"Will you wait for me?" he asked her.

She wanted to lie. She wanted to tell him that she'd thought about it, and her friends would feel uncomfortable about a stranger crashing her farewell, but she couldn't quite bring herself to.

"Mr. Flynn, you must be worn out. On an overnight plane, at the hospital all day," she said.

"Too dingy looking for public consumption, am I?"

"I didn't mean that."

"Give me ten minutes."

"Seriously —"

"Please?" he said pleasantly.

She hesitated, then nodded slowly. Anything else would have been rude. And maybe Mary would greet her warmly enough that she would appear to have at least one friend.

There was an elegant bar just off the lobby, and he indicated that she should wait for him there. "May I hold your bags for you?"

"What?"

"Your shopping bags. We can leave them in my room while we're at dinner, and then I'll fetch them down and see you home for the night afterward," he said.

She was loath to give up the bags, almost as if she would find herself trapped if she handed them over.

But then she grew irritated with herself

for being afraid of the man, knowing full well that he was suspicious of her, and that was why he was promoting their acquaintance. She stiffened inwardly. She was not going to worry about him; she knew what she was doing, and she didn't intend to let him interfere with her purpose.

She'd already missed the chance to say something useful, like, Sorry, but I'm not nearly ready for this trip, and I have to go home and pack. Or, Sorry, but I have to drive out to the country and say goodbye to Mum and Dad.

And now she was standing there looking like an idiot.

Nothing to do but try to appear gracious. And to use this man, if need be, since he was clearly close to the family.

She offered him the bags. "Lovely, thanks."

And with that, she turned and headed into the bar.

4

It had been a long day. A long flight, and a long afternoon at the hospital, time on the phone, time wishing he hadn't come — time wishing he could stay longer. If he'd had any sense, he would have had dinner sent up and gotten a good night's sleep.

But the temptation to find out more about the nurse who was accompanying Sean home had been strong. He didn't tend to categorize people based on looks, and he'd seen plenty of beautiful nurses. But this woman was absolutely striking.

The image of her perfect, porcelain skin and cobalt eyes remained with him as he checked in at the desk, got his key and a welcome speech, and was pointed toward the elevator.

Thoughts of her remained with him as he quickly washed his face, ran a razor over the more-than-shadow he had acquired since he'd last shaved, and hopped in and out of the shower quickly enough to feel the heat of the water and wish he could stay longer.

She was wearing a casual blue sweater dress, so he chose a blue sweater, as well, to go with black jeans and his overcoat. Blue, he thought, taking one last look in the mirror. Deep, dark blue — but still no match for the color of her eyes.

Whoa, buddy, he told himself. He was supposed to be figuring her out, seeing as she was about to be very close to Sean for a while, not assessing the virtues of her appearance. But since they were on his mind, maybe he should assess them and get the subject out of the way. Okay, list time.

Her hair had a blue-black gleam more brilliant than a raven's wing, and judging by the way the sweater dress molded her form, she was built as perfectly as any model who had ever graced the pages of a Victoria's Secret catalogue, and he had the feeling she wouldn't need any airbrushing. Maybe it was the arrangements of her features that made her so compelling. Her face was a delicate oval, her nose perfect, her lips generous and yet cleanly shaped. She had high, elegant cheekbones, and those eyes . . .

He'd noticed that those eyes were often

wary, filled with suspicion. But he was somehow certain that those eyes could also fill with passion and compassion, that they could blaze with anger against injustice, and soften to the warm blue of a summer's day with empathy for those in her care.

So what was his problem? What was not to like?

Something about her just wasn't right, though he couldn't figure out what. They were heading to a pub to say goodbye to her friends, and that was certainly normal enough. She worked in the hospital, was clearly known there. . . .

On the other hand, his brother's old associate was theoretically working in the hospital, too, and he was anything but what he seemed.

He felt that the evening was going to be important; it would be a chance to see her in her element and get a better sense of her.

Why the hell was she willing to drop everything at a moment's notice and head off to the United States to care for an old man with an undiagnosed illness? Maybe that question, more than anything, was at the heart of his curiosity, his suspicions.

Once, she might have been glad for any opportunity to go to the States. Years ago, the economic situation in Dublin had been bad enough to send Irish nurses to the U.S. by the thousands. But Ireland was enjoying a time of solid financial footing these days, and the immigration level of the Irish to the U.S. had definitely dwindled. She wasn't accompanying Sean in hopes of making her way to a new country for good.

He'd had her credentials checked out, and on paper, she was everything she should be.

There was just that something he couldn't put his finger on, something he sensed. Aidan claimed that "sixth sense" was what made a good private investigator, and Zach had to agree.

Sean adored Caer Cavannaugh. He barely knew her, but he already spoke of her with genuine affection. There was nothing lascivious in it, so it wasn't as if he was head over heels — as he had been when he'd decided to marry Amanda. That union had surprised all of them. Not only because of the vast age difference, though that was certainly a red flag, but because Sean was a man who loved books, learning and the sea, and Amanda was interested in none of those things. Sean was definitely well off, but he wasn't stupid enough to be taken in by a simple gold digger. Not even Kat was sure why she was so convinced her stepmother wanted to do in her father. She knew she was protected in his will, as were his partners and his business.

Of course, if Eddie weren't found, there would have to be some changes.

He chafed, thinking about Eddie and how much he wanted to be back in the States, searching for the man.

There was no way he could think of that Amanda could be guilty of Eddie's disappearance. Sean and Amanda had left the States the same day that Eddie had headed out on his fateful trip. Eddie had left at midday, and the O'Rileys hadn't departed until the early evening, but from what Kat had told him, she'd seen Amanda around the house during the day. She had to pack the right jewelry, the right gowns for an evening out, the right casual couture for scrambling around the hills, and heading out of Dublin to view castle ruins and kiss the Blarney Stone. He'd spoken to Kat long enough to know that no, she couldn't swear to Amanda's whereabouts for the entire day, but she'd admitted that she wasn't sure how Amanda could have gotten out of the house long enough to get to Eddie out on the water and do something to him.

So Amanda and Sean had set out after a small goodbye party where people had commented on Eddie's absence but just assumed he'd gotten held up on his afternoon cruise or down at the marina. It hadn't been until the next day that Cal had reported — after arriving at work himself — that Eddie wasn't there, and neither was the boat he had taken out the day before. He'd found the receipt for payment in the drawer. Cash. The name on the receipt had been John Alden, possibly real, but also a good enough alias to pass in New England. With no leads, the police were stymied.

Then, just before Zach had boarded his plane for Dublin, Eddie's boat had been discovered, but with no sign of Eddie. No sign of foul play. Just the boat, drifting alone.

It was winter, but the weather had been mild. There had been no storms to sweep him overboard. There had been no rough water or unexpectedly strong currents, nothing that might have posed any danger for an old salt like Eddie.

Sean hadn't found out about Eddie immediately, because he had been rushed to the hospital just as the police had begun to investigate Eddie's disappearance. But now Sean knew, and he was sick with worry.

Eddie was more than a partner to him.

Eddie had been his support when he was young and determined to take over the business and make a real go of it. Eddie was his best friend.

It was bizarre, Eddie disappearing and Sean coming down with a debilitating and inexplicable illness. Two incidents, across the Atlantic from one another, and yet his gut told him they were related.

Tomorrow night they would be back in the States. In Rhode Island. And then he could find out what the hell had happened to Eddie. If Eddie could be found, he would find him, he thought grimly. But there was one problem.

Sometimes the sea gave back.

And sometimes the sea was an endless black abyss, swallowing all signs of guilt — including the victim. If Eddie had been murdered and cast overboard . . .

He picked up his bedside phone and asked to be connected with Mrs. O'Riley. But Mrs. O'Riley was apparently still at the spa.

She would no doubt argue that she needed to be her absolute best in order to give Sean all the care and attention he would need during the flight home and during his recuperation. Zach didn't care. He thought her place was at the hospital, by her husband's side.

He grabbed his wallet and his overcoat, pocketed his key and headed downstairs.

He wondered if Caer Cavannaugh had really waited for him, or if she had simply headed out the door the moment he had gotten into the elevator.

But she was there. He saw her as soon as he headed toward the open French doors that separated the bar from the lobby. She was sitting by a window with a pint of dark beer in front of her, and seemed to be studying the glass and the beer in it as if they were both something strange and unusual.

Someone walked by on the street outside. The winter evening was already sliding toward a deeper darkness, and for a moment, she was cast completely in shadow. He found himself inadvertently thinking back to Maeve, earlier that day, and the way a shadow had seemed to pass by her on the plane and again in the airport. Maeve. A kind woman who had lived a long life and come home before leaving this world. He felt a tightening in his muscles and a strange sense of fear for Caer Cavannaugh. She wasn't old; she hadn't lived anything that resembled a full lifetime. An urge to protect her washed over him like a whitecap hitting a granite coast.

He gave himself a shake. He'd seen so much that was horrendous and cruel and shouldn't have been a part of anyone's life, and that was affecting his judgment now. It was absurd to connect Maeve's gentle death with his unwarranted fear for Caer.

He'd spent his law enforcement career in forensics; he knew all about science and logic. He knew, as well, that fate was fickle, and no respecter of youth. Infants died; children fell prey to abuse from the adults who should have gone to any end to protect them; people of all ages suffered from terrible diseases. That was sad, but it was fact.

Fearing shadows . . . that was ridiculous.

He was tired, that was all.

Caer looked up, that raven's wing of dark hair framing the perfection of her features.

She even offered him a tentative smile.

He walked toward her, and as he got closer, he felt a sense of being drawn in, replacing his instinctive urge to protect.

A sense of being the hunted, rather than the hunter.

Which was absurd, although he supposed even he deserved a moment to indulge in imagination — especially here in this land of myth and mystery.

His mind filled with a vision of winds that howled, storms that raged, a green that was greener than emeralds, laughter and tall tales. This was a land of belief, in God and in a mythical history populated by fanciful beings that had never lived and breathed except in the imaginations of a population fond of tall tales.

Logic and science, those were the things he knew. He blinked hard and gritted his teeth, determined to cast off the strange fancies no doubt born of exhaustion.

"So where are we going?" he asked Caer casually when he reached her side and sat down. He was close enough to smell the subtle scent of her perfume. Nothing overwhelming.

Just . . .

Seductive.

"Irish Eyes," she told him, signaling to the young man behind the bar to bring her check.

Irish eyes. Was that what hers were? Bluer than cobalt or sapphires, a color so vibrant and deep. Irish eyes.

"Irish eyes," he repeated questioningly.

She stared at him. "Irish Eyes. It's the name of the pub," she said.

He quickly regained his composure, feeling like an idiot. "Right. Forgive an outsider's confusion," he said lightly.

She smiled. "No problem. It's a very popular place at Temple Bar. I'm sorry if that disappoints you, since many an American tourist makes his way there, so you won't be getting off the beaten track, I'm afraid."

"I'll still be with a native," he said gallantly.

He took the check when it came, though she tried to demur.

"Hey, we're both working for Sean, right?" he said.

"Working?" she said, studying him with a frown. "But you're his friend."

"I *am* his friend. A friend who intends to make sure he remains on this earth for a long time to come," Zach said firmly. He signed the check to his room and started to turn away.

"A minute," she told him.

He frowned as she reached for her pint and arched a brow. "We're headed to another pub. You don't have to swig."

"Swig," she said, rolling the word on her tongue and smiling as if she liked it.

"Or we can wait," he said, leaning back.

"It's just that this is an exceptionally lovely beer," she told him.

"Sure," he said.

She didn't swig, but she didn't tarry, either. When she finished, she set the glass back on the table and smiled her enjoyment. She must have sensed that he was watching her, because a slight stain of color touched her cheeks.

"I'm sorry. I don't get out all that often," she told him.

"I see." He didn't see at all, though. Why would a woman who looked the way she did not get out? It couldn't be for lack of invitations.

"Let's go," she said cheerfully.

As she stood, she swayed slightly. He automatically put an arm around her, steadying her, and his libido took a wild leap. She was warm, so vital against him that he found himself instantly lost in carnal thoughts that entwined with the reborn desire to protect her from . . . something. He gritted his teeth, torn between the desire to push her away and the urge to shake her and demand to know the truth.

What truth?

. . . Why was he so convinced that there was more to her than what he saw? Why not just accept her at her very attractive face value and be glad for the chance to spend time in her company?

He didn't know, nor did he have time to explore the thought, because she pulled herself together quickly and apologized. "I am so sorry. I haven't had a drink in . . . I can't even remember. I'll go slow tonight, I promise you."

"Don't worry, I won't let any harm befall you," he said, stepping back and wondering why he'd chosen that particular turn of phrase. For just a moment their eyes seemed to lock.

Images flashed through his mind. Eddie on an open sea. Maeve dying in his arms. Sean in his hospital bed. Blue eyes, bluer than the sea and sky, deep and dark, staring back into his eyes. Eyes filled with enigma and shadows . . .

She turned swiftly, heading for the door. "Chop-chop, then. Let's go on for a bit of supper and get back, eh? Tomorrow will be long."

She had moved, and whatever had held him hypnotized lifted its hold.

Yeah, supper. Something to eat and a good night's sleep. Tomorrow, back to reality, and starting tomorrow night, the search for Eddie.

He would bring logic to bear, and discover the truth behind Eddie's disappearance and Sean's illness.

Cal Johnson usually slept well. But not tonight. Tonight he couldn't stop thinking.

He was the youngest of the three partners, and he knew he'd been brought in because Eddie and Sean had been starting to get tired of handling everything themselves. Face it, they were both getting older — even if Sean had married a woman half his age. The point was, the two older guys wanted more free time. Hell, they deserved it. They'd worked hard.

They loved their history, those two. Loved to pore over books and charts, then sail out to the site of some important event and relive it.

He wasn't all that into history himself.

He was still into making money.

He love sailing, and loved the area. And if he had to learn history to run a successful charter business, then he was glad to do so, but it wasn't anything he would have done otherwise. He was better when his passengers just wanted a look at the scenery from the water, or even a sailing lesson. He was good at that.

And no one could tell a worn-out old story and make it sound exciting again the way Sean could.

It had to be three or four in the morning, he thought, tossing restlessly.

Why the hell couldn't he sleep?

Eddie. That was why.

They'd found the boat, but there'd been no sign of Eddie.

He trembled suddenly. He knew why he

had awakened. He'd had a nightmare. He'd seen Eddie all covered in seaweed, tangled up in ropes and torn sails. Hungry sea creatures had been clinging to him, were almost a part of him.

He'd come in with the shriek of the wind, all darkness and menace and . . .

He'd stood at the foot of the bed, staring down at Cal, but when he'd opened his mouth to speak, he hadn't said anything.

Cal had awakened instantly and sat up, but Eddie, of course, hadn't been there.

There was no actual proof that Eddie was dead, he told himself. Eddie had taken out a single passenger and hadn't come back for the party. Then the Coast Guard had discovered the *Sea Maiden.* Nothing wrong, nothing out of order. Sails furled.

Except that neither Eddie nor his passenger had been seen since.

Cal closed his eyes, exhausted. It was winter, but the weather was good, so people kept wanting to go out, damn them. And with Eddie missing and Sean sick over in Ireland, he'd been left to manage everything himself. Now he was exhausted.

And he was scared.

At his side, Marni stirred.

He didn't want to wake her.

Too late.

"What's wrong?" she asked him.

"I don't know. I just . . . woke up."

She reached out and stroked his face. "It's all right, Cal. Sean will be back soon. Kat sent that friend of theirs, Zach Flynn, to bring him home."

Cal felt a flash of annoyance. His own wife would feel secure if Sean — a sick old man! — came home. She was supposed to feel secure with *him*. But she doted on Sean.

Then he wondered if he was annoyed because Zach was coming. Sean, in turn, doted on the Flynns, especially Zach.

He took a deep breath and told himself to watch it. Jealousy was a curse.

"Cal?" she urged when he didn't say anything.

"I saw Eddie," he whispered, feeling a strange trembling inside. He had liked old Eddie. What hadn't been to like?

"What?" Marni sat up with a jerk. "You saw him? Where? You have to tell the cops. Everyone thinks that . . . that . . ."

"They think he's dead. *I* think he's dead."

"Then what are you talking about, Cal?" Marni asked, a quiver in her tone. "You just said you'd seen him. You're sounding crazy, you know that?"

"I had a nightmare, that's all. Go back to sleep."

She fell back on her pillow, but he knew she wasn't sleeping. She was studying him.

He winced. His wife was beautiful, and he knew he was a lucky man. Sure, Sean was rich and he was just the junior partner, but he should be glad that his wife was so fond of Sean, that they got along so well. He didn't need to worry about her, didn't need to be jealous. She was a good wife, and Sean . . . wasn't interested in her that way. He had his own wife. Amanda.

What the hell was it about Amanda? Women just naturally seemed to hate her. Men couldn't help but notice her. There was something about the way she walked. Sashayed, he thought. Whatever. It was sexy.

He noticed — he couldn't help it — but . . .

She wasn't Marni. No, she was nothing like Marni, with her down-to-earth, natural beauty. Or Kat. Kat was a beauty, too. Vivacious, and refreshingly unaware of her own assets.

Between the three of them, though — Kat, Amanda and Marni — there were definitely some strange dynamics. Kat seemed to like *his* wife, though, and that was all that mattered to him.

He leaned over and kissed Marni's forehead. She wrapped her arms around him, pulled him down and kissed him back, slow at first, then deeper, and finally totally insinuating, as she pressed the curves of her body against him. He felt the tension left over from the nightmare slip away.

She could make love like a high-priced call girl, and in a matter of minutes he had forgotten about his horrific vision of Eddie. A bout of hot-and-heavy sex wiped away thoughts of anything other than his desire to feel himself inside her again soon.

After their lovemaking, she curled against him and he glanced at the bedside clock. Only two o'clock, not as late as he had thought. Seven in the morning in Ireland. Soon time for them to get up there, getting ready to board their plane for the States.

But tonight, Sean would be back and could start taking charge again, even if he was still stuck in bed.

Cal closed his eyes. He needed to sleep.

Just as he drifted off, he thought that he heard the wind rising again and opened his eyes.

Eddie was back, dripping saltwater and seaweed, standing at the foot of his bed and staring at him.

5

Dublin was alive and beautiful by night. Lights from pubs, restaurants and trendy cafés spilled out onto the sidewalk. In the southwest section of the city, the ancient blended with the merely old and the downright new. They headed past Dublin Castle, going toward Temple Bar, the area between Dame Street and the River Liffey. It was a place he knew well, having come often enough in the past few years, since it had filled with shops, restaurants and museums.

Caer looked at him. "You know the area?"

"Not as well as you do, I'm sure."

She smiled. "It's called Temple Bar because the land was acquired by a man named Temple in the sixteen-hundreds. And the 'bar' is the path along the river. And luckily, it's not far from the hotel."

"Luckily," he agreed. "Though I usually take mass transit, I admit."

She flashed him a grin. "Aye, but when

the weather's fair, it's a fine walk." She frowned. "So, is the weather as fierce in New England as they say?"

"They say it's fierce in New England?" he asked her.

"Well, the pilgrims all died, didn't they?"

He laughed. "Not all of them — and not from the weather. I have to admit, I've always lived in the South, but I've visited the O'Rileys often enough to have experienced a few New England winters firsthand. He and my father were friends, and Sean was like an uncle to me and my brothers after our parents died. So New England in winter? You just never know. It can get cold, a lot colder than it usually gets here. But on the coast, unless a storm is coming in, the days tend to be temperate enough. When there is a storm, though, it can get pretty wild. I actually like a good storm — watching from a nice warm room, of course. I've been caught in a few gales off the coast and it's not my idea of a good time, but the old salts — guys like Sean and Eddie — they love the wind and the whip of the waves."

"Sounds dangerous," Caer said.

There had been no storm when Eddie headed out, Zach thought.

"The elements anywhere can be dangerous," he pointed out.

But man could be far more dangerous, he added silently.

"You're thinking about Eddie, aren't you? You're thinking that he's dead, and you're worrying about Sean," she told him.

"Yes."

"You know Eddie?"

"Yes."

"Do you think that maybe . . . I don't know? That he's maybe gone into hiding for some reason?" she asked.

"I wish I did," he answered.

She was silent; then she pointed to one of the spires rising into the night sky and said, "Christ Church Cathedral. It was built by a man known as Silkbeard. He was actually Sitric, a Norse king of Dublin. Did you know the city was founded by the Norse? Then there were the Normans, the Norman English and the English. Can you imagine all the plotting and fighting that's gone on here?"

He was surprised; she sounded as if she were actually trying to lighten his mood.

"You really love this city, don't you?" he asked her.

"What's not to love?" she replied softly. "Dublin is one of the most wonderful cities on earth."

He laughed. "You told me you'd never

been outside the British Isles."

"I've seen the Travel Channel," she said defensively.

"I'm not arguing. It's a wonderful city," he assured her, trying not to laugh at her indignation. And she was right. Dublin *was* an amazing city. So much history, a lot of it tragic, but nowadays the city was as alive and cosmopolitan as any place he knew. Walking along the street, he could hear people speaking in foreign languages, just like in New York, London or Paris, though the majority were speaking in English with the same Irish lilt that made everything Caer said sound so melodic. "The pub is right ahead," she said, breaking into his thoughts. "See? Irish Eyes."

Caer led the way through the groups gathered outside to smoke, and Zach noticed that every eye followed her as she passed. She was not just beautiful but strikingly beautiful.

She would be noticed wherever she went.

He followed her inside, realizing that everyone was looking at him, as well.

Because he was with her.

As they walked in, he was certain that she was about to apologize and tell him that her friends hadn't been able to make it after all.

He was wrong.

She was recognized the minute they walked in. An attractive woman of about forty headed straight out from behind the bar, wiping her hands on an apron with "Irish Eyes" handsomely embroidered on the edge.

"You came!" she said with pleasure.

"I said I would," Caer told her.

He introduced himself. "Zach Flynn."

"American?" the woman said.

"Yes. Wretched accent, sorry. Caer invited me along. I hope you don't mind."

"Mind?" Why 'tis lovely, ye've come. I'm Mary Donovan, Mr. Flynn." She turned back to Caer. "Sit down now. You must be hungry, spending all day in the hospital and all." She waved her hands at a couple of young men in tweed caps sitting at the bar. "Make way, you two scalawags. 'Tis Caer. I told you she might be coming in tonight."

The place seemed to be hopping. There was a family in one corner: parents, a grandfather, what looked like an aunt, a teenager, two smaller children and an infant. A group of blue-collar workmen sat next to them, and a group of thirty-something men in suits was next to the workmen. The various parties didn't seem to be segregated, though. Someone popped up now and then to take ketchup or mayo from one table to

112

another, and now and then one of them called out to someone at another table.

"Caer," one of the men at the bar said, as he tipped his cap. "Glad to hear you were there to be so kind to the old missus."

"It was nothing," Caer demurred.

"We don't need to take your seats," Zach said. "We're not in that much of a hurry."

But the bar stools had already been vacated for them.

"Sit," Mary said.

"Well, thank you," Zach told the pair whose seats they were usurping.

"Dale has to be gettin' home, he's a brand new wee babe waitin' there with his wife," Mary explained.

"I was just droppin' in," the man identified as Dale added, quickly finishing his pint. "I'll be on me way, then. Hope to see you again," he told Zach.

"Thanks, congratulations," Zach said.

"Caer, hope to see you soon," Dale said.

"It will be a bit. I'm leaving for the States tomorrow."

"The States? Well, and isn't that a fine trip, then? Stop in on Mickey Mouse. Glad the wife and I went when we did," Dale said. "It'll be a bit 'til we travel again."

"Good journey," said the man who had been sitting by Dale, grinning. "Guess I'm

113

leaving, too. Dale married me sister, so I'll be stoppin' by their flat to see the babe. Good to meet ya, then."

"Tomorrow? You're leaving tomorrow?" Mary asked. She looked stricken.

Zach could only assume that Caer hadn't said anything to her friends about her trip. A bit surprising, but it had only just come up.

"But I'll be back," Caer assured the older woman, patting her hand where it lay on the bar. "And don't you worry, your mum is going to be fine for years to come."

"She's a dear, she is," Mary said. "Worked so hard for all of us, especially after me da died. Ah, well, this is your last dinner in old Dublin town for a while then. I'm honored ye came here for it. I'll start ye off with the house brew, and it's a fine one, I tell you."

A minute later, Caer sipped her beer with enthusiasm, assuring Mary that it was the best she had tasted since she didn't know when.

It *was* a very good beer. Chilled, it would have been even better, Zach thought. Once again, he found himself inexplicably bothered as he studied Caer. She had friends, obviously. And it seemed she was considered something of an angel at the hospital. But there was just something . . . off about the

114

way she behaved, as if she hadn't had a date or a drink in years.

When Mary left to get them some of the pot roast that was the daily special, Zach turned to Caer. "Is her mother really going to be all right?"

"For now. No man — or woman — is on earth forever." She seemed strangely intent on her beer.

"Old, I take it?"

"Oh, aye. But she'll be all right. Just a wee touch of pneumonia, but they got it under control right away."

"I'm glad to hear that."

He was glad, at least, that she wasn't chugging what she appeared to think was the finest glass of anything she'd ever tasted. Rather, she studied her beer, its color, the way it moved in the glass when she tipped it. And she sipped it as if she were tasting fine champagne.

"I can see that you'll miss home," he said.

He was startled when she turned to him with a sharp gaze. "And *I* can tell that you're chafing to get back to *your* home."

"Not home. Rhode Island. But for tonight, let's just enjoy being in Dublin."

She nodded at him sagely. "All right."

It was then that the music started. Zach was pleased that the group on the dais eschewed the latest pop hits in favor of Irish melodies. One man had a beautifully decorated Irish drum, and Zach longed to get his hands on it. The guitars were something he saw every day; the drum was one of the most unusual he had ever seen.

Caer noticed the focus of his attention and leaned toward him. "Symbols of the old and new." She smiled. "The colors of the flag, see? Green for the Republic. Orange for the Orangemen — the English — and white for the hope of peace. There, on the left, the shamrock, for luck. The rainbow, for the belief that dreams can come true. A leprechaun, because what could be more Irish?"

Mary came back with steaming plates of food. "Homemade," she assured them.

"Zach was admiring that drum," Caer told her.

"Do ye play?" Mary asked him.

"Guitar," he told her. "I just dabble with other instruments."

"That's my Eamon there on that drum. I'll tell him you've a fondness for it."

"It's all right," he said. Too late. Mary had already headed over to the band.

Caer's eyes were bright, and she actually grinned. "Get up and play, why don't you?"

"Because . . . I'm in an Irish pub. And dinner was just served."

116

"You do play, don't you?"

"I do."

"Then get on up, will you? Dinner can wait."

To his surprise, she rose, dragging him from the stool.

At the same time, the lead singer made an announcement.

"We've an American fellow in the house," he said.

Zach wasn't sure what to expect. He'd never experienced anything but courtesy and hospitality in Ireland, but you never knew.

"*The* American fellow who gave Davie Adair his big break, working with Kitty Mahoney, when he crossed the pond. We'll be having him up here to play with us now."

The place was filled with applause.

Zach seldom felt awkward, but he did then. He noticed that Caer was frowning at him, clearly as shocked as he was that he was known here.

"I didn't know you were such a big deal," she said.

"I'm not. Trust me," he replied.

"Whichever, you have to get up there now," she told him, her lips curved in a wry smile. He suddenly felt as if the tables had turned — against him.

117

There was nothing to do. He went to the stage, where the lead guitarist, a young guy with long ink-black hair handed over his guitar with a grin. "What'll it be?" Zach asked.

Eamon said, "We'll just do some of the old standards. You okay with that?"

Zach was, and in a few bars awkward became a touch of magic. Music was a language that always connected people. When he was playing, Zach could forget almost anything. At one point, his fingers caressing the strings, he looked up at Caer, who had moved to the front of the stage to watch him. Her smile was dazzling as she swayed with the music. There was a second, just a split second, when it was possible to imagine that they were more than wary strangers. That life could be like this, being in a place where a welcome was as expected as the sun rising come the morning, and where he felt as if the most striking and enigmatic woman in the world was doing nothing but waiting. For him.

He loved music. It was like breathing for him. He kept his hand in with the studios he owned and the small label he ran, but these days his main focus was on pulling his weight in the investigations business he ran with his brothers.

And with that thought, reality came crashing back.

When the number ended, he undid the guitar strap and waited for the guitarist to retrieve his instrument — a top-of-the-line Fender — then started to step down. But Eamon, Mary's son, stopped him, handing him the Irish drum. "It's yours, man."

"I couldn't take it," Zach said.

"You must. I make them. Maybe you can send some new customers my way."

Eamon grinned and went back to the standard set of drums that also sat on the stage.

"That was great," Caer told Zach with enthusiasm.

"And I have an Irish drum now," he said ruefully. "I didn't mean to take it."

"But you must always accept a gift from the Irish," she told him gravely. "You're not offered a gift unless it's really meant, and it's considered churlish to refuse it."

"Then I'll just be grateful to have it," he told her.

Mary had taken their food back to the kitchen to keep it warm, but she brought their plates to them as soon as they sat back down at the bar. Since the pub was busy, she only had a moment now and then to stop by and check on them. As they ate,

Caer told him more about the city she so clearly loved. He found himself listening to her, enjoying the sound of her voice as much as — maybe more than — her tales of a history he had known, at least to a degree, but perhaps never really appreciated.

She broke off suddenly, as if aware of the way he was looking at her, and he quickly turned his attention back to his pot roast.

She asked him wistfully, "What will it be like, in America?"

He paused, his fork halfway to his mouth, surprised to hear something that sounded suspiciously like anxiety in her tone.

"You'll love the O'Riley place. Sean's grandfather built the house. He bought the land when you could still afford to buy on the coast. The house is on a hill, with a view of the sea that's beautiful on a good day and even better on a stormy one. And you'll love Bridey, Sean's aunt. You'll like Kat, too. She's already home for Christmas. . . . You'll have to take a tour of the mansions, which are amazing, especially when they're all decked out for Christmas. Newport's not as old as Dublin, but it's still got a lot of history. You'll enjoy your visit, I promise." He shrugged, grinning. "Marni — she's married to Cal, the other partner — can be a witch, but just ignore her. Kat and Bridey will adore you. And Bridey . . . well, she might have left Ireland, but as the saying goes, Ireland never left her."

She looked up at him, a slight shadow in her eyes and something vulnerable in her expression, but the look was quickly gone. "We should head out. Tomorrow will be a long day."

"Yes, you're right."

They didn't linger over their goodbyes. Mary gave Caer a huge hug, and Caer returned it warmly. Zach told himself he had to be mistaken. There was nothing suspicious about Caer Cavannaugh.

Except . . . there was.

They walked back to the hotel, where he ran upstairs to get her bags, then assured her that he would call a car and get her home safely.

She told him not to bother, and when he insisted, she said, "I want to go back to the hospital and check on Sean."

"Then we'll go together."

"That's not necessary. You must be exhausted, and you said you have an associate there watching over him."

"Right. So you don't need to go, either. But if you do, then I'll go with you," he said firmly, wondering why he felt so strongly about the subject.

She stared at him in frustration.

What was she afraid of? he wondered. What would he discover if he did take her home?

Maybe she had come from poverty and didn't want him knowing.

Maybe, but she had to be doing all right now; the shopping bags she carried were from high-end stores.

"To the hospital then," she said.

They were long past visiting hours, he assumed, but there were no questions asked. Caer merely said good evening to the guard on duty, who stared at her, smiled slowly, then watched without protest as they headed to the elevator.

They passed the nurses' station with equal ease and headed down the quiet hallway to Sean's room. Just as they reached the door, an orderly stepped out of the shadows. He was tall, heavily muscled, and his face was rough-hewn and showed the signs of a hard life.

"Flynn?" the man asked.

"Travis?"

"Aye."

Zach introduced Caer, but Will Travis smiled and said, "Of course. I've seen Miss

Cavannaugh with Mr. O'Riley."

He took Caer's hand and appeared loath to let it go. She was polite, but she retrieved her hand decisively.

"A quiet evening?" Zach asked.

"Oh, aye." The man's eyes lingered on Caer.

"Was Mrs. O'Riley in?"

"She was. Came about an hour and a half ago, and she was a bit distraught when I told her that I was a friend of your brother, and that I'd been instructed not to let Mr. O'Riley alone for a moment. She was all right in the end, though. Mr. O'Riley had his medication at ten, including a mild sedative, just to give him a good night's rest. I've been watching ever since."

"It's all right," Caer said suddenly. "I'll stay now."

"*We'll* stay," Zach corrected.

Caer frowned. "But you've got your lovely hotel room, and you really need some rest."

"I can sleep anywhere," he told her.

"Now then, neither of you has to stay here," Will Travis protested. "Aidan was a good friend to me when I needed him, and I've no problem being here for the night, as planned."

"Will, thank you. But we'll both stay," Zach said firmly.

Travis, his eyes falling longingly on Caer again, said, "I'll be near my cell through the night, then. If you need anything, just call me."

"Will do, thanks," Zach assured him.

He didn't know why the hell he was so obsessed about staying if Caer was there. He had left the hospital easily enough before, trusting in Aidan's assurance that Will Travis was the real deal and damned good at what he did.

There was a recliner in the room, and he insisted that Caer take it. He opted for a more conventional chair, but leaned it back against the far wall. The darkness in the room, the muted light from the hall and the hum of the heating system seemed to wrap him like a blanket. He tried to keep his eyes open, but he couldn't help it. He drifted. He slept lightly, though, knowing that he would be aware and awake if something out of the ordinary happened.

He wasn't sure about Caer, he thought just as sleep overcame him. He had a feeling that her hypnotic blue eyes remained open in the shadows.

It seemed to Bridey that she was dreaming more than ever these days, and that her dreams were in brilliant color, so real, like those high-definition movies Sean liked to rent.

It was near dawn, and she knew she was asleep, just as she knew that it was just around noon in Ireland. Sean would be on his way back, and this evening he would be home. Zach would be with him, and somehow, she knew, he would set things to right.

She knew all this as she slept and, in her dreams, returned to the sweeping hills and quiet dells of the Irish countryside.

It was all so real. That grass beneath her feet, dew-damp and delicious. And the air . . . There was such a sweetness to it. She was running through the grass, and she was young and beautiful again.

She could see the cottage ahead of her again, and the man in front of the cottage.

Eddie.

She ran toward him, anxious, worried.

And yet, as she neared him, she slowed.

Because the creases formed by time, wind and wear seemed to be fading from his face as she knew they had faded from her own. He had been like a son to her, just as Sean had been. She'd never had her own children, nor even a husband, but Sean was her blood, and Eddie had become family, as well. Like Sean, he was passionate in his pursuit of history and its treasures — real treasures, like gold coins and long-lost gems, and the treasures that came with knowledge and discovery. She'd loved sailing with her boys, as she called them. Fools, in a way, both of them, daring to go out when the wind howled and storms threatened. But they loved the sea, maybe more than either had ever loved a woman, though Sean had married twice, while Eddie had never settled for one.

"Bridey!" Eddie waved to her as he spoke.

But he wasn't Eddie as he'd been of late but the lad she had once known, with a twinkle in his eyes and a love of life. The lad who had brought her flowers on Mother's Day and never forgotten to honor her when St. Pat's Day rolled around.

She kept going, running through the grass, but he seemed to be getting farther and farther away.

"Eddie!" she called with distress.

"You can't come yet, not all the way, Bridey. But I'll be waiting," he told her.

"Eddie, you have to help us. We can't find you," she told him.

He stared back at her, perplexed. "I can't help you. There's too much I don't know, that I didn't figure out. I wish I could help you, but I can't. I love you, Bridey."

"Eddie, lad, we love you, too."

"Bridey, go back now, go on back. I'll be here. I'll be waiting."

Eddie faded. No, he didn't fade. He'd been there, then he simply . . . wasn't. The cottage, too, was gone, and the sweet, rich scent of the grass that had ridden on the air.

The damp grass was gone from beneath her feet, and there was something hard in its place.

She was shrouded in the pale yellow light of the moon. Her old bones ached, as she felt a chill sweep through her.

Startled, she realized that she was fully awake, and that she had risen in her sleep and walked over to the window. The cold of winter was on the pane she touched as she looked out to the sea.

To the bay.

Where Eddie had gone.

Once again she knew the truth. Knew for a certainty that Eddie was dead.

Fear gripped her. Fear for Sean.

Her old heart fluttered. She couldn't lose Sean, too. She couldn't lose both her boys. It wouldn't be right. It wouldn't be the natural way of things, though fate was often wickedly cruel as one generation made way for the next.

Her heart beat hard again. By tonight. By

127

tonight they would be home, and somehow, everything would all be right.

As she stood there, it felt as if a darkness descended again, as if shadow wings beat down around her. It should have been a frightening sensation, she thought, but it wasn't. She felt stronger.

Eddie was dead, but someone out there was listening to her prayers, and Sean would be home by tonight.

Zach didn't know how long he drifted — maybe an hour or two. He woke, senses sharp, eyes flying open. He didn't move, though; he waited silently, trying to discern the source of his sudden alarm.

There was someone in the room. Someone besides Sean and Caer, and somehow he knew the intruder was not a nurse or a hospital employee. Whoever it was had entered quietly, and apparently hadn't noticed him or Caer.

The intruder — attacker? — wore a coat, but there was something odd about it, a strange glint of light emanating from it. He — she? — also had on a strangely shaped hat.

For a moment, pure adrenaline shot through Zach, and he was ready to tackle the figure.

But then he paused, not sure whether to be furious, embarrassed or alarmed.

"Sean? Honey?" the newcomer said.

Amanda.

She swept open the coat.

Beneath it, she was wearing only flimsy panties and a bra adorned with tiny Christmas lights, which explained the glow, and the strange hat proved to be a Santa cap.

Amanda, still oblivious to everyone but Sean, shimmied seductively. "Hey, baby. Amanda is here to make it all better."

She let the coat drop all the way to the floor.

The panties were a thong. Her buttocks reflected blinking red and green lights.

"Amanda?" Sean said groggily, waking from a deep sleep.

Zach rose, clearing his throat, just as a light came on.

Amanda jumped, then looked around, eyes wide. She stared at Zach, but she didn't scream, only smiled slowly. Then her gaze moved around the room and focused on Caer, who had risen to turn on the overhead lights. The flirtatious look she had given Zach turned into something ugly.

Because, Zach thought fleetingly, even fully dressed, with her hair tousled and her eyes sleepy, Caer's far more seductive than you'll ever be, blinking nipples, Santa hat and all.

He dismissed the thought and focused on the situation.

Amanda was angry. "What in God's name are *you* doing in my husband's room, in the middle of the night?" she asked Caer accusingly.

"I'm his nurse," Caer reminded her. "And in case you've forgotten, your husband's doctors said that he isn't to have any excitement — and until he's released, their orders are the law."

Amanda spun and stared at Zach, but she still didn't reach for her coat. Her expression softened. She clearly liked men in general and didn't like other women.

"Zach, you know I'm the best medicine in the world for him," she said.

"Amanda," he said, trying to keep his eyes steady on hers. It wasn't easy. She did have magnificent breasts.

Sean had bought them for her as a wedding present, and there was no way to deny it: they were distracting when blinking.

"Amanda, you heard his nur — doctor's orders."

"Oh, pooh," Amanda said with a pout.

There was a flurry of activity in the hallway, and then one of the nurses on night duty and Will Travis — still dressed as an orderly and having obviously ignored Zach's instructions to go home — strode in.

The nurse gasped.

Will Travis laughed.

"I never!" the nurse said. She was a large, boxy woman, and indignation was clear on her features.

"I'll bet that's true," Amanda muttered nastily.

"Amanda, my love, put on your coat, please," Sean said from the bed. He seemed fully awake and aware, despite the mild sedative he had been given.

"Oh. Oh, dear," Amanda said sarcastically. She stooped smoothly to retrieve her coat.

"Mrs. O'Riley, we'll not have such behavior in this hospital," the night nurse said firmly. "Ye've disturbed Mr. O'Riley, and he needs his sleep if he's to be leaving in the morning."

"Fine," Amanda said with a huff. She looked at Sean, and he looked back with a glimmer of humor in his eyes.

"Sorry, dear," he said, clearly amused.

"You'll have to leave," the nurse insisted to Amanda.

"Me? I'm his wife," Amanda protested.

"And ye canna be trusted," the nurse said.

"Dear, we're leaving in a matter of hours,"

Sean reminded her. Zach noticed that the older man still looked amused, and even a little bit proud. Well, he was in his seventies, with a beautiful young wife. He deserved to puff himself up a bit. "Zach, Amanda was just trying to cheer me up, but I think it would be better if I got some more sleep right now. Will you see her back to the hotel for me?"

Zach glanced at Caer, and she looked back at him steadily. She would be here, and Will Travis had remained on duty. He bowed to Sean's will and turned to Amanda.

"Come on, Amanda, let's get you back to the hotel. We all have to be up early, anyway."

She nodded grudgingly, then smiled at her husband. "Tomorrow night we'll be back home, sweetie," she said.

"Where you'll have to practice a bit of restraint for a while, as well," Caer told her firmly.

Amanda flushed furiously as Caer went on, "You'd be risking his life. Haven't you understood that?"

Amanda at last had the grace to appear abashed.

"I only want to help Sean get better," she announced indignantly. She stared at them all defiantly for a moment, then moved to the bed and kissed Sean tenderly on the forehead. He wrapped his arms around her and held her tight for a moment.

Then he released her. "Get on back to the hotel," he told her.

"Yes, darling," she said, and straightened with great dignity.

Unfortunately, the effect was ruined by the blinking lights that continued to shine from beneath her coat. She started for the door but stopped when Sean said, "Amanda?"

"Yes?"

"Your chest is still lighting up like a neon sign," he informed her wryly.

"Oh!" For the first time she actually had the grace to look embarrassed.

She dug into her coat and found whatever little gizmo turned the lights out. Then she tossed the freshly coiffed length of her platinum blond hair from away from her face and proceeded out of the room.

Zach followed her, glancing back at Caer. She offered him a small smile that she couldn't quite conceal, and yet there was something grave in her eyes, and he knew that they were both wondering if Amanda had come out of love for her husband or . . .

If she understood the gravity of the stress the illness had put on Sean's heart, and had come offering what she knew might well be a death sentence.

6

Amanda sat next to Sean for the flight home, and Zach was next to Caer.

She had told him that she had never flown before, and judging by her nervousness, that was certainly no lie.

She was tense and embarrassed, but he couldn't help being aware of the subtle scent of her perfume. When his arms brushed against hers, he felt her warmth and something deeper, her unique vitality and vibrancy, like pure fire. He moved quickly away, feeling ridiculous for being so entranced by a woman he couldn't help being suspicious of. The thought haunted him constantly, like an otherworldly warning never to accept the obvious, and not to fall too deeply beneath the spell of those cobalt eyes and the lilt in her tone. It was odd, because as much as he sensed that there was something she wasn't telling him, when he watched her with Sean, she seemed absolutely genuine.

As they waited to take off, the flight attendant came by with champagne, orange juice and mimosas. Caer started digging in her purse for money, so he reached over and touched her on the arm to get her attention. "It's all right. It's free in first class."

She put away her money, thanked the flight attendant and took a mimosa, then sat back and sank into her thoughts.

Maybe she was worried about dealing with Amanda, he thought.

In his entire life, Sean had never been anything but courteous to those around him, even when he was working to develop the small, struggling business he'd inherited into the successful concern it was now.

For Amanda, life had been a bit different. Sean had worked for the money he had. Amanda had married into it. He knew that she considered herself superior to the hired help, and in her mind, that's all Caer was. Amanda had made it clear that she didn't see any need to bring Caer back to the States with them, but Sean disagreed. And when Sean had decided on something, not even Amanda could dissuade him.

She knew that. She had tested her limits early in their marriage and finally learned them.

Zach just hoped she stopped glaring at Caer and didn't spend her time thinking up ways to make her stay in the U.S. a misery.

As the plane sped down the runway, he saw Caer grip the armrests so hard that her knuckles were white.

He reached over, placing his hand on hers. "We're just getting up to the speed we need for takeoff," he told her.

"Thank you," she said softly, but he could tell that she was still nervous.

He kept his hand on hers until they had left the ground and were leveling out. Then, slowly, he released her hand.

She made an effort to release the armrest.

What a contrast she was, he thought. Fearless, determined, knowledgeable, cool — until it came to something as simple as riding in an airplane.

It was a long flight, and he spent most of it keeping an eye on what his traveling companions were up to.

Caer got up several times to speak with Sean and make sure he took his medication — despite the chilly looks Amanda shot her way every time. She remained low-key, something Amanda no doubt appreciated. He had to admit, he had found it difficult to look Amanda in the eye that morning.

In fact, he had a feeling he might never

look at her again without remembering her breasts blinking red and green.

He helped Caer with her headphones, and smiled later when she actually enjoyed the chicken pasta she chose for lunch. She also had a glass of champagne, but he noticed that she sipped it slowly. As much as she seemed to savor the taste of alcohol, she wasn't about to overdo it.

She fell asleep shortly after lunch, so he allowed himself to rest, as well. In fact, despite the fact that it was a day flight, when he woke up after a short nap and looked around, he saw that most of the passengers he could see were sleeping soundly, including Amanda and Sean.

He rose and stretched, then walked silently over to check on Sean. He felt a little foolish, like a new father standing over his baby just to make sure the infant was breathing, but given everything that had happened . . .

Sean was breathing.

When Zach turned back, he saw that Caer was awake and studying him, eyes dark and thoughtful. She didn't look away; instead, she lifted a brow and tipped her head to the side, indicating Sean.

Zach nodded, letting her know that the older man was fine.

They were served dinner before landing,

since they were landing at night, despite having left in the morning. Caer seemed bemused to be eating again so soon.

When they deplaned at Kennedy Airport, she seemed a bit overwhelmed, just staring. Dublin was certainly a sizeable city, but no one, he thought, could really be prepared for the reality of New York, the sheer number of people, the speed at which everyone moved, the plethora of accents — *the noise.* She had stepped out boldly, but now he saw her just standing there as people rushed past her. She looked as if she were simply trying to breathe while she assimilated the sounds and sights around her.

"Ah, there you are," Sean announced, as he was wheeled behind her, an airport employee pushing the wheelchair that had been waiting for him. He'd groused about it, but they'd all — including Amanda — vetoed the idea of his walking, Amanda muttering beneath her breath that if *sex* was too much for his heart, she certainly wasn't going to tax it with a long walk.

"First time in New York, huh?" the airport employee asked, smiling. He was a very tall black man, both dignified and friendly. He wore a name tag that identified him as Samuel Smith.

Caer looked at him and smiled, nodding.

"Yeah, yeah, how cute," Amanda said, walking by. "Come on, let's go. We don't have that much time between flights. Let's just get this over with."

"Sorry," Caer said, and started walking. Suddenly she stopped and looked back. "Mr. Smith, am I going the right way?"

"Indeed you are. Straight ahead. Just follow the signs and don't worry about me. I'm so good at navigating these strollers, I could probably win the Indy 500."

When he saw the blank expression on Caer's face, Zach stepped up beside her. "It's a car race," he told her, slipping an arm through hers. Amanda was being particularly annoying, he thought, and felt an urge to make it up to Caer somehow. "Maybe there will be some time to pop back down here. New York is one of the most amazing cities in the world." He flashed her a smile. "With lots of good Irish history."

They cleared customs in good time and changed terminals. The much smaller plane that would take them to Rhode Island was already there and boarding. As they stepped onto the plane, Caer looked a little white again. "No champagne on this one, huh?" she whispered to Zach.

He laughed. "No, but they do carry alcohol," he whispered. She flushed.

There was a row of single seats on one side of the aisle, with double seats on the other. Zach was once again next to Caer, with Amanda and Sean in front of them. Once again, Caer gripped the armrests as they took off.

This time, when he set his hand on hers, she actually flashed him a smile of gratitude. It was a rocky flight; she was gripping his hand by the time they had been in the air for fifteen minutes.

"This is a short flight at a lower altitude, and that's why you're feeling the air, plus it's a much smaller plane, moving at a slower rate. But there's nothing to fear. Think of it as if you were on the water. The air has waves, just like the sea, and we're moving over those waves."

She nodded, but she didn't let go of his hand.

As he'd said, it was a short flight, and after they cleared the plane and collected their luggage, they climbed into the limo that was waiting for them. Zach handled the luggage — and there was a lot of it — with the driver, and at last, they were driving toward the house. Caer didn't seem put off by the limo, Zach noticed. In fact, she seemed to love it. She seemed particularly enamored of the fact that there were bottles of water, soda and liquor in deep built-in wells.

"I'll have a water, if you don't mind," Sean said.

"I'll have a whiskey," Amanda said, sounding bored.

Caer handed Sean a water as Zach reached in and found a whiskey. "Want some ice with that?" he asked Amanda.

"No way. Just hand over the bottle," Amanda said. "I need something to get me ready to face the fury."

"She means Kat," Sean explained to Caer dryly.

Caer looked questioningly at Zach, who merely shrugged. "We all see the world in different ways," he said lightly.

"Of course we do, Mr. Flynn," Amanda said irritably. "*You,* of course, have a vested interest in seeing her as an angel. She's making him a mint," Amanda explained to Caer, as if they were suddenly best friends.

"Amanda, that's not true," Sean put in. "Kat is doing very well *thanks* to Zach managing her career. And he doesn't need anyone to make him a mint — he, Aidan and Jeremy are doing extremely well with their investigation firm." He turned to Caer. "Did you know he was a policeman in Miami? Now there's a city you should see if you can stay in America a while after you're done taking care of me. I don't think I'm going to need a nurse for very long, you know."

"I certainly hope that's true, but you *do* need a nurse right now," she told him gravely.

He smiled. "I know I need a nurse at least through the holidays," he said, winking at Zach as if he were offering him a gift.

Amanda sighed in impatience and looked out her window.

As they entered Newport, Caer looked out at the long row of mansions, each decorated for the upcoming holiday stylishly and tastefully, but to the hilt. One tree was covered entirely in blinking lights of red and green, and she turned to Zach, a small smile on her face, and he couldn't help but smile back, knowing they were sharing a memory of Amanda and her light-up breasts.

The driver slowed down, and Zach watched Caer's eyes fill with admiration as she caught her first sight of the house.

The O'Riley place sat atop a hill on more than an acre of land. The rear of the house sloped gracefully down to the cliff walk. It had massive pillars, and a cupola with a widow's walk. Painted white, it was simply beautiful and majestic. Because it was Christmas, a large crèche had been set up on the front lawn, and holly swags and evergreen boughs had been twined together and were wound around the pillars.

Lights gleamed from within.

Zach let himself out and stared up at the house. He saw someone staring down at them from one of the second-floor windows and waved. It had to be Bridey.

The front door opened, and Kat came racing down the walk. She was a redhead, with her hair cropped short, and she'd dramatically highlighted the color since the last time he'd seen her, so she looked like a ball of fire flying across the lawn.

"Dad!" she cried. "Oh, Dad!"

"Kitten," Sean said in reply.

For a moment Zach was afraid she might throw herself into her father's arms and knock them both backward into the limo. But she stopped a foot away, took a breath and walked toward him before wrapping her arms around him carefully and gently.

Sean held her as if she were the most precious being in the world.

Then Amanda exited the car, slamming the door loudly, as if to make sure everyone knew she was there.

"Hello, Kat," she said coolly.

Kat mumbled something against her father's chest.

"Such a loving child," Amanda said with saccharine sweetness.

Kat pulled away from her father. "Isn't it lovely that he has one — and married one, too?"

"Excuse me. We have visitors," Sean said sternly.

"Visitors? Kat, this is Miss Cavannaugh, the *nurse* your father *hired* in Ireland," Amanda said. "And Zach is really *family,* isn't he?"

Kat looked at Caer, intrigued, as she offered her a hand. "How do you do? Welcome to Rhode Island." She was obviously pleased that her father had found a gorgeous young nurse — one who irked her stepmother.

"Thank you," Caer said. "Lovely to meet you."

Even though the situation's possibilities clearly pleased her, Kat couldn't keep her attention from her father for long and turned back to him. "Dad, are you all right? Really?"

"I am. Really. I have a bucket of pills that Caer makes me take, but other than that, I'm doing great. Now how about we go inside?"

Kat slipped her arm through her father's and started slowly toward the house.

The limo driver was struggling with the

luggage as Amanda brushed past Kat and Sean. Zach and Caer followed, and Zach saw Tom, the caretaker, come out to welcome his employer home. The two men embraced warmly; Sean had always earned not only loyalty but genuine affection from everyone who worked for him.

After welcoming Sean home, Tom came forward to help with the bags, but Zach noticed him staring curiously at Caer.

Zach nudged her and smiled. "You'll like Tom. He's originally from Ireland."

"Glad to see you got the boss home, well and fine," Tom said, still staring curiously at Caer.

Zach quickly made the necessary introductions.

"A pleasure to meet you," Tom said, and he clearly meant it.

"It's my pleasure to meet *you,* Tom," Caer said.

A few moments later they were in the hall, surrounded by noise and confusion. Clara, Tom's wife, the housekeeper and cook, was going on about how glad she was that Mr. O'Riley had come home, Bridey was hugging Sean as warmly as Kat had hugged him earlier and exclaiming over the fact that he was alive and well. Cal, the junior partner, and Marni, his wife, were there, as well,

welcoming the O'Rileys home and con-
gratulating Sean on his narrow escape.
Bridey was particularly happy to see Zach,
her eyes widening with pleasure when she
broke away from Sean and realized he was
there. After a quick hug and a kiss on the
cheek, she said how glad she was, more than
he would ever know, to see him.

"All will be well now that you're here,"
she assured him.

He suddenly felt the massive weight of
responsibility, but he told himself that it was
no different from the responsibility he'd laid
on himself to get to the bottom of Eddie's
disappearance.

Then Bridey noticed Caer, and her hand
fluttered to her throat as she just stared.

Caer stepped forward, offering her own
hand. "How do you do? I'm Caer Cavannaugh. I'm Mr. O'Riley's nurse."

Bridey was still staring. Then, as if operat-
ing purely on instinct, she accepted the
handshake. "I know who you are," she said.

Was he the only one who found Bridey's
tone to be strange? Bridey was actually staring at Caer as if she were a ghost.

"Has there been any sign of Eddie?" Sean
asked Cal anxiously. "Have you talked to
the cops?"

"Nothing," Cal said. "And yes."

"Maybe Eddie's off on a secret adventure," Marni offered. "Sean, you have to worry about yourself right now."

"And . . . Zach is here to look into things now," Cal said. He was lanky, with a wiry strength and a pleasant face. He was handsome in a washed-out way, or maybe it was just that Marni had the look of a playful kitten. Her hair was a sable brown, long and lustrous, and her eyes were a deep matching brown. She was pretty, and so delicately built that she appeared smaller than her actual five-ten.

Kat spoke up with concern in her voice. "Dad, you need to go right to bed. That was a long flight."

"Kat O'Riley, I've sense and a mind of my own," Sean told his daughter, laughing.

"And *I* can take care of getting my husband up to bed," Amanda said.

"Up? Oh, no," Kat said firmly. "Clara and I set up a room down here for Dad until he's feeling better." She turned to Caer. "We've got you in a room on the first floor, too. It's right by my father's room, so you'll be close if he needs you."

"I would prefer to take the room down here," Amanda said.

"Sweetheart, you keep our room warm and lived-in. I'll be back up there before

148

long," Sean said. "I promise."

"Sean," Amanda began.

But Sean interrupted her firmly. "Amanda, I am feeling a bit tired. And I'm not sleeping well. I toss and turn at night, and you need your sleep. It will just be for a little while."

Marni breezed through the awkward moment, striding over to Caer and introducing herself and Cal.

Marni was saying the right words, and she was smiling, but Zach could see that her eyes, as she scanned the newest member of the household, were not so welcoming.

Cal, on the other hand, had genuine appreciation written all over his features as he stepped forward. "Welcome to the States. We'd heard Sean was bringing a nurse, but we never expected anyone quite so beautiful."

"Thank you," Caer said.

"I need to know what's being done about Eddie," Sean said firmly.

"Detective Morrissey will be over in the morning to fill you in, Dad," Kat said. "Now please, go to bed and try not to worry."

Sean started to speak, but Caer stepped in. "Your daughter's right, Mr. O'Riley. You should lie down for a bit. And you have pills to take."

"Sean, do what she says. The business can't afford for you to be laid up for long," Cal said.

"Cal!" Marni chastised. "Stop worrying the man. Sean will be just fine."

"Of course he will," Bridey said. "Zach is here." Then she turned to stare at Caer again.

Once again, the weight of the world seemed to settle on Zach's shoulders.

"I just know someone attacked Eddie, and that . . . oh, God, Zach," Kat said miserably. "He's dead. I'm sure of it. I already didn't like the idea of my father heading across the Atlantic with that woman, and then it seemed like such a bad omen when Eddie didn't show."

The two of them were alone in the kitchen, sitting at the round breakfast table overlooking the water with its trail of reflected moonlight.

"Kat, I spoke with his doctors. They found no trace of poison." Zach sat back, wondering why he was defending Amanda when she had showed up at the hospital, all decked out in her electric underwear, to lure a sick man into a wild romp that she must have known could kill him.

Admit it, he told himself. You just don't think she's smart enough to come up with a poison not even the doctors in one of Dublin's best hospitals could discover.

Kat sat back, staring at him, shaking her head. "She's even gotten to you," she said with disgust.

"No, no, no. I promise you, she hasn't."

But she was still looking at him doubtfully. "Zach, come on. Eddie disappears and my father winds up in a hospital in Ireland the next day, and you don't find that suspicious?"

"I find it very suspicious. Particularly because they had barely arrived when he got sick."

"So you think my father was poisoned here? Before he left?" Kat demanded.

"Kat, I told you. There's no proof that he was poisoned at all," he said firmly, then rose. "Look, Kat, it's nearly midnight. I'd be over seeing Detective Morrissey right now if it weren't. I'll get on it first thing in the morning. But if you love your father, don't go throwing accusations at anyone until you have some kind of proof. Whatever the reason, he chose to marry Amanda, and he *is* of sound mind."

Kat sniffed. "Not when it comes to her."

"Don't cause friction that will create more tension for him," Zach said firmly, staring hard at her.

She stood, as well, distracted, picking up the cups they had used for their late-night tea and their private chat. She had seen Cal and Marni off to their own place, and made sure that her father was sleeping, with Caer in the room beside his, that Amanda and Bridey were upstairs in their own bedrooms, and that Clara and Tom had left for the cottage out back, before they had settled down together. She was trying very hard not to flat out rage against Amanda, but she couldn't keep her antipathy entirely in check.

"All right," she agreed now.

"I mean it, Kat. He loves you, and he loves Amanda. Don't make him struggle to keep the peace."

"I won't," she promised. "As long as you promise you won't stop until you get to the bottom of this." She laughed suddenly, almost carefree for a moment. "Where did you find Caer?"

"I didn't find her. She was your father's nurse when I arrived."

"I love it, oh, God, I love it!" She giggled and caught his hands. "Did you see Marni's face when Cal couldn't stop looking at her? And Amanda's about to burst! She thinks she's so hot, but put her next to Caer and she looks like a bleached-out pile of plastic.

I must say, I am going to enjoy having her in the house."

"No tension, Kat," he reminded her.

"Who, me?" She feigned innocence for a moment, but then the pose dropped away and she suddenly looked very young and hurt and worried. "Zach, I adore my father. I would never hurt him. I'm just afraid that vultures are circling around him. But now that you're here, I really do feel better." She flashed him a sudden smile. "My CD is getting great reviews, Zach, and sales are climbing. And I have you to thank for that."

"Hey, you're the one with the talent."

"Aren't people strange? All these years, there have always been two of you, like a puzzle. The musician who invests in studios and other musicians. And the detective." She shook her head. "It must have been horrible, the stuff you had to deal with back in forensics."

"There you go. You just solved the mystery of me. It's not so strange, really. Death can be ugly. Music is beautiful. The one helps to negate the other."

"Well, I'm glad. And grateful." She studied him with her huge hazel eyes, a touch of tears shimmering in them. "As a musician, you've given me the life I dreamed of. Now you're going to save my father's life. As a cop."

"Private investigator," he corrected her. "And, Kat, as an investigator, I'm telling you that despite my own suspicions, it's possible that the two incidents — Eddie's disappearance and Sean's illness — are totally unrelated."

"Right. And maybe the sun is purple." She started out of the kitchen, then turned back and said, "If you're not down by eight, I'll come get you. Detective Morrissey will be here at nine."

"I'll be up," he promised her.

He watched her leave and wished that he were going to see Morrissey alone. He would have to make that happen later in the day.

He hesitated, then went to Sean's room and opened the door a crack. He watched Sean sleep, watched him breathe. Satisfied that his old friend was safe for the night, he almost closed the door. Then he looked across to the door to the adjoining room. They'd put Caer in there. He could hear her moving, and he found himself thinking of the strange way Bridey had looked at her earlier.

Talk about a puzzle . . .

But there was one thing he definitely

believed about her. She was there for Sean, and she meant to see that he got well.

He closed the door silently and headed up to his room, the same one he had stayed in as a boy, whenever he came to visit. The one he thought of as home.

It was quite a household, Caer thought, unpacking her few belongings in the room that had been assigned to her.

It was perfect. There was actually a connecting door to Sean's room, so she would easily be able to keep an eye on him. He was a proud man, and he had insisted on getting himself ready for bed, but when he had lain down and dutifully taken his pills, she had seen how exhausted he really was. He would see his own doctor in the morning, but she was ready for any questions the man might ask about Sean's care. She had been studying the book Michael had insisted she read, and she had checked out every pill the man was taking. One, taken only at night, was a mild sedative so that he could sleep. Another was to prevent further stomach difficulties, and a third was for blood pressure, with a fourth for his heart. There were vitamins, as well, but she wasn't worried about those, only about seeing that his prescriptions weren't misused. She had managed to politely insist that his medications stay in her room and under her control. Kat and Clara had both been perfectly willing to trust her, and Amanda had retired to her own room to freshen up after the journey, so she hadn't been around to object.

With her belongings all in drawers or the huge closet, she explored her small but elegant space. The room was beautiful, with an old-fashioned sleigh bed, soft beige and blue Persian carpets, and a massive dresser and matching nightstands of gleaming hardwood. There was also an entertainment center; should she feel the urge, she could watch TV on a massive screen that was as thin as a mint.

The bathroom had been stocked with everything she could imagine: a choice of soaps, shampoos, conditioners, bath salts, moisturizers and more.

She quietly opened the door between the two rooms and saw that Sean was resting easily. She stood in the muted light and watched his chest rise and fall.

She closed the door, sat on the foot of the bed and closed her eyes, envisioning the household. There was Amanda, of course. Sean — and Zach, who she was coming to know perhaps too well. And then Bridey.

She had sensed a bit of danger there, in the way the woman had looked at her. She was suspicious. Well, there was nothing for Bridey to worry about. Kat . . . Caer had to smile at how obviously Kat doted on her father and loathed Amanda. As far as she could tell on first look, Tom and Clara were exactly what they seemed to be: honest employees who loved their employer. That left Cal and Marni. Cal, who looked honest. Marni — who honestly wasn't pleased that Caer was here. What dangerous dynamics were at work in this house. So much hatred, and all of it barely bottled up.

She almost laughed, thinking back to the chaotic scene when they had arrived. Sean seemed certain that he could make those around him love one another. Not an easy task, maybe not even a possible one.

She sobered.

Someone was threatening Sean's life, and the only two people she could take off her list of suspects were Bridey and Zach, and Zach only because he hadn't been in Rhode Island when Eddie had disappeared nor in Ireland when Sean had gotten sick.

Zach Flynn was everything he purported to be, she thought. Strong, confident and, she was certain, well-versed in the investigative techniques that would help him figure out what was going on here.

And that would be to her benefit, having someone else there with the ability to investigate.

But he also seemed to be the type of man who wanted to know the truth about everything.

An unnerving thought.

Because she couldn't afford to let him find out the truth about her.

She rose, unwilling to contemplate the matter at that moment, and suddenly thirsty. Kat had shown her around the house and told her to help herself to anything she wanted from the kitchen at any time.

As she stepped into the hallway, the quiet of the house seemed strangely deafening. The others had all gone to sleep, or at least up to their respective rooms.

She headed over to the stove and found the kettle. It was quite a stove, she thought — even quite a kettle, a work of art in well-polished copper. She put water on to boil, then turned, suddenly aware that she was being watched.

Bridey was there. Tiny, slim, yet straight as an arrow. She had silver hair, blue eyes and a face creased with kindness and compassion. She had smiled often in life, Caer thought.

But she wasn't smiling now, as she pointed at Caer.

"I know who you are. What I don't know is just what you're doing here."

7

It was damned difficult to be in a man's house, trying to prove or disprove the idea that said man was the target of a murderer, and that the murderer, according to the man's daughter, was his wife.

Zach tossed and turned for a while, then gave up and got out of bed. He was beyond exhausted, and he knew he wasn't going to be any good to anyone if he didn't get a decent night's rest, but he was awake — wide awake. So he rose, slipped into his robe, and padded out of his room and down the stairs in his bare feet.

He paused just outside the kitchen, aware of the murmur of voices. He held perfectly still for a moment, trying to listen in. He wasn't actually fond of eavesdropping, but right now, anything going on in this house was of interest.

But the voices were too low for him to make out any words, though he recognized

160

both speakers: Caer — and Bridey.

He headed in, glad he had eschewed slippers for his bare feet, even though the hardwood floors were cold where there were no throw rugs. He was almost upon the two before they saw him, though it did him no good. He heard nothing, only saw Caer putting on the kettle, while Bridey sprang to life at the sight of him and headed for a cabinet for an extra cup.

"Zach," the old woman said with pleasure. "You'll be joining us, then, for a spot of tea?"

"It's just what I came down for," he said. "Thank you."

"We're brewing the real stuff, nothing herbal," Caer warned.

"Ugh. Herbal," he said, and smiled.

The two women had been engaged in an intense conversation. Now, they were talking about tea. What the hell had he interrupted?

Bridey, little bit of a thing that she was, pulled out a chair and said, "Sit, Zach."

"Why don't I serve you?" he suggested.

"Because I'm still whole in mind and body, and can manage to pour tea," she said firmly. "Now, sit."

"Yes, ma'am," he said, and did as he was told.

Caer measured tea into the small strainer sitting on the teapot and poured boiling water through, while Bridey set cups, sugar and milk down on the table, along with spoons and napkins. "We've some scones somewhere," she muttered.

"Just tea is fine," he said.

"You'll have a scone," she said.

Caer looked at him, amusement in her eyes, along with a warning that he should simply obey.

She was wearing a flannel robe. Pale blue. Her hair was a cascade of midnight waves over the soft color, and her eyes looked like sapphires in contrast to the light shade of the robe. She was wearing pajamas beneath the robe, and matching slippers. They were new, he thought, and had come from one of the upscale shops whose bags she had been carrying the other day.

She wore the ensemble well. Very well.

"Caer and I were just talking about Ireland and the old ways," Bridey said.

"Ah," he replied, and smiled. *Bull.* Something important had been going on between the two of them. But neither one was going to tell him now.

Divide and conquer, he decided. Tomorrow, he would talk to each of them alone.

"Aha!" Bridey said with pleasure, opening

the breadbox. "Fresh-baked blueberry scones. I'll just pop the little darlings in the microwave and they'll be ready to eat."

Caer brought the steeping tea to the table and flashed the old woman a smile as she said, "Warm scones. That sounds lovely, Bridey." She gazed at Zach. "You must be exhausted. What are you doing out of bed?"

"Overtired," he said simply.

She poured his tea. "Cream and sugar?"

"Of course. Bridey will insist."

"It's the best way," Bridey agreed, popping three scones into the microwave and setting the timer.

"So what were you two saying about Ireland?" he asked, nodding his thanks to Caer as she prepared his cup and handed it to him.

He couldn't help noticing the thick dark lashes that covered her downcast eyes.

Bridey was the one to answer. "Oh, we were just talking about the old beliefs, such things as leprechauns — and the coming of the banshee."

"Now, Bridey, you can't still believe in leprechauns, can you?" he asked.

"*I* do," Caer said lightly. "And why not? Never offend one — you'll have bad luck forever."

"Ah," he acknowledged dryly.

"Hmph," Bridey said. "You might think her highness got off the plane and offended a leprechaun the minute she stepped onto Irish soil, Sean was sick so quickly."

Evidently Bridey wasn't fond of Amanda, either.

"Oh, come on, what could Amanda have done so quickly?" he asked.

Bridey looked around for a moment, as if she thought the walls might have ears. "She thinks that love of the old country is rot," she said, nodding knowingly. "She cares nothing for the past."

"But Sean loves her," Caer reminded her.

Bridey shook her head. "My nephew was so wise for most his life. I don't know what ever compelled him to consort with someone so . . . so empty-headed."

"Now Bridey," Zach said, "Sean's no one's fool, and you know it."

"Every man is a fool when it comes to love," Bridey said sagely, as she took the plate of scones from the microwave, set it on the table and finally took a chair herself. The aroma of the heated scones was delicious and somehow soothing.

Bridey didn't look soothed, though. She looked restless. "And then there's the fact that Eddie is dead," she said quietly.

"Right now he's just missing, Bridey," Zach told her. There had been a curious finality in her voice, though, he thought. As if she *knew* something.

She shook her head and looked at Caer as she told him, "I know he's dead. I've been seeing him in my dreams." She looked at Zach. "You know he's dead, too. The thing is, you have to find out why. And who did it," she said flatly. "They have to pay."

He reached across the table and closed his hand over hers. "I will find out what happened, Bridey," he promised her gently.

"The same person is after Sean," Bridey said.

"Maybe, maybe not," he said carefully. "And no matter what you think of her, you can't go around accusing Amanda unless you have some kind of evidence."

"Well, then, you'd best start finding some, eh?" Bridey said. "And eat your scone before it cools."

Caer was already taking a bite of hers. "This is delicious, Bridey," she said.

Bridey looked at Caer, and it looked to Zach as if she shivered just slightly. But then she smiled, and it seemed to be sincere.

"You can take the baker out of Ireland, but never Ireland out of the baker. You can be gone forever, but you never forget the old ways, or the truths you learned as a child."

"And glad I am of that," Caer told her. "You keep me from being homesick."

Bridey nodded gravely.

Something had definitely gone on between the two women, Zach thought, wondering if he would ever break through and discover what had been said before he arrived. For some reason, it seemed important.

Divide and conquer, he reminded himself.

He finished the last of the scone and his tea, and rose. "Bridey, thank you. I believe I'll sleep like a log now."

She flushed, pleased.

Caer had risen, as well, and was picking up the cups and plates. He couldn't help but think that even if she wore a burlap bag, she would still be seductive. She certainly hadn't set out to entice in her flannel pajamas and robe, but somehow . . .

Bad thought to linger on.

"Good night," he said to them both.

"Good night," Caer echoed.

"Sleep well," Bridey told him.

His eyes seemed drawn to Caer's. It was the color, he told himself, framed by that long raven-dark hair.

He gave himself a mental shake. In a moment, he would be imagining the physical assets beneath the flannel, and that wouldn't be a good thing. He needed to know more about her, not find himself falling victim to her strange Irish spell.

He didn't believe in leprechauns, pixies or banshees. And wasn't it strange that he'd thought of himself as falling *victim* to her spell?

Bridey was most likely right, and Eddie was dead. There was a terrible logic in that conclusion. And as he'd told Kat, there seemed to be more than coincidence at work here, which meant Sean just might be next on the killer's list. A killer who had to be found and stopped.

That was real.

He turned without another word and went back to bed, where he slept at last, and yet, even in his sleep, he was listening.

Listening for what?

Even in dreams, he wasn't sure.

Detective Brad Morrissey was about forty, solid and steady, blunt and, apparently, bluntly honest. He had an iron-gray crew cut, jowls and sad eyes, and though Newport, Rhode Island, wasn't particularly known for being a hot spot of violent crime, Morrissey had the look of a man who'd been around.

"I'm telling you," Morrissey was telling Sean now, as Zach sat nearby and listened, "we've tried. Coast Guard found the boat out there — she was drifting in Narragansett Bay, almost out into Rhode Island Sound, but nothing whatsoever was amiss. We checked the charter office, and Eddie Ray had left the books neat and clean. There was a notation with the passenger's name and reservation time, and another that he'd paid cash. A single passenger, Mr. John Alden. The boat was towed in, and I inspected her with some techs from the crime lab. We dusted for prints and found dozens of them — mostly partials, and mostly, from what we've discovered so far, belonging to Eddie Ray, or other members of your staff and family. We're still sifting through them, but I'm not hopeful for much. It's winter. Whoever Mr. John Alden was, he probably wore gloves. The weather's been pretty warm for December, but even during a mild winter, you know as well I do, it's cold out there on the water." Morrissey sat with his hands folded in his lap as he spoke, addressing Sean, but looking at Zach on occasion, as if seeking confirmation.

Zach knew what the police and he himself were up against. Eddie Ray had gone missing from a charter boat. Clean as the boats might be kept, there were probably prints left over from the last several excursions, and many of the prints that were there were also likely to be smudged.

"There was absolutely *no* sign of a struggle of any kind?" Zach asked.

"No, I swear. I looked the boat over myself," Morrissey said. "Not a thing over-turned, not a thing that appeared to be out of place. It was as if both Eddie and his passenger simply vanished."

"And there's been no sign of either one since?" Zach asked.

"No sign at all," Morrissey replied. "We haven't had a single call on the hotline — although it doesn't help that we don't know what Alden looks like or even if that's his real name."

Morrissey was being patient; Zach had to grant him that. He'd clearly been over all this before, but he was willing to sit through the questions again, to explain everything his department had done, no matter how many times he was asked. It was evident he was frustrated himself by the lack of progress in the case, and perhaps that made him more willing to understand incredulity and frustration in others.

He shook his head then, a flash of his frustration showing.

"Not a single sign," he said again. "It's like they carried a couple of cinder blocks out there, tied a rope around them and sank themselves. I've had police divers down there, and they haven't found a thing, but it's a big bay, and they could be anywhere. I wish to God I had more to tell you. I wish I had an answer. But I don't."

"And you've given up already," Sean said, anger and bitterness in his tone.

Zach held silent. Morrissey hadn't given up; he seemed to be the dogged kind of policeman who never gave up, but who didn't go off in passionate rages, either. Sean, on the other hand, was emotionally involved and couldn't keep himself from showing it, which was perfectly understandable.

"No, sir, we have not given up," Morrissey said firmly. "We have followed every lead. The problem is, those leads dried up quickly, and so far we haven't found any others."

"I'll go down and take a look at the boat, Sean," Zach said, then turned to Morrissey. "I know the boats and the family. If there's anything amiss, something subtle that someone else might not see, it's just possible that I will."

"Fine with me. Cal and his wife were out,

170

and your daughter, too, Mr. O'Riley. They've taken a look around, as I'm sure you know. We don't mind help, and we don't mind being wrong. But don't think that we give up easily. We don't."

Morrissey, with his short iron-gray hair and weary bulldog face, turned to Zach. "The boat is back at the wharf. There's still crime tape around it, but I'll go over with you."

There was a tap on the door, and Sean barked, "Come in."

Kat entered the room. "Dad, Caer says it's time for your medicine. And that she needs to take your blood pressure." She glanced at Morrissey with a hopeful smile.

"Sorry, nothing new. And I was just getting ready to leave," he said.

"And I'll be going with him," Zach announced, rising.

"Where?" Kat asked.

"To the boat," Zach told her briefly.

She studied him gravely, and then, to his surprise, she almost smiled. "Take Caer with you."

"Kat, I'm going out there to —"

"Take Caer. Amanda is going shopping, and I can stay with Dad. It will give her a chance to see a bit of town, not to mention get a sense of what this family's all about —

and to understand that she's going to pretty much have to leash Dad to keep him from trying to get back out on the water."

Sean looked at his daughter impatiently. "I'm obeying every word the doctors said, young lady. And my stomach is right as rain now, by the way."

"But you put a lot of pressure on your heart, and your blood pressure soared off the charts," Kat said.

"True enough," Sean agreed — surprisingly easily, Zach thought. "By all means, Zach, give the girl a chance to get out."

"I'll wait for you out front," Detective Morrissey said.

Sean stood. Kat moved closer to take his arm, and he started to protest, but he loved his daughter, and Zach saw his features soften as he let her lead him out.

"Zach, you can take my BMW and follow Detective Morrissey with Miss Cavannaugh. That way, he won't need to bring you back here."

Zach's coat was hanging in one of the closets by the mudroom that led from the kitchen to the garage. The mudroom had been part of the house before any of the more modern renovations had been done, and it retained its charm, with black and white tiles and etched glass.

He donned his coat, then waited impatiently by the door for Caer.

She appeared a few minutes later. He wondered if he looked annoyed, because she hesitated when she approached him. "I'm sorry. Apparently everyone thinks I need to get out and see my surroundings," she told him.

He nodded briefly. "Where's everyone else?"

"Bridey is still in her room, and Amanda hasn't appeared yet, but Kat says she'll be going out shopping when Bridey gets up." She hesitated again.

He smiled. "And Kat thinks this is a safe time for you to go out, because she'll be with her father and can keep him safe from Amanda," he said flatly.

She shrugged. "Yes."

"All right, let's go."

She looked out the window as he drove, but her expression gave away nothing. Newport had once been a haven for the filthy rich. But, as always, where there were filthy rich, there were those who had to serve them, so once the city had been a place of economic extremes. That had changed with the advent of the federal income tax, and now the population, like that of most cities, represented a continuum of financial wherewithal. Most of the mansions were now owned and maintained by the Preservation Society of Newport County, and were open to the public for a fee. Tourists flocked into the area, even in winter — or maybe especially in winter — to see the way the other half once lived and to enjoy the events the Preservation Society sponsored.

Though the O'Riley house sat high up on a cliff, the offices were at the wharf, where the charter boats could come and go in the comparative calm of the inlet.

When he reached the wharf, he drove into a parking space marked *O'Riley,* then watched Caer as she emerged from the car. The breeze took hold of her hair and swept it lightly around her face. She seemed to love the feel of it, and to enjoy the sight of the many boats in their berths. There were other charter businesses besides O'Riley's, but Sean had the best setup, an old Victorian-style office on a spit of land between docks, with old wooden steps leading up to the front door. The other rental offices were much smaller, some of them just one-person shacks with windows.

The parking lot paralleled much of the waterfront, with a restaurant at the far end, where the docks ended and a sweep of granite rose up from the sea, and they were surrounded by other businesses, all of which were tourist oriented. The Lucky Whale advertised seaside souvenirs, while Narragansett Niceties boasted the finest in New England art. A nearby chowder house claimed to have the world's best clam chowder to eat in or take out. Caer stood for a long moment and simply observed it all.

He saw that Detective Morrissey was waiting for them on the dock next to the O'Riley's Charters office.

"Come on, I'll take you into the office. You can hang out there while I'm talking to Detective Morrissey."

"No problem," she said.

He walked her up the steps to the office and opened the door. Cal was at a desk, doing paperwork, and Marni was dusting the cases holding some of the treasures Sean had found over the years: a sextant from the sixteen-hundreds, the anchor from a long-gone whaler, a display of early American coins, and more. She stopped when she saw them and offered a broad smile, but once again, Zach thought, it didn't seem real.

"Well, hello," she said, walking over to give Zach a kiss on the cheek and nodding at Caer.

"Zach," Cal said with pleasure. "And Miss Cavannaugh." His pleasure at seeing her seemed no less genuine.

Zach suspected the Johnsons' reactions to Caer were typical — and typically split according to gender. She was so stunning that a man would have to be have dead or of a different persuasion not to notice her, while Marni, like most women, might well feel threatened, not just by Caer's beauty but by her own husband's reaction to the other woman. Marni was a very attractive woman herself, but she was in her thirties and insecure that her own youth and beauty were fading. She never reacted this way to Kat, but she'd known Kat a long time, not to mention that Kat was more interested in music than anything as mundane as anyone's appearance, including her own.

Right now, she was obsessed with her father.

And Amanda.

"So Sean is doing well?" Marni asked.

"Very well," Caer assured her.

"And now that he's safely back home, are you going to explore America?"

"I've been retained through the end of the year," Caer told her.

"But you're already checking out the city, aren't you?" Marni asked sweetly, but with an edge.

"Kat wanted some alone time with her father," Zach put in.

"How anyone can be alone in that house full of bitches is beyond me," Marni said beneath her breath, but just loudly enough to be sure the words were audible.

No one *had* asked her, and silence seemed to stretch as everyone tried to think of a way to get back on more casual ground.

"Marni," Cal said uncomfortably, breaking the silence at last. "That was unnecessary."

"I'm sorry," Marni said, and she appeared to be sincere. "I guess I'm not being very welcoming, am I, Miss Cavannaugh?" she asked Caer. "It's been a tense six months here, since Sean and Amanda were married. Kat's so unhappy. And Amanda loathes it when Kat comes back to town. Poor Sean, I don't see how he manages."

Cal rose and set an arm affectionately around her shoulders. "Marni really cares about Sean, and it upsets us both to see him this way."

"Not to mention that Kat's convinced Amanda poisoned her father somehow," Marni said.

"Kat is certainly concerned about her father," Zach said noncommittally.

"And let's face it, we're all fearing the worst about Eddie," Cal said softly.

"Cal," Zach said, "what happened that day? Were you out on another charter? What about you, Marni? You spend a lot of time in the office, right?"

"Of course I spend a lot of time in the office," she said indignantly. "I work very hard. We all know that Cal's the new man, and he and I both put in our fair share of effort."

"Marni, I'm not casting aspersions, I'm just wondering where you were when Eddie booked that charter and took it out," Zach said.

"Oh," she said, then, "Oh," again, as if she realized she had been oversensitive and felt a little silly. "It was the day Sean was leaving for Ireland. I was out buying him some new wool socks for the trip, those special socks that are supposed to support your feet when you're walking," she said. "We intentionally didn't schedule anything for that day."

"And it should have stayed that way," Cal said bleakly.

Marni shook her head sadly. "If only one of us had been around."

"Marni, don't start with that," Cal said. "If only Eddie hadn't accepted that last-minute reservation. If only there had been a storm, and no one had gone out. We could play that game all day."

She nodded.

"So, Cal . . . ?" Zach said.

"What?" Cal asked, frowning.

"Where were you that day?"

"Oh," Cal said. Apparently his mind had been on his wife. He smiled at Marni, then looked back at Zach apologetically. "At home, napping. There was no need for all of us to be in the office. Eddie said he had stuff to do, though I don't actually know what it was." He, too, sounded defensive.

"Hey, I'm just asking, hoping you might have seen or heard something you forgot until now," Zach said.

"How I wish," Marni told him fervently.

"Sorry," Cal said. "All we have is Eddie's note in the book."

"Right," Zach said. "Hey, will you excuse me? Detective Morrissey is waiting for me so I can take a look around the *Sea Maiden*. I was hoping you could show Caer around the wharf, let her get a look at the boats."

"Sure, I can show Miss Cavannaugh our little fleet," Marni said.

Zach glanced at Caer. If she was worried about being left in the care of a jealous she-wolf, she betrayed no sign of it.

"I'd love to see the boats," she said. "And please, call me Caer."

Zach promised to be back as soon as he could, then left to meet Morrissey.

The detective didn't appear to be impatient. He was leaning against one of the dock's support pilings as if he had all the time in the world.

There was crime scene tape circling the *Sea Maiden.* She was sixty feet long, three-masted, beautiful even at rest. She wasn't the largest boat in the fleet, but Zach knew that she was the one Eddie — and everyone else — loved the most. She was so sleek and maneuverable that, despite her size, one man could sail her. One of the prime attractions of an O'Riley's tour, though, was the chance for passengers to help sail the boat, and Eddie had loved to work with people, young and old, teaching them how to read the wind and set the sails.

"You can go on aboard," Morrissey told him. "The crime scene unit has finished up,"

Zach stepped on deck. Her sails were furled, and everything he'd heard seemed to be correct. There was absolutely no sign of a disturbance of any kind. He paced from bow to stern, studied the sails and the helm, and then went into the cabin. There were no suspicious notes lying on the desk, the radar seemed to be working just fine, and there was nothing wrong with the radio. Charts of Narragansett Bay and Rhode Island Sound were pinned to the wall.

Zach went through the galley, the main cabin, the heads and the two sleeping compartments. Everything was just as it should be.

As he passed the head on his way back to the ladder topside, he noted something that he had missed the first time. He hunkered down on the balls of his feet to study it.

Morrissey had followed him down, but had kept his distance, silent as he watched Zach conduct his examination of the vessel.

"Talc," he said now.

"You had it checked out?" Zach asked.

"Hey, we're not the big city, but we do have a decent crime lab," Morrissey told him. "Yes, we checked it out. It's talc."

"Thanks."

"Any idea what it could be doing there?" Morrissey asked. "I mean, who the hell needs talc for a pleasant sail out into the sound?"

"No one — that I know of," Zach told him, straightening. "I can't imagine anyone needing talc for anything other than a wet suit."

Morrissey stared at him, frowning. The man was apparently not a diver, Zach thought.

"Wet suits are tight fitting — they have to be. Talc helps a diver get one on."

"You think Eddie was going diving?" Morrissey asked.

"No. Eddie would never have gone diving in winter."

Strange, he thought. The company hired an outside cleaning company to make sure their boats were always spotless, so the odds of the talc being left over from a previous trip were slim to none.

But it might make sense, even if the sense it made was disheartening. If someone had come aboard with the intention of killing Eddie and getting away with it scot-free, what better way to simply disappear after the murder than to dive overboard and swim to safety, wearing a wet suit for insulation against the cold water? There would be no need for a second conspirator to motor up and pick up the killer, meaning there would be no one to squeal, no one to tell the truth out of guilt or under pressure, no one to break.

"You think someone came aboard, killed Eddie, jumped off the boat and swam away?" Morrissey asked.

"I think it's possible."

"Do you know how cold that water is this time of year?" the detective asked.

Zach nodded.

"If you're right, someone really wanted him dead," Morrissey said. "I'll start checking around the dive shops, see if they noticed anyone suspicious. I don't suppose they offer dives off this boat in winter, do they?"

"No, just cruises," Zach said.

Morrissey shook his head. "Bizarre. How would the killer have gotten an air tank on board without Eddie noticing?"

"I don't know. And, hey, the talc isn't a guarantee. But you didn't find anything else, right?"

"Nothing. She was clean. The guys that found her out there, a couple of Coast Guard officers, said she was like a ghost ship. Nothing disturbed, nothing at all. They hadn't opened a can of Coke or so much as put on a pot of coffee."

"And the weather?"

"Smooth seas and a beautiful day, crisp and cool, but that was it. Light winds, no storms, nothing," Morrissey said.

Zach hesitated. "And no bodies washed up on shore?"

"No. No unidentified patients in the

183

hospital, nothing. I'll start on the dive shops, though, see what I can find out about equipment rental," Morrissey said.

"Our killer — if we're even on the right track with this — probably has his own equipment."

"What about air for his tank?" Morrissey asked.

"True enough. And I'm all for checking the dive shops. Any port in a storm, as they say."

"We'll keep looking for some kind of a lead," Morrissey said. "Or . . ."

His voice trailed off.

Zach finished his sentence for him. "Or a body."

Morrissey only nodded grimly.

"When you make your rounds of the dive shops," Zach said, "can you keep it on the quiet side? This may be a shot in the dark, but if we're on to something, and if there is a killer out there, we don't want him to know we're getting close."

Morrissey smiled dryly. "No problem. And I'll ask you to share your insights with me and keep quiet otherwise."

Zach nodded, smiling in turn. "Yeah, sorry. I know you weren't born yesterday."

He thanked Morrissey, and stepped off the *Sea Maiden.* Forensics could literally be a lifesaver. Few people knew that better than he did. But when nothing was available, when there were no prints, hairs, fibers or useful substances, footwork was in order.

He headed back to the office, where he found Cal, Marni and Caer bent over the desk.

"What's up?" he asked.

"Nothing," Cal said. "Caer didn't know Eddie, but she's been hearing so much about him that I thought she might be interested in seeing some old photos, and then she asked to see his last entry in the register. I figured you would want to see it, as well."

Caer's eyes were clear when they met his. Why the hell did he always find her so suspicious? She'd been Sean's nurse in Ireland — if he could guarantee that anyone was innocent of Eddie's disappearance, it had to be her — but why the hell would she be interested in seeing the reservation book?

"Yes, I would like to see it," he told Cal. "Did they dust it for prints?"

"They dusted everything for prints and came up with hundreds of them — so much for cleaning crews," Cal said, shrugging. "But it's doubtful that Mr. 'John Alden' touched the book anyway. Eddie is the one who made the entry."

Zach nodded, pulling the book closer and turning it to face him.

"Right there," Marni said, pointing.

Eddie had neatly entered the date, the man's name, the price paid and the notation "cash." A side note stated that they would be cruising the bay, then heading for the sound. "Pass Cow Cay," Eddie had written.

Morrissey had told him that the boat had been found not a hundred yards off Cow Cay, a small, uninhabited island where settlers had once raised cattle, hence the name. The Park Service owned it now, and boaters often visited it in the summer, because it was legal to take pets and have picnics. On a hot day the place was frequently crowded, but in December it was deserted.

If someone *had* gotten dive equipment on board, they might have made Cow Cay easily from where the boat was found, Zach thought.

He looked up. "What's on schedule for today?" he asked Cal.

"I'm taking a couple out on the *Sea Lady*," he said. "Two-hour sail, that's all."

"Great." Zach looked at Caer. "I'll show you the area. Cal, I'll take the *Sea Lass*."

"What?" Cal said, blinking. "You want to take out the *Sea Lass?*"

"Yeah, I'll give the Irish lass a spin in the *Sea Lass,* give her a look at the area from the water." And get a chance to talk to her one on one, he thought, and maybe figure out why she kept raising his danger signal

Caer looked white, but she didn't say anything.

"But . . ." Marni said.

"Yes?" Zach stared at her.

"Sorry, sure, whatever you like," she said. She knew Sean had given him carte blanche to borrow any unused boat when he was in town. "No, no, I'm sorry. I just thought you were anxious to look for Eddie, and I thought Caer was working . . . that Sean might need her."

"Sean has Kat right now, and she wants some time with her father," Zach said. "Caer?"

Despite her obvious fear, she nodded.

"Are you going to need a hand?" Marni asked.

"No, we'll be fine," Zach said.

"Are you a sailor, Caer?" Cal asked.

"Not really, but I'm game for anything," she said, making an attempt to sound happy.

False cheer, Zach thought. But that was all right. "Come on, then, I'll show you the *Lass.*"

He caught her by the elbow and led her

out. "I take it you've never been out on a sailboat before?" he asked as the door closed behind them.

She shook her head.

"Are you afraid of water?"

"No." He led her down the dock to the *Sea Lass*'s berth. The *Sea Lass* was a twenty-five-footer, just right for a couple or a small family.

She was also equipped with a first-class engine, which was perfect, since Zach had no intention of taking a leisurely cruise.

"Hop on," he said.

She stared at him.

"Go on."

She didn't exactly hop, but at least she made it aboard.

He released the boat from the dock and directed Caer to a white bench near the main mast.

"I can't help you sail, you know," she called to him over the hum of the engine.

"We're not going to sail."

"What are we doing, then?"

"Motoring out to the spot where Eddie's boat was found," he told her.

The air was crisp and clean; it was a day just like the one when Eddie had ventured out. And disappeared.

Zach eased the *Sea Lass* away from the

dock and past the channel markers.

When he looked back, both Cal and Marni were standing on the dock, watching them head out. He wished he were close enough to read their expressions.

8

Why on earth people would *want* to do this, Caer couldn't begin to imagine. Though the boat moved smoothly enough — and with considerable speed, once they had cleared the dock area — it was cold. And windy. The combination was almost painful.

Zach didn't seem to notice. He held the tiller and kept his eyes on the distant island they were speeding toward.

There was a cabin. He *might* have suggested that she go inside and stay warm, but he hadn't. Then again, he didn't seem to notice the cold, or that the wind, created as much by their speed as anything else, was whipping against their cheeks like a dozen finely honed knives.

She gritted her teeth and sat tight, not about to say a word. It seemed like an eternity before he cut the engine.

Despite having been out for what felt like forever, they had ended up in the middle of

nowhere. There were no other boats anywhere near them, and even the island they'd
been heading for was a good hundred yards
away.

She could barely move; she felt as if her
joints had frozen solid where she sat.

Zach was once again oblivious. He stood,
and strode back and forth along the deck,
looking intently at their surroundings, then
started working a winch.

"What are you doing?"

"Dropping anchor," he told her.

She managed to rise at last, but she hurt.

"Is that how you usually take a sailboat
out?" she asked him.

"No. You usually sail."

"Why does it have a motor, if it's a sailboat?"

"So you don't have to sail."

"Then why have a sailboat?"

"Because you usually want to sail, of
course." He stared at her strangely. "Sometimes," he explained, "there's no wind. And
sometimes, like today, you just want to
move fast."

She followed him to the front of the boat,
moving carefully as she stretched protesting
muscles and tried to adjust to the motion of
the boat. The sea appeared calm, but the
boat still rocked on the water.

"What do you see?" he asked her.

"Water," she told him.

"What else?"

"The sky."

"And Cow Cay," he said thoughtfully.

"What on earth are you getting at?" she asked him, frowning. "Do you think that Eddie is hiding on Cow Cay?"

"No," he said, and looked at her intently. "Eddie is dead."

"How can you know that?"

"Because Eddie isn't a prankster. He would never worry Sean or Kat like this. He wouldn't have missed Sean and Amanda's going-away party."

"Do you think it's possible that he was hurt, that he fell overboard, that —"

"He had a passenger — we know that," Zach said. "It's unlikely they both just fell overboard."

"Right," she agreed.

She watched as he disappeared below deck, then reappeared a minute later with a large storage bin. He opened it, and pulled out something large and yellow. He pulled a tab, then threw it overboard, hanging on to a cord so he wouldn't lose it.

The yellow thing inflated and turned into some kind of a raft.

"What are you doing?" she asked incredulously.

"Going to the island."

"You're kidding."

"I'm not."

"In . . . *that?*"

"You bet. I won't be long."

"Oh, no, no, no. You're not leaving me here."

He looked at her and arched a brow slowly, amused. "You want to come with me?"

"Yes."

"You're better off staying here. I'll keep an eye on the boat the whole time. There's no one on board with us. I checked it out."

"I'm going with you," she said stubbornly.

"You really want to go?"

"Want to? Hell no. But I'm going, anyway."

"Suit yourself."

He went to the side of the boat and pulled out a pair of oars from a bin built into the fiberglass hull, then turned back to her. "Come on. I'll help you down first."

She eyed him warily, not at all certain that she wouldn't fall into the water in the process. But his grip was strong, and she made it safely from the *Sea Lass* into the blow-up dinghy, sitting quickly and care-

193

fully, so as not to rock it. He handed her the oars, then followed.

It didn't take him long to row to the island; still, she felt the icy chill of the water beneath her all the while.

He propelled them right up onto the sandy beach of the small island, then hopped out quickly and reached out a hand to her. "Thank God you're not the stiletto type," he said, eyeing her leather boots, with their broad one-inch heels.

"How do you know I'm not the stiletto type on occasion?" she asked.

He looked at her dryly. "Are you?"

"Maybe."

Her shoes still sank into the sand. "You might have warned me what we would be doing," she called to him. He was pulling the little dinghy higher up on the beach, and as soon as he finished, he started moving purposefully along the shore.

The island seemed strange and stark, she thought as she followed. There were scattered trees, but they bore no leaves. It was winter, she reminded herself. There was some greenish-brown scrub grass, and seaweed teased at the shoreline.

A gull cried forlornly overhead.

Zach walked along the beach, then back, and looked out at the boat. After a moment he turned and retraced his steps, moving further away this time. Hugging her arms around her chest to keep warm, she followed him.

About a hundred feet along the increasingly craggy shoreline, he came to a dead stop.

"What does that look like to you?" he asked her.

She looked down at the ground. It didn't look like anything. Then she studied the area more closely.

"Um, it looks like . . . something was dragged over the sand for a foot or two," she said.

"I don't think so," he said.

"Then what?"

"A footprint."

"A footprint? That would be one big foot."

"A footprint from a flipper, to be exact," he told her. He started to move again, slowly backing inland half a step at a time, looking for a trail to follow. Instinctively, she moved away from the area where he was searching.

He came to a halt again, shaking his head. "We won't get anything from it — too much time has passed. I think it proves I'm right, but . . ." He stared at her for a moment, then pointed. "Walk in that direction. Look for anything, anything at all, that doesn't belong here."

"What doesn't belong here?" she asked him.

"Anything. It's posted no picnicking in winter. The water can get too rough, so they don't want to encourage people to come out here. The park crew goes through at the end of the summer season and cleans, so there shouldn't be anything left to indicate anyone's been here."

Ten minutes later, she decided that the park department did a good job. She couldn't find anything at all.

But when she moved back toward Zach, he was down on his knees in the damp sand and scrub grass. He had taken a small plastic bag from his pocket, and was carefully placing a few blades of grass in it.

"Grass doesn't belong?" she asked.

"There's something on it. Okay," he said, rising, "we're done. We can go."

"No," she said firmly. "We're not done."

"Yes we are."

"Not until you tell me what the hell we were doing," she told him stubbornly.

He glanced at her with annoyance.

"Hey, you're the one who brought me here. If you didn't want me asking questions, you should have left me on shore," she said in exasperation. "I know you're investigating Eddie's disappearance, but —"

"Talc," he told her quietly.

"Talc?" she repeated, confused.

"I don't want you to say anything to anyone, but I think I know how Eddie's killer managed to make him disappear, then disappeared himself." And why on earth was he telling *her* this? he asked himself.

"With . . . talc?"

"He killed Eddie, dived off the boat and came here. I don't think the killer was working with an accomplice. I think he stashed a boat here earlier."

"Wouldn't *that* have taken an accomplice?"

He shrugged, granting her point. The killer wouldn't have needed an accomplice to get back once he had a boat, but stashing the boat would have taken help. There was no other way back to Newport from here. Unless he'd towed it out here, left it, then gone back, hoping no one would wonder why he had started out with two boats and come back with only one.

"Maybe. I keep thinking, though, that the killer was working alone. The thing is, *how?* And does any of this mean that Sean is in danger, as well? Maybe Kat isn't so crazy after all."

Caer exhaled slowly. "Someone would

really . . . jump off a boat into that water on purpose?"

"I think so."

"But . . ."

"He wore a wet suit, and he used talc to get into the wet suit. There was a tiny trail of talc on the *Sea Maiden.* And I think I just found a few traces of it on the underside of this grass." He started walking toward the dinghy, then stopped short when he got there. She'd been following closely and crashed into his back.

He turned around, steadying her. The way he looked into her eyes made her nervous.

"I don't know who or what you really are, but I do believe that you really mean to help Sean."

Her eyes widened. "I swear, I am —"

"Don't lie to me. Just swear that you really mean to help Sean."

"I really mean to help Sean. I swear."

He kept studying her. She didn't drop her lashes, and she didn't look away. How the hell did he know he should trust her, and yet realize that everything about her was wrong?

His gaze turned suspicious. "You're really taking care of him properly? And all his medications are correct?"

"Yes."

"Want to tell me anything else?" he asked her.

She was acutely aware then that they were alone on an island — winter-barren, surrounded by a frigid sea — and that the wind and the gulls were the only witnesses to whatever occurred between them. She was also aware of him as a vital, living, breathing man, the heat of his energy almost palpable even against the chill of the air and sea.

His eyes probed into hers, aqua and hard. Sharp. They seemed to cut like a knife.

"I have nothing to tell you," she said flatly, returning his stare.

"Don't betray my trust," he said.

"What trust?" she asked, a note of bitterness in her tone.

"I'm amazed that you even dare to ask."

She looked out toward the boat. "I swear to you that I am here to keep Sean O'Riley alive and well, and see to it that he lives for years to come."

She looked back at him. His gaze hadn't relented, and she hesitated when he reached for her hand.

"I'm just going to help you back into the dinghy," he told her.

She felt foolish, and offered him her hand.

He was silent as he rowed back, then balanced easily in the little inflatable boat to help her back on the *Sea Lass,* before climbing aboard himself and dragging the dinghy up after him. He deflated it quickly, then restored the oars to their bin.

He didn't head straight back to the helm, though. He found towels below and thoroughly dried the dinghy, then folded it back into its storage bin.

She was staring at him. He looked back at her and spoke curtly. "I don't want anyone to know where we've been."

"All right."

"Grab some sodas from the galley, or a couple of beers. It has to look as if I was showing you the area," he said.

"You *did* show me the area," she told him.

He watched her for another moment, then nodded.

She started to pull two beers from the small refrigerator in the galley, then opted for sodas instead.

She was, after all, a nurse. She was going back to take care of a patient. She shouldn't be drinking.

Apparently he had decided that he did trust her, at least a little bit, or maybe he'd finally noticed that she was freezing and had started to feel concerned for her welfare.

"You might want to sit in the cabin for a

while. The sun's going to start going down soon, so the ride back will be colder."

"I'm all right," she told him.

She wasn't. She was just stubborn. But she sat on the bench just as she had on the journey out and waited for him to raise the anchor and rev up the engine.

The sea spray flew around them, liquid crystals in the air. He kept their speed high until he neared the channel markers, then slowed accordingly. When they neared the dock, he asked her to stand up and help with the tie ropes. She took them as ordered, but she had no idea how they were supposed to be knotted.

He didn't expect her to. As soon as he had cut the motor and wedged the boat exactly where he wanted her against the dock, he jumped out himself and secured the knots. "I'll teach you some of these as we go along," he said absently, then flashed her a smile. "Next time we're in a sailboat, we'll actually sail. It's fun. You'll like it. You don't seem to get seasick."

"No, I guess I don't get seasick," she said.

He stood, having securely fastened the tie around the dock clamp, and stepped toward her, smiled, paused a moment, then moved a wild lock of her hair behind her ear. "You look pretty windblown," he told her.

"I had a great time 'seeing the area,' " she told him.

He slipped an arm around her, startling her, before she realized that Cal had come out of the office and was heading toward them. He was a tall man, sandy-haired, lanky and good-looking in a slightly awkward way; his arms were long, his hands large. He had large feet, too, and yet it all came together with a certain charm.

"How did you like your boat ride?" he asked.

"It was great. Although it was awfully cold. I'm not sure how you all stand it," she said.

Cal smiled at her. "I have to say, you've got a great accent."

"I think *you* have the accent," she said, smiling back.

Enough flirting, however politely, Zach thought with uncharacteristic irritation. "We've got to get back to the house," he said more sharply than he'd intended. "We've been gone a long time. Cal, if you think of anything, if you find anything, let me know right away."

Cal nodded. "I've looked and looked around the office. I've studied that register a million times," he said, and stared at Zach bleakly. "Eddie's dead, isn't he?"

"I'm afraid so."

Marni came out then. She was clad only in a sweater against the cold, and she shivered, then hurried to her husband's side and huddled against him. "You need to come and visit us in the summer," she told Caer. "It's nice then."

"Yeah, and when we have a long winter, summer can be just one day," Cal said.

Marni punched him in the arm.

"Come for it. It's on July fourteenth and you know it," Cal said solemnly.

Marni sniffed. "Hey, trust me, it's better than Florida, where Zach's from. You can fry down there."

"Hey, watch what you say," Zach said, feigning indignation. "We just get more than one day of summer, that's all. Anyway, we really do need to get going. We'll see you later."

His arm was still around Caer as they headed toward the car. She knew that as soon as they were out of earshot, Cal and Marni were going to be talking about them.

"I don't get it. Why do you want Cal and Marni to think you were just taking the afternoon to see the sights — with me?"

He glanced at her quickly. "I like to see people's reactions."

"You like to cause trouble."

203

"Sometimes it's good to stir the pot," he told her.

"You think Cal and Marni wanted Eddie dead?" she asked.

"I think just about anything is possible."

His grim tone surprised her.

"Does that mean . . . you think Amanda might actually have tried to harm Sean? I thought that —"

"I told you. I think just about anything is possible," he repeated. "And," he reminded her sharply, "I don't want anyone to know right now that I'm pretty sure that Eddie was murdered or how his murderer escaped."

He was studying her again.

She returned his stare. She had told him the truth. She *was* there to protect Sean, and she didn't feel the need to assure him again that he could trust her. "I understand," she told him. "And I won't say a word."

Sean was doing well, Zach thought. He'd spent the warmest part of the day, when the sun was high, wrapped in his heaviest coat and sitting outside with Kat.

When Zach returned, he had called Detective Morrissey, and then he and Sean had closeted themselves away and talked about what Zach had discovered on the boat.

Eventually Caer had come in to give Sean his medications, insisting that he rest for a while.

He'd made it to the table for dinner under his own steam, though, and seemed pleased to find that Cal and Marni were joining them.

As they ate, Zach noticed that Marni was as attentive to Sean as Amanda was — and judging by Amanda's expression, she was aware of it, as well, but everyone at the table, including Kat, seemed determined to be cordial to everyone else, and the meal passed pleasantly.

Zach also noticed that Caer was watching the others just as intently as he was, as if she were trying to learn as much as she could about everyone.

Quite a nurse. Except that she seemed to be more than a nurse.

Was he crazy? he asked himself.

No.

Just suspicious of everyone. Eddie had been murdered. He didn't need proof to know that was a fact.

Back in his room, he was still debating the same questions that had been occupying his mind for days.

Why?

Why would anyone want to kill Eddie, and possibly Sean, as well?

The business was worth a great deal of money, true. But the disbursement of that money was controlled by partnership agreements and wills, so killing someone over it wouldn't make any sense. The same thing held true for both men's personal assets.

He couldn't think of anyone who would have wanted Eddie dead for monetary gain.

And Kat would clearly die before she let anyone hurt a hair on her father's head.

Amanda stood to inherit, but it wasn't as if she would receive a windfall. Kat would still inherit the bulk of her father's estate.

So if it wasn't the inheritance, what *was* it?

He put through another call to Detective Morrissey, using his cell phone just as he had earlier, not wanting anyone in the house to be able to listen in. Morrissey assured him that he had his men discreetly checking the dive shops, adding that Zach was more than welcome to double-check his efforts. So far they had come up with nothing suspicious, but they would keep at it.

Zach thanked him, then told him that he wanted to have the substance he'd found on Cow Cay checked out, promising to deliver it the next morning.

He hung up with a growing respect for Morrissey. Cops, he knew, could be jerks. He had been a cop.

He hoped he hadn't been a jerk.

With nothing else to do, he booted up his computer, went online and started going through the newspaper reports on Eddie's disappearance.

They'd run Eddie's picture, but no one had called in to report seeing him. No one had met anyone named John Alden in the last few days.

Tomorrow, he decided, he would do legwork, checking on local hotels, motels, bed and breakfasts and more, hoping someone had seen or heard from a guest by that name. He would also check all the businesses near the O'Riley's office to see if anyone had seen a stranger in the area during the relevant time frame. It seemed impossible that someone had gotten on the boat with Eddie without anyone having seen anything. Someone, somewhere, had to know something.

But the question remained: What had Eddie possessed or known that had led him to become a victim?

What?

Frustrated, Zach shut down his computer and headed out into the hallway. He heard voices coming from Bridey's room, and he hesitated. It didn't sound as if anything was wrong. In fact, he could hear a note of laughter in Bridey's voice.

Heading in that direction, he saw that her door was open, so he paused and looked in.

Bridey was sitting in the loveseat by the window, Caer was at a little table, and Kat was lounging on the bed.

"Zach!" Kat leaped up and gave him a hug. "Come join us. Bridey is telling us stories about Ireland."

"I'm sure Caer knows them all, but she's being a dear and listening to an old woman's ramblings," Bridey told him. "But Zach is too serious a young man to pay heed to any of my tales."

"Tales about what?" Zach asked.

"Leprechauns," Kat told him.

"I have nothing in the world against leprechauns," he said. Then he frowned and looked at Caer, asking a silent question. *Where was Sean?*

Kat answered the question he hadn't voiced. "Dad's physical therapist is here. He's getting a massage, and then he's going to do some light exercise."

"It's good for the heart to begin exercising as soon as possible," Caer told him.

He sat down on the bed, and Kat plopped

down next to him, ruffling his hair, just like any kid sister. Caer watched them, and he was surprised when a veil seemed to come over her eyes, and she looked away quickly, almost as if she felt she were intruding.

"The thing of it is," Bridey explained, "as I was telling Kat, that folks have gotten all confused about the little people these days. They've made some awful films, depicting them as evil. Now, they *are* tricksters, I admit, and thrifty. They hide their treasure, but they only do that, you see, so Ireland herself can hold on to her riches. If you catch a leprechaun, he must be honest with you, but he knows the loopholes in the rules, and he'll take advantage of them if he can."

"Okay, I'm confused," Zach told her. "If I catch a leprechaun, do I get to follow a rainbow to a pot of gold or not?"

"Perhaps. But it's almost impossible for a man to catch a leprechaun. You see, he cannot escape if you remember to keep your gaze upon him, but the second you look away, well, then he escapes, and that is that."

"What about banshees?" Kat asked, giggling.

"Ach," Bridey said. " 'Tisn't laughing you should be. Banshees, well, they are the ghosts of death, don't ye know? When you hear the wind howling like a scream, when the darkness and shadows are all around, then you know the banshee is comin' and all need to take care."

She spoke with such grave seriousness that even Zach was startled, and her words were greeted with a moment of silence.

But then Caer said, "Now, Bridey, wait a minute. 'Banshee' from the Gaelic *bean sidhe,* means 'woman of the faerie mound.' " She looked at Zach and smiled, as if a little bit embarrassed to be so knowledgeable about the old legends. "It is traditional to keen at the death of a loved one, just as it's traditional to rejoice — with a fair amount of drinking — at the life they lived. Some said the banshees were faerie women who had lost their own lives tragically when they were young, so they could join the keening for those who passed over."

"Really?" Kat said. "I saw a movie with a banshee in it once. She was an ugly old hag." She shuddered.

"Excuse me, but that's just not true," Caer said.

"Well, now, that is part of legend, too," Bridey said. "The banshee is sad, for she died too young, and yet she is also kind and generous, for she took the place of another, who needed to rest. She must always stay as

210

she is — remain a banshee — because it would be a terrible sin to force another into her position if that person were evil and cruel. The banshee's role is to ease the journey, so she must be patient and kind. Evil people in life are just as evil when they die."

Caer cleared her throat. "That's one of the legends, aye. The banshee has a serious role in the balance of life — and death. Death is a new beginning, as frightening as being born into this world. A babe comes into this world with a mother to hold it. Into the next world, we go alone. Or so they say." She shook her head as if to clear away dark thoughts and turned to Zach. "The old Irish tales are really beautiful, you know. They explain life, but they also give it a magical twist. And don't we all need a little magic?" She rose suddenly. "Kat, I'm going to go downstairs and see about your father."

Kat nodded. "Good idea." She yawned. "Aunt Bridey, I think I'm off to bed. I'm tir —"

She broke off suddenly, shivering. Zach, still sitting at her side, actually felt the tremor that rippled through her.

"What?" he asked her anxiously.

"I was just thinking . . ."

"What?" he repeated.

Caer had paused to listen.

"The day Eddie went missing . . ." Kat began.

"It was a perfect day, according to the papers. No storms on the horizon, light winds," Zach said.

"The papers are right. We haven't had a real storm yet this season, knock on wood, but the night before . . . well, it was strange," Kat said.

"What was so strange?" Bridey asked, her face knitting intently.

"I dreamt about the wind howling and the sea churning," Kat said.

"Well," Caer said lightly, "we all have dreams." She looked thoughtful for a moment, then asked, "Was — is Eddie Irish?"

"Irish by association, at least," Bridey said.

"Imagine that," Kat said to Zach. "I dream in Irish."

"Well, you *are* Irish," he pointed out.

"I think my mom was what you call an all-American mutt," Kat said, smiling.

"Ireland is in your veins," Bridey told her firmly. "And proud you should be of it."

"I am. Of course I am." Kat stood and hugged Bridey. "If you and my dad are Irish, then I'm *very* proud. Even if it means I have to worry about meeting a banshee someday."

Caer had started out of the room, but she hesitated and turned back. "The thing is, people fear banshees, just as they fear death. But everyone dies. Death isn't evil. It's a part of life, a natural progression. We never really like to go anywhere uncertain, unknown, alone. So a banshee is there to help a person make the transition from life to death, to hold their hand."

"Hey, a death ghost is a death ghost," Kat said, laughing.

Caer shrugged and smiled. "Well, I'm off to see to your dad."

Zach rose, as well. "I'll just say good-night to Sean myself." He walked over to Bridey and bent down to give her a kiss. She caught his hand and smiled up at him lovingly. "Zach, it's good that you're here. So good."

He squeezed her hand in return, a little troubled, because she felt warm.

"Are you all right?" he asked her.

"A wee bit tired," she told him. "But I'm old. I'm allowed to be tired."

"Maybe the doctor should check on you, too, next time he's here," Zach said.

"As you wish," she agreed.

"Definitely, Aunt Bridey," Kat said. "Now I'm worried about you, too."

"I'm all right, but since you're worried, you can help me to bed. And I *will* see the doctor. Maybe I'm coming down with a winter bug," Bridey said. "Zach, you go on now. Good night and God bless."

"God bless, Bridey," he said. Kat nodded, and he left them alone so that Bridey could get ready for bed.

He caught up with Caer outside Sean's door.

"Death isn't always such a natural part of life, you know."

She spun around to stare at him.

"There's not a thing in the world that's natural about murder," he said.

"No," she agreed, her eyes on his unwaveringly. "There's nothing in the world that's natural about murder."

9

The house seemed to moan and whine and whisper by night.

Caer lay on her bed in the near darkness, her fingers laced behind her head as she stared at shadows on the ceiling caused by the night-light. She listened, and tried to define each noise that she heard. The wind played against the wooden shutters on the window, a sound she had come to know. There was a tree whose branches danced against the upstairs wall. Sometimes the place settled, with a kind of ticking sound. But she knew that, too, and it seemed natural now.

Tonight the wind was rising, and it sounded like a mournful cry. It was low, at first. A lament, a soft keening that was barely audible. But as the wind picked up, sweeping across storm windows and shutters and eaves with a greater fury, the pitch of its cry picked up, as well, like someone screaming far away, perhaps in a distant dimension.

All those sounds . . .

Caer listened to them and identified them, certain that the others in the house were resting well.

Then she heard a new sound.

This one was furtive. Slow. It was a creaking, and it was coming from the main staircase.

She told herself it meant nothing. People got up and moved around, even in the dead of night. There was nothing unusual about that. It wouldn't be Bridey roaming about in the wee hours; she had water and whatever she might need right in her room. She was old — and she wasn't stupid. Wandering alone in the dark could mean a fall and a broken hip. She stayed put.

But Kat might be restless by night, and she might have decided to go downstairs and make tea. And God knew about Zach. For all she knew, he might tiptoe around the house for hours every night.

It wouldn't be Sean. For one thing, he'd taken his medication and would be sound asleep, though he was growing stronger by the day and probably wouldn't need a nurse much longer. No matter; she'd been hired, and she was staying. Most of all, though, it wouldn't be Sean because his room was downstairs, and she wasn't hearing someone climbing the stairs but someone descending them.

Amanda might be the midnight prowler. This was, after all, her home. She might decide to wander down to the kitchen. Or — perhaps even with real concern — she might have decided to go down and check on her husband, to see how he was doing.

Another creak.

Another slow step.

A shadow seemed to shoot across the ceiling, but it was just the light flickering. But *why* had it flickered?

She continued to watch the darkness for creeping shadows, the natural consequence of light and darkness meeting.

She had excellent hearing, and she needed to use it.

Creak.

She held her breath and listened. Waited.

Creak.

Yes. Someone was on the stairs, moving very slowly.

Why move so slowly? Anyone in this house had the right to be here and to wander around at will.

And yet . . .

She was certain the sound was coming

from the stairs. A creeping sensation of fear and approaching doom began to sweep over her. She very quietly eased her covers down, and silently set her feet on the floor.

It was late, but Zach found that, as tired as he was, he couldn't sleep. He tried for a while, then gave up. Something had been bothering him all day.

Eddie.

Why had he been the only one to go into the office that day?

Cal had napped, and Marni had gone shopping, but they had both sounded guilty talking about it. As if they'd been caught playing hooky. Then again, if nothing had happened that day, neither one of them would have felt bad. The business was extremely active in the summer; they put in tons of hours. There was no reason to feel guilty for taking some extra time off in the winter, other than the fact that they hadn't been there when something had happened.

But Eddie had said that he had something to do. Cal hadn't been able to figure out what it was, though, so it probably hadn't been business related. So why had Eddie gone into the office to do it?

What he needed to do was go through Eddie's work computer. Maybe the answer was to be found in whatever he had been up to online.

He rose and dressed warmly, adding a scarf, cap and his coat. Late at night, the cold bit most severely. He hit the tiny button on his watch that lit up the dial. Only midnight. Not that late. He would be back soon enough.

He started out the bedroom door, then paused.

His Smith and Wesson .38 Special was locked in his briefcase. Did he need it to go to the office at this hour of the night?

Hell, yes. Eddie was dead. Of course he needed it.

He retrieved the gun, tucked it in his waistband, then silently started out.

It was all that talk about banshees, Kat decided.

She wasn't afraid of the dark, and she wasn't afraid of being alone. At least, she never had been before.

Tonight, it seemed as if she was actually hearing a banshee.

A banshee? It was as if she was hearing a hundred of them screaming, wailing, moaning, caterwauling in the dark. It was the wind; she knew that. The wind had started to pick up late this afternoon and had grown

219

steadily stronger ever since. No rain, just wind.

Maybe there was a storm coming in. Maybe they would even have snow for Christmas.

The shadows seemed to be dancing an evil tango across the ceiling. It was the branches, bending and bowing to the wind, she told herself. But the howl of the wind was utterly unnerving. How could anything that sounded so much like a lonely scream of horror be natural?

The house itself seemed to shake. To breathe in and breathe out.

Kat tossed and turned. She needed to get some sleep. She needed to be alert and aware come morning so she could make sure her father stayed safe. He was doing well now, and at least he was home. He was back in the States, not across an ocean with *that woman.*

The one sleeping in the bedroom down the hall. *His* bedroom. The woman he had married.

For the thousandth time, she felt like crying. Her father had always been so wise. What had made him choose to marry such a tramp? She wished she could believe that Amanda was as harmlessly stupid as she seemed. The quintessential dumb blonde.

No, that wasn't fair; that was giving offense to blondes everywhere. But honestly . . . Her father was a smart man, one who loved culture and books. She wasn't sure Amanda knew that books came in any form other than a shopping catalogue.

Suddenly her attention was arrested by movement along one wall. It was as if a giant black creature with huge bat wings had descended and was spreading its evil shadow over the room. She felt pure, icy terror grip her. She didn't dare to breathe.

Flap, flap, scrape.

Relieved, she let out the breath she'd been holding. It was just the old oak outside her window. The wind had pressed a branch against her window, and that had been silhouetted by one of the outside lights, creating the shadow she had seen. Even now, the oak was moving in the wind.

Why didn't the shadow move?

That question was playing through her mind when she heard the creaking on the staircase.

She burst out of bed. Someone was in the house. Eddie was dead, her father had been poisoned, and now someone was in the house.

She couldn't just stand there, shivering in the night. Zach was down the hall, and he was licensed to carry a gun. She needed to get Zach, and quickly.

Weighed down by dread and a sense of terror greater than any she had ever known before, Kat found herself unable to run, but she forced herself to move, albeit slowly, despite the icy tentacles of fear wrapping around her limbs. She finally reached her door and started to open it. The old knob felt icy, and she could have sworn that there wasn't just darkness around her, but a mist. As if something huge were *breathing* nearby. She swallowed hard and finally opened her door.

Inch by inch, forcing herself to move, she made her way down the hallway. It had somehow gotten longer, and it was frigid and filled with the same mist, as if someone were exhaling hot breath into the cold air. She could hear it inhaling, exhaling. Almost like laughter. She was moving down the hall, and it was moving after her.

Or it was in front of her. She wasn't sure.

She fought the rush of terror that attacked her at the thought of being stalked by some dark, amorphous danger. She didn't believe in ghosts, didn't believe in banshees, voodoo or vampires.

But . . .

She could feel the evil, the menace, cold

as ice, like the touch of the Reaper's hand, coming out of the dark and slipping around her neck.

She wanted to close her eyes. She was terrified that a death's head would suddenly appear before her, out of the mist, laughing in silent glee.

At last she reached Zach's door.

The minute she grasped the knob, she felt stronger.

She pushed the door open, feeling almost normal. She wasn't going to get hysterical, she told herself. Wasn't going to blurt out that the banshees had been crying outside her window, or that the Grim Reaper had been breathing down her neck in the hallway. She would tell him the truth, plain and simple.

Someone was on the stairway.

"Zach?" she called softly.

No answer. For a moment, panic filled her again. *It* had already been here. *It* had gotten Zach.

She rushed over to his bed before she could flee back to her room and hide in her closet. Somewhere out there, she knew, real danger lurked. A danger to her father.

She reached down, trembling in fear at what she might find.

And then she knew.

Nothing had gotten Zach.

He just wasn't there.

Eddie had been to dozens of Revolutionary War sites, and he had studied literally hundreds of maps. Nothing surprising in that, Zach thought. Eddie and Sean had spent days on end rehashing the Revolutionary War and participated in numerous reenactments.

Zach followed Eddie's online trail for an hour, until he realized that the words were blurring on the screen.

He left the office, moving carefully down the steps.

They were icy by night.

He heard the crashing of the waves, the tinkling of the bells and mooring chains on the boats, and the whipping of the wind. Security lights blazed from nearby businesses, but beyond their reach the sea was pitch dark, except when the rolling waves lashed up and the whitecaps were caught in the multi-colored glow of the Christmas lights someone had strung along the docks. What should have looked cheerful instead created a miasma of eerie confusion across the surface of the water.

It was cold. He wrapped his scarf more tightly around his neck, pulled his cap low over his ears and hunched his shoulders as he headed toward the car.

As he moved, listening to the moaning of the wind as it rose and fell, echoing like a screaming harpy in the night, he was startled to hear something else.

At least . . . he *thought* he heard something else.

A footfall, coming from behind him.

He swung around. Flags on houses and boats, Christmas decorations, all of them being battered by the wind, created a confusion of shadows. He could have sworn that he had heard a footstep, but there was no one behind him.

Where could someone be hiding?

Not a hard question to answer, actually. A pursuer could have ducked behind one of the cars still scattered around the lot. Behind a light pole. Behind the giant Santa that was wavering like a trembling jellyfish in front of a souvenir shop.

But the sound had come from directly behind him. As if someone had followed him from the office.

There was no one there now. He slipped his hand beneath his coat and set it on the gun in his waistband, then looked around again, slowly, carefully.

No one. Nothing out of place that he

could see. It was late on a winter's night, the wind was growing wicked, he was tired, and his eyes were playing tricks. And still . . .

It was bizarre, feeling this uneasy when there was nothing there to be afraid of. He was smart enough to be afraid of what was real — deranged people carrying weapons, for instance. But he had never been afraid of the wind, and he didn't intend to start now.

There was no one there. He was sure of it.

He told himself that the wind had torn something loose from somewhere, and he had heard it hit the pavement before blowing off again, this time to oblivion. Determinedly, he strode to the car.

The drive back to the house was uneventful, but as he left the car and entered the house by the kitchen doorway, he was startled to feel a sensation of unease again.

Now he was really being idiotic, he told himself. Even if there had been someone in the parking lot, they sure as hell hadn't followed him here. And back there, the sound had been real, like a footstep on pavement.

Here, it was just . . .

A feeling. But it was almost palpable. Every hair on his nape stood up in warning.

He paused just inside the door, closing it

behind him as silently as possible. Then, even though it made him feel like a fool, he drew the gun from his waistband, certain that something was amiss.

He moved through the kitchen carefully, then into the hallway, passing the formal dining room and Sean's office, and entering the foyer.

There, the feeling seemed to be like something thundering in his heart. No, it *was* his heart. As keyed and attuned to danger as it had ever been.

Over there, a flurry of movement.

A creaking on the stairs.

"Stop! Right there, right now!" he shouted.

Suddenly the staircase and foyer were flooded with light. Looking up, he saw a figure at the top of the stairs, indistinguishable in the glare of the lights it had had apparently just turned on.

Simultaneously, someone gasped nearby, someone else shrieked near the bottom of the stairway, and an irritated woman shouted angrily from the doorway to the ground floor bedroom Sean O'Riley had taken over.

As his eyes adjusted, he saw that Kat, wielding a frying pan, was standing at the bottom of the steps. Caer, standing just outside her own door, was apparently the one who had gasped. Not surprisingly, the irritated woman was Amanda O'Riley.

And it was Bridey at the top of the stairway, standing there like an avenging angel with her hand still on the light switch.

He had the gun drawn and aimed. He quickly flicked the safety back on and shoved the gun back into his waistband.

"What the *hell* is going on?" he demanded.

It was a mistake.

They all started speaking at once, their voices rising in their efforts to be heard above one another.

"Oh, my God, it was you!" Kat lashed out at Amanda, looking as if she were ready to go to war with the frying pan.

"It's my house, whether you like it or not!" Amanda shouted back.

"It's just that it sounded as if someone was creeping stealthily down the stairs," Caer tried to explain.

"I did not creep down the stairs, I walked, and I walked because *I* heard someone creeping — and that someone had to be you," Amanda told Kat, her hands on her hips. Then she spun on Caer. "Or it was you, creeping around where you shouldn't be. You were hired to be Sean's nurse, not spend the night listening to Bridey's ridiculous stories."

"Listen!" Zach commanded, and — miraculously — they all shut up.

And then they all heard it, a sudden, hard slamming sound.

"It's the back door," Zach said. The slamming came again and again, as if the wind was trying to rip the door off its hinges.

He ignored the women and strode through the house, reaching into his waistband for the gun once again, automatically releasing the safety. He reached the rear door that led out to the back porch and the lawn that sloped to the cliff above the sea.

The door was wide open, swinging on its hinges.

He caught it and stepped out onto the porch, scanning the night. There was no sign of anyone anywhere. No sound of an intruder running away into the night. It looked as if the door had been left open, then caught by the wind.

Which was impossible.

They never left the door unlocked, much less open. The house had an alarm, but most of the time no one remembered to set it after Clara and Tom left for the cottage. He cursed himself beneath his breath; he should have thought of that and seen to it himself.

From where he was standing he could see that the cottage was dressed with holiday lights, and that the drapes in the downstairs had been left open, so he could see Tom and Clara's Christmas tree blinking merrily away.

The wind rose again.

Branches brushed against the house.

The door was nearly ripped from his hands.

He walked back in, closing the door firmly, then locking it. And setting the alarm.

When he got back to the foyer, he saw that Sean O'Riley was up and out of bed in his pajamas. Kat was standing at a distance, tense as her namesake on the proverbial hot tin roof. Caer was in her blue nightgown, like a dark angel, and Bridey had come down the stairs to join everyone.

Amanda stood by Sean; his arm was draped around her, but Zach had the feeling that Amanda had been the one to take his arm and put it over her shoulders.

"Well?" Sean asked.

"I don't know," Zach told him flatly. "I didn't see anyone. The back door was wide open, but it doesn't look as if anything was disturbed. I'll call the police."

"You will not call the police, Zach."

"Sean —" he began.

But Sean was adamant. "Every single body in this house was creeping around. Someone didn't close the door properly, that's all."

"Clara," Amanda said with a sigh. "Sean, I think she's just getting too old."

"Too old for what, Amanda?" Kat asked. "Dad, she isn't any older than you are, is she?"

"It's not the age, it's the mileage, and Clara is showing her mileage," Amanda said, holding her temper and not matching the sarcasm that had slipped into Kat's voice.

"Clara is a member of the family," Bridey said. "And that's that," she added firmly. "Besides, Clara didn't do anything wrong."

"Well, if someone didn't break in, then someone *did* leave the door open," Amanda said flatly. "And that someone had to have been Clara."

"No," Bridey said.

They all looked at her.

"There's a banshee in the house," she said, looking around at all of them, shaking her head slightly and smiling, as if they were children and wouldn't understand. "Haven't you felt it?" she whispered softly.

■ ■ ■ ■

Cal silently set his boots by the back door, praying that he could hold the door against the wind, then close it silently. He let out a sigh of relief when he managed to do so.

What a nasty night, he thought. Maybe the weathermen had it wrong again and there was a storm coming in. They had said that it would be a windy night, but that the morning would dawn clear and cold. He locked the door, glad to hear the bolt slide quietly.

Then he tiptoed into the living room.

And went dead still.

There was someone in his house, standing right in front of him.

A scream rose in his throat and burst free just as a person in front of him let loose with an even louder scream.

He reached blindly for the light switch behind him and realized as the lights came on that he'd just been terrified half to death by his wife.

She was clearly as astonished as he was, staring at him wide-eyed, her mouth still open as if she were about to scream again.

Her boots were standing by the front door, and he realized that she, too, had just come in, and had been tiptoeing toward their bedroom in her stocking feet just as he had been.

"You scared me to death," he told her.

"Me? I just about had a heart attack," she told him.

They stared at one another for a long moment. Then he frowned and asked, "Where were you? When did you go out? *Why* did you go out?"

Her eyes opened wider, and then *she* frowned. "Wait a minute. Where were *you?* When did you go out, and why?"

"I heard a . . . noise," he said. "A moaning. I thought someone was hurt in our backyard."

She let out a sigh. "I heard it, too," she told him. "I thought it was coming from the front yard, and quite honestly, I thought it was a wounded hyena, from the way it sounded." She laughed then with relief. "Oh, Cal." She hurried to him, nuzzling into his neck. "I thought you were sound asleep. I was scared, but I thought someone was hurt, and I didn't want to wake you."

He pulled her against him. "My brave girl. I thought *you* were sound asleep. Let's check the locks and go to bed."

She smiled. "I have a better idea. I'm freezing, and that wind is still blowing like a mother. Let's make a couple of hot toddies and *then* go to bed."

He kissed the tip of her nose. "I can one up that. Let's check the locks, make hot toddies, go to bed and fool around. And then sleep late. And screw the business."

She frowned. "Cal, we can't afford to screw the business, especially now, with Eddie missing, and Sean being sick and all."

He nodded. "Okay, we screw each other and not the business."

She laughed. "I doubt if we'll have any charters tomorrow. But we do need to go in."

"Of course."

"Maybe we can go out by ourselves," she suggested.

"Sure, if you'd like," he told her.

She pulled away from him. "You check the doors, and I'll make the toddies. And after that, well, we'll need each other." She wiggled her eyebrows playfully. He laughed and went to follow orders.

10

When Zach entered the breakfast room the next morning, Clara bade him a cheerful good morning as she set a plate of fresh-baked scones on the table.

"Good morning, Clara. You are incredible," he told her, reaching for one of the scones and eating it where he stood. He was ready to run out to the police station. He didn't want to call; he wanted to be out of the house from now on when he spoke with Detective Morrissey.

Last night, after Bridey's eerie announcement, he had soothed her and urged her up to bed. Then, with Sean firmly ordered back to bed by all of them, he had gone over the house top to bottom.

He had wanted to do so alone.

Instead, he had done so with Amanda, Kat and even Caer following him around.

He'd found absolutely nothing out of place.

And no one in the house.

It was a big house, but he had gone through all of it, looked into every closet, every little storage space, and every nook and cranny.

He had even looked under all the beds.

Sean had probably been right, and the back door had just been left open. But he wanted Morrissey to know about the incident anyway. He also needed to give Morrissey the substance he had found on the island. He didn't know what it was going to prove, even if it *was* talc. But it would at least be circumstantial, and with the detective showing him so much courtesy, he wanted to make sure that he returned it.

"Let me get you some coffee," Clara said.

"Thank you, Clara. How you do it, I'll never know. You cook and clean. As huge as this place is, it's clean as a whistle and runs like silk."

"Except for the fact that you left the back door open last night," Amanda announced, breezing into the room. "That can't happen again," she said firmly, taking the cup of coffee Clara had just poured for Zach right out of Clara's hand.

Clara frowned, wiping her hands nervously on the apron she was wearing. "I didn't leave the door open, Mrs. O'Riley. I certainly did not."

"Yes, you did. Or Tom did."

"Tom went to the cottage before me. He had the tree glowing when I came in last night." Her frown deepened.

"You go out the back, right?" Amanda demanded.

Clara nodded. "But I turned the key and threw the bolt," she insisted.

"Are you calling me a liar?" Amanda demanded.

"No, of course not."

"Well, then, there is no other explanation."

Clara stared at Zach, as if asking for help.

"Tell her, Zach," Amanda insisted.

"The door was open, Clara," he admitted unwillingly.

Amanda spun around suddenly to face him. "You were out," she said. "I was so unnerved last night that I only just realized that. You went out."

"I went to the charter office."

"In the middle of the night?" Amanda said, shocked and suspicious.

"I couldn't sleep. And I'm here to find Eddie," he said.

Amanda sniffed. "Yeah? I think you're here because that little bitch upstairs thinks I tried to kill her father."

Clara wore a look of white-faced horror.

Zach tipped his head discreetly in her direction, and she fled.

He turned to Amanda. *"Mrs. O'Riley,"* he said pointedly, "I'm trying hard myself to believe that you're really in love with Sean. But if I were you, I wouldn't go calling his daughter a bitch around here."

She smiled and tossed back the wealth of her hair. "Look, I'm married to the man, which means I'm stuck dealing with the bratty kid —"

"Who's almost your age," he reminded her.

She ignored him. "Not to mention having to deal with that other bitch married to Cal, with his dying old crazy aunt and that senile woman in the kitchen. I really don't know how long my good graces will last. And I wouldn't want you to bet on the fact that Sean would now or will always choose this harem of nutty sluts over me. So maybe you ought to tell the little bitch to behave herself."

She didn't wait for an answer, because she didn't want one.

She simply grabbed a scone and glided off.

Why the hell had Sean ever married that woman? he wondered.

But he was actually pretty sure he knew.

In front of Sean, butter wouldn't melt in her mouth. In front of Sean, when Kat was . . . catty, Amanda replied with calm and patient courtesy. She pretended to be gentle and loving when it came to Bridey.

She didn't keep the act up quite as well for Clara or Tom, because in her mind, they were just servants.

And he knew damned well that she disliked him, pure and simple.

And it was a wonder she hadn't managed to get rid of Caer yet.

He went into the kitchen to assure Clara that they had no idea of who was really to blame, and then he headed out.

He opened the garage door, and then, before he got into the car, he walked out onto the lawn and looked around.

It was a cool, crisp morning, and the wind had died down.

In fact, it had stopped. There didn't seem to be so much as a flutter in the air. It was amazing.

As he drove toward the police station, he found himself wondering about Caer again. Sean had said that she would be staying until after Christmas. He had the feeling Sean had told Amanda that she was staying, and that was that.

Strange.

Why? he taunted himself. He had brought her with him when he should have gone out alone to the island, and he had told her what he wasn't telling anyone else, other than Sean or the cops. He already missed the sight of her when he was away from her. He found himself searching her out when he could.

Hey, he warned himself, watch it, or you'll be imagining a whole lot more about her. Those eyes. That hair. Those impossibly long legs. Wrapped around you.

He groaned aloud.

And drove.

First things first, Caer thought. Sean was getting stronger by the day, but she still sat in the chair in his room while he showered and dressed.

He had an appointment with his cardiologist that morning, and Tom was going to drive them.

To her surprise, Amanda opted not to go.

Along the way, Sean pointed out some of the most famous mansions. "You need to go, young lady. They're all decked out for Christmas."

"I'm working," she reminded him.

"Yes, you are. But I'm doing quite well, and no one works all the time."

240

"I've barely been here, and I've already been out on one of your boats."

Sean just smiled. He was charming, and quite handsome, especially when he smiled. Maybe it wasn't so odd that he had attracted such a young wife.

Actually, it wasn't odd that he would attract anyone; what was odd was that he had chosen Amanda.

Caer pushed that thought from her mind. They were nearing the doctor's office, and anyway, Sean's marriage was none of her business.

Tom opened the car doors, but when he would have helped Sean out, the older man said, "Tom, I appreciate the offer, but I can walk in on my own, and I need to do so."

Tom looked at his boss with real affection and concern, then nodded and said that he would stay in the car.

A little while later, Caer accompanied Sean into the exam room, where a nurse took his blood pressure and listened to his heart, then took his temperature. The cardiologist, a Dr. Rankin, came in then and asked Caer about Sean's medications. She just smiled and said that he should ask Sean, who rattled off the names of everything he was taking, how much and when.

Sean went for a scan of his veins, and Caer

went out to the waiting room.

A woman there was reading the newspaper, and Caer saw that there was a picture of Eddie still on the front page, though it was smaller than it had been. The caption read Local Man Still Missing in Bizarre Mystery.

While Sean was still in the middle of his procedure, the doctor sat down with her in his office and asked her about everything that had gone on in Ireland. She was glad that she'd been in the emergency room as she described everything that had happened and everything they'd done.

Dr. Rankin shook his head. "And they suspected food poisoning?"

"Yes."

"But they couldn't find anything?"

"I assure you, the testing in Ireland is thorough," she told him.

She must have sounded a little indignant. He tried to hide a smile. "I believe you. I'm just completely baffled."

"They were baffled, too," she admitted.

"And you have no idea?" he asked.

She shook her head.

"He's doing well now, right?" she asked.

"Yes, I've checked his heart, his veins, and given him a low-level stress test. Mr. O'Riley's in excellent health overall, thank

God. But no one lives forever. We age. And the body reacts to the kind of stress he's just been through. But he's doing well. I understand you'll be with him until New Year's?"

"Yes."

"That's good. Keep a close eye on him."

She hesitated. "Is he healthy enough to get back to, uh . . . normal relations with his wife?" she managed, looking away at the last. Hell. She was his nurse. This was all matter-of-fact stuff.

To her surprise, Dr. Rankin hesitated. "Medically?" he asked her.

"Of course," she said.

He looked probingly at her. "She was with him when this happened, right?"

"Yes."

"Sean told me he's down on the first floor and she's still upstairs. Let's just keep things that way for a bit."

"Mrs. O'Riley won't be happy."

"Mrs. O'Riley should want to play it safe," Rankin said.

She smiled. "You're the doctor."

He nodded, then excused himself to see other patients. Sean reappeared, buttoning his top button and grinning. "I'm officially in good shape," he told her.

"You're not in the clear yet."

243

"I can drive any day," he said happily.

"But you shouldn't," she said.

"We'll see."

"You have Tom."

"It's a big house, big lawn. Tom is a busy man."

"And Clara. She must be busy, too, keeping up with that place."

"We have maids in a few days each week. No one human being could keep that place clean."

She smiled. "I'm glad to hear it." She paused, frowned and asked, "Sean, do any of those maids . . ."

"Do they have keys to the house?" he asked her.

"Do they?"

"No. Of course not. Clara lets them in, and Clara watches them like a mother hen. A very suspicious mother hen."

She nodded. "It's just that . . . well, that door *was* open last night."

He grinned, then leaned down to whisper conspiratorially, "Did you hear?"

"What?" For some reason, she found herself whispering back.

"There's a banshee in the house." He smiled and winked.

She smiled weakly in return, and linked her arm through his as they made their way back out to Tom and the car.

But when they were settled in the backseat, she looked at him gravely.

"Sean."

"Yes."

She hesitated. "You know . . . Zach is convinced that your friend Eddie is dead," she said quietly.

"I know."

"And I'm afraid someone is trying to kill you, too," she told him very quietly.

He didn't look at her; he stared straight ahead.

"I know that, too," he replied. "That's part of the reason you're here, right?"

She felt as if every muscle within her tensed. "Pardon?"

"To see that some sneaky S.O.B. doesn't do me any medical harm, right?"

"Right," she said weakly, trying to hide her shock.

"I'm going to be fine," he assured her. "I still have things to do."

"Don't we all say that?" she asked softly.

"Of course. And I know that time waits for no man and all that. I just don't think that it's my time. Hey, I've been wrong before. But I have you and Zach to look out for me. And all any of us can do is our best, right?"

She nodded as he dismissed the subject and pointed down the road. "That's the way to Green Animals. It's an old mansion with an impressive topiary menagerie. Bridey loves the place, but you know Bridey. She loves everything magical. Like banshees," he said, and grinned.

Detective Morrissey sat behind his desk, studying Zach gravely. "You should have called. We could have sent out officers to look around the neighborhood."

"Sean refused. He insisted the door had just been left open accidentally, and he could be right. Nothing was stolen."

"Do *you* think the door was left open?" Morrissey asked.

"I don't know. Several people heard noises, but they could have been hearing each other tramping around. I'll make sure the alarm is set from now on. What about the sample I brought you?"

Morrissey shrugged. "I expect you're right and it's talc, but I'm not sure where we go from there." He hesitated for a second, then sighed. "We still don't have a body. Let's face it, we all assume that Eddie Ray is dead, but without a body, we can't be sure. And, I'll admit, I don't think your idea of a diver killing him and swimming away is a long shot anymore. But we've done the rounds of the dive shops and came up empty. But plenty of people have their own setups, so . . ."

"Thanks." Zach rose.

Morrissey leaned back. "You know, people are usually killed for a reason. Sure, you have your psychos, your random killers. But a thought-out murder — and this was well thought out — is committed for a reason. If we can find the reason, maybe we can figure out who did it."

"I know."

"Any ideas?"

"I'm working on it," Zach assured him.

"Keep in touch. I'll do the same," Morrissey said, standing and shaking his hand.

Once he was back in the car, Zach headed for the charter office.

He noted again how different the day was from the night before, with the wind still nonexistent.

Cal and Marni were both in. Cal was on the phone, making arrangements with a cleaning service, and Marni was going over the books.

"Slow day?" Zach asked. It was so beautiful out that he was surprised no one had stopped in to book a last-minute sail. There were certainly plenty of tourists around. A lot of retirees, in particular, came in December to see the Christmas decorations.

"Yes, and a good thing," she said. "If it were summer, we'd have to be hiring extra help, on top of the seasonal employees we always hire. So far, Cal has been able to handle everything we've booked." She sighed. "But the holiday flotilla is coming up — we always show off our fleet then. And then there's New Year's. . . . I guess I'm going to have to talk to Sean soon about hiring on another couple of captains. I don't know what else we can do."

"I can take one of the boats out for the holiday flotilla," Zach offered. "That's just a few days before Christmas, right?"

"The Sunday before," she agreed.

"Maybe Sean will be up to snuff by then."

"Maybe. So what brings you in today?" she asked him.

"Eddie's computer."

"Oh?" She arched a brow. "Well, it's over there. Help yourself."

"Thanks." He didn't mention that he already knew where it was.

Zach sat at Eddie's desk, booted up his computer and went back ten days. As he accessed areas that the casual user might not, he realized that Marni had moved to stand behind him and look over his shoulder.

"How did you do that?" she asked.

"What?"

"Go back so far. I can only pull up the most recent sites I've visited."

"It's not all that tricky, really. A computer — even the worst computer — has an amazing amount of info saved in its memory, and this is a nice setup, so it's got even more."

"Yeah. Eddie insisted he had to have *this* computer. I don't get it, myself. The Internet is the Internet, you know? We have a great business site, though. Eddie did it. Do you believe that? The old guy is the one who figures it all out," Marni said affectionately. She was smiling, but her smile faded as she realized that she was speaking in the present tense about someone who was probably dead.

She didn't walk away, though.

"Hey, you got any coffee?" Zach asked her.

"Sure," she said, and went to pour him a cup.

He thought of the facts he had so far. Eddie had gone out with a man who called himself John Alden. The man had paid cash. The boat had been found by Cow Cay. There was talc on the boat, and talc on Cow Cay. And then he added the facts he couldn't prove but believed all the same. Someone had killed Eddie, used diving equipment to reach the island and disappeared from there. And that someone had killed Eddie for a reason.

Then he moved on to the more questionable suppositions. Someone might be trying to kill Sean. If so, who? Amanda, his wife, who stood to gain? Logical, maybe. She was young and beautiful; Sean was old and rich. A likely scenario. Maybe too likely. Why did people kill? Passion, envy, greed.

Eddie had been accessing all the information he could on Rhode Island and the American Revolution. He had gone to sites that featured maps and charts of the area. He had studied battles and commanders and the congress. He had looked up Nigel Bridgewater, the local hero who had been hanged for treason, on a number of different sites, sites that focused specifically on Bridgewater and sites where he was only mentioned. He had done a lot of cross-referencing.

But hadn't written any notes or conclusions on his computer. At least, none that Zach had found so far.

Zach went to Eddie's calendar. There were notations about work-related events, and then a notation followed by several exclamation points on Christmas Day.

Sean will get the gift and then he'll know!!!!

He exited the calendar and turned around. Marni was behind him, smiling, carrying his coffee. "Black?" she asked him.

"Black is fine," he said. "Thank you."

As he accepted the coffee, she sighed. "Poor Eddie."

"We can still hope," he said.

"Of course. We're all hoping, but . . . Eddie wouldn't just go away without telling someone. I know he wouldn't."

"Thanks for this," he said, lifting the cup to her.

"Sure."

She went back to her own desk. The door opened, and a group of young men came in, hoping they could charter a boat for a sail around the bay. Cal, who was off the phone by then, went over to speak to them.

Zach closed down Eddie's computer. He was pretty sure he had discovered what he could from it, which really wasn't much. He needed to get into Eddie's house, and he needed to talk to Sean.

Passion, envy, greed. People were killed because they knew too much. They were killed because others envied what they had.

What was it that Eddie knew, or had, that had brought about his death?

Did it have to do with Sean, as well?

If they were both dead, did the business fall to Cal and Marni?

No. Kat and Amanda would inherit what wasn't bequeathed to others, including Sean's share of the business. None of it made any sense. Cal didn't really stand to gain anything.

Amanda might do well by becoming a widow. She wouldn't have access to all of Sean's fortune, because of Kat, but she would be better off than she had been going into the marriage.

But Amanda had nothing to gain by murdering Eddie.

There had to be something else. Something he was missing.

He kept returning to Eddie's research. And Sean's. Over the years, they had both gone on and on about Nigel Bridgewater.

He waved to Marni and Cal as they made arrangements to take the men sailing around the bay and headed out, telling him to lock up when he left.

And then his thoughts went back to the Revolutionary War and the missing patriot treasure.

Bridey had come down with something. Clara fussed and made tea, toast and soup. Sean's primary care doctor actually made a point of coming out to see her, and he prescribed an antibiotic. Bridey decried the attention being given to her, but she seemed to like it, as well.

Kat plumped up her pillows and sat with her, reading. Caer popped in to see her, too, then went downstairs for lunch, since Amanda had joined her husband in the dining room. Amanda was completely charming not only to Sean but to her, then left for a pedicure. Zach returned to the house in time to enjoy some of the cod, peas and parsley potatoes Clara had prepared for the meal.

With Zach there, Caer excused herself to sit with Bridey. When Caer arrived, Kat went down to spend some time with her father, and Caer realized that she and Kat had somehow formed a silent team.

One of them was always watching out for Sean.

They were both determined that Sean had to be protected — Caer because she was open to the possibility of danger and Kat because she was certain Amanda was nothing short of evil personified.

Bridey had her eyes closed when Caer sat down at her side and took her hand. She remembered how Bridey had accosted her that first night in the kitchen. She had convinced Bridey that she was there only to protect Sean, but she knew Bridey was still suspicious of her, just as Zach was, even though neither one of them could have said what was behind the feeling.

"You know, there are all manner of stories out and about," Bridey said, and Caer realized that the old woman had opened her eyes and was looking at her.

"It's said, you know, that a banshee can be granted human form. That she can know again what it was like when she was flesh and blood, if she is sent to watch over one who is not intended to die."

"That must be nice for them," Caer said lightly.

Bridey was smiling. "They feel as they once felt. For in taking on human form, they are once again cursed with human emotion."

"Is that such a bad thing?" Caer asked.

"No, not entirely. But sometimes it hurts to feel," Bridey said softly. "Of course, some emotions are genuinely ugly."

"Well, life is good and bad, isn't it? And we need the ugly to be able to see the beautiful, do we not?" Caer said.

Bridey squeezed her hand. "Are you here for me?" she asked.

"What do you mean? I'm sitting here with

you. Or do you mean, *did I come from Ireland to be with you?* I came with Sean, remember?"

Bridey's smiled deepened. "Child, I haven't gone daft. I mean, are you here for me?"

"I . . ."

Bridey stared hard at Caer, then shifted her gaze to a point over her shoulder. Caer turned quickly and saw that Zach had come into the room.

To her surprise, she felt vulnerable. Whatever he had overheard, she doubted it would mean anything to him. What bothered her was that she kept hearing Bridey's words about emotion and how it could hurt.

And in fact it *did* hurt.

She had been fascinated by him from the start. And as she had come to know more about him, she only liked him more and more. His eyes, the way his hair fell across his forehead, the color and texture of it. She liked the movement in his face when he flashed a grin, and she loved the tone of his voice. His walk. The kindness and affection that touched his features whenever he looked at Bridey. His respect for others, his patience. His intelligence and sense of responsibility. The fact that he was clearly a man who would do anything for the people who mattered to him.

She was attracted to him. She wanted to touch. To feel.

To know all the vitality and heat that were part of him, to hear him speak words of passion to her as he moved against her in the dark.

"What's this I hear? You can't get sick before Christmas, Bridey," he said, coming over to the bed and planting a kiss on her forehead. "We have to get you over this thing right away."

Bridey laughed, but her laugh became a cough. "Here, take a sip of water," Caer said, quickly rising to help Bridey with the water. Zach was next to her. Touching her. It was as if she could feel his heartbeat. He breathed, and she breathed in time with him.

She set the water down when Bridey had finished, and quickly backed away.

"I'm all right," Bridey assured them both.

Zach looked at Caer with concern, voicing a silent question.

"The doctor has been in, and she's taking an antibiotic," Caer said.

Zach nodded.

Bridey waved a hand dismissively. "Get out of here, both of you. I'm going to take a wee nap now."

"A nap, and don't forget your medicine," Zach said.

She waved him off. He stood in the doorway and watched as Caer moved back over to the bed, drawing the covers up. As she leaned down, Bridey whispered to her, "Eddie is dead. I know he is. I saw him. Did you come because of Eddie?"

"Bridey, I swear, I know nothing about Eddie," Caer said, hoping Zach couldn't hear them. She touched Bridey's cheek and smiled reassuringly.

Bridey caught her hand and squeezed it. "You're a sweet child," she said simply. "Now, go. Get out of here, so I can rest."

Caer joined Zach in the hallway. He was frowning. "When did this all happen?" he asked, as she closed the door.

"I think she just woke up this morning with sniffles and that cough. The doctor saw her when he came to check on Sean, so she's in good hands."

He nodded. "Good. Thanks."

She stared up at him, uncomfortable. She wanted to step away, or step closer, forget time and place and all convention, and cup her hand around his face, feel his flesh beneath her fingertips. Wanted to step closer and press herself against him, rise on her toes and touch her lips to his. She saw it, felt it so clearly, that a flush rose to her cheeks.

She stepped back.

"Hey, want to come with me?" he asked her.

"Um . . . where?"

"Eddie's house."

"Oh? I, uh, I shouldn't. I should keep an eye on Sean."

"No need. He's going out with Kat. They'll be gone at least an hour. He wants to do some Christmas shopping. It seems the doctor gave him the okay to get out a bit, so long as he doesn't overdo things."

"Yes. He said Sean's doing well and can start easing back into day-to-day life."

Zach nodded. "Sounds good." He smiled. "So come on. Let's go to Eddie's house and see if we can find out what's going on."

She had to smile back. "We? You mean you trust me? Really?"

"Not really. Just where Sean is concerned. So, are you coming with me?"

She nodded, trying to not to let herself feel bad that he still distrusted her. "Aye, that I am. Thank you. I'll grab my coat."

Eddie's house was only a couple of blocks away. It was a rustic nineteenth-century saltbox, small, but big enough, and with plenty of charm. A huge leather sofa faced the fireplace, and a reinforced rolltop desk held his computer. He apparently liked TV; his plasma screen was huge. Caer noted that he had dozens of DVDs, virtually all of them documentaries on the American Revolution, sailing, treasure hunting, archeology and the like.

"He did love history, didn't he?" she noted.

"He sure did."

Zach went straight for Eddie's computer. "I talked to Sean. He and Eddie have spent years studying their favorite Rhode Island native son together. His name was —"

"Nigel Bridgewater," Caer supplied.

Zach looked at her in surprise. "Yes. How did you know?"

"Sean told me about him when he was in the hospital in Dublin."

"Ah," Zach said, and turned back to the computer.

"Just look around and see what you can see," he told her.

"All right."

"The police were here, so I don't think you'll find much of anything, but it's worth a try. I'd love to find out exactly what he'd been up to before he went out."

Zach was already scrolling through data

as he spoke, so she started looking more carefully through Eddie's books and DVDs. Most were on the Revolution. Some were on the Civil War, and some were on history that was closer to home for her. There was a biography of the first president of the Irish Republic, Eamon de Valera, and another on Brian Boru, and the Vikings in Ireland.

"Nigel Bridgewater was something of a northern Swamp Fox," Zach said, talking absently as he worked. "He knew the northern waters like the back of his hand. He'd been a Royal Navy man at one time, and then he opened a print shop. . . . He took all kinds of letters and documents up and down the East Coast, and he even carried payroll at times. Legend has it that not long before his capture, he met with a French ambassador before the French were fully committed to the American cause, and received a large sum in gold, silver and jewels to be delivered to the Continental Congress. The British knew about him for years, but he eluded them time and time again. He was young — only twenty-six — when he was finally apprehended. And he was caught because his ship — a fast moving sloop too light to be heavily armed — was outgunned in Rhode Island Sound. The ship went down in flames, but the British captured him. And they were furious with him. He'd made a fool of them too many times. He was taken off the ship before it could sink, brought down to Boston, given a sham of a trial and hanged on the spot. They say he was tortured first, but that nothing the British did could make him talk. He died without telling them anything they wanted to know. He knew the names of American spies throughout the Colony, and even in Britain, but he never revealed a single one."

"How extraordinary," Caer said. "What courage. But if he was caught and hanged, what's the big mystery?"

"Most people believe that the treasure and his last dispatches went down with his ship in the Sound. The ship has never been discovered. Of course, it's deep out there, and cold, but they've found the Titanic, so it's possible that one day his ship will be found, too. The thing is, some people say that he was afraid he might meet up with the British on that particular trip. They believe that before he set out he hid the treasure and all the letters he was carrying somewhere around Rhode Island. If so, though, there's no record of it. His men went down with his ship, or were killed outright in the fighting."

"Do you think it's possible that Eddie figured out where the treasure was?" Caer asked.

"I don't know. I think he might have found some kind of clue, at least. On his calendar, at the office, he made a note on Christmas Day about a gift for Sean. He wrote 'Sean will know.' So I'm assuming Eddie found out something Sean wanted to know, and that Eddie's gift was going to be that knowledge."

Caer had been trailing her fingers over the rows of books and DVDs. She paused suddenly, staring at something stuck between two books.

Frowning, she tugged at it.

"Zach."

"Yeah?"

"I think it was more than knowledge that Eddie intended Sean to have," she said.

"Why?" he asked, turning around, then getting up to join her.

She showed him what she had found: the remnants of a sheet of wrapping paper and a courier receipt.

Zach's fingers brushed hers as he took the receipt. "It's insured, but it's coming parcel post," Zach said.

"What do you think he sent? Not just information, right?"

Zach looked at her. "No, definitely not. Not if it weighed twenty-five pounds, five ounces."

11

"We're going to have to wait until it arrives," Sean said pragmatically, when they showed him what they'd found.

"But it's . . . in the system somewhere," Caer said, looking hopefully at Zach.

He shook his head, smiling. "I doubt that even Aidan's FBI buddies can break into the postal system, Caer." He shook his head. "Leave it to Eddie. He would trust the mail."

"I can't even get the electric bill half the time," Sean said.

"Oh no, you mean this could be lost in the mail forever?" Caer said.

Sean laughed. "Probably not. But it *is* frustrating. We're just going to have to wait until it gets here, then we'll know what he sent."

"It should come soon," Zach reasoned.

"It's almost Christmas, don't forget. They'll be rushed off their feet," Sean warned.

"Even so . . ." Zach said thoughtfully, figuring the time since Eddie had disappeared.

Still not quite a week.

"Even so. Yes, hopefully, we'll see it soon," Sean said.

Sean yawned and stretched. "Well, I think I'm off for a nap. I told Kat I'd spend some time with her tonight. She wants to try out a few new songs on me." He looked over at them, and Zach realized they were both staring at Sean with concern.

He sighed. "Look, you two, you can't watch me all the time. Please, I'm not a fool. I'm taking everything very slowly and very carefully, all right?" He shook his head. "It's like I'm the king or something — pretty soon you'll be thinking I need a food taster." He groaned. "Oh, God, stop looking at each other like you think that might be a good idea."

Caer shifted in her chair, looking away silently, leaving it to Zach to reply.

"Sean, it's just that —" he began.

"Maybe whoever killed Eddie is trying to kill me," Sean said flatly. At their shocked looks he added, "We all suspect that, and hell, it's better just said out loud. At least, between the three of us."

265

"Where do we go from here?" Caer asked.

"We wait. There's nothing else to do," Sean said.

"I'm getting back into Eddie's computer," Zach said. "He knew something, and he'd been somewhere. I have to figure out what and where."

"Let it rest for the night," Sean said. "Mull things over. You can get back to it tomorrow, when you'll be fresh."

"But —" Zach started to protest.

"I'm telling you. Let it go for now. You'll be better off. Now," Sean said, "you two need to go out. Shake all this off. The mind, like the body, works better when you move it around a bit."

"Out?" Caer said. "We've just been out."

"No, no. I mean *out,*" Sean said. "Have dinner somewhere. Go listen to some music. It's a beautiful day, it's supposed to be a beautiful night. It may get up to forty-five. I'll be with my daughter, who has decided that she has to stick to me like glue. Not that I don't love to be her sounding board. It makes a father proud, and I don't want you around, stealing my thunder. So I'm ordering you both, get out for the night."

"But —" Zach began again.

"Amanda is having dinner with the women from the garden club. She won't be back until late herself," Sean said.

Zach looked at Caer. She was staring at Sean, and she seemed to be blushing.

"It's all right by me," Zach said. "Caer?"

"I have to say, I don't seem to be working very hard," she said quietly.

Sean laughed. "In my mind, you've gone above and beyond."

She still hadn't looked at him, Zach thought, just as she finally turned to him.

"I guess I'll go change, then," she said.

Zach smiled slowly, then laughed. "Sean, are you going to tell us where we should go, too?"

"Sure. American Pie," Sean said. "It's a new place up on the highway. And after dinner, stop of at McCafferty's. They have a jazz quartet up from Louisiana. Give Caer a taste of the country along with her meal."

"All right," Zach said doubtfully. "I still don't like the idea of leaving —"

"I'll set the alarm, and I'll be with Kat, plus Clara and Tom are right out back. And I'll phone you if anything comes up. All right?"

"All right," Zach said. "Just one more thing."

"What now?" Sean demanded impatiently.

"Just how dressy is this place?"

■ ■ ■ ■

Caer was glad she'd gone shopping in Dublin. She wasn't even sure why — except that she'd been leaving for the holidays — but she'd purchased a long-sleeved, cobalt-blue slinky cocktail dress and appropriately delicate heels to go with it. Once she was dressed, she played with makeup, washed it off, then heard a knock at her door.

It was Kat, whose only response was, "Wow."

Caer blushed. Again. "Thanks."

"Are you crying?" Kat asked her, perplexed.

"Crying? Oh. No, I just washed my face. The makeup wasn't right."

"Well, sit, I'll give you a hand."

Caer sat.

Kat went to work. A few minutes later she stepped back to survey her handiwork. "You look perfect," she said.

"Thanks," Caer said, and blushed yet again.

"And you really don't know it, do you? That's why you blush so much." Kat laughed suddenly, a touch of wickedness in the sound. "I have to tell you, I loved it when you walked in here with my dad and

268

Zach. I could just see how much it burned Amanda to have you around."

"Kat," Caer said seriously, "what makes you so certain that Amanda is . . . after your father?"

"My dad is in his seventies," Kat said flatly. "And Amanda spends half her day in front of the mirror. All he is to her is a meal ticket. I think she'd cut my heart out, too, if she could."

"But she wouldn't inherit all your father's money," Caer said.

"No. My father believes in his flesh and blood. Sometimes I wish he hadn't been so brilliant with business, though. But the thing is, he did what he loved and still does. He just happened to do it better than all the rest, him and Eddie."

"What about Cal?"

"Cal's good," Kat said. "And Marni is great with the books. I'm sure they're both sweating this whole thing, though. My dad really is that company. With Eddie gone . . ." Her voice trailed off. "Well, I'm sure Cal is praying that Dad gets well soon, and that nothing else happens."

"Do you think something else is going to happen?" Caer asked her.

"Don't you? Isn't that really why you're here?"

"I'm here to see that your father takes his medications, and to be around in case there's an emergency with his heart or his blood pressure," Caer said, wondering if there was anyone here who *didn't* think they knew why she was really there.

"Yeah, right," Kat muttered.

"What?"

"You're working for Zach, aren't you?"

"Pardon?"

"The Flynn brothers brought you in. Don't try to tell me differently."

"No, really, that's not true," Caer said.

"Whatever. I'm just hoping you and Zach really do have a thing going, because it's time for him to find the right person, and you're either an amazing actress or one of the most 'right' people I've met in my life. You care about him, I know. I've seen your eyes when he doesn't know you're watching him, and I've seen the way he looks at you. Then again, I guess a lot of guys look at you that way." She laughed. "You are refreshing. Marni loves a mirror, and I think Amanda worships at one. But they can't hold a candle to you. You just walk into a room and it's game over. Plus you're younger than Amanda."

"You're younger than Amanda, too," Caer told her, grinning but perplexed.

"Yes, but I'm my dad's daughter. She hates me, but she's not jealous of me the way she is of you. Or Marni. She's always hanging on my dad. She told me once that she lost her father when she was really young, and that's why."

"Maybe that *is* why."

"I don't think so. She flat out flirts with him. Honestly? I think she'd have an affair with him in a heartbeat"

"What?" Caer asked, shocked.

"Don't worry. My father would never do anything like that. He doesn't get all hot and bothered over a pretty face. That's why we were all floored when he fell head over heels for Amanda. My mom has been dead a long time, so it wasn't anything like that. It's just that . . . he was barely dating, and then . . . Amanda. But watch Marni when she's around my dad. I'm surprised Amanda hasn't thrown a fit yet and tried to get Dad to fire Cal just to get rid of Marni. You've seen how she treats Clara, but I promise you, Tom and Clara will outlast Amanda, and so will Cal and Marni. My father believes in loyalty. Anyway . . . I have Dad covered tonight. You two go out. And stay out late. Oh, and fool around if you get a chance," Kat teased. "Dating the boss is exciting, don't you think?"

271

"Honestly, I met Zach for the first time when he came over to Ireland," Caer said.

"Whatever you say. Now go. You look like a million bucks."

Caer stood, shaking her head. Maybe it was all right if she left Kat thinking she worked for Zach. She certainly didn't seem able to convince her otherwise.

Kat caught her hand, dragging her out of the room just as Zach was coming down the stairway.

He'd donned a suit, and Caer felt her breath catch. He was gorgeous. He was fixing a cufflink when he looked up, saw her — and froze.

"Hey, get a room, you two!" Kat said. "You both clean up real nice. Now get out of here."

"We're going, we're going," Zach assured her. "Miss Cavannaugh?" He made a slight bow, directing her toward the kitchen and the way out. In the garage, he opened the car door for her, and she slid into the passenger seat.

She felt awkward. This was like . . . a date.

They were going out.

And anything could happen.

She sat stiffly in the car as he drove. She found herself staring at his hands where they lay on the wheel. Musician's hands.

His fingers were long, and his hands were neither too rough looking nor too manicured. They had a strength about them, the kind of strength that made her shiver down to her bones.

He flashed her a glance. "Are you all right with this? You look tense."

"I'm fine," she said.

He grinned. "I'm not evil."

"I promise you, I'm not evil, either."

His grinned deepened. "Evil or not, Miss Cavannaugh, you really are quite stunning."

"Like Kat said, we both clean up well."

He laughed. "You're stunning even when you don't clean up. Not that I've seen you running around in the mud or anything."

"Only in the sand," she said.

"That's a taboo subject for tonight," he told her.

"Really?" She turned to him and smiled skeptically. "I know you. You're already planning your next move."

"Am I?"

"Yes."

"Well, it *is* what I do," he said. "I find the missing. I solve the mystery. It's the family business."

"Right. So you have a plan, even if you're not going to talk about it with me. You're not going to sit around just waiting."

"I'm going to find out what Eddie found out. There. That's it in a nutshell. Now, let's move on. Tell me more about yourself, Miss Cavannaugh."

"There's not that much to tell."

"Oh, I have a feeling there's a massive tome behind you."

"You first, then, since you seem to think I'll be talking for the rest of the night."

"Okay. My parents died when I was in high school. They were great. My dad could be tough, but my mother was just as strong. Irish. Dad's family went way back. He was a cop. He and Sean had been friends for years. We all spent time together when we were growing up. Aidan's the oldest. He joined the military, and they paid for him to go to school so he could keep the three of us together until we were all legal. We all love music, and we all went into law enforcement. A little over a year ago, we inherited a plantation down in New Orleans. Aidan, his wife and their baby live in it now. And you'll meet Jeremy soon, I imagine. He's down in Salem, Massachusetts — he just married a woman who lives there. Let's see, I own some small music studios. I saved up and invested in the first one, and that one made enough for the second one, and so on, and I used some of the money I made to start a music label. I love stuff that's new and exciting — or old but done in a new and exciting way. A few of the artists I've picked up — like Kat — have been bought out by major labels, so it's been a very nice sideline. That's it. I was in forensics when I was a cop, but I think you know that. And now I work with Aidan and Jeremy. It's a great gig. Now you," he said pointedly.

"Aidan is the oldest?" she asked.

"Yes, I told you that. Your turn."

She looked ahead. "Isn't that the restaurant?"

"Yes, but you're not getting out of this."

He drove into the valet lane. A few moments later they were walking into what appeared to be an original colonial building. It was whitewashed, boasted grand pillars and was decorated with American flags.

The staff members were all dressed in colonial garb, right down to the Martha Washington caps the women wore.

They were ushered to an elegantly set table in an alcove and presented with a wine list.

"Wine?" he asked her.

"Whatever you'd like."

"I'm fond of a good beer on tap, actually, but you're welcome to whatever you'd like."

"A good beer on tap will be lovely," she

assured him.

As they waited for their drinks to come, Caer studied the menu intently.

He leaned closer to her and said, "You're not getting out of it, you know."

"Out of what?"

"Telling me your life story." He took the menu from her. "Will you let me order for you? I'm not trying to be chauvinistic, I'm just trying to make sure you get a great American meal."

"Please. By all means."

Their waitress returned with their drinks. They'd both ordered a dark seasonal beer from a local brewer. She sipped, loving the flavor, as he ordered.

He chose turkey, stuffing, cranberry sauce, mashed potatoes and green bean casserole for both of them, with mini hot dogs and mustard for an appetizer.

"As American as apple pie — which we'll have for dessert," he told her. "Now. Go on."

She took another sip of her beer, grinning. "You are persistent."

"Have to be. It's the only way to solve a mystery. And the Irish can make any story dramatic, I've learned."

She laughed. "Really? All right, then. My father was one of the faerie folk, and my mom was . . . a banshee. They lived around the Giant Stones near Tara. I have one sister who disgraced the family by running off to live with the leprechauns."

"How about the truth?"

She looked at him, noting the tone of his voice, and set her glass down. "My father was killed fighting when I was fifteen. My mum died soon after. She was very sick. My siblings wound up spread out around Ireland. My baby brother was adopted and taken to Australia. And I've been lucky enough to acquire a good education and a job that gives me a great deal of satisfaction."

"Sounds like you had a tough time of it, growing up," he said, but he didn't apologize for making her bring up what must have been sad memories. They were just part of life.

"But you do have good friends," he said.

"Pardon?"

"Mary and her family. They were lovely people. I really enjoyed that pub — Irish Eyes. And they think the world of you there."

"Oh. Aye, well, thank you."

He was staring at her again. She met his eyes and found herself wondering about his thoughts.

She almost started when his hand touched hers across the table, his fingers moving gently. It wasn't a sexual gesture, but it seemed to be the most erotic thing she had ever experienced.

"What is it about you?" he asked, and his voice was husky.

"I . . . don't know?"

He laughed, and the sound was deep and rich, as sensual as the brush of his fingers.

"I can't figure out what you're really up to, but the more time that goes by, the less I care. I look at you, and I trust you, even though it's against everything I've ever done, been or known. You speak, and I'm nearly hypnotized by the sound of your voice."

She didn't know what to say. She was frozen in place, and her throat had closed up. She was afraid that if she tried to speak, she would squeak.

Salads arrived along with the mini hot dogs, which were accompanied by delicate little cups that held mustard and ketchup. He drew his hand back. She straightened in her chair and thanked the waitress, who smiled, told them to enjoy their salads and their appetizer, and moved away.

Caer tasted a hot dog and pronounced it delicious.

"There's an American treat for you," he promised.

She chewed delicately, taking her time. He seemed to enjoy them himself.

"You like my story because it's similar to yours," she told him.

"I don't like to hear anything that's painful," he said. "People shouldn't have to lose their parents when they're young. It's as unnatural as a parent losing a child. I've seen that happen, too. All in all, I've seen some pretty horrible things out there. So I'm glad to hear you've done well on your own, and to know that you have good friends."

"What if I really had been the child of a faerie and a banshee?"

"Are you?" he asked.

"No."

"Then . . . ?"

"There are strange things in this world that could be true," she told him.

He hesitated. "I've seen some strange things, I admit, but usually it's strange people who cause everything around them to seem . . . strange."

"So you don't believe in ghosts?"

She was surprised by his hesitation, but then he grinned and said, "Actually, even my very tough oldest brother might believe in ghosts. I've never been really sure."

"Ghosts are real," she said softly.

"Have you spoken with any lately?"

"Now you're making fun of me."

"No, I'm not." He shrugged. "There's real — and there's not real. That's just the way it is."

A string quartet — dressed in colonial style — was playing chamber music in a far corner. She turned to watch them.

"Beautiful, isn't it?" he asked.

"Aye."

"Puccini," he said.

Their appetizer plates were whisked away and their dinners arrived. She found that she especially loved the stuffing, which had corn, nuts and raisins in it.

They ordered more beer.

He told her more about Louisiana and the family plantation, insisting that she really had to see it one day. He talked about Florida, as well, growing up in the north of the state, working in the far south. She talked a bit about her work as a nurse and educated him on Irish history. The time passed quickly.

When they finished, she was relaxed. As they returned to the car and headed to the pub, he entertained her with stories about the scrapes he had gotten into with his brothers, and how their mother only had to grab one of them by the scruff of the neck or speak a single word to make them shape up.

"She was that scary?" Caer asked.

"She was that wonderful," he said, looking straight ahead. "We loved her to pieces. We were a little wild, but we all adored her. And my dad, of course. We all wanted to grow up to be just like him. In a way, we've managed that."

At the pub, she was introduced to jazz. She loved the sound of it. They sat in a booth, and she leaned against him, his arm resting easily around her shoulders.

She didn't think she'd ever felt more blissful.

There's real — and there's not real.

That was what he'd said.

At the moment, though, it was real. And she loved it.

They listened to the music for a long time, the silence between them a very comfortable thing. When they left, she was loath for the evening to end.

"I don't want to go back," she admitted out loud.

He glanced at his watch. "Well, I can show you one more thing in Newport, if you'd like."

"Really? What? It's late, isn't it?"

He laughed. "Yes, it's late, but I can get us in."

"Oh?"

He drove for about five minutes. They weren't exactly off the beaten path, but neither were they in the midst of a commercial area.

He parked in front of a long commercial building that looked both very old and very well cared for. She realized that small placards on the different doors advertised an art gallery, a piano store, a photography studio and, on the last door, a music studio.

"Yours?" she asked him.

"My latest acquisition. On the upper level. Just up these stairs."

He drew out his keys and started up, and she followed.

The reception held a desk, a sofa and several chairs, all tastefully antique. Magazines of all sorts covered the coffee table, and it seemed a very comfortable place to wait. "The sound studios are this way."

He walked along the hall, opening doors as he went. She was fascinated. There were monstrous machines with all kinds of buttons, and glass cubicles that held nothing but microphones and stools. Headphones hung neatly on rungs by the doors.

"I'm amazed," she told him. "And extremely impressed. But when do you find time to work here?"

He laughed. "I don't, really. I send people here to do the work for me. These days I have managers and technicians who do most of the work."

"It's incredible."

"It's a good studio," he told her. "People like it. The important thing, of course, is the quality of the sound you produce. But it's good to be comfortable. There's more."

He led her down to the end of the hall, where there was a full kitchen, and behind it, a bedroom, sleek and inviting, with a lush private bath. The carpet was a rich blue, the bedspread a shade deeper and piled high with pillows.

"Who lives here?" she asked him.

"No one. It's for visiting artists, but there isn't one at the moment."

At that moment, Caer made a conscious decision.

This was her night.

She might never have another one.

She walked into the room. It was lit only by the glow coming in from the kitchen, and she thought she had never seen anything more inviting.

Zach had remained in the doorway.

She turned to him. "Aren't you supposed

to make a move now, or something?" she asked softly.

"I can't say it hasn't occurred to me," he told her. "But it wasn't my intent when we started out tonight. It wasn't even my intent when we came here."

"It wasn't my intent when we started out this evening, either," she said. "It *is* my intent now."

Still, he didn't come to her. She didn't know how long she could hold out before she felt like an idiot and went racing from the room.

She didn't have to find out.

He strode over to her, and she was suddenly grateful for the dimness, because she was shaking, tremulous, not at all sure. Then his arms came around her. She had visualized so much before. . . .

But this . . . This was real.

All the wonder, warmth, strength and vibrancy she had imagined were there in his embrace. And then . . . the tenderness in his fingers as he lifted her chin, and the hot, deep wonder of his kiss when his lips found hers, a touch at first, molding shape against shape, and then a burst of hunger and his tongue deep within her mouth, amazingly intimate, a harbinger of things to come, searing and frantic.

The kiss could have lasted forever and she wouldn't have complained. But then she felt his hands on her, and she instinctively moved her own. She felt the silky brush of fabric as her dress was pulled over her head; her fingers were awkward against his buttons, but she learned quickly.

Naked was even better.

Flesh against flesh. The quickening of muscle, the feel of his heart, the rise and fall of his breath, mingling with her own. They tangled together, falling upon the bed, and she was curled in his arms, locked in another passionate kiss. She was half atop him. She was beneath him. She lay, barely able to breathe, as his lips moved from hers and touched flesh, tenderly, erotically, with fever and heat. Her fingers moved over his shoulders, nails raking lightly.

His mouth . . .

His kiss . . .

So intimate. She felt her blood racing, every inch of her flesh so alive, so unbelievably alive and vital. Felt him, his caress upon her breasts, her throat, her ribs, her inner thighs. She yearned for greater intimacy even as she feared it. Awkward and tentative at first, she touched him in return, learning that her instincts were all she needed, that she could touch and thrill him, that her kisses spurred his fever. And then they were an incredible tangle of give and take, limbs and torsos, fingers and hands . . . lips caressing, a shattering ride of wild and liquid movement. There was nothing that did not seem incredible, the wickedly sweet arousal, the feel of him inside her, the staggering, blinding ecstasy that came at last in a shuddering moment of climax, and the euphoria that swept over her again and again like an ocean tide as she drifted down, held in the curve of his arms. And all the while, she felt the rhythm of beating hearts, and the rise and fall of their breathing, the sweet and precious pulse of life.

This was real. . . .

His face was in shadow, his expression difficult to read, as he rose up on one elbow, tenderly touching her cheek.

"What is it about you?" he asked her.

She turned to him, glad that a note of laughter escaped her lips. "What is it about *you?*" she asked him.

"Honestly, this room is for visiting musicians."

She laughed again. "Of course."

"I'm serious."

"I know a few Irish tunes."

"I'll bet you do."

"And what does that mean?"

"Only that I'm sure you do. And that you sing them well. And that your singing will be as great an enigma as everything else about you."

She ran her fingers through his hair, studying his features in the half-light, praying that her own remained as well hidden.

"I'm not so sure about that," she said huskily.

"You know what's frightening?" he asked.

"What?"

"I feel as if I could stay here, right here, forever."

He was a man, she reminded herself. Words came easily to them, emotions and the memory of those words . . . not as much.

Not fair . . .

"We can't stay here forever," she said.

"A lifetime might not be a bad thing," he said.

"We have to go sometime."

"Yes." She saw his smile. "But not just yet. I mean, if that's all right with you."

She wrapped her arms around him and pulled him close. She felt the sleekness of his body, the length of his limbs, the pulse of his blood and the heat of his skin.

Just to touch.

Just to feel.

Just to know . . .

It was amazing again. It was another dimension, sensations so strong and rich and vital that she felt as if she'd died and come back to life, only to die again and ascend to some strange heaven. Yes, it was sex, physical beyond a doubt, and yet it was also magic, something ethereal. She was certain that hearts didn't always beat together, that two people didn't always feel as if their minds and souls had joined so intimately into a single whole. . . .

Eventually, finally, they had to rise and dress and head back to the house.

As they got settled in the car again, she looked at him gravely. "Don't ever try to tell me that the fantastic does not exist, that magic isn't real."

He smiled, then leaned over and kissed her slowly, holding her chin, studying her eyes.

"Careful," he teased, his eyes warm, alive with tenderness. "You seem to be magic yourself. You just may make me fall in love with you."

She looked back at him without smiling. "It's life itself that is magic, Zach." She turned to look out the window, and he turned on the car and drove. She kept looking out the window, thinking that she didn't have to worry about falling in love with him.

She'd already done it the first time she'd seen his eyes, and that had only been in a picture. And then she had seen him.

And gotten to know him, and to care.

It *was* magic.

And with magic, there was always a price to pay.

12

The next evening, Zach was in Sean's office studying the local sea charts kept there.

A scream cut through the air.

"What on earth was that?" Clara cried, practically dropping the sandwich she was carrying, her eyes darting to Zach's.

Without answering, he tore from the room and down the hallway toward the dining room, where everyone else — except Bridey, who was still sick — was having dinner.

When he got there, it was like looking at a tableau. Everyone was so completely motionless, they didn't even appear to be breathing.

Caer was standing slightly in front of Marni and Amanda, who were flanking her as if they were backup singers, although Zach had to admit he'd never seen a backup singer holding a plate of blueberry pie, as Marni was. Cal was on his feet as if he had just leaped up from his chair. Tom had ap-

290

parently come rushing in from outside, because his hands were dirty and his face was flushed. Sean was standing next to Kat, at the end of the table, her hand locked around a silver pie server.

"What the hell?" Zach demanded, and all eyes shot to him.

"Glass," Kat announced, and lifted the hand that held the server.

A thin trail of blood was oozing along the side of her palm.

Confused, Zach strode forward to Kat, took the pie server from her and grabbed a cloth napkin, which he held tightly against the cut. "You cut yourself slicing a pie and screamed?" he asked, puzzled.

She shook her head. "I cut my hand *on* the pie."

Clara had come in behind Zach, and she said, "Child, you can't cut your hand on a pie."

"Yes you can," Kat said. "If there's glass in the pie."

Marni let out a sudden howl, grabbed a napkin and held it to her mouth, and started spitting out blueberry filling.

"Did you swallow any of it?" Cal asked anxiously.

"No!" she gasped.

"Clara!" Amanda snapped.

291

"Wait," Sean began.

"There is no *wait,* anymore, Sean. Clara cooked glass into a pie. Someone could have eaten that and —"

"Could have? It was in my *mouth!*" Marni cried.

"You spit it out soon enough," Amanda pointed out. "But it could have been much worse. Sean, I know you love Clara, but we can't keep on living like this."

"Oh, Mr. O'Riley!" Clara gasped with horror. "I would never, ever, make such a mistake. I have no idea how that happened, but I promise you, I . . ." She burst into tears, and Tom hurried to her side to put a protective arm around her.

"Now, now," Sean said firmly. "Amanda, we don't know what happened. Clara, please stop crying. You know how much I treasure you."

"Excuse me, but *I'm* the one who almost swallowed glass," Marni said, then hurried from the room. Cal rushed out after her.

Zach already had his phone out and was dialing Morrissey's number.

"What are you doing?" Kat asked him.

"Calling the police."

"The police?" Amanda asked.

"Yes. We're going to give this pie to Detective Morrissey and find out just what the hell is in it," Zach said.

"I don't think we need to bring the police into this," Sean said.

"What do you think they'll find?" he asked. "Ground glass. Where will it have come from? Somewhere in this house."

Zach ignored him and was put through to Detective Morrissey, and quickly explained the situation, extracting the other man's promise to come over right away.

"Zach, this is just crazy," Sean protested.

"Maybe there was glass in the blueberries when they were purchased," Caer suggested.

"It's her!" Amanda said suddenly, pointing at Caer.

"Pardon?" Caer said.

"Our lives have just been a mess since you brought her home with us, Sean." She looked at her husband with concern. "Ever since Caer came into this house, things have been going wrong."

"Oh, Amanda, don't be ridiculous," Kat said with disgust. "It seems to me our lives have all gone to hell since *you* came into them."

"Sean, I told you that your daughter was never going to be able to accept me," Amanda said plaintively.

"Everybody, stop!" Sean snapped. "This

is my house. Amanda, I love my daughter, and, Kat, Amanda is my wife. Caer had nothing to do with Eddie's disappearance or me becoming ill in Ireland, Amanda, so, please, let's just calm down on that. In fact, let's all go into the living room and have a drink while we wait for Detective Morrissey. Caer's right. There might have been something wrong with the blueberries themselves. Fresh or canned, Clara?"

"What?" Clara said, as if still dazed. "Oh, the blueberries. They came in a jar, Mr. O'Riley."

"You're right, Zach," Sean said with a deep sigh. "We need Morrissey. There might be more jars of bad blueberries out there. I, for one, am having a drink. You should all join me."

"Dad, you shouldn't be drinking," Kat said.

"I'm having a whiskey," he said firmly, and left the room.

The others began following him. Zach waited for Caer, who left last. Her eyes met his, big and blue and questioning.

He shrugged. "One swig of whiskey isn't going to kill him. Something else might, but . . ."

She nodded, then followed the others from the room.

Soon after drinks were poured, Morrissey arrived. By then, Caer had headed upstairs to check on Bridey. Everyone started talking all at once, until Morrissey gained control. Marni made a point of mentioning that she and Cal didn't live there, so of course they didn't know anything about the jar, the pie or anything else that went on in the house. Morrissey wanted to know when Clara had purchased the blueberries, and she was so distraught that she had to think for a while to remember that she had bought them exactly one week before. Morrissey was by turns grave, thoughtful and patient with everyone there, earning Zach's continuing respect. In the end, he left with the pie. Since the garbage had already been picked up, there was no jar to salvage, but Clara remembered the store where she had purchased the blueberries and the brand, so he had that information to follow up on. In the end, it took hours, but Morrissey had doggedly gotten everything he needed from everyone.

Zach walked the detective out.

"This is a strange situation you're in," Morrissey said. "Maybe you should all take separate hotel rooms for a while."

"Sean will never accept that a member of his family or circle of friends is trying to harm him," Zach said. "And as to glass in a pie . . . if Kat hadn't gotten cut right away, anyone might have eaten it, which would make it a rather random method of committing murder. Marni did take a bite," he added thoughtfully.

"Maybe she should head to the hospital and have herself checked out," Morrissey suggested. "Just to be safe."

"She never actually swallowed or even chewed it," Zach said.

"Your prime suspect would be anyone who didn't want pie — if the tampering was done in the house. If Clara isn't homicidal."

There was no pun intended. Morrissey's features were dead flat.

"I'd bet my life that Clara isn't homicidal," Zach assured him. "And everybody wanted pie."

"Well, first things first. The pie, and the blueberries," Morrissey said. "I'll get things in motion right away. You just make sure everyone is careful." He looked at Zach. "Anything else you think I should know?"

Zach stared back at him with a level gaze. "No."

Morrissey nodded and left.

Cal and Marni emerged from the house before Zach could reenter.

"We're going home," Cal said, but he

looked apologetic, as if he felt guilty, leaving when everything was such a mess.

"Yeah, sure." Zach looked at Marni. "You're sure you didn't swallow any of the pie?"

Marni nodded. "Trust me — I'd have been screaming for an ambulance if I had. I'm all right. And someone has to keep the business going."

"Of course."

They still stood there awkwardly.

"Well, we'll talk tomorrow, I'm sure," Marni said.

"Yes, I'll be in," Zach told them. "I may take off around the area, do a little boating, clear my head."

"Oh?" Marni asked.

"Nothing like sea air to clear the mind," Cal agreed.

"Well, of course, but . . ." She grimaced apologetically. "Zach, shouldn't you be following the blueberry trail?" She hesitated. "So many scary things are going on around here."

"Morrissey is a good cop," Zach said. "He can take care of that. My focus is this family right now."

"Of course," Cal said.

"Well, good night," Zach told them both, and they departed at last.

When he returned to the house, it was quiet. He found Tom and Clara in the kitchen, cleaning up. Tom told him sadly that, no matter how much they cared about Sean O'Riley, they doubted they could stay much longer if Amanda continued to be abusive toward Clara. Zach assured him that he understood, but asked him to try to be tolerant a little while longer.

Tom looked at him sadly and assured him that he would try.

Sean and Kat had apparently retired to their rooms, Caer had already gone back to Bridey the minute Morrissey had finished talking to her, and Amanda was nowhere to be seen. He hurried upstairs to check on Bridey and Caer himself.

Caer was seated by Bridey's side, holding her hand, speaking to her soothingly. The lilt was in her tone as she talked about the old country, the sweeping emerald hills and the beauty of the great tors, and the sweet sounds of fiddles and harps. Bridey was smiling, listening to her.

He found himself lulled, as well, almost mesmerized, listening to the rise and fall of her voice. Caer laughed and reminded Bridey that a leprechaun was required to polish a person's shoes, so if she really wanted a pot of gold, she needed to leave her shoes out to compel a leprechaun to stop, giving her a chance to catch him.

Bridey's eyes opened. "Remember, when you catch the evil, you can't allow it to roam the world. Remember that the banshee must be good, Caer. Swear it."

"I swear," Caer assured her.

A moment later, Bridey was sleeping peacefully.

Caer rose quietly and spotted him standing in the doorway.

"Do you think she's all right?" she asked him anxiously, joining him.

"Yes. Why would anyone want to hurt Bridey?" He shook his head. "She's no danger to anyone. I don't think we need to worry about Bridey."

"I *am* worried. She's taking her medication, but she doesn't seem to be getting any better," Caer said. "Pneumonia is a real danger for her now."

"It is for anyone her age, Caer. Bridey is up there."

"Some people live to be a hundred," she said.

"True, but we get vulnerable as we age," he assured her, noticing that she seemed distraught. "Why don't you head to your room, where you're closer to Sean?" he suggested. "Tomorrow I'll ask Kat if she'll watch over him for a while. You and I are going exploring."

"Oh?"

He nodded gravely. "Eddie left a clue."

"What?"

"Just be ready to head out around ten," he told her. "Now go on. It's still safest when either you or Kat is near Sean."

She slipped past him, and he stepped into the room, anxious to make sure that Bridey really was sleeping easily. Her breathing sounded a little raspy, but her sleep appeared to be peaceful.

But as he stood there in the muted light, she opened her eyes. She seemed to be staring at him, but he could tell that she wasn't seeing him at all.

Her lips formed a word, and he leaned closer, trying to hear her.

"Bridey, I'm sorry, what?"

Nothing.

Her eyes were closed again, and he hesitated. He straightened and was about to leave when her lips moved again.

He leaned close and heard her whisper a single word.

"Banshee."

Outside, the winter wind suddenly rose with a vengeance, like an ominous echo.

Banshee, banshee, banshee . . .

He rose, shaking the strange spell of the wind, and looked down at Bridey.

She was sleeping soundly again, her smile completely serene.

He left her room to return to his own but paused at the end of the hallway, where a high arched window looked out into the night. No one had drawn the drapes, and the view by moonlight was breathtaking, all jagged rocks and the silhouettes of boats lying at anchor. Lights along the docks cast a gentle glow on the eighteenth- and nineteenth-century buildings that lined the waterfront, and Christmas lights twinkled, adding a holiday touch to the peaceful scene.

Then he saw the birds.

Ravens, maybe, or crows.

They'd begun appearing as he looked out the window. First one, then two. Then a flock — a *murder* of crows. Sweeping through the sky, their great dark wings appeared larger as they caught the moonlight and shadow. Then they began to settle on the roof of the cottage where Clara and Tom lived.

He gave himself a shake.

Birds. They were just birds.

Yet it seemed as if they had spread their wings like an ominous blanket.

Unable to stop himself, he went back and checked on Bridey again.

He touched her face gently, and her eyes opened.

"Sorry. I didn't mean to wake you."

"I wasn't sleeping. I was listening to the birds. They're out there, aren't they? I hear the wings. They come first, you know."

"Bridey, what are you talking about?"

"The birds come first. They foretell the fate of those who are blessed or damned, so that a soul may make peace with God."

She was rambling, and he was worried that she was feverish, but she didn't feel warm.

"Bridey, you're scaring me."

"Ah, Zach, I'd not scare ye. Don't be worried, and don't be sad. Few know their place in heaven or hell, but I'm one of the lucky ones, for I do know mine."

"Bridey —"

"It's sorry I am to be muttering on and on. I've a mind to sleep now, though, and you should get on to bed, too. We need you here, you know. Rested and well."

He kissed her forehead again and returned to his own room.

But he couldn't escape the echo of the wind that rushed against his ears like the laments of the damned, or the shrieking cries of the crows.

And all the while his mind whispered . . .

Banshee.

When she headed for bed that night, Kat was mad.

It was Amanda. Amanda was trying to kill her father, even though he didn't believe it, *wouldn't* believe it. The woman was nothing but a monster who was able to put on airs because of his money. Why he didn't see right through her was a complete mystery. Were all men, including her father, unable to combat the call of their hormones?

At least the cops were in on things now, thanks to Zach's insistence . . . She didn't know whether to hope that the latest incident was a case of some psycho with a grudge engaging in product tampering, putting the whole community at risk — and, if so, how coincidental — or that there was a monster living in their midst. There was simply no good answer for that one.

She brushed her teeth, washed her face, slipped into a pair of her most comforting flannel pajamas and lay down to sleep. Grinning, she hugged one of her favorite stuffed toys, a very lifelike collie her dad had bought for her years before.

She closed her eyes.

The old house creaked and groaned.

And she started to listen. Nervously.

She couldn't help it. She knew that her father and Zach had taken to making absolutely certain that the doors were locked and the alarm was on, but still, she couldn't help listening to every sound and wondering what it meant.

She strained her ears and heard the sounds of an old house settling.

But there was more. *Wings.*

A thick beating in the air, as if great dark wings were all around the house.

She lay there, telling herself to stop acting like a scared little kid. She lasted for a few minutes, and then it was suddenly too much.

She leaped up and stood still, listening.

She was scared, even terrified, but she had to know the truth. She felt ridiculous, as if she were a character in a horror movie, but this was her house and she was not going to let her fear control her. Besides, Zach was near, just a few doors down, and her father and Caer were downstairs.

No way was she going to count on Amanda for help, but Bridey was there, too.

Great. She could call on her ill great-aunt to come and be brave for her while she stood there, trembling, in her bare feet.

And what on earth was she afraid of, anyway?

The sound of wings in the night? Big deal.

She gave herself a mental shake and walked to her window, pulled open the drapes — and gasped.

Crows, or maybe ravens.

Scores of them.

They were perched on top of the cottage, on the garage, in the trees, everywhere around the house, and more were surging through the air like harbingers of evil. Birds. At night. In the dead of winter.

And that was all they were, she told herself. Birds. Just birds. What the hell did she care about birds?

She looked down at the ledge beneath her window and barely choked back a scream.

One of them was sitting on her ledge. Staring at her. With just one eye. . . . When it turned its head, she saw that it had lost the other.

So it stared at her, so close that it could have pecked at her if not for the glass between them.

She dropped the drape to shut out the sight of the bird, then found that her fear was not so easy to erase. She had a terrible picture of the bird suddenly slamming through the glass and attacking her, talons clawing at her face.

She thought about racing down the hall to Zach's room. He was her friend. He would understand.

But she couldn't do it. Zach had his own demons. Zach was falling for Caer.

Caer!

She could ask to spend the night in Caer's room downstairs. She wouldn't even have to admit that she was a coward; she could make some excuse about being worried about her father.

She stepped out into the hall with that plan in her mind, but then she saw Bridey's door and found herself tiptoeing in that direction instead.

Bridey was sleeping, but she was such a tiny little thing that there was plenty of room for Kat to slide in right next to her.

She almost screamed when Bridey spoke.

"Hush, darling, it's all right. Don't be scared."

Kat was too startled to wonder how Bridey knew why she was there and said only, "There are birds."

"I know. But you mustn't fear, child."

"Have you seen them?"

"I hear them. They are the forerunner of darkness, Kat, but light remains in the world."

Great. Bridey was going off into some kind of delusional fantasy.

"I'll protect you, I promise," Bridey went on.

Kat gave her a hug back and said, "I love you, Aunt Bridey. And I'll protect *you.*"

And then, at last, Kat slept.

Cal was standing at the back of their house, where the sliding glass doors led out to the porch and a spectacular view of the sea.

"Are they still out there?" Marni asked him.

He nodded.

She came up to him and slipped her arms around him, shivering.

They had a great backyard, perfect for parties. Both were covered now, for winter, but in summer the barbecue was often lit and the in-ground pool was uncovered, and the lawn chairs were full of friends having a good time.

Not tonight.

Tonight the yard was filled with . . .

Birds.

"Damnedest thing I've ever seen," Cal said, studying them. He didn't seem afraid, just fascinated.

Marni, however, was unnerved.

"Shouldn't they have flown south?" she

whispered.

"Maybe it's global warming."

"Just make sure all the doors are locked and drapes are closed, and please, let's go to bed and shut them out. They're creepy."

He nodded, but he didn't move. Marni couldn't stand looking at the birds anymore. She wanted to keep holding him, but she was afraid, so she let go and turned to walk away.

"I'm going to bed," she told him over her shoulder.

"Sure. Be right there." He sounded mesmerized.

"I could have died tonight, you know," she reminded him.

He turned suddenly and pulled her into his arms. "I'm sorry, baby. I can't believe I could have lost you."

"Let's go to bed," she whispered.

"Just one more minute," he said, looking back out to the yard.

She pulled away from him, hurt, and headed for the bedroom. "I'm pretty tired." She yawned loudly. "I won't be awake that long." Maybe the fear of missing out on sex would get him, she thought.

He only nodded absently. Angry now, she went into the bedroom and shut the door loudly, then slipped into her side of the bed, upset that she could hear the sound of wings. She closed her eyes, though, and began to drift.

She suddenly sat bolt upright, shaking off the vision that had invaded her mind as she had started to fall asleep, a vision of a giant black bird, crashing right through the glass and sweeping Cal away.

She shivered, about to jump out of bed, then realized that she must have fallen more deeply asleep than she'd realized, because Cal was lying beside her, sleeping soundly.

He was even snoring.

She snuggled closer to him, and tried to fall asleep again, but she was suddenly angry. Zach was a frigging P.I., and with everything going on, he wanted to go boating.

Screw them all.

Caer was sitting with Sean in the breakfast room, reading a coffee-table book on New England and sipping coffee, while he read the paper. Clara was bustling about, straightening things that didn't need straightening.

When the phone rang, it was as startling as if a bomb had gone off.

Caer must have jumped, because Sean glanced her way, amused. "Sorry, house phone. Pretty loud, huh?"

He rose and walked over to the little marble table where the old-fashioned telephone sat. "O'Riley," he said as he picked up the receiver.

For a moment he frowned, and then a smile split his face. "Yes, serious, very serious. I'm sorry to hear that, but let's hope that at least this will keep anyone from being hurt."

He hung up, still smiling. "What is it?" Caer asked him.

Clara had frozen and was looking at him expectantly.

"That was Detective Morrissey," he told them.

"And you're smiling," Caer noted.

"They found several jars of those blueberries that had been tampered with. There were three others with ground glass — all of them at the back of the shelf, where they were unlikely to be picked up anytime soon, interestingly. We're actually lucky that Kat cut herself slicing the pie. Without that, someone could be dead."

"So — so —" Clara stuttered.

"It means that no one in this house did anything to the blueberries or the pie. They're investigating now, trying to find out how the jars got on the shelves."

"I knew it!" Kat said triumphantly from the doorway. "Amanda was just being a troublemaking bitch."

"Now, Kat," Sean remonstrated.

"Sorry, Dad."

"Thank you."

Kat walked over to pour herself a cup of coffee, saying, "I'm sorry your wife is a troublemaking bitch, not that I said it," she told him flatly.

"Oh dear," Clara said, and fled toward the kitchen.

"She does speak her mind," Sean said, winking at Caer.

"Where *is* your dear and devoted wife this morning?" Kat asked.

"Still sleeping, I believe."

Kat sat down at the table. "Dad, come out with me for a bit today, will you? I've asked Tom — he can drive us around."

Sean looked at her with a question in his eyes. "Are you just trying to keep me occupied?" he asked her.

"Yes." She aimed a smile in Caer's direction. "I want you to myself for a while. Is that such a bad thing?"

"No." He reached across the table and squeezed her hand. "I'll be happy to run around town with you."

Zach breezed into the breakfast room

then, his hair still damp from the shower, dressed in jeans and a thick sweater, a heavy Windbreaker over his arm.

"What's up with you?" Sean asked him.

Zach set his jacket down and headed for the coffee. "I talked to Morrissey," he said.

"Yeah, he just called," Kat said. "Weird, huh? And scary." She shivered. "I hope they catch whoever did it soon."

"Morrissey and his crew are on it," Zach said. "And I thought I'd do some boating today. I want to get out on the water, but I don't want to mess with the sails, I just want to zip around."

"And you don't feel you need to look over the cops' shoulders?" Kat said, grinning. "You must be mellowing."

"There's nothing I can do that they can't — and plenty that they can do and *I* can't," Zach said. "They'll be running prints, checking credit card bills. . . . They're on it. Caer, are you ready? You can grab a waterproof parka at the office."

Just as they got up to leave, Tom walked in with the mail.

"Bill, bill, bill, letter from an antique dealer for Sean, letter from Kat's webmaster, Christmas card, Christmas card, Christmas card . . . letter for Caer."

"What?" she said, startled.

He handed her an envelope. She saw Michael's name on the return — just the first name — and the address of the hospital in Dublin.

What the hell did he want? she wondered. She would have to find out later, because she wasn't about to read his letter in public.

"A letter from home already? How nice," Sean said.

She nodded and stuffed the envelope in her pocket. "A friend," she said briefly. "I guess he misses me."

"A friend, huh?" Kat teased.

Caer tried to laugh easily. She knew they were all studying her. "Not that kind of a friend. Just a guy I work with," she assured them.

"Friends and family are the stuff of life," Sean said gruffly.

"Okay, then, we're out of here. Later, folks," Zach said, sounding impatient.

He hadn't said a word about the letter. And she knew he was still suspicious of her, no matter how close they might have become in some ways.

As he ushered her out, she felt the letter burning against her flesh through the layers of her clothing, as if it were on fire.

13

"What the hell are we doing out here?" Caer demanded, sitting next to Zach as he drove them to the wharf.

"Even I would have expected you to be investigating those blueberries."

"Product tampering is a federal crime," he told her. "The police and the FBI will be doing everything that can be done. Although I have to admit, I think the person behind it is in Sean's household."

She gasped. "What?"

"We have to go back to the beginning," he said. "Eddie missing, Eddie dead. Sean sick — but so soon after he left the States that it's more than possible that he consumed whatever caused it while he was here. They tested for every bacterium in the world, but they never tested for metals. Arsenic. More exotic things."

"You think someone has been dosing him with arsenic?"

"Maybe. It's possible. Or it might not be a metal at all. There's always the gyromitra family."

"I have no idea what you're talking about."

He laughed. "Gyromitra. The false morels. And some of them don't cause any physical effects for hours."

"And then they cause severe abdominal pain, vomiting and diarrhea?"

"You guessed it. It's unlikely the doctors would have recognized it, because by the time he got to the hospital, nothing would have been left in his stomach to act as evidence."

"Do you think Sean was meant to die, then?"

"Definitely."

"But why would someone want to kill him?"

"He's rich."

"But . . . his share of the business would go to Kat, and neither of us thinks she would ever hurt her father. So . . . why?"

"I think someone wanted him out of the way because Eddie had discovered something.

"Sean and Eddie had a whole separate business. You know how fascinated Sean is with Nigel Bridgewater. I've been using Eddie's computer to check out his research.

Here's the thing, both Eddie and Sean believed that Nigel was carrying huge sums of money, as well as crucial documents, when he learned that the British were on his trail. When he was apprehended, he had nothing on him. It was important to him not to implicate anyone who had financed or otherwise helped him. Remember, the British considered the Revolution to be an act of treason. It wasn't called a war until it was over. Anyone who signed the Declaration of Independence was ready to accept a hangman's noose if apprehended."

"They signed it anyway."

"Yes, and we take what they did for granted because the war was won, but it might not have been. Back then, plenty of people prayed for independence from Great Britain, but that didn't mean they were ready to die for it. Nigel Bridgewater was a careful man with a great respect for those who wanted to help him but might not have wanted to die for it. So he hid whatever he was carrying, papers *and* money, which means it's possible he really did leave behind a buried treasure."

"And Sean and Eddie were hunting for that treasure," Caer said thoughtfully.

"I may be way off, but Eddie also loved Sean like a brother, and we know that he sent him something that he considered a big deal. With any luck, whatever it is will show up soon, because I think it will prove me right. I think Eddie discovered the treasure."

"But . . . if Eddie did find the treasure and was killed for it, wouldn't whoever killed him have taken the treasure and made off with it by now?"

"Not if Eddie didn't actually have the treasure in his possession but had only left some kind of clue, which this person hasn't discovered as yet," Sean explained. "I'm assuming the killer wanted timing. Eddie and Sean gone at once, or practically at once, or why kill Eddie without having the treasure? Unless the killer was certain there was a clue that would lead him — or her — to the treasure whether Eddie was around or not. *Or,* Eddie was growing suspicious and the killer had to take the chance that he/she would still find the treasure."

"So we're going out looking for treasure?"

"Yup."

"And you think we're going to be able to find a treasure no one else has been able to find?" she asked skeptically.

"Exactly. Not even the killer, who probably thought he had it figured out, then discovered he'd killed Eddie and gone after

Sean prematurely. Why is he still trying to kill? Fear of exposure. Or fear that he won't get to the treasure first."

"You're crazy, too," she told him.

He smiled. "There are a number of charts in Sean's office."

"Maritime charts," she agreed.

"One of them was taken out of the frame, and lines were drawn on it," he said.

"And no one else noticed?"

"No, it's subtle, just a darkening of some of the original markings. If Sean were to really study it, he would see it. If I hadn't been in there looking around last night, I might not have noticed it, either."

"So you have a line on a chart?" she asked him.

"Yes."

"And it leads to . . . ?"

"Cow Cay. Eddie's boat was found right off of Cow Cay," he explained.

She frowned, and met his gaze. "Zach, do you realize that you've passed the wharf?"

"Of course I do."

"So where are we going?"

"To buy supplies."

"Like?"

"Shovels. How else do you dig for buried treasure?"

"You *are* crazy," she told him.

"I don't think so."

"Crazy people never think they're crazy," she said.

He shrugged. "All right, maybe I'm a *little* crazy. I guess it was the birds last night."

"The birds?"

"You didn't see them? There must have been hundreds of them."

"What kind of birds?"

To Zach's surprise, Caer appeared agitated.

"Crows, I think. Maybe ravens. They were big crows, if they weren't ravens."

"No, I didn't see them," she told him. She was looking straight ahead. Had he imagined the tension she suddenly displayed?

"Are you afraid of birds?"

"What?"

"Birds. Do they frighten you?"

"No, of course not. It would be sad to go through life afraid of birds, don't you think?"

"I'm sure plenty of people do," he told her. "Bridey thought that they were a foretelling of something."

"Maybe she's right," Caer said, and he realized that she was studying him closely. "I mean, we all go through life believing in what we see and feel, but most of us have some kind of faith, as well."

"So you think that a bunch of birds flying around last night means something?" he asked, and he couldn't help sounding slightly amused.

She hesitated. "Don't you sometimes believe in something that you can't see or feel? Don't you adhere to some kind of faith?"

"Are you asking me if I believe in God? Yes, I do. Probably a legacy of my Irish mother," he told her.

He was surprised that she seemed to be watching him with such intent passion in her beautiful blue eyes. "If you believe in God, then why not believe in ghosts, in miracles, and even in the devil?" she asked quietly.

"Because I believe that God expects us to go through life with common sense. And common sense says birds are just birds," he told her flatly.

She laughed suddenly.

"What?" he demanded.

"All right, granted I haven't seen much of Cow Cay and it's not a large island. But you're just going to buy two shovels and in the course of this afternoon we're going to solve a centuries-old mystery?"

"I'd say you're forgetting the birds," he said, "but I didn't fully explain."

"So please do."

"There's a border around the chart with pictures of various landmarks in the area. One of them is rather interestingly named."

"What is it?"

"Banshee Rock."

"What?"

"Banshee Rock. It's an outcrop of granite that just happens to sit on —"

"Cow Cay?"

"You guessed it, gorgeous," he said lightly.

She blushed, and he found himself wishing desperately that they weren't going out looking for buried treasure, that they were heading out to a remote ski cabin that boasted a whirlpool and a fireplace, where they could sit and bask in the glow of the fire, and make love without inhibitions.

He returned his attention to the matter at hand and drove into the parking lot of the little strip mall where he could purchase what they would need.

He hadn't come to a major chain store but a smaller, mom-and-pop place run by Slim and Sally Jenkins, a couple he had gotten to know during his trips up this way as a kid.

He sent Caer to look for the shovels while he went to get a pick and a couple sieves to sift the sand. Even having a fair idea of what

Eddie had been up to, he knew they would be looking for a needle in a haystack.

He recognized the young man behind the counter as Slim's son.

"Hey, Jorey, how are you?"

"I'm fine — going to college down in New York now. How are you? Haven't seen you in a long time." He looked at Zach with a sad expression then. "I know you're close to the O'Rileys. Will you tell them I'm really sorry about Eddie? I don't know what he was thinking, taking out that weird dude."

"You saw him?" Zach asked, startled.

"I saw Eddie at the coffee shop that day." Jorey went pale. "Wow, the way you're look-ing at me . . . is something wrong with that?"

"No, no, it's just — you never said any-thing to the cops?"

"No. I — I guess I should've, huh? I only got a glimpse of the guy when I was buying coffee for the drive back to New York, so I never really thought about it. I saw Eddie meet the guy after he left the coffee shop. I'd never recognize him. He was wearing a heavy coat and carrying a duffel bag. And he had on a hat, like a fedora. Who the hell wears a fedora on a boat? Have I done something wrong?"

"No, of course not. I was just curious. The cops have been asking for any kind of help, though, so you ought to give them a call."

"I will. I'm really sorry — I wouldn't keep back information on purpose."

"Jorey, do you think the bag was big enough to hold scuba gear?"

Jorey's eyes widened. "Yeah, maybe. It was a big bag. The dude was kinda short, too. The bag seemed heavy for him."

"What did he look like?"

"I didn't really see his face. The hat was pulled down, and he had a big ugly mustache."

Caer returned with the shovels just then and Jorey looked at her, then kept looking.

"Hi," he said.

"Hi," she returned pleasantly.

"Can I help you?" Jorey asked.

"We're together," Caer told Jorey, indicating Zach.

"Irish?" Jorey asked her, still staring and smiling. Smitten.

"Yes, I am."

"Jorey, is there anything else you can tell me?" Zach asked.

"What?" Jorey sounded as if he'd completely forgotten Zach existed, then collected himself.

"Oh, yeah. Let me think. . . ." After a minute, he said, "He was out of place, know what I mean? Eddie was making fun of him in the coffee shop, asking who the hell went around with that much cash these days. Oh, and Eddie said he'd insisted on the *Sea Maiden.*" He paused. "You think this guy killed him, huh?"

Zach nodded grimly.

"I wish I had paid more attention," Jorey said. "Tried to stop him, even."

"Hey, you didn't know," Zach reassured him. "Eddie was a grown man, I doubt if you could have talked him out of taking a paying customer."

"I guess not."

Zach scribbled down Detective Morrissey's phone number. "Give this guy a call. He's a good cop, and he may think of a question I haven't. But, listen, I need a few more things, and you know what? If anyone wants to know, you never saw me today, okay?"

"Anything you say," Jorey said, but he was looking at Caer again, grinning foolishly.

In no time, they were ready to go, with their shovels, sieves, a pick and two metal detectors, and a canvas duffel to carry everything in.

When they reached the dockside office, Zach pointed out the *Sea Sprite,* a small, one-masted boat with a powerful motor and shallow draft. "I need you to go inside, and if Cal and Marni are both in there, give me a wave, then keep them occupied for a few minutes."

She stared at him as if she thought he was nuts for playing at being James Bond.

"Caer, please, we have no idea just who might be involved in all this."

"What do I say to them?"

"Ask Marni if she's all right after the incident with the pie yesterday."

Caer nodded.

A few moments later, she opened the door and waved to him, then stepped back inside. He hauled his bag onto the little boat, checked the gas gauge and looked her over, then headed for the office.

"Morning, Zach," Cal greeted him. "Did you see the paper this morning?"

"Actually, no. Sean was reading it when we left."

"They're recalling those blueberries," Cal said grimly. "There was a big article on how they think some psycho is out there, maybe some ex-employee with a grudge."

"I'm glad they got right on it," Marni said. "They can make sure no one else winds up with a mouthful of glass."

"Are you absolutely sure you're all right?" Caer asked her with concern.

"Oh, I'm fine. Honestly," Marni said.

"We could have sued," Cal said indignantly.

"And what would that have done? We're far too litigious in this country," Marni said firmly, shaking her head. "And I'm just fine." She lowered her voice, though they were the only ones there. "It's such a relief to know that some stranger did this, and that it wasn't someone in the house. You know what I mean. It was awful, Amanda accusing poor Clara, on top of Kat being so certain Amanda has it in for Sean." Marni dropped her voice even further. "Although who can blame her? Let's face it, we all think the woman is a total bitch."

"Sean loves her," Cal reminded his wife. "And who knows? Maybe she loves him, too. Who the hell are we to judge? Not to mention that it's pretty insulting to him to think there's no way Amanda is actually in love with him. Did that make sense?"

"It did," Marni said, looking at her husband affectionately. "It's just that she and I are about the same age, and I look at Sean like a father figure."

"Well, I'm going to show Caer around some more," Zach interrupted. "See you folks later."

"Any action on the wharf?" Marni said. "I get restless when we're not busy."

326

"I saw some people walking around checking things out," Zach told her, but it was a lie. He didn't want either Cal or Marni out on the water, not until he and Caer were long gone.

Cal led the way to the door, with Marni following close behind them. Zach was anxious to get going, but Cal opened the office door and stepped outside, then gasped sharply.

"What is it?" Marni demanded, pushing past Zach and Caer to reach her husband.

It was a bird. A dead bird — and a huge one.

Not a blackbird. Not a crow.

A raven.

It was lying on its back directly in front of the door, talons curled in, sightless eyes wide open.

Marni let out a frightened scream.

Cal put his arm around her and pulled her close. "Marni, it's just a bird. A very big, very dead bird."

"What the hell was it doing, dying right in front of the office door?" she demanded. "Oh, God, it's a bad omen. Something awful's going to happen."

Zach stepped forward, ignoring her, and said firmly, "You got a garbage bag in there? I'll pick up the poor thing and set it aside.

You can call someone to pick it up."

"We can just feed it to the fish," Cal said.

"I wouldn't," Caer said quickly. They all turned to stare at her. "What if it died because something was wrong with it, because it was sick? Maybe animal control ought to incinerate it or something."

"She *is* a nurse," Marni said. "And it's a good point. But get it away from me."

With a shudder, she hurried back into the office, where she got a large garbage bag. Cal and Zach bagged up the bird together, and then Cal laid it by the Dumpster, saying that he would call animal control.

At last Zach and Caer waved goodbye to him and headed to the *Sea Sprite.*

"Hop on," Zach said, loosening the mooring ropes after she stepped lithely to the deck, then boarding himself. As he took a seat at the helm and turned on the motor, he told her that she would find both the galley and the head in the small cabin.

"Thanks, but I love being up here."

He smiled as he steered the boat through the channel markers slowly, then opened up the throttle until they were whipping over the water. The air was cold, and the wind was stinging, but he saw that Caer didn't flinch; indeed, she seemed to love the feel of it. Her arms were wrapped tightly around herself as she sat across from him, staring out at the water and the passing scenery.

Newport was beautiful from the bay. The rocks jutted dramatically, the lighthouse was a piece of bygone charm, and mansions stood sentinel on the cliff. The bridge connecting the city to the mainland rose so high above the waves that the cars crossing it looked like toys.

When they reached Cow Cay, Zach anchored just offshore and found a couple of pairs of waders. Caer stared at him. "We're walking? In those?" she asked incredulously.

"It's only a few feet, but it's worth it to stay dry. Trust me — it's not deep. You'll be all right."

She didn't look as if she trusted him one little bit, but as he set about zipping himself into the waders, she followed suit. After carefully lowering himself into the water, he reached up to help her. She was skeptical, but she carefully dropped into his embrace.

She smelled sweet — but not too sweet — from some elusive perfume, and no amount of clothing could impede his instinctive response when he felt the vivid crush of her body against his own. He held her close, grinning, as he let her slide slowly down until her feet touched bottom. "It *is* a deserted island," he said teasingly.

"And it's freezing," she told him primly.

"You're not much of a romantic," he said, mock accusingly, then reached for the bag of tools he had left on deck.

"Walk carefully. You don't want to get a dunking."

She nodded, preceding him through the shallow water to the shore.

"It's great out here in summer," he said.

"Really?"

"Well, if you ask me, the water is still freezing, but it's bearable. Northerners love it. You're Irish. You would like swimming here."

She looked at him as if she didn't have any idea what he was talking about.

"Are you telling me you've never been swimming?" he asked her.

"Actually . . . no. I mean yes. I mean, I haven't."

"You need to learn to swim. And then to dive. Being underwater . . . it's another world." He heard his voice growing husky as he added, "I have to take you south. Home, or to the Caribbean. You can't imagine what it's like to dive the reefs. The colors of the fish, the coral . . . it's like nothing you've ever seen."

"I'm sure it is," she agreed, suddenly cool,

then asked, "So where is this Banshee Rock?"

He pointed. "Right there."

He passed her and strode over to the rock. It was an oddly shaped piece of granite, standing by itself as if placed by a giant hand. It stood about ten feet high and four feet wide at the base.

"We'll be systematic," he said. If she was going to be all business, so would he.

Opening the canvas bag, he took out the metal detectors, pick and shovels. "We could get lucky and find it immediately, but I have a feeling it's not going to be so easy." She watched as he walked around the rock, trying to figure if there was a spot where it looked as if someone might have dug centuries before. It took a while, as he kept circling with the metal detector. Caer watched him, then started using her own.

At one point she cried out with pleasure and dropped down to her knees in the sand. "I found something!"

He hurried over and started to dig. A moment later, he held up a spoon.

"I don't suppose it's an antique?" Caer asked hopefully.

"Sorry — it was swiped from a local fish place," he said, showing her the engraving on the handle. "But now we know your metal detector works. We'll find more."

"There might not be anything to find," she said glumly. "Nothing that matters, anyway."

"There is. I know there is."

He went back to searching, and a few minutes later he paused, standing dead still and staring. But not at the rock itself. His vision was focused on a spot twenty feet away, toward the shore, where he suddenly realized that someone else had been digging.

"Look," he said, striding toward the area. As he got closer, he could see that there were a number of places where someone had been busy with a shovel.

Zach used the metal detector to systematically search the sand. Caer started working nearby, emulating the grid pattern he was walking.

There wasn't a sound from either of their instruments.

"Maybe, if there was something, it's been found," she suggested.

He shook his head. "We'd know."

"How?"

"Because something would be different," he said, turning back to stare at her. "Something in the O'Riley household would be different. Whoever killed Eddie would . . .

well, they wouldn't be a part of the household anymore."

She walked over to him. "Maybe a stranger killed Eddie. Isn't that what we're all hoping? Maybe Sean getting sick was just coincidence."

She was staring at him earnestly, as if wanting could make it so.

He sighed. "We don't know anything. Except that someone else is looking for whatever Nigel Bridgewater might have buried. Let's get to it, shall we? We'll start over by the rock where we got a couple of potential readings."

"Maybe there's nothing there except for some kind of tarp protecting the documents he was delivering. Maybe there's no metal to find," Caer said.

"I'm willing to bet there are coins."

He started with an area by the south face of the rock, digging industriously. However long it took, he was going to keep digging until he found something.

Caer started working alongside him, but he was so preoccupied that he didn't realize how hard the going was until she set down her shovel and let out a sigh. "I'm sorry, but my muscles aren't accustomed to this. This is hard work," she said. It wasn't a complaint, just an observation.

"I shouldn't have brought you. I'm sorry. This is real labor." He was developing blisters himself, he realized.

"I don't mind. I just need to stop for a bit."

"Go ahead, take a break," he told her.

"I'm going to walk around a bit, see the island."

"All right. Stay within yelling distance."

"Zach, we're the only idiots out here."

He leaned on his shovel, indicating the dug-up area of the beach. "Someone else has been here — and they could come back."

She stared at him, then at the previous dig, and shivered. "Good point. I won't go far."

She walked off, and he started digging again. After a while, he realized that even though he was in good shape, *his* muscles were aching, too. Time to take a break himself.

"Caer?"

He couldn't see her.

"Caer?"

He dropped his shovel and walked north, toward a copse of trees, skeletal and forlorn in winter.

He still couldn't see her, and he looked out toward the water with a sense of rising unease. The *Sea Sprite* was still drifting at anchor just off shore, and no other boats were near.

A screeching caught his attention, and he looked up.

Birds. More birds. And not gulls. Gulls would have belonged.

They were black birds.

"Caer?"

His unease became an inexplicable fear for her, and he hurried into the copse of trees. Barren branches, pathetic in the winter air, brushed his shoulders. He looked up and realized that the sun was already beginning to set.

"Caer!"

Then he saw her. Her back was to him, and her head was bent over. She was staring at something in her hands.

For a moment he thought she had made a discovery in the sand, but then he realized that she had taken her letter from her pocket and was reading it.

He approached slowly. She was studying the words as if disturbed by whatever they said.

"Caer?"

She jerked, hearing him at last, and looked up.

"Is something wrong?" he asked her.

"Oh, no."

"Then what is it?"

"Just . . . my friend. He's here. In the States. I have to figure out how to meet up with him somewhere along the line, that's all."

She quickly folded the letter and shoved it back into the pocket of her jeans. "I'm sorry. I was just distracted."

He knew he generally had a good poker face, but it must have failed him then, giving away his suspicions, because she quickly smiled and rose. "I'm sorry. I should have been digging, not reading my mail."

He nodded, but he held his arms still by his sides as she came closer and pressed the full length of that glorious body against him.

The wind picked up. He heard that wild screeching again and looked up to the sky.

It was a scene out of an Alfred Hitchcock movie. There were birds everywhere.

Black birds.

High above the winter-barren trees, they swooped high, then low, circling and making that terrible noise.

Caer obviously didn't like them, staring up with what could only be dread in her eyes.

The sun was well and truly setting, he saw. It was time to abandon their efforts for the day and get back to the wharf. And since he hadn't managed to find anything on his own, he needed to speak with Morrissey.

"Want to help me pack up?" he asked her.

"Of course," she said, looking embarrassed by his unresponsiveness, and moved away.

She headed back toward where they'd been working. Zach pulled out his cell phone, keeping an eye on her and praying that he would get a signal this far out.

He was in luck, and he punched in Morrissey's number, wondering if the detective might be regretting the fact that he'd given Zach his own cell number. Apparently not, because he didn't sound upset when he picked up and heard who was calling.

"I need help," Zach said. "I'm out on Cow Cay, and I think I've figured out something important. I think Eddie was killed because of a discovery he made. I think he figured out where a bunch of historical documents and a good-sized treasure were buried out here, and someone killed him for it. They've been digging for it, but they haven't found it yet, and neither have I. I can't exactly stay out here, though. Any possibility of sending an off-duty officer or two out to keep an eye on the place? I'll see that they're paid."

Morrissey wasn't that easy. He thanked Zach for sending Jorey to him, though he admitted nothing he'd said had helped much, then asked a lot of questions. Zach answered them honestly — this wasn't the time to be evasive.

"I'll make some calls," Morrissey promised finally. "The island is actually under the jurisdiction of the Park Service, so it's a little complex." As the other man talked, Zach watched the birds warily. "And where are your funds coming from?"

"Sean O'Riley. But I want the whole thing kept secret. I want guards here to see who comes out here and tries to dig again."

"Okay, I'll get right on it," Morrissey said. "Cops are always underpaid, always looking for some extra cash. I hope you're on to something. We're doing everything by the book, and we haven't got a clue. So getting you someone to guard a sand pile and a big old boulder shouldn't be a problem."

"You'll need guys with boats who aren't afraid of a little weather."

"This is Newport. Like I said, shouldn't be a problem," Morrissey assured him.

"As soon as possible."

"You want them there twenty-four/seven?"

"Yup."

"Okay, I'm on it," Morrissey said, then

hung up.

Zach finished packing up with Caer, toted their equipment back to the boat and helped her aboard. The weather had taken a turn for the worse. There were no storm clouds in the darkening sky, but the wind had picked up, and the temperature had dropped.

And the damn birds followed them all the way back.

When he brought the boat into her berth at the dock, the streets were empty.

The O'Riley's office was closed.

But the birds still circled overhead, letting out their horrible cries.

Zach wasn't as disturbed by the birds as he was by Caer. She tried not to let him see her, but she kept glancing toward the heavens and the night sky.

And the birds.

The black birds.

Circling.

14

Gary Swipes was sixty, but still in excellent shape, a big, muscled guy, nearing retirement — and embittered by that fact.

He had lived here all his life. He'd watched people come and go from mansions so self-indulgent that no one person should ever have had the bucks to live in them. He'd watched the yacht owners come and go — modern-day men who had the money to own massive three-masted vessels with state-of-the-art fixtures and electronics and multi-person crews kept on retainer.

It was a money town, but somehow he'd managed to be born to a maid and a gas station attendant. No great schools in his life, no frat parties and cushy career in Daddy's company. Just work.

He'd been a cop most of his adult life, and just because he'd acted like a cop now and then, he'd gotten nowhere.

Once he'd been reprimanded because of

the way he'd treated a batch of drugged-out high-school kids. Hell, their pockets had been full of ecstasy, but somehow he'd still gotten in trouble for being too brutal.

As if they would have handed over the drugs without a little . . . convincing.

Then there was the matter of the money.

There hadn't even been all that much of it. He'd found it in the back of the car driven by a guy high on cocaine who'd hit a kid in the street. Drug money. He'd forgotten to turn it in right away, and he'd almost faced charges.

So he had a temper. Big deal. He'd become a cop to uphold the law, and he had never meant to break it. Teachers couldn't discipline kids these days, and parents didn't — and cops had to jump through hoops to arrest perps. It sucked.

He'd been married, once. She said he had too much of a temper, too. He didn't get women, either. It was okay for them to get mad, slam a fist against a guy's chest, but if he so much as pushed her an inch away, he was an abuser.

Job, life, women, they all sucked.

At least Morrissey had offered him this chance to make some extra cash.

He didn't mind the cold. And he'd indulged in an iPod, so he didn't mind being alone out on the island. The wind might be blowing like a mother, and the temperature at night dropped like a stone out here, but he didn't mind. He'd sailed all his life — crewing on rich guys' yachts just because he loved it so damned much — and the wind and cold motoring over here hadn't mattered a damn to him.

He liked his solitude, too, and what was the difference whether he was alone at home or alone here on Cow Cay?

He had a blanket with him for extra warmth, and a thermos of coffee — spiked coffee. Why the hell he was guarding a barren island and a big rock, he didn't know. Someone had been sniffing around. Digging up the place. The Park Service didn't even give a damn.

But if O'Riley wanted to pay him to watch a rock, hell, he'd watch a rock.

He found a place by Banshee Rock and sat down on the blanket, setting up his lantern and his thermos, and flipping through his iPod. Not a bad gig. He'd asked for a bonus because of the cold, and no one had even questioned it.

He leaned back against the rock and turned up the volume. The blanket below him kept his ass from freezing, and his parka did the rest.

Not bad, he thought.

There were some stars, and the moon was a crescent. Over on the main island of Newport, Christmas lights were flickering everywhere. Colorful.

Only the thatch of trees on Cow Cay seemed to be really creepy. They shifted in the wind, like something from a Halloween fantasy. He could imagine the skinny damned things picking up their skinny damned roots and starting to walk, waving their bony little branches around in an attempt to snag the hair of some high-school girl balling her boyfriend in a bedroll.

Then there were the birds, big black things screeching overhead.

Man, it seemed like they'd been around all day. Creepy as hell, watching the stinking birds swoop around those trees.

He hated birds. All of 'em.

Gulls, terns, seahawks — hell, he hated canaries.

Birds were messy. They were loud. They were always hanging around the docks, wanting handouts, and their shit was everywhere.

But birds like these, flying around as if paying homage to something in those trees, something awful, something that demanded a literal flock of subjects . . . they were unusual.

Screw the birds.

He had a bunch of old comedies on his iPod. He was going sit there and laugh all night, collecting the big bucks without having to do squat.

And his thermos was next to him, filled with nice hot coffee. Well, half-filled with nice hot coffee. There was some good old American bourbon in there, as well. He took a long swig.

The bourbon went down with a pleasant burn. Another swig, and he was warm all the way through.

He didn't drink on duty. Not *real* duty.

For off-duty jobs . . .

He'd done a stint in the service; he'd been a hunter. He could listen. But screw this. He was on a freezing island in the dead of winter, on a ridiculous job. Who the hell was going to come out here tonight and dig?

As a matter in fact, who the hell was going to come out here tonight, period?

There was only one way to get through the long hours: his way. Lots of bourbon and a very small-screen TV.

He swore and got up, thinking he would relieve himself against one of those scrawny, creepy trees before settling in to wait and watch.

The good thing about being all alone on an island, he thought, was who the hell cared what you did? He took a piss in full view of the beach, and then, that taken care of, he belched loudly and settled down again.

Not bad. All the money he was going to make, and all he had to do was sit here, drink and laugh.

Money. It was all his ex-wife wanted, and for some reason the courts had decided she deserved it.

She was a bitch.

Work was a bitch.

Life was a bitch.

Life sucked.

And that was that.

But he was a man's man, tough, smart and not about to take any shit. Even if the whole world *had* gone over to the pansies and the P.C. crowd, he wasn't going to take any shit.

After a while he settled into his show, drinking steadily all the while. He would probably doze off soon enough, but even if he did, who the hell would know? Or care?

He was laughing at one of his shows when, with an awful thud, *it* landed on the blanket, almost in his lap, and his laughter became a scream.

"Anything on those blueberries?" Zach

asked Morrissey over the phone.

It was nearly ten, and he was alone in his room at last. He and Caer had joined Amanda, Kat and Sean at a seafood place down by the wharf. Cal and Marni had come in on their own, and they had all laughed awkwardly over the fact that not only did none of them want to eat at home, they had all been drawn to the same restaurant.

Because, Zach realized, it was a buffet.

Whatever they ate was also being consumed by the dozens of other people eating there that night.

Only Clara, Tom and Bridey weren't there. Clara had cooked for the three of them and then sat with Bridey.

Kat had talked about going out to a club, and she'd tried to convince him to come along, but he'd decided against it. He was too consumed with the mystery of Eddie's death and the treasure, examining the charts in his mind, trying to figure out if he was misunderstanding or missing something.

Meanwhile, Sean was worried that Bridey didn't seem to be getting any better and wanted her to go to the hospital, but she was refusing, so now one of them was sitting with her nearly all the time.

Zach reflected now that somehow, during

dinner, they had managed to keep the conversation light. They hadn't talked about Eddie or the sabotaged blueberries, or anything evil.

Even Kat and Amanda had managed to be civil to each other.

They had all talked about the birds, though. Except for Caer.

Caer didn't want to talk about the birds. She was quiet for much of the meal, pleasant when spoken to, but her mind was elsewhere.

Maybe on the letter? The letter that had clearly upset her earlier?

Back at the house, he'd put her out of his mind and called Morrissey.

Zach had been relieved to hear that the detective had gotten a man out to the island. "Gary Swipes. An old cop — guy's been on the force since he was a kid, nearly forty years. He was glad to head on out, especially when I told him I was sure you'd pay a bonus on account of the cold. Big guy, tough guy. He'll stay on until morning, and then there's a kid, a new officer but a good one, relieving him."

With things on Cow Cay well in hand, Zach had asked about the blueberries.

"I don't have anything. Not yet. We've got no prints other than those of a stock boy, and those are smudged — looks like the jars were taken off the shelves, tampered with and returned. We're looking through all the video from the last week or so. They track their stock well there, so we know the jars in question came in during that period. The thing is, the video shows the cash registers, not the aisles. Still, we'll know who came in and out. It's just slow, tedious work, and there are only twenty-four hours in a day."

"I'll head out by myself to Cow Cay again tomorrow and play with the metal detector some more," Zach told him.

"On parkland. You know that's illegal." Morrissey laughed. "Don't worry. I'm not looking and my man won't be, either. And if you get the urge, come on down to the office — we can use some help staring at those tapes. At least the newspapers are full of articles about the blueberries. Hopefully no one else will wind up involved."

Involved? Zach thought.

Innards cut to ribbons.

Dead.

Yes, hopefully no one else would wind up *involved.*

There was a tap at his bedroom door, light and hesitant. He frowned and quickly finished his conversation with Morrissey, then flipped his phone closed, walked to the door and opened it.

Caer was standing there, a strange, wistful look in her eyes.

"Hey," he said. "Is anything wrong?"

She shook her head.

"Sean — is he all right? Where is he? Who is he with?"

"Sean is out with Tom and Kat, seeing that jazz trio she was talking about. Amanda is locked up in her suite, and Clara went back to the cottage."

"Bridey?"

"Sleeping peacefully. I just checked on her," Caer said.

He studied her with a frown.

"Are you going to ask me in?" she asked him.

He stepped back, stunned, realizing for the first time that she had prepared for bed. She was in a soft flannel gown and robe; small white roses fell lightly upon a creamy beige background, and there was lace around the collar and cuffs. Her hair was loose, falling like blue-black waves around her shoulders.

"Come in," he said.

She entered and closed the door, and there was nothing coquettish in her manner. She rushed against him, burying her face against his cotton T-shirt and slipping her arms around his waist.

"Is this too terrible?" she asked quietly. "I feel . . . I feel time slipping away, I guess. . . ."

Was what they were doing right? Wrong? He had no idea. But it was impossible not to welcome her. Everything about her was the ultimate in sensuality and seduction. Not contrived, not artificial. He remembered opening his arms, drawing her to him, feeling the rush that swept through his muscles and into his blood whenever she was close and the curves of her body were flush against his. He stretched his shirt to the ripping point, he was so eager to get it over his head and discard it. He was slightly more circumspect with the little buttons on her gown, seeing as at some point she would have to return to her own room.

Even so, he moved with the maddened speed of a schoolboy, afraid to lose the moment. Then she was against him, naked flesh to naked flesh, hunger and electricity driving away thought, words, past, future — even the present. She was not in the least shy, trembling against him as her lips moved over his skin, as their tongues met and tangled and dueled in wet, feverish kisses. She slid against the length of his body, the satin of her hair teasing his flesh, her hands, lips, teeth and tongue following suit.

She was sweeter than any woman he had ever known. He was ravenous, but he forced himself to lavish care upon her shoulders, breasts, belly, limbs and beyond. She tasted of life and vitality, sweetness and light, and his every touch seemed to arouse her almost unbearably. They fell together on his bed in a wild jumble of arms, legs and bodies, striving to touch each other, gasping at an erotic touch received. Their caresses were beyond intimate. He roused her to a series of mini orgasms that left her moaning and him desperate to control his own frantic urge to climax.

But it was a lost cause. Her fingertips, just brushing his shoulders, his thighs, were like a physical aphrodisiac. The feel of her lips against him so sexually was enough to make him tremble and surge in a frantic desire for release.

The torture was exquisite. To receive, to give. He finally shifted his weight atop her, teasing every inch of her flesh, as he had been teased. He laced his fingers together with hers after he had trailed fervent kisses down the length of her perfect form, feeling drunk on the feel and taste of her. He met the brilliant blue beauty of her eyes and saw there a trust and need and vulnerability that tore at his very soul. And then he was inside her, and instinct took over. They moved together, and somewhere in his mind he heard the wind at sea, the waves in a storm, a force of nature that was beautiful and almost violent, and, above all, as passionate as heaven and hell and all that reigned in between.

The world and the night seemed to explode as he did, and he was gratified to feel the quaking of her body as he held her, basking in the spill of heat and fire that erupted between them. He held her, examining the lines of her face and form, the tangle of her hair against his flesh and pillow. She looked up at him as if marveling at the experience of being with him, and that look was something he was certain would gratify any living, breathing man in the entire universe. He touched her hair, and she caught his hand and kissed it, and the look in her eyes was suddenly pained and wistful.

"I've got to go," she said.

"What? You've just arrived."

"I have to go."

She kissed his lips again, passionately, so passionately that he was tempted to drag her back down, but just as she had arrived with no hesitation or pretense, she was equally determined that she had taken all the time she could and now had to leave.

"I have to go."

"Like Cinderella, and the clock is about to strike midnight."

"Cinderella?" she asked.

He frowned. "Even in Ireland, I'm sure you know all about Cinderella."

"The fairy tale?" she said. "Of course."

He smiled. She was stumbling back into her clothing, watching him. She tossed her hair back as she buttoned her robe and then kissed his forehead. "It's just that we have so many fairy tales of our own. . . ."

"Every country has its fairy tales," he agreed.

"Tales of magic, fantasy and what lies beyond," she said, her voice trembling and hinting at mysteries undreamed of.

"What lies beyond?"

"It's real, you know," she said softly.

"What's real?"

"The world beyond. Heaven, hell . . . more."

She seemed strangely worried and distracted, he thought. She'd been his so completely in bed. So real, a creature of flesh and blood and bone, breathing, hot and damp, twisting and writhing and holding tight. And now . . . it was as if she were a million miles away.

"Caer . . ."

"I've got to go."

He started to rise, but she stretched out a hand to stop him. "Midnight. The witching hour. Sean will be back soon, and I have to be in my room. I have to watch over him," she said.

Short of chasing her buck naked through the house, he had no choice but to let her go.

"Weren't they great?" Kat asked, leaning her head on her father's shoulder.

He squeezed her hand. "Thanks for inviting me. I had a good time."

"Thank you for coming," she told him sincerely.

Her father was looking out the window at the Christmas lights, still holding her hand. "Do you remember when you were younger, just starting out as a musician? You'd play that trance stuff that just about made me crazy. And that hip-hop."

She laughed. "Dad, I still play those now and then."

"But your music has matured. You've expanded your horizons. You love every form of music, and even if I don't like all of it, I can accept that you do. It's like that with people, too. Amanda —"

"Please, Dad. Stop. I accept that you're married to her, but I just can't imagine . . . Dad, she isn't your type. I'm not jealous because she's young — and I don't care about money, you know that."

He laughed. "I do know that. You told me when you were just a kid that you were going to make your own money, and the hell with me. You're doing a damned fine job, too."

"Thanks to Zach," she said. "I wish he had come tonight."

"He's focused. Have you noticed that about Zach? He's into his music or he's on a case. One or the other, never both at once. He uses the music to cleanse himself after every tough case." He let out a sigh. "But . . . back to the subject. Amanda's my wife, even if that makes me an old fool."

Kat drew away, stunned. "You mean that you agree with me . . . that Amanda did —"

"Kat, don't go thinking that I agree with you about that, because I don't. Just because I've realized that Amanda isn't . . . well, that she can be rude, that she's shallow, that I may have been thinking with other parts of my body than my brain, it doesn't mean she's an evil human being."

The word *evil* was a strange choice, she thought. Her father should have said *bad*.

". . . it doesn't mean she's a *bad* human being."

It was just a word. . . .

"Almost home," Tom said cheerfully. "Just a few more minutes."

Kat tried to read her father's expression, but he had turned away, watching the lights once again.

"Amanda has been a lot nicer since the blueberry incident," Kat said, trying to sound nicer herself.

"She coops herself up in our room a lot, that's for sure. I've barely seen her myself lately," Sean said. "It's as if we're all on hold, in a way. Waiting."

"Waiting for what?"

"Eddie to be found," he said quietly.

Tom drew to a stop at the front of the house to let them out. Kat thanked him and stepped from the car, reaching in to offer her father a hand.

"Thank you, kitten," he said, kissing the top of her head. "It was a nice night."

He headed for the house, and Kat started to follow.

But then she froze. There were birds everywhere.

They were high over the house, swooping on the air currents like vultures. Were they vultures? She narrowed her eyes against the night sky, trying to ascertain what they were. Not vultures. They were big, but not that big. They were darker silhouettes against the dark night sky, moving in strange circles, rising and falling.

She remembered the bird outside her window, and suddenly panic swept through her.

"Dad!" she cried, and raced to catch up with him.

He waited for her, and she took his arm. "Look at all those birds," he said.

"They're creepy," she told him. "Let's get inside."

"They're just birds," he said, and shrugged. "Maybe it's global warming."

"It's freezing tonight."

"They're just birds, Kat. They won't hurt you."

He was convinced and started heading toward the house again. Kat looked up at the sky as she walked alongside him and could have sworn that the birds were swooping lower. She was sure they wanted to come after her and peck her eyes out.

Cal was dreaming. Dreaming that he was running, about to grab the brass ring and achieve a life of ease, a house that wasn't owned by the bank, credit cards that weren't maxed out and the power to make someone else work when he didn't feel like it.

He was reaching out, about to grab it. . . .

But Eddie was there, in front of him, laughing at him, telling him that he was a fool, that he had to learn to work, like all the rest of them, had to pay his dues. Eddie was going to block him from his dream.

Then the birds came. Great flocks of them, with huge eyes and wide dark wings. They cawed and flapped around him, tearing at his hair.

He cried out and ducked.

And woke up.

He was standing outside, barefoot, and the ground was freezing. At least there weren't any birds, he thought in relief, and then he realized that yes, there were. They just weren't flying around and screaming.

Two of them were perched on the cover of the barbecue.

A few more were on the eaves of the house.

He swore softy and glanced at his watch. It was late, but he wasn't tired at all.

Might be the fact that he had all but frozen his feet.

Well, hell, this just might be the time to get a few things done.

■ ■ ■ ■

When Caer had gone, Zach took a long hot shower and dressed in long flannel pajama pants. It was late, but he felt restless. He slipped into a robe and stepped out into the hallway.

He stood outside the door of Amanda's and Sean's room, listening. He could hear the television; she was either watching a late-night talk show or she had simply fallen asleep with the television on.

He quietly walked away and went to check on Bridey, cracking the door open and looking in.

He thought she was asleep, but then she spoke to him. "Hello, my boy. Are you all right? Restless, and walking about in the night."

"I'm fine, Bridey. How are you doing? Think those pills are starting to kick in?"

"I'm all right, Zach. I'm all right. They're not here for me, y'know."

"Who's not here for you, Bridey?"

"The birds."

Bridey wasn't all right, he thought. She was growing stranger by the day. She'd told stories forever, but always with a twinkle in her eyes.

Now she seemed to believe every thing she said.

"Bridey, those birds are just birds."

"No, they've come on account of the evil. I wish Kat understood," Bridey said, distressed. "The birds only come because of the evil. I'm not evil. I'm where I should be, and it will not be the birds comin' for me."

"The birds will go away, Bridey."

"Aye, just as evil goes away. Always, it is beaten somehow. But the birds have come now because of it. Don't worry about me. I'm not afraid of the birds."

He pulled a chair over to the bed and sat down. "It's all right, Bridey. There are evil people, we all know that. But you're going to get well, and I won't let anyone else get hurt."

"You'll try, you'll try hard, and I believe you are the man who can win."

"Bridey —"

"Eddie . . . will be there. Eddie will wait for me."

"Bridey, I —"

"I'm an old woman, Zach. Now, you. You're young and in love with her, aren't you?"

Her change of subject threw him.

"Pardon?"

"You're in love with her. It cannot be. Because she must bide and do her duty, and when her duty is done, she must go."

"Bridey, don't you worry about anything now. All right? I'm here, and I'll protect you and Sean and everyone else."

"Aye, Zach, what a fine lad ye are, but ye canna protect me from time." She closed her eyes. "I think we all love her. She has such a goodness about her. Such beauty and sweetness. But she must do as she must do, but it's from Ireland she sprang, and it's to Ireland she must return."

"Bridey, I'll let you in on a little secret. I am a little bit enchanted. But that's not something we need to worry about right now."

"I don't want to see you hurt," Bridey said.

"I'm strong, Bridey."

"No man is ever as strong as he thinks. Sean, my nephew, he's a strong fellow, too, but strength canna always win out over deceit."

Her eyes closed.

"Bridey?"

But she had fallen asleep — or she was faking it. Either way, she was done talking to him. He kissed her forehead and tiptoed out.

Despite the late hour, when he returned to his room, he put a call through to his brother Jeremy, who was just a few hours away in Salem, with his new wife, Rowenna. He needed a fresh perspective, and Jeremy was just the one to provide it.

"Hey, bro. What's up?" Jeremy asked once he was awake enough for conversation.

"Everything all right with you?" Zach asked.

"Everything is great with me. But you wouldn't be calling so late if you didn't need something, so spill. Kat okay? Is Sean all right?" A note of worry had crept into Jeremy's voice.

"Kat's fine, and Sean is doing extremely well. It's hard to tell he was ever ill."

"So Kat was just being paranoid, thinking Amanda was trying to kill her father?"

"I don't know. I really don't. I need you to see what you can find out about arsenic poisoning — and mushrooms."

"If you think there's too much arsenic in Sean's system, he needs a heavy metals test," Jeremy said.

"I know. I'm leaning toward the mushroom thing, though. There's at least one kind of poisonous mushroom that causes all the symptoms he had — and they can be delayed. But I'd like you to talk to some medical people who aren't from around here, keep things quiet. See what you can find out from the experts." He went on to tell Jeremy about Eddie Ray and his hunt for Nigel Bridgewater's treasure, and his discovery that Eddie had left a clue on one of Sean's charts.

And about the crushed glass in the blueberries.

"You think all those things are connected?" Jeremy asked.

"Well, the blueberries came from a local store, but no one else reported having any problems, so I don't know about them. But the other two things? Yeah, and I'm looking for the answers."

"All right, you work your end, and I'll get all the info I can for you on this end. If I can't get everything I need, I'll have Aidan ask some of his FBI buddies to snoop around. Anything else?" Jeremy asked.

"Bridey's ill," Zach said.

"Damn," Jeremy said, then fell silent for a moment. "She's old, Zach," he said finally. "She's lived a long life, but we can pray she'll get well. I'll head up in a few days, after I talk to some people. Rowenna can see Sean's place, and she'll love Newport at Christmas. Anything else you need from me?"

Zach hesitated. "Yeah. Study up on Irish legend for me, will you?"

"What?"

"Banshees, to be specific."

"Banshees."

"Yes. See if there's any legendary association between banshees and birds."

"Banshees and birds?"

"Yeah. Especially crows or ravens."

"All right, you got it," Jeremy told him.

Zach said good-night, and they hung up.

Zach tried to sleep after that, but he could still see the birds, swooping so strangely around the sky.

His mind was racing. It felt as if there were something he should be able to see or touch or understand, and it was eluding him.

He sat up suddenly, picturing Caer as she had been that afternoon. She had gone off on purpose, he thought. She hadn't wanted to open that letter in front of anyone else. And whatever it said had disturbed her greatly.

Bridey had been right. He was falling more deeply for Caer every hour. And he trusted her. He shouldn't, because he knew there was something she wasn't telling him. But she wasn't out to hurt anyone — he was certain of that.

Eddie was still missing and undoubtedly

dead. They might never find him. And if he'd been in the water all this time, there wouldn't be much to find.

The gift.

He clenched his teeth and spoke aloud.

"Damn it, Eddie. I hope that gift gets here soon."

Because it might well be the answer.

Gary Swipes stared at the thing that had landed in front of him, almost in his lap.

It was the biggest damn bird he'd ever seen. Big and black, but other than that, he didn't know what kind it was. Crow, raven, whatever . . . it was big, and judging by the thud it had made as it landed, it was heavy.

It was also very dead.

Its claws were curled and constricted.

It was open-eyed.

It was lying on its side, and the one eye he could see seemed to be staring at him in horror, as if it could still see him. He felt uncomfortable, as if he would see himself reflected in that one awful eye if he looked closer.

He swore violently, fear suddenly blossoming in the pit of his being. He kicked out, half expecting that the dead bird would rise up and fly at him.

It didn't.

It was dead.

But the kick did nothing to stop that eye from staring at him.

He was dimly aware of the sound of canned laughter coming through his headphones as he realized he hadn't kicked the bird far enough away. It was still lying on its side.

Staring at him.

"Son of a bitch," he swore aloud. "You creepy *mother*. You just had to die here, huh?"

He took off the headphones and got to his feet. There was only one thing to do — get rid of the damned thing. Dump it in the ocean and let the fish eat it.

He looked up, aware suddenly of a noise that didn't fit, something he shouldn't be hearing. He realized that he hadn't really been *listening* at all. He knew the sounds of the sea and wind. Knew that sound could actually bounce over the water from the wharf far away or the traffic on the bridge. He knew all those sounds, but this was something else.

The bird distracted him again. That eye. That frigging eye. It had caught the reflection from his lantern, and now it was gleaming, as if the bird had come back to life.

He swore again, moving away from the rock.

He heard a whizzing sound, and the pain that blossomed in his back was instant and staggering.

He fell down on his knees, instinct kicking in as he reached around, trying to grab whatever had struck him. He could still see the bird, but something about it was different now. It had been splashed with something red. In fact, it was lying in a pool of red.

He tried to reach out, but his hands wouldn't obey. He could see them, though. They, too, were covered in red. In blood.

What an idiot he'd been, letting someone attack him from behind.

Knife? Hatchet? Axe? What had made that sound?

What the hell difference did it make? All that mattered was that it was something steel and sharp and lethal.

He swore again, internally now; he didn't have enough breath left to make a sound.

Life sucked, but he'd still planned on living it.

Death sucked worse. He hadn't even fought; he hadn't even faced his enemy. He was just going to die, and he was never going to know why.

He pitched forward.

He couldn't stop himself. Numbness came sweeping through him as he fell, landing on his side.

One eye visible, he thought.

One eye.

The bird was staring at him with one bloodstained, gleaming eye.

And there lay the irony.

Because he knew he was staring back at the bird . . .

With one bloodstained, gleaming eye. . . .

15

Michael was seated at one of the booths in the coffee shop when Caer arrived. He was reading the newspaper. He wore a heavy sweater and jeans, blending right in with everyone else in the rustic, oceanside town.

He knew Caer was there as soon as she slid into the booth opposite him, but he still took his time to finish whatever article he was reading.

"Coffee?" he asked her when he finally looked up. "We have a lovely waitress. I'm sure she'll be right here."

"Michael, you're not here just because of me, are you?" she asked.

He set the paper down. "Well, one might have hoped you'd be further along by now."

She frowned at him fiercely. "You know, I don't have a badge or a license to go snooping around. I'm here as a nurse. I'm observing people, and I'm doing my best to follow Zachary Flynn around and learn what I can from him. He *does* have an investigator's license, and he's on the trail of whatever's going on. If you had given me better credentials to work with, I might have been able to beat down a few doors."

"Don't be ridiculous. It's your job to study people, to understand them. You need to discover how they think and why — and, most importantly, when they're lying and when they're not. But, since you brought it up, no, I'm not here just because of you. I'm here because there are a number of items that need my attention on this side of the Atlantic."

"Great. I'd hate to think that any failure on my part to move swiftly enough brought you out on a journey to the New World," she told him sarcastically.

He shrugged. Michael was not easily goaded. "You're usually very good at what you do, Caer."

The waitress arrived with his food, and it looked to her as if he'd ordered half the breakfast menu. The waitress set down a plate that held an omelet, hash browns and toast. Smaller plates held side orders of pancakes and biscuits.

Caer ordered coffee.

"What, nothing else?" Michael asked her, already cutting into the omelet with gusto.

"Pancakes. Will you look at those pancakes? Light and fluffy. I'll bet they're delicious," he told their waitress, whose name tag identified her as Flo.

Flo blushed with pleasure. Michael's smile could be absolutely charming. "We make the best pancakes in the state, I swear."

"There you go, Caer. Pancakes."

She forced a smile for Flo. "No, thank you. Just coffee for me."

Flo lingered a moment. "I just love hearing you talk. My great-grandfather was Irish."

"Lovely," Caer assured her.

Flo walked away. Michael seemed to be giving his attention to his food when he told her, "Let's see, not so thrilled with the concept of breakfast. Foods that tease the taste buds and the palate. Hmm. There's a flush about you. Something in your face, in your movement, that I find intriguing. Is it . . . could it be . . . dare I suggest that you might have discovered a few of the other joys of the flesh during your time here in Rhode Island?"

She gritted her teeth, trying hard to stare at him with an unreadable expression. "That's really none of your business."

"You're right." He set down his fork. "It's none of my business. But you *are* my business, and I'm getting worried about you."

"Why?"

"You can't stay here. I'm seeing far too much emotion in you, you know. I think that you believe, or wish to believe, that you might have some kind of future here, and you do not."

She looked down, startled, and suddenly feeling vulnerable.

"I'm trying to save a man's life, remember?" She waited as Flo returned with her coffee, thanked the woman, and waited until she was gone to lean in and say, "Michael, there are black birds everywhere. Crows, ravens, black birds."

"I see," he said. "So it's drawing closer."

She shook her head. "It? Nice euphemism. Michael, it's becoming more and more evident that Eddie was murdered, so *it's* not closer — it's *here*."

He studied her for a while, and then spoke softly. "Caer, you've seen the world for a long time. You know how it works. Bad things happen. The birds come when evil grows, when tragedy threatens, when the death toll will be high. When the normal order is seriously disturbed. You have a lot of work to do."

"But . . . you're here," she said.

"This is your assignment, and you must

handle it. And it's not going to be any easier now that you've allowed yourself to become so involved."

"It's not fair," she said. "Michael, this isn't a place I know, it isn't home, and now you're here. You have more experience, and you have much more *power*. And —"

"Whoa. Who ever said that life and death were *fair?*"

"I've always done what I was asked to do, and I've done it well."

"Human flesh is weak," he said. "Take me — I do relish a good pancake."

"Pancake!" she protested.

"Temper, temper," he warned.

She let out a sigh of aggravation. "Michael —"

"I saw that you were attracted to the man, to the picture alone. It's a natural thing, perhaps. He's a handsome man, with strength of purpose and real decency, but, Caer . . . a *fling* with the man was fine. Now you've become far too involved. You're dreaming of a life with him, and it isn't to be. Cannot be."

"I'm not dreaming —"

"You are. And you are forgetting the havoc you can cause if you upset the natural order." His features grew harder. "There are birds. All around. They foretell great evil. You will remain here and do whatever is necessary to complete your assignment and keep that evil at bay. Most importantly, you'll not let that evil take on a life that will create only agony in what should be gentle and natural crossings. You know that. I know you know that. Ah, Caer! I'm trying to make this as easy as possible for you."

She sat silently staring at him. She hated having a heart. It was just an organ, she knew. An organ of the human body. Hearts didn't really break. Emotion lay in the soul. In the essence that made a man a man, that raised human beings above the other creatures sharing the earth.

He reached into his pocket and handed her a slip.

"Back to regular business . . . this one is yours."

She looked at the paper he had handed her. Then she stared at him with pure horror in her eyes.

"No!"

"Aye, my dear. And don't look so stunned. What did you think? No one lives forever."

"You're a monster," she told him.

He smiled sadly. "No, I'm not, and you know it." He gripped her hand and stared at her seriously. "I am counting on you. And when the time comes and evil must be bested, I know you'll remember that it cannot be set free in this world or the next."

She looked at the paper in her hand and asked him dully, "When?"

"Now."

Zach had left the house early, grabbing coffee and a scone and taking them with him. He drove to the wharf, arriving so early that the office wasn't even open yet. He was glad. He boarded the same boat he had taken the day before, gunned the motor and navigated out of the channel, then let the throttle go.

The day was colder than the one that had preceded it. He felt the bite of the wind, the spray like needles against his face, but he hardened himself against the elements. He planned to start digging again, and to spend the day at it.

He drew close to Cow Cay, dropped anchor and waded in. There were two boats anchored nearby, both small motorboats. Both the cops Morrissey had hired must be there; the night man had probably stayed on chatting to the day man. He didn't really need someone here while he was working, but it wasn't such a bad idea, either. If the treasure *were* here, whoever had killed for it might well return, and it surely wouldn't hurt having a man to watch his back.

He stripped off the waders and headed for Banshee Rock.

Before he could reach it, a young man in jeans and a rough-weather jacket came rushing toward him.

His face was white.

"I can't find him. I've looked everywhere, and I can't find him."

"Who? You can't find who? And who are you?"

The man regained his composure. He couldn't have been more than twenty-five; beneath the huge jacket, he was slim. He had tawny hair that topped a somewhat bony face.

"I'm Phil Stowe. Officer Phil Stowe. Detective Morrissey hired me to come out here for the O'Rileys. I was supposed to relieve the guy who was here last night — Gary Swipes — but he isn't here. I've looked everywhere. But that's his boat. It's as if he just vanished."

"Men don't just vanish," Zach said.

Stowe suddenly backed away. "Who are you?"

"Zachary Flynn. I'm working for the O'Rileys, too, and I'm an old family friend, as well."

Phil seemed to relax. "I swear, he *has*

vanished. There's no sign of him anywhere."

Hell, Zach thought. First Eddie Ray had vanished.

And now a man Zach hadn't known, but who had been hired on his say-so, had also disappeared.

He started past the young policeman and headed for Banshee Rock.

As he walked around it, he saw the bird.

Dead. Talons curled, one eye wide open.

Wide open and blood-covered. As a matter of fact, the bird's entire body was covered in blood.

He hunkered down to study it.

Stowe had followed him. "It's just a dead bird," the young policeman said. "I found *it,* but no sign of Gary."

Zach rose. "There's a sign of Gary all right," he told him. "That isn't the bird's blood. I'm willing to bet it belonged to Gary Swipes."

Phil Stowe was fumbling in his pocket. "I'll . . . I'll call this in."

"Yeah, do it. Right away. Let's get Morrissey out here. Tell him to bring the crime scene team, too."

Stowe kept staring at him. "It's a bird. Just a dead bird," he said.

"There's going to be a dead man somewhere, too," Zach told him. "Tell them to get out here as soon as they can."

Bridey knew the time had come.

She had known for a while now that it was coming, and she wasn't afraid.

She'd seen Eddie by the cottage down the emerald slope, and she'd felt the rattle in her chest. She had loved her time on earth, loved her nephew Sean, her beautiful Kat, and so many of those who had surrounded her.

There were others who had gone before her, and they, too, would be waiting. Her father, her mother, brothers . . . so many friends. The years, the rough ones and the easy ones, they had all in their way been good. But her time had come.

She wasn't afraid.

Aye, she was, she thought, laughing at her own brave lie.

There was a flurry of activity all through the house, and she was aware of it. They thought that she had slipped into a coma, and that she couldn't hear them. But she could.

The doctor was there, and her priest, Father O'Malley, was intoning the last rites in Latin.

Sean was there, sitting gravely at her side, holding her hand. Kat was sobbing, and

Bridey wished that she could do something, say something, to help her. Bless Kat; she knew how to love.

Amanda didn't come into the sickroom, and she had heard someone say that Zach had left early that morning. She missed Zach, of course. He was such a support to her, and to the others. But it was Kat and Sean who mattered most.

They were certain she was already beyond them. The doctor had given her morphine to ease the pain in her chest. He had told them that it was just a matter of time.

Caer was there, too. She wasn't in the room the way the others were. She was there as she really was.

The others couldn't see her; they didn't know.

She was holding Bridey's other hand, and she was with her as they rose above the others, as the room and all those in it began to fade into the distance.

"I am here," she told Bridey. "I'm here with you, and it will be an easy voyage, I promise you. You'll smell the earth again, the sweet flowers of the fields. The air will be soft, and you'll ride through the heavens. You'll feel the warmth and comfort, and you'll touch love, all the love of the ages, of all those who knew you and have gone on.

You'll feel no pain, not ever again, and you'll cross into a world of beauty, a reward for all the kindness you've shown others. You'll have my hand and my strength while you need them, and you will find only glory."

How sweet her voice was! So many never understood. They thought the banshee came in darkness and evil. But the banshee came as a mourner, one who loved, one who helped.

"You won't leave me yet? Please, I know I shouldn't be afraid, but — Lord, help me, I am," Bridey said.

"I'm here, and the coach is coming. It's a grand coach, Bridey. Plumed horses will pull you through the darkness to the light. The coach is black, because it blends with the shadows of life and death, and it is hidden from mortal eyes. Don't fear the darkness, for it brings you to the light."

"There were birds, but I knew they weren't for me." Bridey frowned suddenly; looking downward, she saw her body — so frail and thin — on the bed far, far below, and she was even more afraid, but not for herself. She looked at Caer, who was dressed in long black silk, her beautiful dark hair blowing in the breeze where they stood on a great green hill above the world. She was so lovely, her features filled with such gentle compassion and tenderness. "I can't go. Not now. There are birds. It *is* my time, I know, but Sean . . . it isn't his time. And my precious Kat . . ."

"I will be there to guide and protect them." Caer looked at Bridey. "And Zach is there, too. He loves your family. You and Sean were there for him and his brothers, and now he'll be there for them. He will not fail them."

As she looked down again, Bridey heard Kat let out a sob, saw Sean move to hold on to his daughter.

She wanted to touch Kat so badly, to comfort her.

"Lean down," Caer said. "It's not as far as you think, and you may touch her cheek, help her understand that you're all right."

Bridey reached down and stroked her great-niece's cheek.

Kat looked up, wonderingly, and touched her face where Bridey's hand had been.

"She felt me," Bridey said, awed.

"Aye, she'll know," Caer assured her. "And look at you! Already, I see the youth and strength returning to you."

Bridey heard the horses then. Heard the coach approaching. There were eight black horses, beautifully plumed. They pawed the air in a strange majesty. Then they set down upon the emerald hill, and the coach door opened.

Caer led her over. The step might have been high to her once. No more. And there was a warmth and light within the coach that beckoned.

Bridey turned, and hugged and kissed Caer. She was ready. She stepped into the coach, then turned, looking into Caer's eyes. "If you ever need me . . . You love him, I know. It must be so hard, knowing you'll have to leave him. Protect him. Protect them all, and especially protect Sean."

"I will," Caer vowed.

"I will be watching over you. Somehow, I know I will be watching over you," Bridey said. She did. She *knew* it. Already she felt so strong. Like running again, skipping, laughing . . .

The carriage would take her to the emerald hills, and there she would see so many people she had missed so badly for so many years, and she *would* run and skip and laugh.

Caer smiled. "Aye, I know you will be looking out for us."

Bridey took her seat in the coach, no longer afraid.

As the coach took to the skies again, she looked back, and she felt a little pang. Caer was still standing on the hill, the breeze catching her beautiful dark hair and lifting it around the porcelain sculpture of her face. The air caressed the black silk mourning gown she wore, outlining her form. Caer lifted a hand, smiled and waved.

And Bridey rode on.

"It looks as if he was killed right here," Zach told Morrissey.

Morrissey was apparently not a cold-weather fan. He was trying not to, but he was visibly shivering.

Four crime scene techs had accompanied Morrissey in the police patrol boat that had brought him out.

"I'd say he's right," one of the techs said. "No bird bleeds that much. And the sand . . . right there. You've got drag marks. Stay back, or you'll compromise the evidence."

There were drag marks. They had been smoothed over with some kind of makeshift broom, probably nothing more than a branch, but if you looked for them, they were there.

And they led to the water.

Two of the techs went out to Gary Swipes's boat. Zach didn't expect them to find anything there, since it was unlikely he had returned to it once he had reached the island, but they had to be thorough.

The police combed the island again, using waders to search the shallows, but there was no sign of Gary Swipes.

All he had left behind was a pool of blood on a dead bird.

Zach found himself searching through the small copse, examining the ground under the skeletal trees. Scrub grasses and a few hardy shrubs were clinging to existence there.

The area directly under the trees afforded no clues, but digging around in the shrubs, Zach discovered an object that didn't belong.

A thermos.

A thermos covered in blood spatter.

He called the photographer over to get a picture of it in situ, then put on a latex glove and picked it up gingerly, and took it over to one of the crime scene techs to be bagged.

Phil Stowe looked at it forlornly.

"He was a tough guy," he said thickly. "He could be a jerk, but he was a . . . decent guy at heart. He sure as hell didn't deserve this."

"What the fuck is going on out here?" Morrissey asked. "Shit!" It was the most anger — the most emotion of any sort —

Zach had seen the guy display. "I thought I was giving him a break, giving him a chance to pocket some money — that ex-wife of his took everything. Some damned favor." He shook his head.

"Someone will have to be out here all the time now. On the clock."

The three of them were standing there, just staring at one another, when Morrissey's phone rang.

He took the call, frowned, then looked at Zach as he flipped his phone closed. His expression was leaden.

"Zach, you've got to get back right away."

Zach tensed. "What's happened?" What the hell could it be? If there had been a problem, why hadn't someone called him?

"That was Clara. She couldn't reach you. They need you back at the house. Bridey passed away. I'm sorry."

Amanda had taken to her bed in a fit of dramatics. Caer was with Kat, who was inconsolable. Sean and Tom had headed out, following Father O'Malley, to make arrangements with the church and the funeral home.

Clara was in no shape to deal with the situation, Marni thought. The old woman was family, too emotionally involved to be the hostess, so she decided to stay and help out.

Cal kept standing about awkwardly, or following her around, until he finally got on her nerves. She sent him off to the grocery and liquor stores with a list of things to buy. The O'Rileys were well-known in town. Everyone would be coming by to pay their condolences, and someone needed to be ready to welcome them.

Thank God the doctor had been there when Bridey died. That meant the O'Rileys wouldn't be subjected to the official questions that were obligatory when someone died at home without a physician present. It was just the law, of course, but she knew it was difficult on those in the household. Her father had died at home, and the police had been forced to ask how and why. Without a doctor's assurance of illness, a body would be subject to autopsy. Family members could wind up accused of murder. It was horrible, and Marni couldn't even imagine Kat having to deal with such a situation.

She was just arranging glasses on a silver serving tray by the bar when she heard the door open. She rushed out to see who it was.

Zach.

He was grave but calm. "Where are Sean and Kat?"

"Tom took Sean to talk to Father O'Malley about funeral arrangements. I'm not sure when they'll be back. Amanda is in bed 'recovering,' " she said sarcastically. "Kat and Caer are up in Kat's room, Clara is out back, and I just sent Cal to pick up some things we'll need once word spreads and people start coming by."

"Thank you, Marni," he said. "I'm going to go up and see Kat."

"Is there anything I can do for you, anyone you need me to call or anything?"

He shook his head. "But thanks. I know your help will mean a lot to everyone, especially to Sean."

He'd been gone a few minutes when she thought she heard someone at the front door. It was beginning already, she thought, as she went to let them in. The next few days would be hard, but she intended to be there for the O'Rileys all the way.

She looked through the peephole in the front door and saw no one. She frowned. She was certain she had heard something.

She opened the door and looked to both sides.

Still no one.

Then she looked down, and a scream rose

to her throat.

It was another one.

Another dead bird.

Horrible, contorted, lying there on its back, looking up at her.

Its eyes were open. Both of them. And they seemed to be staring at her.

Fear shot into her heart, and she gasped for air, only then realizing that she had been holding her breath.

Dead birds. Everywhere.

First at the office.

Now here.

She closed her eyes. She couldn't deal with it; she just couldn't deal with it. Bridey, yes. Bridey's death had been natural and smooth and easy, and she knew that things needed to be done, so she would do them.

But another dead bird . . .

She closed the door and locked it, then realized how ridiculous that was. As if a dead bird could get in!

Shivering, she walked away.

"Zach!" Kat exclaimed when she saw him.

She had been lying down, her eyes huge and puffy from crying. Caer, sitting next to her, wore a deeply sorrowful look. She met his gaze and smiled weakly, but she stayed where she was as Kat rose and threw herself into his arms.

"Oh, Zach," she sobbed.

"She was a wonderful person, and she lived a long, full life, Kat," he said, holding her, soothing her.

"I loved her so much," Kat said.

"And she loved you, Kat. She always said you were the light of her life. And she was so proud of your success."

"Oh, Zach, I know she was old. I know she lived a full life. But I'm going to miss her so much. I can't picture life without all her stories about leprechauns and banshees. Oh, Zach . . ."

"Kat, it's all right."

"I can't stop crying."

"It's all right to cry."

Kat pulled back slightly. "She loved you, too, you know."

"I know. And I loved her back. We all did."

"Have you called Jeremy and Aidan?"

"Not yet, but I will. I wanted to see you first."

Kat started to cry again. "She was old, but people can live to be older. And if she's old, then my father isn't that far behind her. Zach, I'm so scared. If I lost my father now . . ."

"You're not going to lose your father."

She wiped her tears away, tipped her head

back and studied his eyes. "You believe me that someone is trying to kill him, right? So this . . . This . . . won't stop them," she said in a whisper.

"I'm going to protect your father."

"Oh, God, Zach, the birds. The birds came, and that's why she died."

Zach smoothed back her hair. "The birds are birds. Kat, Bridey was old. She caught a cold, and it turned into pneumonia."

"She knew the banshee was coming for her. She told me that. I tried to tease her out of it, but she was right. She *knew*," Kat said earnestly.

"Kat, people often know when they're going to die. At least, that's what they say."

"Where were you?" Kat demanded suddenly.

"Out on Cow Cay," he admitted.

"Cow Cay? Why? What happened out there?"

He realized that Caer was studying him, too, frowning in concern.

He didn't want to say. He didn't want to tell Kat that another man had disappeared, only this time, he'd left behind a trace of his existence and pretty irrefutable proof of his death.

His blood.

"Something is going on out there — I'm

not sure what yet. A guy was out there and now . . . they can't find him," Zach said.

"He's disappeared? Like Eddie?" Kat demanded.

"Yeah, I'm afraid so."

"Oh, my God! Eddie, Bridey . . . my father getting sick, and now this man? What the hell is happening, Zach?"

"Kat, Bridey was sick. And old. It was just her time," Zach said.

"Well, it was wrong. She should have lived to be a hundred. Time . . . The time wasn't right, not for us, not at all." Kat started sobbing, and he held her tightly again. There was little else he could say or do. He looked at Caer, feeling helpless.

She rose. "Kat, you may want to rest for a bit. It's all right to cry, though. We cry because we miss people. But we have to believe that there is a plan, and a time and a place where we'll meet one another again, where we'll see them again and all will be well."

Kat drew away from him and looked at Caer. "Do you really believe that? You sound so sure. . . ." She actually managed a smile. "So . . . Aunt Bridey died in peace, and the banshee came for her just like she expected?"

"Aye," Caer agreed gravely, and flashed a

glance at Zach. "She was Irish, so the banshee came for her and showed her the way, so she wouldn't be afraid. And as she left, she left behind all pain, and she left behind age, and her soul was as young and beautiful as ever she was."

Kat released Zach and walked over to hug Caer, who hugged her in return. "It's all right to mourn — in fact, we need to. But we need to celebrate, as well. She's gone home."

Kat nodded.

Zach straightened. "I have to go call my brothers. They'll want to be here for the funeral."

"Of course," Kat said.

In his own room, he called Jeremy, who assured him that he would get in contact with Aidan, and that they would be there as soon as possible.

Then he went downstairs. People were already starting to arrive to tell Sean how sorry they were, although Sean himself wasn't back yet.

It was all right. Marni was dealing with everything.

Zach slipped out and headed for the police station.

Morrissey was back in his office. "I'm sorry about Bridey O'Riley," he said, "but . . . we've got another murder on our hands, so you'll have convey my condolences for now."

"Of course," Zach told him.

"Awkward time, isn't it?" Morrissey asked him.

"Yes," Zach said flatly. "There should be something to do. But there isn't."

"There is."

"What?"

"That young man you told to call me is in with a few of my men. They're going through the tapes from the grocery store. Why don't you go in and see if you can help his memory along?"

With the presumed murder of Gary Swipes, Zach was suddenly worried that any association with the case might be dangerous for Jorey, who probably hadn't thought to keep it a secret that he was talking to the police. Which meant word could reach the killer. Damn, he should have thought of that.

Morrissey stared at him, his eyes narrowing. "Who knew that you were digging up Cow Cay?" he asked.

"Caer Cavannaugh," he said. "And you." He stared at Morrissey, who stared back at him.

Zach couldn't prevent the unbidden

393

thought that came to him.

Morrissey. No. Impossible. No one could put on that smooth an act.

Oh yeah?

Anything was possible. He'd learned that through the years.

"I don't know if it's even relevant or not," Morrissey said. "Although, it's one of two things. Someone knew that the island was being guarded and went out there anyway to do or get . . . something, figuring he'd deal with the guard if he had to. Or that same person headed out to the island, stumbled onto Gary and felt he had no choice but to kill him. All of which gets us precisely nowhere."

"I'll step in with Jorey. Maybe my presence will help," Zach said.

Morrissey nodded and rose. "Follow me."

Jorey and two policemen were in one of the interrogation rooms, watching videos. Jorey smiled when he saw Zach. "Hey, Mr. Flynn."

"Jorey, thanks for trying to help."

One of the officers suddenly spoke up. "Look. There's Amanda O'Riley."

"And Kat," Zach said.

"And there's Clara. I recognize half the city," Jorey said, shaking his head with dismay. Then he froze. "There — look.

There's the guy who went out with Eddie that day!"

16

It was a sad household, Caer thought.

The O'Rileys' place in the community was obvious; people stopped by the house all through the day, quietly, respectfully, and with genuine warmth.

Once Kat had fallen asleep, there was little for Caer to do except sit in her own room or wander around the house, but she was lonely in her room, and Marni had the house under control. She didn't want to leave Kat alone forever, but she didn't want to just stay around doing nothing. It had already been a long and painful day.

Finally she decided that even though it was a bit of a walk on a cold day, she was going to head down to the charter office, which was officially closed due to Bridey's death, and see what she could discover there.

It was a longer walk than she'd realized. Maybe in summer it was pleasant, but today she was cold.

And empty.

It wasn't surprising that Michael had assigned her to assist Bridey. Age would always be man's enemy; no matter how science progressed, there would always be things that robbed a man of life, and life of its value.

The human body was not immortal.

It was, however, amazing.

There had been other times over the years when she'd taken this form, the one with which she'd been born. And it was always a pleasure and a revelation.

People so often misunderstood her role. She did not take life. Life was lost to the natural order of the world. She simply helped those who died. There were evil banshees, of course. Evil men and women made evil banshees. Michael was always on guard against such creatures, who caused only havoc and pain.

Michael had been around since the beginning of time, but he never explained where the evil banshees had come from; he only warned those who served him that they must never make more of such creatures. He knew so much, she thought, knew all about humans and mortality. Banshees were Irish and it was their role to help the Irish, though sometimes they assisted others, as well. For the most part, though, every ethnicity had its own beings who came to escort the dead.

The ancient Greeks had crossed their river Styx.

The Norse were taken to Valhalla.

And always it was the escorts who controlled the experience, who made the journey one of joy or, on those rare occasions when evil slipped in, of horror.

A new banshee had to be chosen with great care, and always the choice was Michael's. It was the banshees' job to take the hand of those who had lived good lives — they didn't have to be saints, they simply needed to have treated their fellow humans with the same kindness about to be given to them — and escort them into the next world. The coach that came, the black carriage drawn by the plumed black horses, was strictly Irish.

Hers was a compartmentalized duty. What became of others, she didn't know, nor did she have time to worry about it. The Irish had populated all corners of the globe, so banshees tended to be very busy.

Death in old age was not a tragedy. It was the natural progression. Death at a young age was wrong, against nature, against the great plan. It occurred, and when it did, sometimes a new banshee was born. She herself had been a victim of ages of conflict, of hatreds that had been bred into people for hundreds of years. Murdered for love — both sad and poetic.

It was said that at the moment of someone's death, a banshee who had taken on human form, as they were sometimes required to do, could convince the dying soul to take her place. But that soul had to be a worthy one, for there was no sin greater than allowing someone cruel, someone evil, to become the escort of the dead as they made their journey to the land beyond, where the hills were green, and youth and beauty and happiness were returned.

She had always enjoyed her work, which she saw as the final kindness for those who had led deserving lives. She slipped into their minds to take them gently to whatever rolling hills and old loves reigned in their souls. She had seen men who had been strong in their convictions, women who had quietly been the strength behind great men, and all those in between, as well as those who had learned, at the end of their days, that the things they had fought for, the wars they had waged, had not been everything — they had learned late that killing in the name of God was not always just and never done with God's approval.

She had taken those who had given their own lives to save others, and she had been glad to be there, to say thank you, to let them know that their love and sacrifice had not gone unnoticed.

In human form she had enjoyed the fashions of many ages, seen sights of incalculable beauty, and reveled in sweet and subtle perfumes.

Like Michael, she'd savored many good meals.

But she'd never indulged in such physical pleasure before, and now she knew too well why she had been wise not to do so.

Pain.

Allowing herself the pleasures of the flesh could, in the end, bring only pain.

She could not be killed again. She might feel it when she bruised herself, if she tripped or received a cut. But it would be gone in a wink. But in the great dilemma of life and death, internal suffering was far worse than any physical pain.

Love.

Was she really in love? Was it possible to fall in love in a matter of days?

Indeed, did kindred souls exist?

Was it possible . . .

To be immortal, then look into the eyes of a man and know that he was everything she desired?

To fall in love with a strength that had nothing to do with muscle, nothing to do with the way he walked or talked, and everything to do with a quiet code of honor and ethics?

Even a love for music.

She yearned to stay. Had allowed herself to dream.

She should have known better.

Once, long ago, in another life — in her mortal life — she had loved. She should have learned. She had thought that love was greater than hatred, that love between those born to be enemies would be understood, even celebrated. She had thought that she could change her tiny corner of the world, make people see that they should no longer nurture the hatreds they had nurtured for so long.

But she had been wrong. And she had died for her mistake.

Now, only now, while the rest of the world exploded, were the Irish finally learning that each day was new, that no child born today deserved to suffer for the sins of the past.

Far too late for her.

She couldn't help the yearning, though.

401

She could forego the feel of silk, the taste of honey. There was no place on earth that she could not bear to leave.

But the heart and soul she saw in this man's eyes, the way he touched her . . .

She brought a hand to her cheeks. Tears.

She straightened her shoulders. She was what she was. And not only that, but what if he *knew?* Dear Lord, she could imagine trying to tell him. "I canna stay with you. I am a banshee, you see. Yes, seriously. A howling banshee who comes with the great black coach of Death."

He would loathe her; he would be repelled.

Tears. She had not shed them in . . . forever.

She realized that she had reached the wharf.

She looked around and saw that the birds were everywhere.

Poor birds, she thought, even though they unnerved her. She was here to prevent tragedy. Sean was not due to die yet, not for many years. She had been certain that she could protect him, and that with Zachary doing the real work, the investigation, the identity of Sean's enemy would soon be discovered.

But the birds . . .

Their presence meant that many people were threatened, and she had watched them arrive with fear.

I'm not equipped for tragedy, she thought. *How do I stop what is happening?*

She didn't need to be afraid of the birds themselves, she knew. They were mortal. They lived; they perished.

But their presence in such numbers foretold great tragedy. Nothing so sweet as the passing of a woman as loving as Bridey. They foretold something evil, a mass murder, a blood spree.

For now, she ignored them.

The office door was locked, as she'd expected it to be. Michael might have arranged to get her the proper credentials for a nurse and not a spy, but she had been picking locks for decades.

This one was actually quite easy.

Inside the office, she looked around. Where to start? Was there even anything to discover here?

She began to rifle through the drawers. Carefully.

They rolled back the tape. They enhanced it.

But the quality was grainy, and no matter how much it was blown up, no matter how the pixels were rearranged, there was little they could do to get a clear picture.

But there, on the screen, was the man Jorey had recognized.

He wore a hat pulled low over his eyes and a massive coat, and he had the bushy mustache Jorey had seen.

"Well, it's something," Morrissey said.

"Yeah, shave and a haircut, and you'd never know the guy," Zach said. "The mustache looks fake, anyway. But I'll tell you one thing."

"What's that?"

"I'd lay odds that the man who killed Eddie is the same one trying to kill Sean. If there was video of the aisles, I'd guarantee you'd see this guy putting that glass in those jars, then telling Clara how good a blueberry pie would be. We're on the right track. He's after whatever Eddie found, and he's certain Sean will find it, too, unless he gets Sean out of the picture first."

"I agree. We'll get teams out on that island and dig where you suggested," Morrissey assured him.

"Thanks," Sean said. "I have to get back to the house."

"What about me?" Jorey asked. "Do you still need me?"

"No, son, thank you. Thank you very

much," Morrissey told him.

"Jorey, you went above and beyond," Zach assured him. "I'll walk you out."

As they left, Jorey told him, "I'm sorry about Bridey. Everyone who knew her loved her."

"Thank you. I think Sean is going to be all right. It's Kat I worry about."

Jorey looked at him and grinned sheepishly. "Can I make a suggestion?"

"What's that?"

"I've known Kat forever, and whenever anything upsets her, she likes to play her guitar. Maybe you can get her planning the music for Bridey's memorial service."

"Thanks, Jorey. I think you have something there."

Zach looked around. Those damned birds were still everywhere.

Birds. Just birds, he told himself.

"Hell of a thing, those birds, huh?" Jorey asked.

"Yeah, hell of a thing."

Jorey got in his car, and Zach leaned down to speak to him. "Jorey, do me a favor. Lay low. Stick around other people for now, huh?"

Jorey's eyes widened. "Why? You think I could be in danger?"

"I think someone is killing people. You just

don't need to be one of those people."

"I'll be careful. I like living," Jorey assured him.

Zach watched him go. He needed to head back to the house, but he decided to take a detour and check out the charter office. He didn't think that, under the circumstances, anyone would be there, but something urged him to go by anyway.

He drove onto the wharf. It was a true winter's day. The sky was gray, but then again, it was growing late. Darkness would come soon enough.

He parked the car, and his muscles quickened. There was a light on in the office. It was a just one of the desk lamps, but it cast enough of a glow to show him that someone was there.

He exited the car, reaching to his waistband for the gun he always carried now. He approached the office door from the side, moving with speed and stealth.

At the door, he hesitated, then tried the knob.

It wasn't locked. He pushed the door open with a foot, used it as a shield and shouted, "Freeze!"

To his complete surprise, Caer jumped and turned to face him. She was in the process of going through Eddie's desk, but she froze, as commanded, and stared at him.

"What the hell are you doing?" he asked her.

"Looking."

"For what?"

"For whatever everyone else has missed," she said.

He let out a sigh of relief, clicked the safety back on and slid the gun back into his waistband, then closed the door behind him.

"Have you found anything?"

"Poems," she told him.

"What?"

"Poems. He liked to write poetry. Well, they're more like ditties, really. Funny little poems. Here, listen. 'One if by land, two if by sea, oh, I'm so happy, it's all me, me, me.' "

Zach arched a brow. "Deep," he said.

Caer shrugged. "He seemed to like to write them. Look, there's nothing on the computer. I mean, there's lots on the computer — but you've already found it. This is what I think. I think Eddie found something on Cow Cay, but he moved it."

"What makes you think that?" he asked, realizing that she might not yet know that a man had been murdered out there sometime last night.

"I'm not certain, but I think these poems were his . . . his way of leaving something behind. Insurance, maybe."

"Take them. We can go over them later. We should get back to the house."

"All right."

She gathered up the poems, which had been written on all kinds of paper, then shoved into a file folder.

"How did you get in?" he asked her a few minutes later, as they were driving back to the house.

She hesitated, and he wondered if she was about to lie, to tell him that the door had been open when she'd arrived.

"I picked the lock," she admitted.

"You did a good job. I might not have known."

She shrugged.

Suddenly he veered the car to the side of the road and slammed it into park. She stared at him, startled.

"Who are you, Caer? And what are you doing here?"

"I told you —"

"Everything you've told me is a bunch of horseshit. Who are you?"

"Caer Cavannaugh."

"All right, let me try again. Who and what are you — really?"

She stared at him, her eyes hard. "You've accepted that I want to save Sean's life. Can't we just leave it at that?"

He shook his head. "No. A man was murdered out on Cow Cay last night, the man I hired to watch over the area where we were digging."

Her eyes widened. "Murdered?"

"Presumably. We found a lot of blood, but his body has disappeared, just like Eddie's."

"The birds," she murmured. "It's starting."

"Who are you working for?" Zach demanded.

"An Irish agency," she said after a moment.

"The name of it, please."

"It's just referred to as the Agency," she said.

"That's bull."

He saw her take in a deep breath, then she said, "All right, Zach. You want the truth? Here it is." She practically spat out the words. "I'm a banshee. They refer to us as *death ghosts*. I guess that's an appropriate label. We *are* ghosts, and we *do* deal in death. But anything you might have heard that's frightening or bad about banshees isn't true. We come to ease the burden, to be a friend. We help people cross over."

She spoke so seriously.

He felt his temper soar. "That's the biggest pile of crap I've ever heard," he told her angrily. "And you know what? Gloves are off. I wanted to trust you. I *did* trust you. Hell, I started falling in love with you. But you need to tell the truth. If you're some kind of Irish secret service, spit it out. I'll get on your credentials. Governments share information. My oldest brother has contacts almost everywhere."

Her expression had gone implacable. "Do what you have to do, Zach." To his amazement, there was a quaver in her voice.

His fingers were locked on the wheel. "People are dying. Tell me the truth."

"I just told you the truth," she said dully, looking ahead. "Why is this so hard for you? Can't you just accept that I'm here to save lives, and . . . and can't you give me what time we have before I have to go?"

He stared back at her. God, she was beautiful. He wanted to draw her into his arms. He wanted to tell her that he didn't give a damn if she was an alien from planet Zardov, he just wanted *her,* wanted a life with her, waking up to her eyes every morning, to the feel of her close against him. He wanted to grow old with her.

A banshee?

He swore, determined not to touch her. He'd trusted her — and she returned the favor by coming up with a bunch of Irish claptrap.

He revved the motor far too hard and jerked the car back onto the road. He didn't say another word as they drove back to the house.

When they arrived, there were cars lining the driveway.

The Irish mourning process had begun.

Caer found it difficult to concentrate. The house was full of people, and this first night following Bridey's death was long and draining. At eleven, despite the continuing crowd of visitors, she decided that she had to act like a nurse and make sure Sean got to sleep.

She firmly insisted that he go to bed. As she gave him his medications, he told her, "You know, Caer, I could handle these on my own."

"You hired me through the end of the year, and I'm going to earn my salary." She smiled to take the sting out of the words.

"You're a very special young lady," he told her. "Hell of a thing. I'm starting to worry about you. Another man was killed today. A stranger, but he died in my employ. I'm thinking I should send you back to Ireland."

"I wouldn't go."

"And why am I not surprised to hear that?"

At last he was in bed. Kat had spent most of the day resting, though she had finally come down for a while to accept condolences, then returned to bed. She was young, and she felt the loss keenly. But she was going to be all right.

As long as her father was all right.

With Sean in bed, Caer curled up in her own room to read more of Eddie's poems. By themselves, they were just silly, but then she began to put them in a semblance of logical order. "Me, me, me," led to "clever boy, I've found the joy," and they went on from there.

"The clue is left, the clue is right, follow the North Star tonight."

And then, "I dream, therefore I am. Careful, must not be a sacrificial lamb."

She set the sheets of paper down on the bed, cursing Michael for not staying to help. Then again, not even Michael had all the answers. People had that whole "free will" thing going on, and he never tampered with the rules that applied to his place in the grand scheme of things.

Men had choices, and choices meant

chances.

She herself had done well that night, she thought, helping with the guests. Amanda had come down, but she had only swanned around regally, the lady of the manor. She loathed Marni, but that hadn't stopped her from letting the other woman take over the hospitality arrangements while Clara stayed in her own small house, mourning privately, while Kat had been a zombie.

Caer hadn't given herself much time to think, much less to feel.

And she was glad. She didn't like feeling. It was far too painful.

Now she prayed for sleep. Flesh and blood were so weak. Without sleep, she couldn't function, and when she was awake, she hurt.

Sleep. At last it came.

The next day, Aidan and Jeremy arrived.

Aidan was alone, because his wife, Kendall, couldn't leave the community theater that they ran on the plantation so quickly, not to mention that traveling with an infant took preparation.

Jeremy came with Rowenna, his new wife, and the two of them were settled on the second floor, while Aidan took an attic room. Clara was happy to have all three Flynn boys to fuss over, Sean was grateful for the show of support, and Zach was pleased that he would be able to talk over the situation with them.

Rowenna and Kat seemed to hit it off right away. She told Kat that she needed to pick up a few things and actually convinced Kat to go out shopping with her. Since Sean was closeted in his office, Zach decided it would be a good time to bring his brothers up to speed, not to mention go over the information they both had for him.

"Where do we start?" Jeremy asked.

"I'm oldest — and wisest — so I'll go first," Aidan said, smiling. "Zach, I've had your friend completely checked out, and I can't come up with anything that contradicts what you've been told. She has no known association with any intelligence agency, either in the States, Great Britain or the Irish Republic. She's absolutely clean. She got her nursing degree five years ago. She's lived in Dublin all her life. Good grades in school . . . the whole kit and caboodle. She's clean, Zach. Pure as the driven snow."

Jeremy picked up when Aidan was done. "As to the arsenic, my experts all say it's not a weapon any killer is going to use these days if there's any possibility of an autopsy. It's too easily detected, for one thing. They

414

think you might be spot-on with the toxic mushroom theory. The delay in the advent of symptoms causes doctors to look for other possibilities first. By the time they've ruled those out, even if someone thinks of mushroom poisoning, the victim has passed the toxin via the violence of the very illness it caused. It can be especially dangerous in the elderly, because of the wear and tear it causes on the heart. In can even — as certainly happened in Sean's case, whatever the cause — bring on cardiac arrest."

"So, assuming that Sean was poisoned, it almost certainly happened here, in the United States," Zach said.

"It's a theory, but a good theory, I think," Jeremy told him.

"So where are you with this?" Aidan asked. He'd always been the most serious of the three of them, and the death of his first wife had only made him more so.

Remarriage, however, had done wonders for him. His wife was filled with life, with a touch of the psychic about her, and Zach knew that they were both convinced that they shared the family plantation outside New Orleans with the remaining spirits of the past. But they were happy, and Aidan was a crack investigator.

"At the moment it's impossible to know

what happened first, Eddie disappearing or Sean becoming ill. Chances are the two things more or less coincided," Zach said. "A few nights ago, we found ground glass in a pie Clara made, and more was found in several other jars of the same brand of blueberries. Not exactly a foolproof method of killing someone, but I'd bet cash money it's connected. Yesterday, at the station, Jorey Jenkins — you remember him, his parents run the hardware store near the wharf — recognized someone on the grocery store security tapes as the same person who went out with Eddie. Problem is, the guy was obviously wearing a disguise. A very bad disguise. I don't believe that Bridey's passing had anything to do with any of this, by the way. It was just her time." He took a deep breath and looked at his brothers. "I started digging out on Cow Cay after studying the charts Eddie had been reading, and then seeing the way someone — I'm assuming Eddie, since I know it wasn't Sean — doctored one of the charts in Sean's office. Detective Morrissey sent a man out to the island to keep an eye on things, and that man has disappeared and was presumably murdered. Again, no body. But this time there was blood. A lot of blood. Then there's Caer."

416

"She seems charming, and she's absolutely gorgeous," Jeremy told him. "Though I get the feeling you know that," he added with a wink.

"There's something . . . not right about her. She acts like she's some kind of investigator, even though we know she's not," Zach said.

"You've never just asked her?" Aidan asked.

"Sure."

"And what did she say?" Jeremy asked.

"She started out acting all innocent and swearing she was only here to take care of Sean," Zach told them.

"As a good nurse should," Jeremy said.

"Well, you met her in Ireland. Did you meet any of her friends?" Aidan asked. "How much time did you spend together over there?"

"Not much."

"Maybe you should just take her at face value. Maybe everything about her is true," Aidan suggested.

"Oh yeah? Last night she told me she's a banshee," Zach said dryly.

To his surprise, neither of his brothers laughed. They just stared at him.

"I did some research," Jeremy said. "Like you asked me to. The legends are fascinating. Supposedly they were once beautiful women, and when they died, they were . . . recruited, I guess you'd say, to mourn and to help people cross over from this world to the next one. There are banshee laws, even. A banshee can take on human form, and it's said that she actually enjoys it when she does. She gets to enjoy the pleasures of life once again. But she can't remain, not unless she can find someone to take her place. But it has to be someone with a good soul. If she loses sight of honor and justice, and chooses someone evil, she'll be damned for all eternity."

"So you're saying you think Caer Cavannaugh might really be a banshee?" Zach asked incredulously.

"No, of course not," Jeremy told him.

"Then what *are* you saying?"

"Nothing — I'm just giving you the information you asked me for," Jeremy said.

"I think we should all head out to the island," Aidan said.

"The cops are out there now," Zach said.

"I still think we need to get out there," Aidan said. "And we should get going, so we can be back for tonight. Sean is having an old-fashioned Irish wake at the house, and we all need to be there to honor Bridey."

"Right," Zach said. "Let's go get a boat

and head out."

It was a harsh day out. Fitting, maybe.

The black birds still lined the wharves. They were huddled on perches, feathers fluffed against the rising wind. Zach noticed that signs were out all over, advertising the Christmas flotilla. It was just four days away.

He wondered if Sean would still participate, then realized that of course he would. It was tradition, and he would feel honor-bound to participate, if only in Bridey's honor.

It was raw out on the water, but they'd taken one of the larger boats, in order to have a dinghy to bring them right up on the island, so they took turns staying warm in the cabin.

Morrissey hadn't lied. There were a number of men there, some still searching the island, and some digging around Banshee Rock. The three of them explored the island, too, but with so many others traipsing around, there was little to find. Zach found Aidan just standing, looking at the rock and beyond.

"Do you see something?" Zach asked his brother.

"No," Aidan admitted. "But it's always good to look at the whole of a place, memorize it, map it in your mind. Later on, you may get information that literally falls into place."

A moment later, Jeremy joined them and asked, "What are we doing?"

"Memorizing the island," Zach said.

"Oh, good. I thought we were just standing here."

At last they left and went back to their boat.

Zach wasn't sure why, but he thought maybe Aidan had been right. Memorizing a place, seeing it as it was today, couldn't be a bad thing. And he was getting nowhere else fast.

By the time they got back to the house, everything was set up for the wake.

Bridey lay in a beautiful coffin, adorned with flowers and crosses, in the parlor.

Zach stopped by the coffin before going upstairs to change and thought how strange it was to say that a corpse was beautiful.

When life and light were gone, beauty usually departed, too. Morticians could be artists, but they couldn't restore the flash in the eyes, the vibrancy that came with living.

Except with Bridey. She seemed merely to sleep, her lips curved in a slight smile. Her skin was clear, and many of her wrinkles seemed to have disappeared. She was tiny, as she had been in life. And she was at peace.

She was beautiful.

"Rest well, old friend," he said softly.

It was a long night, a night of mourning, and yet also a night of joyous memory. Zach, Aidan and Jeremy were glad to be there — moral support for the family and literal support for Bridey's elderly friends, who used their arms for balance.

Kat would smile, even laugh with someone, and then she would cry.

Clara spent most of the night in a chair near the coffin, with Tom at her side, holding her hand.

Amanda was the lady of the house again, treating Marni and Cal, who had once again taken care of the arrangements, like hired help.

Sean was often lost in his own thoughts, his own memories, and he spent much of the night sitting by Kat's side.

Caer stayed in the background, but Zach saw that she was watching everyone with keen attention.

The priest spoke, and his words were important to them because they would have been important to Bridey. Then Sean talked about his love for his aunt, about how her help had taught him to survive in a new world, and how she had been a link to a past that was as dear to his heart as it had been to hers.

Then Zach suggested to Kat that she sing one of her beautiful laments. Guitars were brought out, and Zach wound up at the piano.

One song became two, then three, and as the mourners joined in, the mood became Irish indeed. As if the very air had lightened, people began to talk about Bridey with love and laughter. Ale and whiskey flowed, food was produced, and sorrow was leavened with the joy of memory.

At one point Zach looked up and caught Caer's eyes. She wanted to smile, wanted to beg him to forgive her.

To love her.

To what avail?

He did neither, but he did say, "Caer, come and give us an Irish tune."

She shook her head.

"I can't. Believe me, I can't."

"Sure you can," he told her.

"Come on, lass!" Sean encouraged. "All the Irish can sing — except for the banshees, of course. 'Tis said if they try to hum a tune, it sounds like the wind howling in the midst of a storm, or a wolf, crying to the moon."

She froze. Then she quickly smiled and said, "Trust me. I love to listen, but even a wolf would be insulted by having its cry compared to my singing."

Somehow, the moment passed.

She looked at Zachary again.

He studied her speculatively, then turned back to the piano.

There was so much noise in the house that none of them heard the birds.

Not until everyone else left and they tried to sleep.

Then there was no avoiding the cacophony of screeching and cawing, or the wind's howl.

It was like a chorus from hell or some dark legend.

As if all the banshees of Ireland were singing as one.

17

Bridey was buried the next afternoon. It was a beautiful winter's day. The sun was shining, and the weather had taken a turn upward; the temperature had reached the midforties.

Her service was a mass, just as she would have wanted. At the graveside, the mourners joined hands to sing "Danny Boy."

Caer liked the other Flynns very much, and she found Rowenna to be charming, but Zach had taken to keeping a distance from her. He seemed angry.

She should have expected it, she thought.

She had told him the truth, but he didn't believe her. Perhaps he didn't want to, or perhaps he simply couldn't. What had she been thinking to blurt things out as she had? She'd had to say something, and she'd had plenty of time to think up a clever answer. So why hadn't she?

She didn't know.

They held the post-funeral gathering at a large pub, which they'd rented for the evening. There were at least two hundred people in attendance. Caer found herself constantly in the company of one of the O'Rileys, Cal and Marni, or Tom and Clara. She was made to feel valued, almost a part of the family.

There was plenty to eat and drink, and Bridey was honored, but, as always among the living, people couldn't keep from talking about the latest news.

That morning, the newspaper had reported the disappearance of Gary Swipes. The article noted that he was a highly trained police officer, that he was well versed in self-defense, and that the amount of blood suggested that he had been murdered.

Eddie's case was brought up again, one disappearance leading the reporter to try to link it to another.

Detective Morrissey was there, along with a large number of off-duty officers, Sean and Bridey being fixtures in the community. Lots of local businesspeople were also in attendance, including Jorey, who kept trying to park himself near Caer.

Looking up at one point, she noticed that Zach was watching the two of them and frowning.

She excused herself and walked over to join him. "What's wrong?"

He looked at her for a long moment, then seemed to relent. He shook his head. "Nothing. I guess I'm just worried about Jorey now. He did what I asked him to do — he called Morrissey. And then he went above and beyond, and went down to the station. So now I'm worried about him, too."

Sean called Zach over to say hello to an old friend, and Caer turned to rejoin Jorey, but she didn't see him anymore. Perhaps affected by Zach's fears, she wandered through the crowd looking for him, but she still couldn't find him.

She left the restaurant and walked down the steps. The day had been warm, but the temperature was dropping as darkness fell. She hugged herself, feeling the chill ripple through her. Flesh and blood. Not always comfortable.

"Jorey?" she called. Nothing. She called louder.

Then she saw him, caught in the glow of a streetlight further down the sidewalk. His hands were in the pockets of his jacket, and Caer watched as his shadow lengthened. He must be going home, she thought.

She almost turned to go back in.

But then she saw the birds.

They were covering the roof of the restaurant. They were perched on nearby fences, and even atop the cars in a nearby parking lot.

"Jorey," she called again, genuinely uneasy now; she hurried along the sidewalk in the direction he'd taken.

She couldn't tell who, but someone else was passing beneath the streetlamp. His shadow was huge, stretching up and out. It was a trick of light, she knew, yet . . .

Caer started running. She suddenly knew that she had to reach Jorey.

The second figure turned as she ran past. She ignored him and had almost reached Jorey, who heard the sound of her footsteps and turned.

And then she felt the pain.

Staggering, horrible, numbing pain.

She had felt it before, but . . .

This time it was different. Now . . .

There was something in her back. A knife.

Oh, yes, she knew exactly what it was!

She knew she had to remove the object, and quickly. She caught hold of the hilt and strained to pull straight out.

Jorey ran back toward her, and he was staring at her in horror.

"Help!" he screamed. "Help!" He caught

hold of Caer, who held the knife in her hand as Jorey helped her gently down to sit on the curb.

"My God," he said to her. "You saved my life. That was meant for . . . for me. Help!" he shouted again. "You're bleeding . . . you could bleed to death. We have to get you to a hospital."

The knife was covered with blood, but she could already feel the pain receding; the wound was closing quickly.

"I'm all right. I don't need to go to the hospital."

"Are you insane? You were stabbed in the back. Help! Someone help!"

"It's all right," Caer told him.

By then people were spilling out of the pub. Caer swore silently. Whoever had attacked her had either run off or merged into the crowd.

The first person to reach her was Zach. Jorey was talking a mile a minute, trying to explain what had happened, but she barely heard him, because Zach was there. He was on his knees before her, his eyes naked for once, their pain and concern vivid as they met hers.

She could hear the roar of a siren; an ambulance was coming.

"Caer," Zach said, his voice soft, concerned, a little desperate.

"What the hell happened?" It was Morrissey, shouting over the din. And then she was aware of the paramedics, insisting that she lie down on the stretcher so they could take her to the hospital. Aidan and Jeremy Flynn were there, and then Sean and the rest of the household pushed their way up front.

"I'm going in the ambulance," Zach told his brothers, who nodded, and she realized that she was suddenly . . . *jealous.* They had a family; they were close. Brothers. When one of them needed something, the others were there. She ached terribly just thinking about it.

She wanted to be loved. To feel that bond of family. To know there was someone in the world who would move heaven or hell for her.

"I don't need an ambulance," she said, holding tight to Zach's lapel. "I swear to you."

But it was no good; she was being taken to the hospital.

They didn't let him in with Caer, and Zach understood, so he paced the waiting room, trying to think. He had been afraid for Jorey, and he hadn't been wrong. But Caer had stepped in front of a knife. *The knife.*

429

They had to examine the knife. No, it was all right; the cops were still there, and so were his brothers.

He felt a chill sweep through him. They'd just been at a funeral.

And they had almost been required to hold another.

"Mr. Flynn?"

He spun around to see the E.R. nurse. "You can go in. Miss Cavannaugh is waiting to see you."

"How bad is it? Is she going to be all right?"

"She's already healing. It really was just a nick." The woman smiled.

"There's no internal damage? You're certain?" Zach demanded anxiously.

"She's fine. She thinks the knife was stopped by the underwire in her bra, and I suspect she's right. Now go on in and see her."

He walked into her cubicle and saw her lying on the bed, her eyes closed, her porcelain skin even paler than usual, her hair a raven-black frame around her features. Shaking, he sat at her side and took her hand.

Her eyes flew open and she smiled slowly, then asked anxiously, "Jorey is okay, right? I mean, nothing else happened? Did they catch who did it?"

"Are you kidding?" he replied in disgust. "There were a hundred people out there. But you . . . Caer, how the hell can you be all right? You must be the luckiest damned woman in the world. Even so, you shouldn't go throwing yourself in front of knives."

"I didn't, really. And I'm all right, Zach. I really am all right."

"Good, but you're still staying here tonight. If you're good, you can come home tomorrow."

"But I'm fine."

"They call it observation, and you're staying for it."

"There's too much going on," she said.

He smiled. "I'll be here with you."

"But . . . what about Sean?"

"You don't need to be worried. My brothers are there."

"You know how on TV the killer always makes a mistake?"

"Yes?"

"Well, he did. Jorey saw him, and he's afraid of being recognized, even though he was wearing a costume, so he tried to kill Jorey, but Jorey is alive."

"Hiding in plain sight," Zach said thoughtfully.

"What?"

431

"I think the killer was there at the pub, enjoying the hospitality of the O'Rileys. I bet he stole that knife from the kitchen, then followed Jorey when he left." He paused, looking at her. "Caer, I think my heart stopped. My God, there was so much blood. . . ."

"The luck of the Irish," she said lightly.

Her eyes were starting to close. They'd given her something, because no one would believe that she wasn't in pain. His face was blurring in front of her.

"I told you, Zach. I'm a banshee," she said. But the drug was getting to her. "All right. I'm part of a worldwide spy organization. No, just a branch of Irish nationals determined to watch over our brothers and sisters across the world. I'm . . ."

She never finished. Whatever they had given her, it kicked in fully then. She slept. And she dreamed.

And in those dreams, her future was bright.

They let Caer out the following afternoon. Zach had spent the night with her at the hospital, but the doctor had told him that he would need to be treated for a bad back before Caer had a problem. "She barely needed stitches, and the wound is practically healed. It's amazing, a real miracle."

The minute they returned to the house, Kat rushed out to meet her, as if she'd been watching at the window, and even Amanda was downstairs, ready to fuss over her. Zach was glad to see it, and especially pleased that Caer and Kat seemed to have grown close.

And as to Amanda . . . well, Caer had made the news and was a guest in her house. Maybe it was a novelty — and would wear off.

But at the moment Caer was a heroine. The paper had even carried her picture.

Zach suggested she rest, since she must still feel weak and tired, but she refused to be put to bed, and though he wanted answers, he wasn't leaving her.

Not that day.

He had checked in with Morrissey that morning, and the detective had assured him that the department was working overtime to find the killer, so Zach decided to let them do their work without him looking over their shoulders for a day.

Aidan and Jeremy had gone out earlier to cut down a Christmas tree, which was now being set up in the parlor. Caer insisted that she was going to help decorate it.

Everyone ended up getting involved. Cal

and Marni came over, since they and Sean had decided to keep the business closed for a few more days, and Clara and Ted were in the parlor with everyone else. Amanda wasn't even making them work as if they were indentured servants. While the younger men struggled with strings of lights — and Aidan said he'd done all the work, actually chopping down the tree, while Jeremy claimed he had done more than his share by paying for it —

Sean came into the room bearing a tray of steaming cups.

"Bridey's Christmas concoction," he announced. "Tea, sugar, whiskey and a touch of cream. Enjoy."

He lifted his cup. "To Bridey!"

Around the room, the others scrambled for their own cups, then toasted.

"In her honor, we'll be happy," Sean said. "She's watching over us, I know, so we'll decorate just as we always have, as if she were sitting in that corner with her knitting, telling us when something's uneven."

"Hear, hear!" Kat managed, with only a glint of tears in her eyes.

The doorbell rang while they were still at work on the tree. Zach told Clara to keep hanging tinsel and went to answer the door himself.

It was the postman. He was carrying packages, along with the usual mail, and Zach carried everything into the parlor. Then, as he started to set them down, he froze.

"What is it?" Sean asked.

Zach held up a box that was no more than six inches square and bore Sean's name. Written above the address, in Eddie's big, identifiable style, were the words *Sean, you old buzzard, do not open 'til Christmas.*

Marni let out a gasp.

"What?" Amanda demanded.

"It's from Eddie," Cal said.

"Then he's alive!" Marni said, a smile splitting her face.

"No," Zach corrected her. "I'm sorry, but he sent it before he went missing."

Sean stared at Zach, hope in his eyes.

"Sean," Zach said. "We found the mail receipt. But under the circumstances, I think you should open it now."

Sean sat down on the overstuffed chair nearest the tree. His hands were trembling as he worked at the outer wrapping.

Zach stepped forward with a pocketknife.

Under the brown wrapper, the box was covered in cartoon Christmas paper. Happy little dogs leaped about wearing Santa hats. Once again, there was a note. *Sean, lost your eyesight? Do not open 'til Christmas.*

"Oh, Eddie," Clara said softly.

Sean tore into the wrapping with determination. Underneath there was a leather box that advertised Boston Beginnings. Sean lifted the lid.

He gasped, then drew out the ornament from within.

It was a coin, set into a frame of delicately worked gold. Sean held it up, staring.

"English issue silver piece," he said. "My God, look at the date. Seventeen-seventy-nine."

"He . . . he . . . found that treasure you two were always talking about," Amanda said in awe.

"He did. He really found it," Sean breathed.

"I believe he found it," Zach said. "And then I think he moved it."

They all turned to stare at him. Zach wasn't sure why he had spoken, except that Eddie's gift had convinced him that something had to break, and throwing out information that would be bound to reach the killer's ears could be just the way to do it.

"He moved it? Where?" Sean demanded. "And where did he find it?"

"He found it on Cow Cay," Zach said. "I thought it was still there, but it's not. When he took out his passenger that day, I think he let it slip that he had found the treasure there, which was what his killer wanted to know. . . . And I think the killer thought, as I did, that it was still on Cow Cay, so he killed Eddie and any chance of finding out where it really is. And because I didn't know it had been moved, either, I had Gary Swipes guarding Cow Cay, and he ended up getting murdered for nothing."

The room was silent. They were all staring at him open-mouthed.

Except Caer.

And his brothers.

"I'll call the company, this Boston Beginnings," Aidan said. He took the box from Sean and headed out of the room.

"Where would he have taken it?" Sean asked. "If Eddie found it, what did he do with it?"

"I think he hid it somewhere, and then he died with the secret," Zach said.

"Poor Eddie," Marni said. "To find his treasure . . . and then . . ."

Clara gasped, stood up and left the room. Tom hurriedly followed his wife.

Aidan came back into the room a minute later. "I'm going to drive to Boston tomorrow. I spoke with the man who made the ornament. I'm not sure he can help, but I'll go talk to him anyway. Maybe Eddie told him something."

"Right," Zach said, and thanked him.

"I need another drink," Amanda said.

"I'll get you one," Sean offered.

"That's all right. I'll get it myself. And I'm not bothering with the tea this time, either. I'll take my whiskey straight, thanks."

She wandered off to the kitchen.

Cal cleared his throat. "Um, Sean. The flotilla. Are we . . . are we still going to go out?"

"You bet. We'll take out the *Sea Maiden*. In Bridey's honor. And Eddie's," Sean said thickly.

The room fell silent again, until finally Rowenna Flynn rose. "Well, shall we finish the tree?" she asked, breaking the tension.

"Sure," Jeremy said, and rose to join her.

Sean stood and looked about to speak, but then, as if he couldn't say a word, he just waved and headed out.

"I think we'll be going home," Marni said. "Cal, I just feel . . . worn out all of a sudden."

"Sure. Whatever you say." Cal went over and put a supportive arm around her shoulders.

"Good night, then," Marni said.

They left, and then it was down to just the Flynns, Caer and Kat.

"Turn some music on," Aidan suggested.

"Good idea," Zach said.

Kat shrugged unenthusiastically, but she went over and put on some Christmas music.

"O Little Town of Bethlehem" was the first cut, and Zach thought it seemed somehow strange and out of place.

"All right," Aidan said, sitting down and starting to untangle a string of lights, "where could Eddie have hidden the treasure?" He turned to Zach. "Assuming you really think he took it off the island and weren't just saying that to see who you could stir up."

"I really think so," Zach said. "Eddie was leaving clues to where he found it, but he must have become nervous. Maybe someone was asking him too many questions, who knows? But I'm sure he moved it, and equally sure whoever killed him didn't know that. Someone besides me had been digging out on Cow Cay."

"Of course. Eddie," Kat said.

Zach shook his head. "Someone else. The ground was freshly disturbed. The thing is, for the moment, the killer still thinks the treasure's on the island. That's why the guard was killed. Okay, the killer did away with Eddie, tried to get to Sean and tampered with the blueberries. The blueberry jars — only three of them — were tampered with here, either taken from the store and returned, or else the killer managed to tamper with them and then reseal them right in the store. I don't think anyone was meant to die because of the blueberries, though."

"You're losing me completely," Kat said.

Zach grinned at her. "It's all right. I keep losing myself. But in a nutshell, I think the blueberries were a red herring."

"A red herring?" Rowenna repeated questioningly.

"You don't read enough mystery novels," Jeremy teased her.

"I know what it is, I don't know what you mean," Rowenna said.

"Whoever did away with Eddie and Gary Swipes is smart, and he knew he would be caught on the grocery store's camera. He wanted the blueberries to be found so someone would check the tapes and he would be seen — seen wearing the disguise he wore when he went out to kill Eddie. That way, everyone starts looking for someone who doesn't look anything like the killer really looks."

"In other words," Aidan said, "the killer is someone close, someone Eddie and Sean would have recognized." He paused, then asked, "Zach, who knew about the island being dug up when Gary Swipes was killed? Let's go over it again."

"The family, basically. And the cops."

"The cops?" Kat said. "My God, you're not suggesting that . . ."

"We need to find out everything we can about Morrissey and the rest of the men working the case," Aidan said.

"I've got an idea," Jeremy said to Aidan. "You can investigate the cops, and I'll drive to Boston with Rowenna. You have the most friends in high places," he reminded his brother.

"Sounds good," Zach said, and Aidan nodded his agreement.

"I'll stay here and keep an eye on my dad," Kat said, then shivered. "She's trying to seduce him, you know. Amanda, I mean. What if she's trying to kill him . . . that way, since nothing else worked?"

"I know you hate her, Kat," Zach said, "but we don't know that she's the killer, so try to keep an open mind, okay?" He smiled, trying to cheer her up. "I'll go over the *Sea Maiden* with a fine-tooth comb tomorrow," he went on. "See if maybe Eddie left a clue to where he hid the treasure."

"I'll keep reading his poems," Caer said

thoughtfully. When everyone but Zach turned to stare at her in confusion, she explained, "I found a bunch of silly poems that Eddie wrote. They're pretty terrible, but I don't think quality was the point. I think if I can put them together into one long poem, we'll find a clue to where the treasure is."

"Well," Kat said, and stood. "We have a plan."

That night, when the house fell silent, Zach headed to Caer's room. When she opened the door, he glanced around quickly to make sure the door connecting her room to Sean's was closed, then entered.

"What?" she whispered.

He didn't speak. He just took her into his arms, and when she didn't protest, he kissed her long and hard, all too aware that he had almost lost her. He kept his hold gentle, afraid to hurt her injured back.

But she was so passionate in return that he forgot that she had just been in the hospital. They made love, struggling to remain silent, and then struggling not to laugh, almost as if they were high-school kids trying to keep it down out in the family car. They made love again, and when they finished, they were both breathless.

"I almost lost you," he told her.

The happiness faded from her eyes. "You wouldn't have lost me."

"Caer . . . you have to stay. You can't go home."

She rolled away from him.

"I have to go home."

He stroked the satin skin of her arm. "You can't. We have to take the time to explore this — to explore *us*."

She rolled back into his embrace and stared at him. "Zach, don't you understand? You know the truth. You've *seen* the truth."

"What are you talking about?"

She stared at him, then shook her head. "How can you even talk like this when there's still a killer out there? We can't talk about anything until he's caught, Zach. We . . . just can't."

"You're still hiding something, aren't you?"

"I'm an open book."

"Caer, I'm falling in love with you. You've hypnotized me; charmed me. No, it's more than that. You're beneath my skin, in my soul, you're . . . I don't know what, but I know we can't let what we have slip away. Don't you feel it?"

"You don't know how I feel?" she whispered.

"Then it's easy," he told her gently. "Just

tell me whatever it is you're hiding."

"I *have* told you. I really am an open book. You just have to read the pages and believe," she said, and then, because she couldn't bear to talk anymore — to dream anymore — she curled against him again, the softness of her hair brushing his flesh, the whisper of her kiss light against his lips.

When dawn came, he rose, dressed and slipped back to his own room.

He paused in the hallway, looking out the window.

Birds.

There had never been more of them. They were covering the trees as thickly as leaves in summer. So many of them.

As he stared out the window, they let out a horrible cry and, in one violent mass, rose from their perches and soared, a blanket of black to hide the rising sun.

Eight o'clock came quickly, and with it, a call from Morrissey.

"They've found a body. It's with the M.E. in Providence, and we need a family member to identify it. They think they've found Eddie."

Zach flinched inwardly. "If it's Eddie, he's been in the water more than a week. What makes them think they've got the right man?"

"The remains of a tattoo are visible on the upper left arm. It says *Sea Maiden*."

18

Sean was grim, his face set, as they discussed the possibility that Eddie's body had been found. Sean wanted to go, felt he should be the one to make the identification, but at the same time he dreaded going and didn't want to do it.

He had accepted Eddie's death slowly over the days since his disappearance, and he would be glad to know the truth, if the corpse was indeed Eddie's, but he also knew that then all hope would be lost.

It was a painful emotional tangle.

"I should go," Sean said. "He was my friend, my partner."

"You shouldn't go for that exact reason. I've already told Morrissey that I'll go."

"Do they know the cause of death?" Sean's voice was hollow.

"Apparently, nicks on an exposed rib indicate that he was stabbed."

"A knife. Someone threw a knife at Jorey

and hit Caer," Sean said, then looked up at Zach, his eyes betraying an uncharacteristic vulnerability.

"I should send Kat away," he said.

"Sean, a bulldozer couldn't get Kat out of here any more than I could get you to leave. If we could just find some clue . . . We need to find the killer. It's the only way any of you will ever be safe."

"Amanda?" Sean said as if unwillingly.

"I don't know. I do believe it's someone in your household. Not Kat and not Caer — Kat would die for you, and Caer wasn't here when everything began. She didn't even know any of us until you were taken ill."

Sean stared at him angrily. "Bridey is dead. I guess that exonerates her."

Zach knew the other man's anger wasn't directed at him. Sean just didn't want to believe that anyone close to him could be guilty of murder.

"No, not Bridey," Zach agreed dryly.

Sean stared at him, his eyes suddenly burning. "What about Morrissey?"

"He's a cop."

"So?" Sean leaned forward. "He knew everything everyone was up to. And who better to hide evidence than a cop?"

"Yes, a cop knows how to hide evidence

better than anyone else. But I'm not convinced. Morrissey knew what was going on with you and Eddie and your hunt for Nigel Bridgewater's treasure. Besides, anyone knows enough to wear gloves to avoid leaving prints, and that the sea, especially in winter, with the currents, is a great place to toss a body. It wouldn't take a rocket scientist to figure that out. As to the attack on Jorey . . . I don't think that was planned. Stealing a knife from the kitchen when the pub was crowded and no one was watching . . . that was an act of improvisation, and luckily no one was badly hurt." He shuddered, remembering how afraid he'd been that he was about to lose Caer. "Listen, I'm going to go identify Eddie, and I want you to stick with Caer and Kat — and Amanda, unless she has other plans. I was going to check out the *Sea Maiden* again myself today, so you three have to do that now. See if anything is amiss or if you can find anything that looks like a clue to where Eddie might have taken the treasure. No one knows her like you do, Sean."

"No one but Eddie." Sean sighed. "She was his love. He knew her backwards and forwards. But yeah, so do I. So do I."

"Good. Jeremy and Rowenna are heading to Boston to talk to the man Eddie ordered the ornament from, and Aidan is checking into a few things himself. I want the rest of you to stick together. I don't think you'll be in any danger in a group. Oh, and eat out."

"Now you think Clara is the murderer?" Sean asked dryly.

"I think Clara was manipulated — made to look as if she were guilty — and that means someone could try it again. Besides, I haven't ruled anyone out yet."

"Including Morrissey?"

"Including Morrissey. Aidan is on that one. You just make sure not to leave the others' sides. You four stick close together."

"Zach, I swear. I'll keep the other three in my sight all day, every hour."

When Zach left Sean, he found Jeremy and Rowenna ready to leave for Boston. Aidan had already headed out to find a patch of private territory far from the house and all possible suspects where he could call his contacts.

Zach decided to eat something before he left. He found Caer and Kat already in the breakfast room. Caer's eyes met his, a wealth of sadness and resignation in them.

"Well, this sucks," Kat said, settling into a chair with her cup of coffee. "Dad said *she's* coming."

"I take it she means Amanda?" Zach asked

Caer, taking a bite of a Danish.

"She does," Caer agreed.

"Well, just ignore her. She'll probably go sit in the cabin in a huff anyway. I want you two to go over the *Sea Maiden* with Sean. Sorry," he said, smiling at Caer, "but you'll have to check out Eddie's poetry another time." His tone grew firmer. "And be careful. Make sure you have your cell phones. If anything weird happens, anything at all, call me or call Aidan."

"What about Morrissey?" Kat asked.

"Call Aidan first," Zach said. Did he mistrust Morrissey now? Or was he just being paranoid?

Morrissey had been decent from the beginning, a good cop.

He *was* being paranoid, he decided. He didn't like the idea of going to Providence; he felt as if he should stay with them. But someone had to go. And it needed to be him.

He paused, watching the two women: Kat, the feisty little sprite who was like his sister, and Caer, beautiful, regal, strangely sad and serene.

He gave Kat a kiss on the cheek, then pulled Caer up into his arms and kissed her lips tenderly.

Kat whistled.

Caer pulled away, blushing. . . .

"Go," she said. "We'll be fine. Maybe we can even convince Sean to take us out sailing. We can check out the boat and have some fun at the same time. We'll be fine."

He nodded, turned and left.

Everyone was dressed and ready.

Amanda even seemed excited.

"I actually think this will be fun," she said, packing a canvas tote bag in the kitchen. "Coffee, we have to take coffee. And some whiskey."

Caer, gathering things from the kitchen as Amanda suggested them, was startled when her cell phone rang.

She answered, thinking that it might be Zach.

But it wasn't. It was Michael.

She smiled weakly at Amanda and stepped out of the kitchen, knowing the other woman was watching her suspiciously.

"Michael, what do you want? I can't talk to you now."

"Have you been outside?" he asked.

She frowned. "Why? Are you out there? I thought you had a lot of business to attend to here. Why are you hounding me? I'm doing my best."

"Go outside."

Caer made her way along the hallway, through the foyer and out the front door.

There were birds everywhere. They were on the eaves of the house. In the trees. Flying above in great swooping crowds.

Black birds.

Dozens of them were even sitting on the lawn.

"Michael, what's going on?"

"The list . . . *your list,* to be specific — is changing. Names are appearing and disappearing. Right now, Caer, your purpose is what matters. You've got to forget your . . . entanglements and pay attention. This isn't supposed to be happening. You'll upset the entire scheme of things if you don't prevent what's coming."

"Michael," she said, desperate, "help me. What should I do? What should I *not* do? What's coming?"

"You know I can't tell you that. It's not even that I *won't* tell you, but I honestly can't foresee what's next. Too many things are in flux. Keep on as you are, but be on the lookout. Be careful, and stay sharp."

The phone went dead.

She hung up and looked around. As she did, the black birds blanketing the front lawn suddenly let out a shrieking, dreadful cry, en masse, and with a thunderous flurry of wings, they rose into the sky like one giant omen of doom.

After he arrived at the morgue, the receptionist took Zach to meet Dr. Jon Wong.

He was cordial and serene, which Zach supposed was one way to cope with death on a daily basis.

He asked that the body be brought into autopsy room A, and the two of them chatted idly as they waited for the remains.

Zach had seen just about everything during his days in the forensic department in Miami-Dade. Body parts in barrels, bones that had been dug out of the Everglades, fresh bodies, looking as if they might leap up from the gurney, slashed flesh, burned flesh, shot flesh, mangled flesh.

But Eddie was bad.

That was what happened after so many days in the water. So many days as the target of hungry fish. His finger had been chewed to the bone.

Where once his eyes had been, only empty sockets remained. The corpse was hardly recognizable as Eddie.

But it *was* Eddie.

Dental records would clinch the ID, but the tattoo remained, along with the medallion he wore, a piece of Spanish gold drilled through and hung on a chain.

"It is Edward Ray?" Wong asked.

Zach nodded. "Cause of death?"

"The soft tissue around the wound was eaten way," Wong said, showing Eddie's exposed ribcage. "But there are marks on the bones made by something very sharp."

"Did you find anything that could help us find his killer?" Zach asked.

Wong shook his head sadly. "No, but that kind of wound . . . I think the killer took him by surprise. My guess is that he was killed and thrown off the boat almost simultaneously, maybe caught off balance as he died. What was left of his clothing is with the forensic department at the police station. Feel free to stop by there and see what they can tell you. Meanwhile, I expect we'll be releasing the body in another few days."

Zach thanked him, and headed to the police lab.

Amanda looked at the bags and hampers she'd readied for the day. "What a shame. We had all those strapping Flynn brothers here before, but now that we could use their help with all this, they're gone. Oh, well. Tom, I'm sorry, but would you mind grabbing that bag?"

Kat looked at Caer, incredulous that Amanda was being so nice. As she walked past Caer, picking up one of the hampers, she said, "Almost scary, huh?"

"You know what, Tom?" Amanda said suddenly. "I think you and Clara should come along today."

Kat and Caer stared at her.

Tom gaped.

"You want the two of us to come sailing with you?"

Clara, standing at the sink, said, "Oh, no. We couldn't."

"Of course you can," Amanda insisted. "I've invited Cal and Marni, too, but Tom would be a big help. Sean still shouldn't be doing anything strenuous, you know."

Tom looked at his wife. Her eyes widened, and she shrugged. "All right, then." She still looked stunned by the offer.

Cal and Marni arrived just as the car was being packed up. Entering through the open garage door, they gave the others a start.

"Sorry. We thought we'd see if you needed some help getting ready," Marni said, apologizing for startling them all.

"I think we're good. Let's get going," Amanda said.

"We've got a bottle of Irish whiskey," Marni said. "We can drink to Eddie. It was his favorite. Hey, where's Zach?"

Everyone went still for a moment.

"I guess Dad didn't want to tell you until they were sure," Kat said. "A body washed up near Providence. Zach went to see if it's Eddie."

"Oh, God, no," Cal said, his shoulders drooping.

"Let me go get my father so we can get out of here. Let's let Dad have a good day," Kat said.

"Good idea," Amanda agreed. "Sean? Are you ready? It's time to go," she called, her voice rising.

Sean appeared, zipping up his waterproof Windbreaker. "This is it? Let's roll."

He took it in stride that Tom and Clara were joining them as Tom opened the rear door of the black sedan, and Sean and Amanda slipped in.

Kat wedged in next to them. She wasn't leaving her father. "Caer, sit up front with Tom and Clara," Kat told her.

Amanda giggled and squeezed closer to Sean. Kat was tight-lipped. Caer saw Tom exchange glances with his wife. They both smiled, but they looked wary.

They reached the wharf and started loading the boat. With that many people, it was quick work. Caer was in the galley with Kat and Amanda when Marni came down the steps into the cabin. "She's ready to go as soon as Cal gets here. But you know how he is. He ducked into the office the minute we got here and got hung up on a call. He'll be a few minutes, so I say, let's break out that whiskey. We'll toast Eddie, and by then Cal should be back and we can get under way."

"Where's the whiskey?" Kat asked.

"Topside," Marni told them. "So come on up."

"I'll get the glasses," Amanda said.

On the deck, Sean was seated at the helm. He had on sunglasses, so it was impossible to tell what he was thinking. "Not a lot of wind, but enough," he told Marni as she approached. "Besides, we always have the motor, and it's not like we're actually going anywhere." He looked at her and frowned. "Where's Cal?"

"That guy from the flotilla committee called. He said he'd be right along." She appeared to be struggling with the seal on the bottle of whiskey.

"I can do that for you," Kat said, coming up on deck, followed by Amanda, who had a tray of glasses.

"It's okay, I've got it," Marni said. "Caer, would you pass the glasses?"

Clara came over from where she'd been standing by the rail, offering to help, but Caer smiled and shook her head. "I've got it, Clara, thank you. Here, take a glass."

"Oh, I need to watch out for the whiskey," Clara said.

"This is for Eddie," Marni said. "One drink won't hurt you."

Birds screeched, and Caer looked around, almost dropping the glass she was holding. It seemed as if the flock of black-winged demons had left the O'Riley lawn and followed them to the boat. A chill went through her as the whiskey was passed out.

Marni lifted her glass. "Down the hatch in one big gulp, everyone. Just like Eddie took it, 'neat and hard as an Irish whore,' as he liked to say."

"For Eddie. A friend like no other," Sean said, and downed his whiskey.

"For Eddie," Kat said, then swallowed and winced.

"Eddie," Clara whispered.

"Eddie," Tom echoed.

Caer downed her own glass of whiskey. It seared down her throat like fire, and seemed to light a fire in her blood.

The birds took flight. Unease, like black lava, burned through her with an even greater fire than the whiskey.

"Stop. Something's wrong," she said suddenly. "Something's wrong. We can't go out today."

She pulled her cell phone from her pocket, her movements awkward, as the others stared at her in shock and confusion. "Kat, Sean, we have to get off this boat. Now. I know it. I . . ."

She couldn't dial. Her fingers were going numb.

The phone fell to the deck, and she looked around, her vision hazy.

The birds seemed to join together to form one monstrous black shadow-beast and descend over the boat.

Zach talked to the forensic tech who had examined Eddie's clothes, but, as he'd expected, there were no clues for him there. He thanked the man, left and called Aidan from the car.

"Is it Eddie?" Aidan asked, before Zach could speak.

"Yes. He was stabbed in the chest. The M.E. thinks he was stabbed and went overboard pretty much simultaneously. The body is a hell of a mess."

"To be expected, after that long in the water," Aidan told him. "I have some interesting information for you."

"Shoot, please, and quickly."

"Where are you?"

"On my way back from Providence."

"Good. I've checked out Morrissey. He's spotless. More than spotless, actually, and there's no way he'd kill anyone for money."

"Why?"

"He's the grandson of Cornelius Sharp."

"Who's Cornelius Sharp?"

"Well, he's dead, but he was one of the richest men in the state. Morrissey has a ton of money in trust. He doesn't even have to work, but he's one of those men who don't want to live off family money. He made it through the academy with flying colors, and he's never had so much as a parking ticket."

"And that's so interesting because . . . ?"

"That's not interesting, but I'll tell you what is. Mrs. O'Riley."

"What about her?" Zach asked sharply, acutely aware that Sean and Kat — and Caer — were out with the woman even now.

"She was born Amanda Marie Jenkins."

"So?"

"She was married and divorced ten years ago."

"Lots of people have been married and divorced."

"The divorce was instigated by the husband, and there was a child, a little girl. The husband has her. Amanda didn't even ask for custody or visitation."

"You're kidding? That *is* surprising. I can guarantee you that Sean doesn't know. He's such a family guy, and that would really bug him."

"I'm heading down to New York City now, about to get on a plane."

"What? Why?"

"I found someone who won't talk to me on the phone but says that he can tell me something unusual about the case. He was working for her attorney at the time. And I've heard from Jeremy. Eddie insisted on picking up the ornament so he could mail it himself. He wanted the timing to be exact, and he didn't want anyone to know about it. He said that 'they' were watching him all the time, and that he was going to protect everything he knew until Christmas. That was all the guy knew. Anyway, I feel like we're getting close. You need to stick with the family. Sean trusts you. Jeremy is heading back, so he and Rowenna will be there soon if you need them."

"All right."

Zach realized that he was going to have to call Sean with the truth, and it was not a call he was looking forward to making.

"What about Cal?" Zach asked. "Anything on him?"

"No, no record. He married Marni five years ago. They met in New York and married there."

"Lots going on in New York City, huh? Well, stay in touch. I'll get back to Newport as fast as I can."

Caer crashed down to the deck, her eyes still open. And then, as she watched, she saw them fall, one by one.

Clara, Tom.

Kat.

Sean.

Oh, God, it had been her job to protect Sean.

Amanda. No, Amanda was still standing.

Kat had been right all along, Caer realized. Amanda *was* the killer.

Flesh was weak, Caer thought, but though hers had reacted to whatever drug she'd been given, she would recover — and quickly. Meanwhile, she had to think, had to figure out what Amanda had given them — or had it been Amanda? She was still standing.

But so was Marni.

Caer prayed fervently that they had only been drugged, not poisoned, that their names had been the ones that had wavered on Michael's list, indicating that they were in danger but not necessarily slated to die.

It was up to her. She had to keep their names from solidifying, had to keep herself from becoming only air and the stuff of the dreams — the death ghost, there to take them home.

So she lay there and narrowed her eyes until they were almost closed, then watched and listened.

"Let's get them below," Marni said.

"Why didn't we just do this down there?" Amanda demanded crossly.

"Stop complaining and hurry up," Marni said. "I've already rigged the engine to explode, but we've got to get out on the water first, and I don't want them dead until we've found what we need. I know one of them knows where Eddie moved the treasure. Let's get them down to the cabin, get away from here, then start going through their things. I'd rather find what we need that way than have to wait for them to wake up and question them about where Eddie took that damn treasure."

"Marni, I'm not sure this was such a great idea," Amanda said nervously. "Zach and his brothers are still out there somewhere, plus they found Eddie's body. You said that he'd never turn up."

"Hey, at least I killed Eddie. You're the one who screwed up with Sean."

"Oh, right, like I did that on purpose!" Amanda protested. "How did I know the old fart would survive? *You* got the mushrooms. *You* told me he'd die, and it couldn't be traced. Well, he didn't die, though at least they didn't figure out what made him so sick. And what's the story with Cal? I thought he was supposed to be out here, too? Or did you chicken out?"

"I've taken care of Cal," Marni said curtly. "When I set out to kill someone, that someone ends up dead. I took care of him back at the house, then pretended he got hung up here, in the office."

"You killed him back at the house?" Amanda said incredulously. "What are you? An idiot?"

"I have it all figured out. It was the faithful servants, who were jealous all the time of the O'Riley money. They killed Cal when he caught on, then killed the rest of these fools and got caught up in their own explosion. Luckily for us, you and I were thrown clear."

"And instead we're going to freeze to death out in that water," Amanda accused her.

Marni grunted. "Give me a hand with Tom. He's heavy. We're not going to freeze to death, but you may get a little cold. The boat won't explode until we're close to the island. We'll have on life jackets by then."

"You're crazy. That water's frigid."

"Hey, I killed Eddie and swam in. No biggie."

"You were in a wet suit."

"Amanda, if we pull this off, not only will we have that treasure, you'll be the only heir to the entire O'Riley fortune. Don't you think that's worth being cold for a few minutes? Dammit, Amanda give me a hand. Then you can go through their things while I get us out of here. We have to hurry. Some other asshole is going to think it's a good day to sail and see what's going on. Come on!"

As the two women hauled Tom down the steps to the cabin, Caer tried to struggle up; she was conscious, yes, but still too weak and dizzy to manage it. What the hell drug had the two used this time? Poison mushrooms, ground glass, knives and cunning. Marni was cold. Icy. Why hadn't she seen it? And why had no one suspected that the two women might be in collusion? Because they'd carefully made themselves look like rivals, that was why.

She fought to regain her strength without betraying that she was awake, listening to every word. Marni had said that she'd murdered her husband, but wouldn't he have been on her list as someone to cross over? It didn't *feel* as if Cal was dead.

Her mind raced. She had to talk to the two women, get them off guard, find some kind of weapon to use against them.

And she had to get the others off the boat while they were still moored, before the rigged engine blew the *Sea Maiden* into a million pieces.

How?

Marni and Amanda got Tom down the five steps to the cabin below, then came back for Clara.

Then Sean, then Kat.

Then they paused, breathless. Marni laughed. "Wow. They're heavy. Even Kat."

"Only one more to go," Amanda said. "But . . . one second. I just have to breathe."

"Poor baby, poor precious baby. But it's almost over. And no matter what anyone thinks, they'll never be able to prove any-thing," Marni said. "Come here."

Caer watched the two embrace and share a kiss. "You were such a convincing bitch in that house," Marni said with a giggle.

"It wasn't hard. You got to marry the cute

466

young guy. I had to marry the corpse and act as if I was turned on all the time. That would make anyone bitchy." She laughed. "Over! This could really be over."

"Could be? It is," Marni assured her.

"Cal's body will be found."

"I killed him with gloves on, with one of Clara's big broiler pans. They can't trace it to me. I went into that grocery store in the same disguise I wore when I killed Eddie. No one will ever get anything useful off that security tape. They'll never figure out what made Sean so sick, and what do you think they'll learn from Eddie's body? Nothing, that's what. He'll be chewed to bits by now, and when they find that cop I had to kill when I stumbled on him, he'll be just as chewed up as poor old Eddie Ray. Come on, Amanda! We've earned this. We've worked for it ever since we met Eddie years ago, in that bar in the Village, bragging about the great discovery he was going to make. Now, whether we ever find that stupid treasure or not, we'll be rich. We can do anything, go anywhere, because *we're all that's left* of the O'Riley empire. Even that old biddy, Bridey, went and died, saving us the trouble of killing her. Amanda, we deserve the money, and we deserve happiness together. Lord knows, we both paid for

467

it, married to an idiot and a corpse. Grab the Irish bitch. I want to get us out of here. Go through her things first, because she's been snooping around the most, with that damn Zach Flynn. Kat was too busy hating you to figure anything out, and if Sean had really known something, you would have wheedled it out of him already."

Marni started up the engine. Caer cursed herself for not having dragged herself onto the dock, but she hadn't been able to move, and she'd also been afraid to leave the others.

Amanda bent down to grip her by the arms and started to drag her. Hers would be a bruising descent down the steps to the cabin.

Caer opened her eyes fully and gripped Amanda right back.

Amanda screamed.

19

Zach's mind was racing as he drove back to Newport as quickly as he could.

Eliminate the possibilities. Then, no matter how improbable, the possible became the plausible.

Morrissey appeared to be upright and honest. Zach had felt a decent vibe about the man from the time they had first met. He was a rare breed, a self-sacrificing individual, maybe determined to pay back the world for the life of luxury he might have enjoyed. Fact or instinct?

Gut feeling.

Tom and Clara. Hell, he'd known them both for years. Since he'd been a kid, since he'd known Sean.

Was it possible that they were killers? One of them was almost always at the house. They'd both been there for the party when Amanda and Sean had been about to leave for Ireland, the party where, if his theory was correct, Sean had been fed the mushroom that made him so sick. But what about earlier in the day, when Eddie had disappeared? They would both have been there at the house, preparing.

Was there a way one of them could have crept away from the house? Tom, yes, Clara, no. Could Tom have killed Eddie and Clara have poisoned Sean? Yes, possibly.

No hard facts there, only instinct again.

Gut instinct.

Which told him that scenario was possible but unlikely.

What was possible and also likely?

Amanda. Kat hated Amanda and was convinced the woman wanted her father dead.

Cal and Marni. Cal could easily have put on that disguise.

So could have any of them, but . . .

Cal was young and strong. He would have been able to tackle both Eddie and Gary, and throw a knife with enough force and accuracy to have hit Jorey, if Caer hadn't gotten in the way.

Providence and Newport were no more than thirty miles apart, though traffic could turn the drive into an hour or more at the height of tourist season. But this was winter, and well before rush hour, and Zach made it to the house in good time. He was feeling confident, because information was coming in now, clues were beginning to add up. The truth was going to surface, because it was true: eventually, even the most careful killer got careless.

He pulled into the long drive in front of the house, and stopped. The yard was black with birds.

It was eerie. No matter how often he told himself that they were just birds, he'd never seen birds do anything like this before.

He remembered the way Caer had seemed to dread their appearance.

She claimed she was a banshee. Maybe that was what her group in Ireland called themselves. The Banshees.

No, she wanted him to believe that she was the real thing. A howling, flying, crying, screaming, mourning, escorting-the-dead kind of banshee.

Impossible. Banshees did not exist.

And massive raven migrations did not take place, bringing the creatures to Rhode Island in the midst of winter.

He slammed his way out of the car, a sense of dread filling his heart as he burst into the house through the kitchen.

Immediately, he discovered one truth. Cal was not the killer.

Cal was lying on the kitchen floor, blood streaming from a wound to his head and one of Clara's heavy, old-fashioned iron frying pans lying nearby. The blood on it made it clear that it had been the weapon that felled the younger man.

Zach dropped to his knees at Cal's side and lifted his wrist, looking for a pulse, fearing the worst. The man looked dead.

But there *was* a pulse. Faint, but real.

Zach pulled out his phone, called 911 and asked for an ambulance. As soon as he hung up, he called Morrissey. When he got no answer on the detective's private line he momentarily doubted himself, but then Cal opened his eyes, the pupils uneven, and mumbled, "Go . . . she's crazy, they're crazy."

"Tom and Clara?" he asked incredulously, looking at the frying pan by the man's head.

"Marni," he managed. "Marni and Amanda."

"Where are they? Are they on the boat?"

"It's rigged. Gonna blow up. She's crazy. Marni is crazy. I figured it out this morning . . . caught her and Amanda . . . whispering . . . in it together. . . ." He groaned. Speaking was costing him a tremendous effort. "Stop them. Got to stop them."

Zach could hear the sirens. What could be

done for Cal would be.

He lit out of the house; he didn't have time to talk to the cops or the EMTs, but with Cal conscious, he could take care of that.

Back in the car, Zach raced down the driveway, jerked out onto the street with reckless speed, then tore down the road, cursing every other car he encountered.

When he reached the wharf, he saw the *Sea Maiden*. She was about twenty feet out and moving steadily away.

'*She's crazy,*' Cal had said of his wife. Marni and Amanda had been in it together.

The *Sea Maiden* was moving slowly, making her way past the channel markers. Whichever woman was steering her would be careful, wouldn't take a chance of being stopped by the shore patrol.

Who was the brain behind the crime? he wondered. Marni or Amanda? His money was on Marni, plotting and planning, in the office every day, with access to charts and logs, listening to Eddie's tales. With Cal as her husband, she had access to Sean, as well. He would even bet that she had introduced Amanda to him.

He couldn't just dive into the water and start swimming after them. He would freeze before he reached them. He couldn't motor up, either. Too obvious. Cursing, he burst into the charter office, and found a wet suit and diving gear, then headed out.

Even in the state-of-the art wet suit, he thought he was going to solidify before he could catch up to them. *Move!* he told himself. Moving generated body heat. The flippers he'd chosen were designed for speed, and he shot through the water, following the sound of the motor.

Just as they reached the last channel marker, after which he knew he would never be able to keep up, Zach surfaced and caught hold of the anchor ring. He was so exhausted from the cold that he was afraid he wouldn't have the power to drag himself up, but adrenaline could do amazing things. Fear — for the others as well as for himself — was a potent impetus. Straining, he pulled himself up, checking to make sure he wouldn't be seen before hauling himself to the deck.

He made it over the rail just as the boat picked up speed and began to streak across the water.

When Amanda screamed, Marni streaked over like a bolt from the blue, and Caer had a moment of truly appreciating physical pain. Marni hit her, and she saw stars.

"She's not out!" Amanda cried, shaking. "I laced that whiskey with plenty of Seconal. Plenty! She should be out cold."

"It's all right," Marni said. "It might even save us some time. There's something about her, anyway. I think she knows something." She reached down and drew Caer to her feet.

In seconds, Caer, her head still reeling, felt a knife at her throat.

"You know where Eddie hid the treasure, don't you?" Amanda asked.

"What do you need with the treasure? You'll be inheriting all the O'Riley money."

Amanda shook her head. "I want it all. I earned it."

"Save it for later, honey," Marni said. "We need to get out of here first."

She dragged Caer with her to the helm, keeping the knife against her jugular as she forced her down on her knees and took the wheel.

"You do know where Eddie left the treasure, don't you?" Marni said.

"No, actually, I don't. I do know there's a clue somewhere on the boat, so you might not want to blow it up," Caer lied desperately.

"What the hell are you talking about?" Marni demanded harshly.

"She'll cut you if you won't tell," Amanda taunted. "Stupid Irish bitch. You could have stayed over there, but no. You're just as greedy as anyone else. You used Sean to come here, and then you went after Zach. You're trying to find the treasure yourself now."

"Shut up, Amanda," Marni said wearily.

"Be careful, Marni," Caer said coolly. "Amanda inherits the fortune, not you."

Marni's hand twitched, and Caer felt a trickle of blood slide along her flesh.

"Shut up about Amanda and tell me where the treasure is," Marni said. "Or we'll just drag sweet little Kat back up here and start ripping her apart. That will make you talk."

"You're going to kill her anyway," Caer said with a shrug. What the hell was she going to do? She could stall them, but what was the point? There was no hope on the horizon.

"Aren't you a smart little potato?" Marni said. "There's killing, and then there's killing. I can let her die as she is now, totally unconscious. Or I can wait 'til she comes to and make sure she dies slowly and in agony. Trust me, I know how to kill."

"I believe you," Caer said. "But do me a favor, since you're going to kill me anyway.

Fill me in, tell me how all this happened. . . .
The plans — the sacrifices. I mean, you two
are obviously in love, so it must have been
hard pretending to care about your hus-
bands."

"Not so hard, given the payoff," Marni
told her, amused. "Things just kind of fell
in together once we met Eddie. I had to arrange to meet Cal, make him fall in love
with me — which wasn't hard. Men are so
easy. Then I played matchmaker, introduced
Sean to Amanda. It was easy, really. The
hard part was waiting for that idiot Eddie
to actually find the treasure. Too bad you
didn't figure it out a bit earlier."

"You were good, I have to admit," Caer
said. "You pretending to flirt with Sean to
make Amanda jealous, and Amanda, you
pretending to hate Marni. And you, Marni,
always siding with Kat in any argument.
Brilliant. I tip my hat to you both."

"That's enough. What do you know about
the treasure? If you don't start talking now,
I *will* bring Kat up here and dice her into
fish food."

" 'The clue is left, the clue is right, follow
the North Star tonight,' " Caer quoted.

"What?" Amanda said.

"Keep going," Marni said.

"There's nothing more. It's Eddie's poem,

477

and that's what it says."

"She's playing us, Marni," Amanda said.

"No, I'm not," Caer assured her.

Marni stared at her with narrowed eyes.

"That's the clue. It's Eddie's poem, and his clue to where you can find the treasure."

Zach could hear voices from the stern, so he shed and hid his tank, mask and flippers, then slipped down the back steps to the cabin, hoping that neither Amanda nor Marni would be there.

They weren't.

But what greeted his eyes, once they had adjusted to the dim light, caused his heart to skip a beat and then slam like a jackhammer against his ribs.

Bodies.

Clara draped over Tom. Sean lying in the center aisle. Kat in a heap at the bottom of the stairs.

Tom was closest, so Zach hunkered down and felt for a pulse at Tom's throat first, then Clara's. They were both alive. He stepped around them quickly, relief filling him.

What drug had the women used? What would put them out so completely? What the hell did it matter, if he couldn't gain control of the boat? And how was it rigged to explode? He had to know so he could stop it from blowing sky-high.

He started to rise, so he could station himself on the steps and listen to whatever was going on, but just then Sean's eyes opened and he tried to speak.

Zach shook his head and brought a finger to his lips.

"Caer," Sean mouthed. "Stalling them."

"I know. It's all right," Zach repeated.

All right? A maniac had Caer. Nothing was all right.

Zach stood and retrieved the gun he had tucked into his waistband under the wet suit.

Sean was out again, he saw. Just as well. With his gun drawn, he moved to the steps and silently started to climb.

Simultaneously, Amanda came to the top of the steps, saw him and screamed.

He rushed her. He had no choice.

He grabbed her bleached blond hair and pulled her against him as a shield, his gun to her head, as Marni stood, dragging Caer up with her.

Standoff.

"Let Caer go," Zach said.

Marni laughed unpleasantly. "You must be joking."

"Actually, I'm not. Let Caer go or Amanda

will be dead before you can flick your wrist."

Marni shrugged. "Kill her."

"Marni!" Amanda shrieked.

"I'm going to have the treasure," Marni said. "If I have it alone, so be it."

"No!" Amanda cried. She was shaking in Zach's arms, betrayed.

"Stop crying," Marni snapped at her. "He isn't going to shoot you. He's a man. He's in love. Or lust. Didn't I teach you all about men? Trust me. He'll let you go, and he'll toss his gun overboard, or else I'll slit his girlfriend's throat and fillet her like a fish, and let him watch."

"Like hell you will!" Caer exploded. "Zach, shoot her."

"We can figure this out," Zach said flatly, buying time, trying to figure out a way to convince Marni to let Caer go.

He could see it in Marni's eyes. She wasn't the kind of crazy that would make her do anything stupid. She was smart-crazy. She had planned this for years.

"Don't bother with Amanda," Caer pleaded. "Shoot *Marni*."

Holding Amanda tightly against him, he felt her shivering body through the wet suit. He aimed the gun at Marni.

"You won't take the chance," Marni taunted.

"You have to kill her," Caer said. Her eyes were brilliantly blue and pleading as they met his. "Zach, I've told you the truth. You've seen the birds. You have to save Sean. There's a reason. I don't know what it is, but Sean has to live out his natural lifespan. That's why I'm here. Please, Zach. You have to believe me, believe what I've told you. *Everything* I've told you."

He stared at Marni, who only laughed coldly.

"Shoot her, Zach," Caer said again. "You have to believe me. Believe *in* me."

"Drop the gun, Zach," Marni said again, and pressed the knife harder against Caer's neck. "See? I can make her bleed."

And he knew. He couldn't give up his weapon, not even if his heart was tearing as if the knife shimmering in Marni's hand was slipping into his own flesh.

Because there was something . . .

Something in Caer's eyes that spoke of truth and wisdom.

But she wasn't a banshee.

Couldn't be a banshee . . .

Could she?

The image of another knife flashed into his mind, a kitchen filleting knife, razor sharp, slicing through the air and into Caer's back.

She had lived, had only been nicked. She had explained it away as coincidence, the knife hitting the wire of her bra, but . . .

Did it matter? There was no choice. They would all die, Sean, Kat, Tom, Clara, not only Caer, if he didn't stop Marni.

"Zach, do it!" Caer cried.

"Don't do it unless you want to see her bleed," Marni taunted. "I'll make her bleed just a little more now, just to prove it to you."

His finger twitched, and the gun exploded, the knife slicing into Caer's throat just as Marni caught the bullet in her forehead, pulling Caer to the deck with her as she fell.

Amanda began screaming hysterically. Zach thrust her away from him as he hurtled toward Caer, clutching her against his chest, searching frantically for something to stanch the flow of blood at her throat.

There was a roaring in his ears, and he looked up. The sky had gone black, but not from weather, he realized in shock. It was the birds, hundreds upon hundreds of birds, swooping down toward the deck.

Amanda continued to scream, her cries merging with those of the birds.

He held Caer, his hand over the wound at her throat as he tried to stop the bleeding. Then he saw. Her eyes were open, and she smiled slowly.

"Ah, Zach. I told you. She couldn't kill me. It's all right."

He didn't have a chance to reply. The darkness in the sky was taking shape. To his amazement, he heard something like thundering horses' hooves.

"It's the coach. The death coach," she told him. Tears stung her eyes as she balanced herself against him and stood.

He lifted his hand as he rose with her and saw that the bleeding had stopped. He stared at her incredulously, wondering if he was hallucinating. He must be, because when he looked up . . .

He saw a coach in the sky, hovering over the boat and drawn by black horses with plumed headdresses.

"I have to go. I always told you that I'd have to go," Caer said quietly. Then she pulled him close, pressed herself against him and touched her lips to his. She kissed him, and he tasted her tears as she whispered against his lips, "I love you."

Then she jumped, as startled as he was when they suddenly heard a voice, rich with a very cheerful Irish accent, say, "No, my dear, ye need not be goin'."

They spun around together. A woman had stepped from the coach. She had Bridey's voice, but she wasn't Bridey — and yet she was. It took Zach a long moment to realize that it *was* Bridey, but Bridey with the years peeled away, Bridey beautiful and young, dressed in a flowing black gown that waved around her in the breeze.

"Bridey?" Caer whispered. "But . . . I sent you on. I sent you to the emerald hills and fields, and the cottage in the woods, the light and —"

"Aye, but I couldna' stay," Bridey said, then turned to Zach. "A banshee is not evil, my boy, for 'tis her job to escort the good folk to the promise and rewards that await on the other side. But sometimes, like Caer here, she takes human form. And now our Caer has fallen in love with you, just as you have fallen in love with her, so I made arrangements, if you will, to take her place. So you see —" she turned to Caer "— you are free now to remain. I do na mind a bit taking your place, child. Indeed, I'm quite eager, and you must stay here and love Zach 'til the end of both your days. And as I was coming to see you anyway, I've been asked to see that these two go where they should, a place where no green fields await."

"Two?" Caer said blankly.

"Aye, two." Bridey lifted a hand and pointed.

Amanda O'Riley was lying on the deck, blood pouring from a head wound. Zach could only assume that she had panicked at the sight of the birds and had fallen, hitting her head on the rail on the way down.

"I must be goin' now," Bridey said. "Michael said to tell you that you did well, Caer. He's proud of you. Ye'll not be seein' him again, so he said to warn ye that ye must be careful with that flesh and blood ye've been given, because from now on, a knife in the back or a blade against the throat, and ye'll not be healing."

"But —" Caer began.

"What the hell is going on here?" Zach whispered.

Bridey laughed with delight. "Ye've been given a gift. The gift of life," she told him. "Caer's life."

A loud and terrible sound began to vibrate through the air. A wail, a scream, something both hollow and sharp, something that seemed to come from the sea and sky, carrying the threat of terror and doom. Darkness swirled around Marni and Amanda where they lay, and as he watched, their spirits rose from their bodies, rose and saw the dark shadows, like birds, like hundreds of black birds, sweeping around them.

They screamed. They frantically batted

and scratched at the darkness, but the shadows consumed them and dragged them, kicking and screaming, to the waiting coach.

"Life is a gift. Appreciate it, and use it well, me lovelies," Bridey said.

Then she turned, leaped atop the driver's seat of the coach and waved.

Zach blinked, and the coach was gone.

The sea was calm, the sky brilliantly blue.

He looked at Caer and tried to speak, but couldn't. He tried to touch her, and then, to his absolute embarrassment, he crashed to the deck, out cold.

He came to, still on the boat. Caer was bending over him, her eyes anxious, her Windbreaker bloodied, though the cut on her neck was already healing, and her hand strong on his. She offered him a tentative smile.

"What the hell happened?" he asked her.

"They're dead, both of them. You shot Marni. Then the boat lurched, and Amanda crashed into the rail. She's dead, too."

"Sean, Kat, they were alive and —"

"And they're going to be fine."

He stared at her. "That's what happened?"

"Yes."

He shook his head, his eyes searching her face, studying it, reading it.

"You *are* a banshee," he said in awe.

"No more, but . . . aye, I was. Can you live with that knowledge?"

He pulled her to him, then realized that he must have been unconscious for a while, because there was all kinds of activity on the boat now. Policemen and medical personnel were everywhere, and he overheard someone, apparently from the bomb squad, saying that they'd disabled the device Marni had rigged up.

Zach slipped his arms around Caer's neck and pulled her close, then kissed her lips very tenderly. "I don't believe in banshees," he whispered.

"Really?" She smiled teasingly. "Then maybe it was just a dream."

"Life is a gift," he said, smiling back. "And love is what we make of it."

EPILOGUE

" 'The clue is left, the clue is right, follow the North Star tonight,' " Caer said, quoting Eddie, her eyes twinkling.

Christmas Day. So much had happened since she arrived, but still, Christmas had dawned, bringing the peace of the season with it. And for Zach, life had never held so much promise.

They were out on the *Sea Maiden.* They'd all nearly met their deaths there, but, as Caer had said, a boat couldn't be bad, only people could be evil. When the day had dawned so beautifully, after the church bells had pealed and the carols had been sung, going out on the boat had seemed like the right thing to do.

They were all there together, celebrating the fact that they had survived. Sean was a widower again, but he didn't seem to mind too much. In the end, his ego had suffered more than his heart had from finding out that the woman who had pretended to love him had only done so as part of a conspiracy to kill him.

And Kat had wisely refrained from saying, "I told you so" for having distrusted Amanda all along. Cal was along, too, still suffering from the aftereffects of concussion but relieved to have been forgiven for the actions of the wife who had deceived him as much as everybody else.

Tom and Clara were there, even though Clara had once said she would never set foot on a boat again. With everyone else determined to go, she had changed her mind, claiming she wasn't about to spend Christmas away from the people she considered her family.

Jeremy and Rowenna were there, and Kendall, Aidan's wife, had flown up so they could be together with the rest of the family for Christmas. They even had a baby on board, the next generation of Flynns, Aidan's and Kendall's son, Ian.

The others were all in the cabin at the moment, leaving Caer and Zach huddled together at the helm. It was crisp and cool, a stunning Christmas Day. The sea stretched out endlessly, smooth and calm. There was just enough breeze to fill the billowing sails. And it felt fine to be there, she thought, sharing the warmth of their bodies.

"Do you really think there are clues in Eddie's poems?" Zach asked her.

"I do," she said gravely.

"Do you know where the treasure is?" he asked her.

"No, but I know where the last clue is. At least, I think I do."

"Where?"

"Right there."

She was pointing at the wheel. There was a compass set into it. "The clue is left, the clue is right, follow the North Star tonight. Look at that compass. The *N* has a star above it."

Zach stared at her. The compass could be removed, in case it needed to be repaired. He looked at her curiously, then unscrewed it.

And revealed a piece of paper.

"Another clue," she said.

He nodded.

" 'Tick-tock, Banshee Rock, it's twelve o'clock,' " he read.

"Eddie really wasn't much of a poet," she said ruefully, "but I wish I had known him anyway."

"He was a great guy. And not such a bad poet."

"Oh?"

He remembered the day on Cow Cay when, as Aidan had suggested, he had imprinted the layout of the island on his mind.

"He said everything he needed to say, and isn't that what counts?"

He pulled out his cell phone, called Morrissey and told him to get people out to Cow Cay again. "Eddie never took the treasure off the island, he just shifted it. Whatever Nigel Bridgewater left, you'll find it due north of Banshee Rock, probably in that copse of dead trees. Take metal detectors and start there."

Zach hung up and smiled at Caer.

Her eyes widened. "You don't want to go after the treasure yourself? You don't think Sean wants to dig it up?"

He shook his head. "For one thing, it's on state land, so it's not up for grabs. For another, Sean will be happy if the world has the historical documents and the coins go to museums. We've both learned what real treasure is."

"Oh?"

"Family," he said. "And love."

He took her into his arms and kissed her. "And you."

From the cabin, they could hear Kat singing Christmas songs, and then the others joining in.

As the *Sea Maiden* sailed smoothly across the water, Zach and Caer were content simply to hold one another and know that life stretched before them.

The most amazing gift.

ABOUT THE AUTHOR

Heather Graham is a *New York Times* bestselling author of over 70 titles, including anthologies and short stories. She has been published in more than 15 languages and has over 20 million copies of her books in print.